BRENI ASHORE

The Adventures of an Irish Lad Seeking his Fortunes in Liverpool in the Early 1960s

David R. McCabe

*To Mully
with very best wishes
David McCabe
Sep 2017.*

Beaten Track
www.beatentrackpublishing.com

Brendan Ashore

Published 2017 by Beaten Track Publishing
Copyright © 2017 David Raymond McCabe

All rights reserved.
No part of this publication may be reproduced, stored in a retrieval system, or transmitted, in any form or by any means, without the prior permission of the publisher, nor be otherwise circulated without the publisher's prior consent in any form of binding or cover other than that in which it is published and without a similar condition including this condition being imposed on the subsequent publisher.

The moral right of the author has been asserted.

ISBN: 978 1 78645 145 3

Beaten Track Publishing,
Burscough, Lancashire.

Table of Contents

Introduction 1
Part One 5
    1. Return to Liverpool 7
    2. Working in Lewis's & Visit to Anfield 13
    3. Meeting New Friends 23
    4. Mugged – Meet New Girl 31
    5. Driving Test 43
    6. Brendan Meets Mother! 47
    7. Promotion from Sub-basement 55
    8. Maureen Disappears 65
    9. Game of Hockey 67
    10. Job Hunting 73
    11. The Landlady Gets Drunk 79
    12. Back to Sub-basement 83
    13. Interview for Sales Post 89
    14. Moving House & Leaving the Department Store 93
Part Two 97
    15. Broons Biscuits 99
    16. Visiting the Cavern – Marriage in the Air ... 109
    17. Look to the Future – Another Job Offer ... 117
    18. House Hunting 125
    19. Job Offer – Who is Maureen's Father? ... 131
    20. Buying and Selling 145
    21. Area Sales, Sabre Sword Edge 153
    22. New Family Development 159
    23. Meet the Grandparents 169
    24. What Does Grandma Want? 175
    25. Moving House 183
    26. The Wedding 189
    27. Interesting Offer 201
    28. The Funeral 213
    29. Accept Offer 217
    30. Leave Sabre Sword Edge 223
    31. The Operation 229
About the Author 232
By the Author 233
Beaten Track Publishing 234

Introduction

"Are you there, Mr. Harris? Can you hear me…? No movement, Nurse, he's still away with the fairies. No, wait… Can you hear me, Mr. Harris?"

Brendan, coming out of the drugged sleep, could hear the voice but didn't relate it to himself. His head was aching, and all he could see was darkness interrupted by flashing red arrows that bored into his brain.

The male voice repeated its questions. "Do you hear me, Mr. Harris?"

Is he talking to me? Oh, yes, I remember the operation on my eyes. Will the double vision be gone?

"Yes, I hear you," he answered in a slurred voice.

"Good, good," was the relieved reply. "You're back from theatre, Mr. Harris, and your eyes are covered. We're going to take the cover off. Close your eyes tight now, and open them slowly when I take the bandage off."

Feeling hands at the back of his head loosing the tape holding the mask over his face, Brendan crossed his fingers, hoping the operation had corrected the damage from his road accident.

What will I see? A single world…just one of everything…no more double images? No further need to wear the eye patch? Oh! What a difference that will make.

With a sudden movement, the blindfold was removed, and light pushed its way in.

Dare I open them? God! They're stuck together. Force the right one open…

At the blinding flashes of white light intermingled with red and blue, he quickly shut it and tried again, slowly.

"How many pencils can you see, Mr. Harris?"

"To hell with pencils. All I can see is white light."

"God, will somebody pull the curtain?" ordered the voice.

In the darkened room, Brendan began to see a pencil in front of him with his right eye.

Now, open the left slowly. Will there still be one pencil or will there be two? Slowly now, concentrate on the pencil, concentrate…concentrate… Only one pencil? No…is that another below? Oh, no, there are two, one above the other.

Brendan concentrated and moved his head to the right; the pencils came closer. To the left, and they drifted further apart.

Oh, no! It's worse than before.

"What do you see, Mr. Harris?" asked the disembodied voice in a resigned tone, realising there must be something wrong with the result of the operation; Brendan's tears expressed his great disappointment.

"It's worse...it's worse than before," Brendan cried. "The gap between the pencils is greater than before. Oh! Shit! Shit! Shit!"

"Early days, yet, Mr. Harris. Early days. It may improve," mollified the voice.

"At least I only see one pencil when I shut my right eye." Brendan sighed. "Now give me my eye patch and let me go home."

***

This is the third book in a gathering of stories about Brendan Harris. Brendan was born in Dublin, Ireland, in 1940, when Ireland was recovering from hundreds of years of occupation. Most Irish people had accepted Britain's rule, and ridiculed the small number of rebellious young men and women who were dissatisfied with and loath to accept the occupation. But through fair means or foul, independence was gained in 1922, and Ireland was now on its own.

However, there was no industry to speak of, apart from farming, and the country was led by the Roman Catholic Church, which revelled in the freedom gained through independence, to practise without restriction. This was after some four hundred years of dominance by the Protestant occupiers, so it was with a relieved cheer in 1922, that the people renounced the British dictat and embraced Rome.

Many of the richer and land-owning Protestants in the country chose to leave. Brendan's parents, Alice and Henry, being followers of the Protestant faith—or Church of Ireland—kept a low profile whilst they lived in the southern suburbs of Dublin City. In 1946, the family moved to a small village just outside the port of Dunlaoghaire and took out a £1,000 mortgage on Laurel Cottage.

Brendan Harris had left Ireland in 1957 to seek his fortune and fame in the British Merchant Navy. After four years serving his apprenticeship and travelling the world, Brendan returned to Dunlaoghaire to sit his officer's exams...and found fate had other ideas.

Late one summer's evening, Brendan, in full health and youthful vigour, was returning home from the city on his brother's Vespa motor scooter, when his dreams and aspirations came to an abrupt end. A carelessly driven car pulled out from a side road, causing Brendan to collide with it. Brendan was rushed to hospital, where he remained, concussed, for three weeks, and spent the following months recuperating from his injuries. Memory loss, eyesight complications and severe leg injuries had ended this young man's dreams.

While his memory was gradually returning, and his right leg—which had gone through the closed side window of the car, severing his thigh muscles—was still a bit stiff but mending, the damage to his head had resulted in severe diplopia or double vision. To ease this, he made use of a black eye patch over his right eye. His employers in Calvex Tankers offered a contract as a uncertified Third officer; with the boom in oil requirements by the developed world, tanker companies were quite desperate to hold onto deck officers and were ready to re-employ Brendan.

Dismayed by the probability that he would have to wear an eye patch for the rest of his life, Brendan decided—rather than accepting or, more likely, rejecting the kind offer from Calvex—to have the eyesight impairment corrected.

Reporting to the eye and ear hospital in Dublin, he joined the queue as instructed, and after some hours was ushered into a dimly lit side room. There, he underwent a multitude of sight tests, at the end of which he was informed that surgery could be effected to correct the double vision, but with the proviso there would be no guarantee of success. Brendan agreed to undergo the operation and was told to await a letter from the hospital when they could offer a bed.

By now, Brendan was getting very frustrated. His memory was improving in leaps and bounds, aided by re-reading his diary of his exploits whilst at sea. He was, however, daunted by the studies required to continue his career as an officer with Calvex Tankers and started to consider studying for another profession.

Accountant, solicitor, doctor, or maybe become an astronaut…

Part One

1

Return to Liverpool

Returning to Laurel Cottage—his home in Dunlaoghaire—after the abortive operation, Brendan reassessed his position. He was twenty-three years of age, reasonably fit, a bit underweight, suffering from double vision and a gammy right leg. His chosen career as an officer in the Merchant Navy was over, the studying over the past four years all wasted due to his scrambled memory. What to do now? That was the question. Stay in Dublin and try to start another career?

He knew how to drive a car, or, at least, he'd bought a driving licence; that didn't guarantee he could drive. His brothers were both in chosen career paths. But where were the opportunities for the future, in Ireland?

His good friend Doc Courcy was all for him going back to sea, but Brendan didn't feel he was up to the mental rigours of navigating and ship control. The doc even offered an introduction to a couple of firms in Dublin city.

After due deliberation, Brendan decided to return to England, and the doc kindly gave him an address of a family in Liverpool who welcomed lodgers. So it was with a sense of a new adventure that Brendan Harris, grateful to be alive, boarded the Dublin ferry to Liverpool, again waving goodbye to his parents and to Ireland.

***

Now here he was, a tall, underweight Irishman wearing a brown duffel coat and with a black patch over his right eye, standing outside a small terraced house in the Bootle district of Liverpool, with a packed suitcase and cheap holdall on the ground beside him. It was a cold and damp October morning in the year 1963. Brendan knocked on the door and turned to the taxi idling behind him.

"How much?" he asked, delving into his pocket to produce some silver coins.

"Five Bob, mister...but I don't take paddy money," was the startling response from the diminutive taxi driver as he saw the coins being proffered.

Sensing the door opening behind him—as far as the security chain would allow—Brendan turned to see a shadowy face through the narrow gap and a female voice exclaimed, "Oh, it's you, Hector. What do you want?"

Then, noticing Brendan, she shut the door, released the chain, and reopened it. There stood a tall woman in a red dressing gown and carpet slippers with her hair somewhat askew. In a sleepy voice laden with the Liverpool accent, she greeted Brendan, standing back to allow him to enter.

"Hello there." She smiled. "Of course, you must be Mr. Harris. I got your letter. Do come in. How are you keeping, Hector?" she asked the taxi driver, who was still awaiting payment. "How's yer mum?"

Before the taxi driver could reply, Brendan—who was very, *very* tired, given he'd only just disembarked the B&I ferry boat from Dublin after a very uncomfortable sleepless night—smiled in his most pleading manner and said, "Mrs. Brown, can you help? I've only got Irish coins an' Hector here—" he looked accusingly at the taxi driver "—won't take them. I'll go to the bank later an' pay you back."

"That's all right, Mr. Harris. Now, wait a moment, Hector, how much do you want?" On the driver's reply, she remonstrated, "Five shillin's? Good God! Five shillin's from the dock to Bootle? No wonder you can go on holiday to Blackpool. Away wid you now, wid yer stealin' ways... Are they all his bags, den? I suppose I've got to pay. I'll go get yer five bob." She half smiled.

"Yes! Mrs. Brown, it's five bob, an' I have a family te support, you kno'. Three children an' a missus sufferin' from the tiredness an' of course me mum with the forgettin'," retorted the driver in indignation.

Mrs. Brown turned away to find the money, a bare foot with red-painted toenails searching for the errant slipper on the coir doormat.

"Ye see what I have to put up wid, mister?" sighed the driver, looking up to Brendan who towered above him in with his six foot height. "Ye kno', I can't take the Irish money—wish I could. She's all right. She'll treat you OK... Oh! Yep! Missus, five bob an' not'n less. A tip of a shillin' or two... Oh! All ret, I kno' when I'm beaten. Day to ye, sir." With a scowl, the taxi driver pocketed the silver coins, climbed back into his cab, loudly revved the engine of the ancient Ford and drove away, leaving a plume of smelly exhaust behind him on the stone setts.

"Now come in, then, Mr. Harris, I'll put the kettle on. Being from Ireland, I'm sure you'd like a cup of hot tea."

Having recovered her slipper, Mrs. Brown stepped back from the doorway, holding the door open with one hand and adjusting her dressing gown over her tall body with the other.

Brendan followed her inside, somewhat taken aback by the dark interior of the house and the pervading smell of…was it boiled cabbage? He deposited his luggage in the hallway, awaiting instruction from Mrs. Brown, who he realised was not much older than himself, maybe in her late-twenties.

"Your room is up the stairs, Mr. Harris. Hold on, I'll shut the door and take you up. Jeesus, the noise the trains make," She exclaimed as an electric train went swishing by on the raised track across the roadway. Hitching her dressing gown up to her knees, she took Brendan's holdall and beckoned him to follow with the suitcase.

"Thanks, Mrs. Brown, these stairs are a bit steep. Will you call me Brendan, by the way?"

"Sure, den, Bren. Ha! Ha!" was the gasped reply from the staircase heights. "I'm June 'burstin' out all over'. God, what am I sayin'? There you are, Bren, I hope you find it comfortable enough. Now, come on down for a cuppa. That Hector…that Hector, his wife is sufferin' badly from some complication. But you, Mr. Harris…Brendan…don't want to hear about that." She laughed in excuse. "There's the kettle boiling. Do you want a cup?" she offered again, brushing past Brendan on her way out of the small room as he stepped aside in the doorway.

Slightly overcome by the effusive welcome, he placed his suitcase on the lino-covered floor and walked over to the window: two panes of dirty glass, the bottom of which had a crack making its way from left to right, with the frayed sash cord dangling at the side.

Better leave that alone for the moment, the catch looks a bit rusty.

Turning around, he examined the bed crouched in the corner of the small room; it had a rounded metal headboard and a thin mattress over a metal sprung frame. The white sheet folded down from the white pillow was a contrast to the dark, heavy blanket over the bed. A wooden cabinet, with a ceramic lampstand holding up a paper-thin, brown shade, stood forlornly beside the bed. Shivering a little as he shed his duffel coat and threw it on the bed, Brendan noted the tall wardrobe, which was lacking a handle, as the small hole in the left side of its single door seemed to suggest. Alongside that was a flat-topped deal table with a small table light balanced on it. A bookcase housing some worn Penguins clung precariously to the plain dusty wallpaper. The wooden chair pushed under the table was at odds with the rest of the room's contents, its dark gleaming rounded back with cushioned seat stood out in stark contrast.

What are you doing here? You should be with the rest of your class around the mahogany dining table in a large comfortable house with log fires and embossed wallpapers. One day, chair…. One day… Brendan mused as he made his way down the steep stairway on the well-worn carpet, following the smell of frying bacon.

"Oh! There you are...Brendan," called Mrs. Brown peering around the kitchen door. "I'm making some brekkie for myself. Would you like some? I've got the eggs, a couple of slices of bacon an' could do some fried bread."

"That would be great, June. Is there a paper shop close, by any chance?"

"There's Frank's just around the corner. I'll have a plate full ready for you when you come back, Bren," answered the cook/landlady before she switched to singing the top song of the day, 'Confessin' by Frank Ifield.

"Oh, yes!" she called. "Here's a shillin' you'll need for the paper."

"Thanks, June. That's six bob I owe you."

Humming the tune to himself, Brendan went outside into the dirty air of Bootle.

Feeling on top of the world, he strolled along the wide pavement with its rows of terraced houses divided by the narrow street. Everything was shrouded by the all-pervading dust with gaps in the neat rows where the bombers in the 'forties had left their mark. Being close to the docks, he could see the tops of the masts of some of the ships in the distance, and hear the doleful sound of horns as they moved around the basins.

Must get down to the docks and look at the ships, thought Brendan to himself, feeling somewhat sorry his sea-going career had now ended. *But I've got everything to look forward to. I've got a few bob in the bank, and I'm in pretty good health.* After the accident in '61, encouraged by his parents, Brendan had taken a case against the driver who had caused the accident, and had realised a couple of thousand pounds in settlement. But having reimbursed Jono—his elder brother—for the cost of a new motor scooter and paid his parents something towards the cost of looking after him, he was left with close to a thousand. This he had put into shares in the UK market.

He laughed to himself. *Got a wonky right leg, and this double vision and the eye patch are a bit of a nuisance, but I can put up with it. Now, I must get work and start on another career path.*

***

"The stores in Liverpool are all looking for temporary Christmas staff, I see, June," Brendan called out as he looked over the job section of the morning newspaper. "How far are we from the city centre?"

"Well, Sandhills station is just up the road an' you're five mins from Central. You've got Blacklers, Owen Owens and Lewis's just around the corner from Central. I've been to Lewis's—got the hall carpet there."

"By the way, June, I never asked you. Where's Mr. Brown at the moment?"

"Oh, John…he's way out in India or somewhere. I'm hoping he'll be back for Christmas. He's a second officer with Blue Funnel, you kno'— the Alfred Holt Line. They're based here in Liverpool," she announced proudly. "There's a photo of him." She patted the small, framed photo of a tall man with thinning hair and a ghastly grin in an officer's uniform, obviously taken in a studio.

"That was taken about three years ago. Isn't he lovely, my John?" She gushed and gave the picture a kiss. To Brendan's relief, no comment was expected from him.

"That was a hell of a breakfast, June. I'll go get my head down for a couple of hours and pay some of those stores a visit this afternoon and, most importantly, get to a bank."

"OK, Brendan. Here's a quid. It should get you into town. Will I give you a call in a couple of hours? I'd better get on with the washin'."

Over the next few days, Brendan visited a number of the large stores, and within the week had offers from two of the largest: Owen Owens and Lewis's of Liverpool. As Lewis's offered a slightly higher hourly rate and the promise of an interview for a trainee manager's post, after the Christmas rush he gladly accepted this.

2

Working in Lewis's & Visit to Anfield

"Mornin', everybody. I'm Marsden, John Marsden, personnel. Glad to see all your shinin' mornin' faces."

With a pronounced sniff and cough, Marsden positioned himself behind the large desk in the office reserved for Personnel, on the fifth floor of the department store in the centre of Liverpool, and glowered at the small group of newly recruited temporary staff standing before him.

"Yep, everybody, you have all come through the selection process, and now what do we do with you?" With a further sniff, followed by a controlled sneeze, Marsden wiped his nose on the back of his hand and called through the open door to the adjoining room, "Mary, personnel files, please. Why are they not on my desk?"

"Yes, I have dem here, Mr. Marsden. Sorry," was the cry from Mary as she grabbed the files from the mound on her desk and came through the door, stumbling on her high heels and adjusting her miniskirt with her free hand.

Catching the eye of another recruit of his own age, Brendan grinned, as Mary nearly dropped the bundle of papers and leaned over Marsden's desk, showing a lot of stockinged upper leg in the process. All eyes followed the unbalanced, self-conscious Mary as she returned to her desk.

"Attention, you lot!" Marsden barked, glowering at the three young men standing before him. "I know what's going through your minds, gentlemen—" Marsden nodded towards the open doorway "—but what I've got to say is far more important than your obvious lewd thoughts. Now, I've decided that you, Baker—" Marsden advised the man alongside Brendan "—report to Mr. Speakeasy on Toiletries. You look slightly less scruffy than the others. You, Smith, to Mrs. Nolan on Confectionary. Don't eat too much of the product, it won't help your pimples—Ha! Ha!—and you, Harris, to Mr. Jones on Toys. You look like you could do with some cheering up. Any questions?"

With no response, Marsden dismissed the three recruits with a wave of his right hand as his left paid attention to his reddening nose.

Brendan, bristling slightly from the negative comments, left the room with the other two, Baker smiling to himself and Smith fingering his pimples. As neither made any effort to communicate, Brendan strode ahead and made his way to the lifts to discover Toys was on the next floor down.

Right, Mr. Jones, your best recruit of the year is coming to help run your toy department—though I'll probably be given the job as tea boy. Anyway, what of it? As they so rightly say, this is only temporary until Christmas, and eight pounds a week is not to be sneezed at.

What, I'm twenty-three now, single, no debts, no friends here, no home, got a bit of money in the bank, pretty fit, a bit woozy in the memory stakes, a bit of a perfectionist, I'll admit. Somewhat old-fashioned in my ways... Must find a dance hall... Wow! There are some cute-looking ladies around. Right, now, let's find Mr. Jones.

Brendan faced the lift's trellis gate as it concertina'd back. Six foot tall, dressed in his double-breasted, well-worn grey suit with twenty-two-inch trouser bottoms and turn-ups. There were two biro pens protruding from his top pocket; his black shoes, highly polished, were quite remarkable; a white shirt and dark tie, surmounted by his straight uninteresting thick brown hair, completed the dramatic scene.

Alas, the effect was somewhat reduced by the unknown-to-him large red pimple with white head beaming out amid the varied inactive and less colourful pimples on his forehead, not to mention the black eye patch over his right eye.

Did heads turn? Did the girls all gasp at this saviour of their humdrum lives as the figure strode into the toy department? No. The only reaction he got was from a young woman in a long, brown coat, who looked at him questioningly as he strode between the stacks of Meccano and Hornby trains before she continued with pushing a large metal container full of boxed toys.

Brendan looked around the floor, which seemed to stretch into oblivion, to find someone in charge.

Maybe that young lad behind the tills over in the corner can help.

A dapper middle-aged man stepped out from behind an unsteady looking display of tall spaceships and made his way through the many counters displaying a multitude of toys. "Yes, sir, may I be of help?"

"Oh! Hello! Are you Mr. Jones?" Startled, Brendan questioned the diminutive figure before him.

"Yes, I am—"

Before Jones had time to finish, Brendan had shot out his right hand, which was met by Mr. Jones rather weak, small, cold hand. Brendan shook it vigorously and announced, "Brendan Harris, Mr. Jones. Personnel advised I contact you to discover my duties. I am looking forward to workin' in Toys with the Christmas coming."

"Glad to meet you, Harris." Jones released himself from Brendan's light grip by pushing Brendan's hand away with his free hand. "Please speak with Miss Byrne over there. She will tell you what to do." With that, Jones turned and strode away.

Bemused by this dismissal, Brendan stood for a moment. He was astonished his friendly approach could be spurned in such an abrupt fashion.

Sensing movement behind, he turned to find the said Miss Byrne standing a couple of feet away from him with a large box of Meccano in her arms and a knowing grin on her face.

Leaning forward, she confided in a marked friendly Liverpool accent, "Pay no attention to him, Mr. Harris—the miserable Welsh moron. He's been like that for the last two years. Never mind, dear. You're under my wing now…call me Maureen."

"Maureen," Brendan repeated. In her oversized brown dust coat and flat black shoes, on first glance, she was none too attractive, but a closer look revealed she was in her late-twenties and had a beautiful smile and sparkling brown eyes. Brendan was instantly smitten. "Call me Brendan," he managed to utter, smiling as he considered what might be underneath that shapeless brown coat. "What do you mean, under your wing, by the way?"

Maureen cautiously glanced around. "Didn't Taffy tell you you've to work with me in the basement?"

"That sounds pretty OK to me, Maureen."

"Our job is to bring toys up from the store as needed, an' with Christmas comin' up, to give a weekly stock check. We're goin' to be busy, Bren. So you'll need to cover up your dapper suit. There's a couple of coats in the store. Help me unload this lot an' I'll take you down after. We also keep the floor tidy here…ye know…if there's any paper lying about.

"Oh! An' there's Noel Danster, the assistant manager. I'll introduce you when he's finished with that customer."

Delighted to be taken in hand by this positive young woman, Brendan looked across the floor to see a tall, dark-suited male figure attending to an elderly woman who was pointing at a row of colourfully dressed dolls.

"Bet she's askin' about the Sindy doll." Noticing Brendan's puzzled look, Maureen continued, "The Yanks brought out a Barbie doll and now Lines Brothers, here in Britain, are producin' the Sindy. Should be with us in a couple of weeks."

The first thing Brendan did, upon being introduced to Danster as the 'assistant store man', was enquire when the Sindy doll was due in the store—no harm in making an impression in management's mind, he thought.

Danster was a tall but slightly built man with very highly polished brown shoes and a matching waxed brown moustache, which he smoothed as he considered Brendan's question before answering in a squeaky southern English accent, "The Sindy doll is *hush-hush*, Mr. Harris, but it will be in the store quite soon. In the meantime, I would suggest you go ahead and do what you're paid to do."

Brendan bristled slightly at the put-down. *OK, Mr. Moustache, I may only be a temp, but I'll see you off one day.*

"Thank you, Mr. Danster," he answered as the man turned on his heel with a lift of his shoulders and a pronounced sniff of disdain. Brendan looked at Maureen, raised his eyebrow and gave a loud pretend sniff himself, provoking a muffled snigger from Maureen as she made her way towards the staff lift, signalling Brendan follow her.

"It's comin' up to eleven, Bren—coffee time," Maureen said as she pushed the large heavy manual Otis lift door shut and pressed the button. "We'll head for the basement first, get you a coat, and as I have a list of toys they're short of on the floor, we'll get them on a trolley. Show you where everythin' is and go to the canteen. I'm lookin' forward to showing you off to the girls and hearing about the eye patch." She grinned and punched Brendan on the arm.

The roomy lift started to drop rapidly down the shaft, giving a fleeting glance of the exit doors as they descended. They arrived at the basement, and with an authoritative smile, Brendan gently pushed the brown coat aside and, catching the handle of the heavy lattice gate, found he had to put some effort into pushing it fully to the side. He took a deep breath and caught the handle of the outside door, pushing it open with a flourish.

"Well done, Tarzan!" Maureen called out as she stepped into the badly lit basement. "The toys are over there, behind the toiletries. Grab a trolley, Bren, an' follow me into the jungle."

Delighted to find someone with his own sense of humour, Brendan dutifully followed her instructions and pulled out a blue low-down storage trolley on wheels and followed the rapidly moving Maureen who, with a light step, was dancing her way between the tall stocked shelves and singing. Brendan recognised it from the radio—the latest hit song by Gerry and the Pacemakers, 'You'll Never Walk Alone'—and sang along where he could. By the time they reached the toy shelves, they were both singing together.

"You'll never walk…a—" drawing out the last word "—lone."

Both laughed heartily, enjoying the moment. Maureen procured a coat from a small alcove between the mountainous shelves of toys and produced a list from her pocket.

Brendan donned his office robes, and for the next short while gathered boxes of Meccano, Mousetrap, Scalextric and Corgi toys while Maureen talked away about her visits to the Cavern night club and dances in Reece's ballroom.

"Oh! By the way, Brendan," Maureen suddenly advised, "all deliveries must be checked by me. I mean only me, as there have been some shortages in the past few months, you understand?"

"Sure, Maureen, anything you say." Brendan was more interested in speaking about his visit to the Cavern Club back when he had joined the *Calvex Faith*. "Yes! I remember, back in 'fifty-nine going to the scruffy Cavern Club. There was a band they called themselves…the Quarries, or, something like that."

"Yes! I went to the Cavern back then, Brendan. God, the fun we had. You mean the Quarrymen. Do you kno' who they are now?" Maureen stopped reaching up for a box of Etch-A-Sketch and turned to Brendan.

"Haven't a clue." replied Brendan, squaring up the stack of boxes on the trolley.

"Careful there, Bren, you've got too many… Careful, Bren—Oh, God, they've fallen over. Look, put the bent boxes to the side. We'll look at them later. As I was saying, you've heard of The Beatles, haven't you?"

"Yes, of course I have. You're not going to say—"

"Yes I am, you dodo. The Quarrymen are now The Beatles. They play at the Cavern every now and then. The Cavern is hummin' at the moment. There's a group playing there now called the Rollin' Stones. They're great. I like Little Richard and Bo Diddley. You should go sometime."

Brendan recalled his visit to the claustrophobic Cavern with its glistening walls and the noise and the smell of sweating bodies.

The Beatles…a noisy group of adolescents. Wonder how long they'll last? And those Rolling Stones. What a bunch of wallies with their long hair.

He thought maybe not, but…

"I might take you up on that, Maureen. Maybe sometime soon. Won't they be wondering where we've got to up on the floor? We've been gone nearly an hour."

"God, is that right? What, it's ten to eleven. Down tools, Tarzan. Let's go for a coffee."

***

They joined the short queue at the glass-covered canteen counter, with its sandwiches and various cakes, where Brendan bought two large cream buns and two teas. Balancing the buns and two plastic beakers on the small tin tray, he joined Maureen at a crowded table.

"This is Brendan Harris, my protégé. He's learning the trade," announced Maureen with a big grin as she pulled out the metal chair beside her and turned to Brendan to help him unload the tray. "That's Mike over there, Bren. Beside him is Sheila and Bill, and Pru the other side. That'll do for now. How are you all keepin', everyone? Gettin' all geared up for Christmas?"

With a degree of shuffling and movement, the newcomers settled into the close-knit group and the hum of conversation picked up. Maureen, sitting alongside Brendan, gave him a smile and continued her conversation with a girl sitting beside her.

Listening and smiling to all around, Brendan scooped out two small spoonfuls of sugar from the semi-congealed lump in the bowl, being careful not to upset the flimsy plastic cup, and stirred the hot liquid with the dirty metal spoon. Holding the thin container under the slightly pronounced lip on its top edge, Brendan raised the hot cup to his lips and was about to take a sip of the steaming liquid when there was a sudden startling noise from the adjoining table. Involuntarily gripping the plastic tighter, Brendan squirted the hot milky tea into his face and chin. The cup slipped out of his fingers, spilling the rest of its contents onto his trousers.

Pru—sitting to his right—jumped back in alarm. There was a gasp all round with a few embarrassed giggles.

Brendan, now the centre of attention and quite mortified, delved into his trouser pocket for his handkerchief and commenced to dry off, but in his haste to mop up the brown liquid from the crotch of his trousers, he lost his balance on the narrow seat, and in an effort to save himself fell against the table, putting his free hand on the cream bun.

With laughter all around, Brendan sat back again on the chair and licked the cream from his hand, keeping his head down and blushing furiously and grateful as, once again, conversations started up all around him.

Football seemed to be the main topic—how Liverpool and Everton were succeeding in the First Division. Liverpool was at the top of the division, with Everton lying seventh. The next match was apparently Liverpool playing against a side called Fulham at Anfield the following Saturday. When he asked Maureen if she was interested in the game, she launched into a mock tirade against 'that side of donkeys' and professed herself to be 'a blue'—an Everton supporter.

Well, I shall be here for a while. I'll have to pick a side. Red or blue? As Liverpool are at home in Anfield this Saturday, I'll have a look at them first and see for myself who're the donkeys.

***

The next Saturday at one o'clock, Brendan set off from Bootle to make his way to the famous Anfield football ground, first on the smelly train from Bootle to the famous Lime Street station, which immediately brought back memories of 1957, as the naïve sailor-to-be, taking the train from Lime Street for his journey to Newcastle on the North East coast where he had joined his first ship.

He noticed a group of obvious fans with their red scarves and bonnets, some wielding football rattles, and shouting to each other with the f-word dominant. They were like a bunch of schoolboys, showing off to each other their independence from their mothers. Brendan smiled to himself, comparing their amateurish profanities to that of the typical seaman, whose natural language contained a greater and richer variety of swear words.

Feeling quite grown up, and anticipating the hours ahead, Brendan, dressed in his brown corded trousers, white jersey and his old faithful brown duffel coat, finished off with his black eye patch, boarded the single-decker football bus in Paradise Street. He had to force his way past a group of arguing supporters to sit beside the window on the shiny, scruffy plastic seating.

Alone in this hive of jostling bodies, all laughing and arguing with each other, Brendan peered out the dirty bus window and noticed, amongst the hurrying figures, a group of rather oddly dressed young men: six of them, slouched against the dirty wall and all dressed in tight-fitting jackets with velvet collars, some brown, some white, and one even a shade of pink. Each had their legs encased in very tight trousers, the colour of which complemented their jackets, and each was topped by a sweeping head of hair greased into a gloriously shaped form. The tight trousers melted into large, ungainly shoes with thick soles, the prominent colour being white.

There was one member of the group taller than the rest, with a smoking cigarette dangling from his lips as he talked in bursts of speech, emphasising his words with elaborate gestures. Another of the group, a smaller lad of about eighteen, seemed to take against something the taller lad said and squared up to him. Looking quite ridiculous in his big white shoes and thin body encased in a pink sheath surmounted with a crown of black shiny hair, he was pushed aside by the taller lad with a scornful smile.

Two of the others went to confront the taller male when the coach started moving out from the kerb; Brendan sat back in his seat and lit up a cigarette, thinking the world was full of strange people. While his attention was centred on the events on the pavement, he'd been joined on the seat by a tall, gaunt, older man wearing a red peaked cap over a worn face with the customary cigarette dangling from his lip. Dressed in a well-worn brown leather jacket over a roll-necked sweater, the caught Brendan's glance and responded with a broken-toothed smile.

"Hello there," offered Brendan, tentatively wondering what his newfound companion would come out with.

"They're a poor imitation of the teddy boys of the 'fifties. I remember them well," was the surprising comment made in a deep musical voice accompanied by a generous slap on the knee to emphasise the point made. "More to the point, isn't Shanks doing a great job?"

Shanks... Now, I think he's the manager. "That's right, he's doin' a great job. I agree."

"He should scrap Melia and put St. John in his place in the midfield an' put John Arrowsmith up front..."

For the next fifteen minutes, Brendan's new companion regaled him with his in-depth knowledge of the Liverpool team, its past and its future. With "Ould Shanks, they were goin' places."

Nodding wisely at certain points in the flow of information and opinion, Brendan asked where the best place was to watch the game. What was the Kop?

"The Kop, son, is a terrace at one end of the ground, an' way back in the 1900s, there was a battle during the Boer War in South Africa at a place called Spion Kop, near Ladysmith. A lot of Liverpool lads were killed, so I suppose it's in their memory. Unfortunately, the British were defeated."

Brendan nodded his thanks for the information and, looking out the window, noticed the pavements were becoming quite full of men and children bedecked in an assortment of red scarves and caps, all walking purposefully forward.

"We must be close to the ground now?" Brendan said.

"Yeh! Just a couple of minutes more an' we'll be there. By the way, son, do you wanna join me? I'm meeting a few pals, an' we're going to the Kop."

"Why, that's great, thanks very much. By the way, my name's Brendan."

"Mine's Mick," replied the older man, rising from his seat as the coach pulled to a stop on the road alongside the looming ground. "Aye, come along, Bren. There's the guys."

"Hiya, Mike," was the united greeting from the group, all in their late-twenties or early thirties and all displaying their support for Liverpool with red blazers and red hats, red scarves, red shirts—one even had red shoes.

Feeling somewhat overwhelmed, Brendan shook hands with Dave, Robin, Ron and Bob, making the customary 'hiya' greetings as they made their way to the turnstiles.

"Right, lads, first stop the bar," announced Dave, sporting the red shoes, red bonnet and leather wind cheater. "Ten bob all round for the first drinks. OK with you, Bren?"

With some trepidation Brendan agreed and passed over the note to Dave, who advanced to the bar followed by his pack of six, or, should we say, five thirsty men. Brendan—not one to drink alcohol, particularly in the middle of the day and on an empty stomach, too—accepted the glass of whiskey and followed the role of the others by gulping it down in one swallow. This was, apparently, the rite followed by the group at every match.

"Right, pints of ale next, lads. Here ye are, Bren. Knock that back." Dave passed a glass pint of brown liquid with wisps of white foam on the surface. Brendan was already feeling a bit groggy from the whiskey but took the proffered glass of brown mixture from Dave and giving an 'I'm with you, lads' smile, took a sip of the sickly brew.

"Go on, Bren, knock it back!" the others encouraged as they all gulped down at least half of their own pints of noxious brew. The guy called Tom, short in stature but built like a brewery, drained the whole pint.

OK. Never liked the stuff, but if these guys can do it, I'll have a go.

Taking a deep breath, Brendan dug his nose into the cauldron of tepid brew, tipped his head back and took a large mouthful. With beer dripping down the sides of his mouth, he took one gulp, and even ventured into another, to find he could not take any more and snorted back into the glass, spraying beer over those close to him.

With his nose full of beer and his head going around in circles, Brendan, feeling very foolish, passed the pint glass back to Mike and rushed to the men's toilets, where he vomited the lot into the bowl. He flushed and sat down the wooden seat, feeling quite miserable. The last time he'd felt like that was in Barcelona, where he'd ventured on a pub crawl and, after three glasses of wine, lost consciousness in the outside toilets.

I can't go back out to those guys. They must think me a right softie. I was stupid in trying to drink the stuff—must be something wrong with me.

With his head whirling, he staggered his way out into the noisy crowd now making their way to the stands. No sign of his lost friends, he followed the main movement of bodies and ever-increasing noise of singing voices, and suddenly stepped out into daylight.

What a sight. Over the heads of the singing crowd, he could see a stand at each side and one ahead of him, all packed with thousands of eager bodies waiting with anticipation for the players to emerge onto the well-manicured green stage. Brendan lurched his way forward to the nearest metal barrier, getting a few dirty looks and the ever common f-word thrown at him, and gratefully leaned on the welcome support.

Maybe if I stand still for a few moments, my head will clear.

There was a mighty roar from the crowd.

Emerging from under the stand on the left, the visiting side, in their white shirts and black shorts, came running out in single file and started kicking a football between them. The roar increased in volume as the red shirts of Liverpool appeared, and the players trotted towards the Kop. Some waved to the crowd, and for the next few minutes stretched their limbs. Each time a player kicked a ball towards the Kop goal, a further roar of sheer enjoyment and anticipation filled the air.

Brendan became aware of the press of bodies behind him as the stand filled up. On the pitch, the referee and linesmen, in their black shirts and shorts, trotted out to their respective places, and the ref called the two team captains to the centre circle. After the toss-up of the ref's two-bob piece, Ron Yeats, the Liverpool captain, decided to defend the Anfield Road end of the ground; the players all changed ends, with the Fulham team getting a round of friendly boos and references to their nickname of 'The Cottagers'.

The Liverpool side dominated the first half, with a forward—a man of short stature but with immense speed, Ian St. John—scoring the first goal at the Kop end. Brendan, still feeling somewhat sick, noticed some of the male supporters were relieving themselves against the side walls of the stand. One guy, who had been drinking from bottles stowed in his coat pockets, urinated into a folded-up newspaper. Many of the supporters standing in the vicinity drew back in disgust, but the rather inebriated drinker shouted at them to 'eff off' and continued with his exercise.

At half-time, with the score standing at one-nil to the home side, there was a concentrated rush to the toilets. Following the throng, Brendan—in dire need himself—found he could not enter the toilets as there was a long queue. Rather than waiting, the majority relieved themselves where they were standing. Brendan found he had to follow suit.

In his shock and dismay at his own actions and those of his fellow man, Brendan made his way out of the ground and, after asking directions, traced a slow and wavering path to his digs in Bootle.

3

Meeting New Friends

"Hey, June, what does a fella do on a Saturday night, here in this Liverpool?" Brendan had returned to the flat in Bootle after a long weary day in the department store. It was now a Saturday evening in early December, two months since Brendan had arrived in Liverpool, and he was beginning to feel a bit restless.

He had got to know his landlady fairly well, due to the shared intimacy of the accommodation. June had been married for two years and had only bought the house in Bootle twelve months ago. John, her husband, had been away at sea most of the marriage.

Patting her blonde hair into place, June turned around from the gas cooker. "I dunno, Bren. Suppose you could go dancing or maybe the pictures. Do you dance, then?"

"I can get around a dance floor. Did a bit of dancing back home in Dunlaoghaire." Brendan looked over the rim of his mug of tea at the tall woman dressed in a shapeless working dress, her face reddened by the heat from the stove. "Which is the best to go to? I've heard mention of a dance at the Grafton Rooms and another at a place called Reece's. Reece's is quite close to where I work—"

"If you like, Brendan," interrupted June hesitantly, "you could come along with us. I'm meeting a few of the girls, and we're going to Reece's Ballroom tonight. Sheila an' Mary. Sheila's husband is with the Bibby Line, and Mary is single. She's about your age, had a fella in one of the passenger ships, Cunard I think—though I think they've split up. Anyway, we meet for a chat an' a bit of a dance. I'm sure they would love to meet with you."

Three women out for a chat doesn't sound like a big night out. Wonder where it all could lead? No, it would be too much, be nice, though, to have the company.

"OK, June. I'll come and say hello. Perhaps you and I could have a dance…?" Brendan offered a sidelong glance with his good eye, bringing a slight blush to June's cheeks.

"Yes, that would be nice," June said, no doubt thinking to herself, *there's no harm in a dance, and I get to show off my new lodger to my friends.*

"What would you like to do? Are you meeting the girls at the dance or before? Maybe we could go together? Or, I could go ahead on my own and meet you there?"

"Yes, Bren, maybe that would be better. I'll see you at the dance. Now, what would you like with your fried eggs? A bit of fried bread and a sausage or two?"

After his tea and a good wash, Brendan donned his best suit, the grey double-breasted jacket and trousers with twenty-two-inch bottoms. With a few quid in his pocket, he waved to June—"See you later"—and took the train into Lime Street. Alighting in the large bustling station brought back memories of six years ago when he was seventeen, arriving in Liverpool with his seaman's trunk full of ambition and expectation to take the train to Newcastle on the east coast to start his career in the Merchant Navy. *Now, here I am, seven years later, an assistant in a department store, working in the sub-basement with a gammy leg, wearing an eye patch and with a dicky memory instead of being an officer on a merchant ship sailing the oceans.*

Shrugging his shoulders, Brendan adjusted his black eye patch, rubbed his aching right leg and, pulling up the hood of his brown duffel coat to avoid the drizzling soot-laden air, stood with the famous St. George's Hall ahead of him. Knowing how to get to Reece's from Lewis's store, he turned to his left, pushing aside the entreaties from the rain-soaked beggars, and made his way to Reece's ballroom in Parker Street.

Or so he intended, but as walking down Ranelagh Street with the rain getting a bit heavier, he stepped into an open doorway for shelter, to be assailed by the smell of beer and cigarette smoke and the sound of voices with the odd burst of laughter.

I'll have a drop of whiskey, might as well. The night is young, and I've got a few quid in my pocket, he thought as he stepped aside to allow two girls in brightly coloured macs to pass through into the interior.

He followed the two girls into a large room with a well-stocked bar to one side and large etched mirrors on every wall. Looking up, he was struck by the impressive ceiling and, of course, the many Christmas decorations draped over everything. Quite envious of the animated groups dotted around the room, he noticed the girls being welcomed by two smartly dressed beaus at the bar. With a few curious glances as he strode towards the bar in a John Wayne saunter, he caught the barmaid's eye and, in his best American drawl, ordered a shot of 'Paddy's'.

Not to be caught out, the barmaid immediately retorted with, "Will it be a Powers or a Jameson sir will be wantin'?"

"Thank you, miss. I'll have a Jameson." He glanced around at the very few customers in the room. "Not many in tonight," he stated in a dismissive manner, delving in his pocket for his cigarettes: a twenty packet of Rothmans tipped.

The barmaid—more a madam than a maid—laughed and placed the expensive—to Brendan—drink in front of him. "No, der's not many in at the moment, mister. Whereabouts in Ireland are you from? That'll be three bob to you." She leaned over the bar counter, showing an eye-catching amount of cleavage.

Do I drink this drop of liquid in one mouthful? Got to draw it out a bit. "Give us a drop of the Mersey in it, please, miss." He managed not to comment on the nice pair she had and passed a ten-shilling note to the barmaid, who took it in both hands, flattened it out and held it up to the light.

Accepting that the note was genuine, she gave Brendan a semblance of an apologetic smile and went to deposit the note in the till further down the bar, returning with a handful of silver change, which she placed on the bar and pushed them towards Brendan with an expectant smile.

What do I do? Do I leave a tip? Do I give her a threepenny bit, or, sixpence, or, a shilling? Luckily, a customer further down the bar called for service, giving Brendan the opportunity, as she turned away, to pocket the silver coins.

Lighting up his cigarette, John Wayne adjusted his eye patch and swivelled around on the bar stool, noticing—amongst the silent couples sipping their drinks and a group of young men talking loudly at a table close to him—three men with a cribbage board between them. Two of them were concentrating on the game whilst the third man, quite a bit younger than the players, sat looking quite bored.

I know that guy, Brendan realised. *He was on the Calvex Renown—now, what was his job? Yes, of course! He was the 'sparks'—the radio officer. Wow, those were the days, when I was a naïve seventeen-year-old, first time away from home. A grand guy...what was his name? Paul? That's it. Paul—wireless—sparks—larks—Marks—Paul Marks. He'd just got his radio cert and it was his first trip. Went ashore with him in BA—wonder if he kept in touch with that girl he met—wonder how Joan Turbitt is?* These were the fleeting thoughts that flitted through Brendan's mind about the four years he had spent at sea, as he made his way across the crowded floor. *Wonder if he will remember me.*

Looking up, the target of Brendan's interest notice his approach and rose with a beaming smile of recognition on his lightly bearded face.

"Well, if it isn't Brendan Harris, the Irishman. What a nice surprise," greeted the suntanned young man in his early twenties, dressed in a smart suit and company tie. "I see yer as tall as ever." He grinned as he stretched up his hand. "Are you on your own, then? I'm here on my way from a funeral. Let's go sit." He pointed to a couple of spare chairs at a small table. "I'd like to hear what brings you to Liverpool. John, Mike," he called to his fellow cribbage players. "Met an old shipmate, going for a talk over old times."

After replenishing their drinks, Paul explained he was on leave between ships and was staying overnight in Liverpool before taking the train to join his ship in London.

"And what's the eye patch for, Bren? I notice you've got a bit of a limp as well. Been in the wars, have you?" Paul replaced his pint glass of stout on the glass-topped table, giving a snort of satisfaction and licking the beer froth from his moustache in readiness for the story from Brendan.

"Well," grinned Brendan, "it was like this..." And he began to relate the events leading up to the reason why he, the deep-sea sailor, was now land-bound and instead of commanding a ship's crew was now a lowly assistant in a department store.

Receiving the expected sympathies from his newfound friend, and feeling a lot more relaxed after the pint of stout and the expensive whiskey—John Jameson, of course, the Irish whiskey his father favoured and much softer than a Scotch—Brendan brought up the invitation from June and enquired if Paul was interested in a bit of female company.

"I'm a bit nifty at the rock 'n' roll, an' could do with a bit of cheerin' up. Let's go, buddy." Catching Brendan's shoulder, he rose somewhat unsteadily from the low chair.

"Hold on there. Let me finish my drink. Cost a lot of money, you know." *God, I'm feeling a bit tipsy myself, but I can't leave all this.* He lifted the half-full glass of beer and downed it in a couple of swallows, nearly choking himself in the process.

"Bren, yer eye patch has moved over your nose. Don't see anything wrong with the eye. What's going on?"

"It stops me seein' two of you, Paul. Brendan readjusted the patch over his right eye. "It's the dip-dip-lopia I have. Like I said, my eyes are not in line after the accident. Come on, let's get going to the dance."

With that, the two pals took a quick visit to the men's room and made their way, slightly unsteadily, into Parker Street. After a suspicious examination from the doorman at Reece's, they were allowed into the large ballroom on the first floor, where the two beaus surveyed the field looking for a conquest.

The three-piece band—piano, clarinet and drums—were playing the Cliff Richard hit of the day 'Bachelor Boy'. There were tables to the side of the dance floor, with groups of girls talking animatedly and some men standing near a small bar while a few couples traipsed slowly around the floor.

"Where's your date, Bren? It all looks pretty dreary," Paul said with a dismissive laugh. "What's that, Bren?" Paul suddenly changed his tone of voice. "There's a couple lookin' our way. I like the one with the short hair. Look, Bren, she's waving at me."

"Who are you kiddin', Paul? That's June Brown, my landlady." With a derisory snort, Brendan elbowed his friend. "Come on, I'll introduce you."

"Hello, Brendan," June greeted, touching a chair alongside her in an invitation for them to join the small party. "Who's your friend?"

"Hello, June. This is Paul, an old shipmate. Paul, meet June. Who are your friends, June?"

"This is Sheila." June indicated a smiling woman in her late-twenties—"and Mary"—a younger woman with blonde hair tied in a ponytail standing alone. "This is Brendan Harris, girls. I told you about him. He's staying with us for a short while. Another seaman." She tossed her hair as if to dismiss the relevance of the association. "And you, Paul? It is Paul? Looking at you, I'd say you're probably a seaman as well."

"Yes! A radio officer," Paul confirmed as he took the chair Brendan offered. "A sparks. Joining my ship in London tomorrow—staying overnight in the Adelphi and catching the first train in the morning."

"You guys are so lucky," voiced Mary in a disgruntled tone. "Here am I, stuck as sales assistant whilst you lot travel the world. Though I've been to the Isle of Man on the ferry for a day," she reflected. "Going to New Brighton tomorra, wid me mum, to visit me granny."

"Forget about your granny, Mary," Paul said. "I'll put you in a spare suitcase and we'll see the world together."

"Aw, come on, Paul. I might take you up on that to get out of this miserable place." Mary laughed resignedly. "Thanks, but I'll go back to my weary job behind the counter in Lewis's."

Well, that's interesting. Here's June implying I'm a seaman only staying for a short while. Mary obviously doesn't know I'm also working in Lewis's. Will June tell her or will I?

The band was now playing a jazzy quickstep. Brendan noticed June's fingers tapping away with the catchy rhythm and inclined his head towards the dance floor, now occupied by some actively moving couples. He was pleased to receive a nod in agreement and caught June's hand as they stepped onto the dance floor.

They found it quite easy and relaxing to go with the music and get into the swing. After a few stumbling steps, Brendan realised June was an experienced dancer, so for the moment, he was quite happy for her to lead. He knew some of the basic steps in the dance from practising with his mother many years ago and found he could merge in with June's obvious better ability. As the dance progressed, he gained more confidence and began to improvise, resulting in a few stumbling mix-ups. He took control and made a passable attempt at the quickstep.

"Look, Bren," exclaimed June with delight in her voice, "your friend has taken Mary up. Crikey, he's good. Mary got some medals at Martins. She'll be pleased to get a dance. Will you give Sheila one next?"

"I will," Brendan said. "Hadn't I better tell Mary I'm working in Lewis's? She obviously thinks I go to sea, and she'll be very surprised—" he laughed "—when she sees me pushing a trolley around the sub-basement."

"I'll tell her when we get back to the table, Bren. Let's enjoy the dance. Oh! Damn, that's the end." June sighed in exasperation as they went into a last swing at the end of the quickstep. Returning to the table and reluctantly letting go of June's hand, Brendan made a point of sitting beside Sheila, whilst Paul and Mary returned to the table with their arms around each other.

"Nice to meet you again, Bren," was the surprising greeting from the flushed Paul. "Goodnight, ladies. Mary an' I are going for a little walk. All the best, Brendan laddo, in your new career."

"Good luck, Paul. Nice to have met you again." Brendan waved, thinking to himself *what a lucky so-and-so, getting the girl and also going back to sea and the novelty of a new ship. Here am I, landed with two married women and a miserable job to go back to on Monday.*

"Right, girls, I'll up and leave you. I've got the spare key, June. I'll let myself in if you're not back. Nice to meet you, Sheila. Brendan rose from his chair and, receiving a startled glance from the two women, bowed slightly and collected his coat to the sound of the band playing 'Fools Rush In'—the recent hit by Ricky Nelson.

Walking self-consciously to the exit, Brendan wondered what he was going to do now, at ten in the evening: go to the pub or walk back to Bootle? He decided to walk back to the house rather than buying another expensive drink he didn't need.

I'll go along the dock road, he thought. He remembered the way the taxi had taken him when he first arrived, and strode out in the cold night air, down towards the river, past the B&I ferry tied up in Prince's Dock on the left, noticing the few remains of the overhead railway, or the 'dockers' umbrella', which had been dismantled in the late 1950s. As it began to rain slightly, he pulled the duffel-coat hood over his head, put his hands in the pockets and strode onwards, his leg aching a bit after the unaccustomed dancing.

Feeling somewhat downcast, Brendan trudged through the wet street with warehouses to his right, a busy port to his left with cargo ships of many nationalities tied up and discharging their cargoes. He passed Waterloo Dock, closely followed by Nelson Dock, and when he came to Canada Dock on his left, he thought he remembered the turn taken by the taxi and turned right into the street showing the depressing sight of bombed-out buildings. Certainly, he would have to leave the digs in

Bootle; living in close proximity with June would not be good for either of them.

Not paying too much attention to his surroundings, thinking about his future, he heard running footsteps behind him and was shocked to receive a blow to the back of his head. As he fell to the cobbled street, he felt a boot in his side and tried to recover, but gloved hands caught at his coat and tore it open. He could smell stale beer fumes on his face as his assailant searched his jacket for his wallet.

Somehow, Brendan got his legs under him and butted the smaller man in the face, praying the attacker would not hit him again with the heavy object he'd used for the initial attack. A car's headlights blinded him as it entered the roadway.

Thank God, some help.

The assailant immediately let go of Brendan's coat and raced away into the darkness.

Relieved, Brendan sank down onto the wet road, shivering violently with his head aching.

"How are you? Are you hurt? Can we help?" were the anxious calls heard by the now semi-conscious Brendan.

"Blow on head...kick in side...best hosp...please."

"Should we move him, John? He might be injured bad. Where's the nearest phone box?"

"Just a moment, Mary," said a soft Irish male voice. "Can you move there, fella?"

"Yes, I can, thanks. Just feeling a bit woozy."

"OK. I'm going to lift you and get you into the car, and we'll take you to the David Lewis—that's the nearest...God, he's a weight. OK, Mary, I've got him. Hey, fella, what's yer name? Do I hear a Dublin accent there?"

"Brendan Ha...rris. Yes," he slurred. "You're right. Thanks...both of you. I feel terrible."

"That's all right, then, Brendan. We're both from Wexford. Now, drop yer head and stretch out on the seat. Hop in, Mary."

Brendan drifted into unconsciousness as the car drove away.

4

Mugged – Meet New Girl

Where am I? I smell hospital again. Where am I? Oh! Yes! That guy hit me on the head. How did I get here? With these thoughts running through his head, Brendan opened his eyes slowly to see he was in a darkened room with a high ceiling. He could hear the odd cough from a male body echoing around the room. There was the sound of a female voice behind a white screen across from his bed…

"Come on, Mr. Maloney, lift yer bum, we haven't got all night." The young Liverpool voice hid an obvious wish to laugh.

"That's better, Mr. Maloney. Now, do yer business an' we'll be back in a mo."

Yes! It's definitely a hospital, realised Brendan. *I feel fine. What am I doing here?* His eye patch was missing and there was a cloth around his head. *These aren't my pyjamas. Oh! I feel a bit groggy.* Lying back in the uncomfortable, metal-framed bed to ease his head—and shutting one eye to cancel the problem of his double vision—he realised he needed to urinate and carefully swung his legs out from under the bed clothes. He sat on the edge of the bed, feeling quite unsteady, and when he attempted to rise, the pyjama trousers fell around his ankles. There was another bed alongside him, with an older man lying on his side, watching him. Brendan hastily recovered the trousers and sat back on the bed.

"Where am I, then, mister? Where the hell am I?" he asked loudly.

There was no reply from the recumbent male, but with a rush of white clothes, starched cap and commanding voice, a female advanced from across the room and stood before him with hands on hips.

"What are you up to, Mr. Harris? you should be in the bed. Now, come on, git back under the clothes."

"OK, OK, Nurse, if you say so, but where am I? An' I need to go to the lavatory. What time is it please, and where is my watch?"

"No, back into bed. I'll bring a pan for you. You're in the Liverpool Hospital, came in early this morning. It's six o'clock Sunday morning," the nurse answered sharply. "Now, back into yer bed like a good man."

"But, Nurse! I feel fine an' I could really do with a visit to the lav," Brendan pleaded, giving his woebegone look while standing beside the bed in his bare feet, his right eye shut tight, and holding up the thin pyjama trousers with his right hand.

"If you're all right? I'm rushed offen my feet—down that corridor first door on the left. All right, Mr. Murphy, I'm coming," cried the overworked angel of mercy as she hastily made her way back up the large room to Mr. Murphy, who had apparently fallen out of bed. "Will you hurry up, then, fella?" came the sudden growling voice from the neighbouring bed. "I need me bloody sleep."

"Sorry, sir," Brendan muttered as he gingerly stepped off the coir mat beside his spartan bed and onto the cold wooden floor. He made his way, unsteadily, to the dark corridor, holding his left arm out to grab anything secure if needed. His right hand gripped tightly to the pyjama trousers.

Quite relieved to reach the corridor entrance without falling over, he held on tightly to the doorpost whilst his spinning head returned to his shoulders.

A dark-robed large figure surmounted by a wide white headpiece suddenly materialised out of the gloom, and a female voice, laced with authority demanded, "Where are you going, young man? We can't have patients wandering around the wards. Now, back to bed. Nurse!" In one smooth movement, she turned Brendan around, causing him to lose his balance, and in his need to prevent himself from falling, he grabbed the nearest solid object—the well-rounded figure of Matron—letting his pyjama trousers fall to the floor.

"Ah! There you are, Nurse," said the matron, who, in one professional movement, untangled herself from Brendan's grasp and left standing, quite disorientated, with his trousers around his ankles and his right eye closed tightly to reduce the surrounding objects to one apiece.

"Take charge of this patient, Nurse, and…why is he wandering around in a state of undress?" With a loud disdainful sniff, she looked at Brendan and asked, "Isn't this…the Irishman with the head injury admitted earlier?"

The harassed nurse, carrying a rather full bedpan at arm's length, acknowledged the questions with a hurried smile and continued past Brendan to the lavatory, muttering under her breath, "Work all damn night, an' she comes in, laying down the law. Who does she think she is?" then at normal volume, "Yes, Matron, I'm coming!" and to Brendan, "I'd like to pour this over her head." She disappeared into the lavatory and emptied the bedpan with a loud splash.

Returning to the entrance door to the ward, she was taken aback to find Brendan back in bed with the matron standing over him.

"Mr. Harris, Doctor Porteous and our almoner will be in to see you at eight-thirty. From the contents of your wallet—do excuse us for the intrusion, but I am sure you will understand—" the Matron nodded her head to enforce Brendan's agreement "—we see you are from Ireland. Are you resident in England?"

Brendan started to tell the matron what he remembered of the night before, but before he could finish, she stopped with a short smile and a condescending pat on the head. "Not to worry, Mr. Harris. Everything will work out all right." She turned and started to walk away. "Enjoy your breakfast," she called back, "and your stay in David Lewis Hospital and thank the Lord." And off she went, headdress bouncing.

Brendan, becoming somewhat annoyed with this treatment, called out to the retreating body, "Where is my wallet, Matron? And my watch and my clothes and the rest of my things?"

Turning in a sweep of dark dress and cape, the matron glanced back and said again, "Not to worry, Mr. Harris. Everything will work out all right."

Brendan lay back in the uncomfortable bed, resigned to await the hoped-for visit from the almoner. He guessed the time to be about seven-thirty, as further staff appeared pushing trolleys with trays of food, the glorious smell of cooked rashers wafting around them.

After a reasonable breakfast, Brendan considered discharging himself. He felt quite all right, apart from a tender spot on the back of his head. *Where's my clothes and my wallet? There was a pound note in it. I'll give this almoner creature until ten o'clock, and if nothing happens, I'm getting on my bike. Wait, now...I wonder if there is anything in this locker.* Leaning over the side of the bed, and feeling a bit faint with the blood rushing to his head, Brendan tugged at the door of the metal locker, but he couldn't get it open.

Just then, an important flotilla of uniforms, led by a severe-looking male in a white coat—presumably Doctor Porteous—swinging a stethoscope in his right hand, entered the ward and advanced towards Brendan's bed.

"What have we here?" The doctor snatched up the clipboard from the end of the bed. "Ah! I see," he continued in a very refined English accent. "I see this is the case which came in overnight—assault and battery. A blow to the head, was it?"

"Yes, I was hit—"

"Sit. Now, lean forward."

Brendan did as he was told, and the doctor coarsely examined the back of his head.

"Yes. Light contusions. Sit back...sir," was the first recognition that there was a person carrying the injury. "Why have you your right eye closed?"

Brendan explained.

"I see. Follow my finger, keep your head steady. Look right... Hmmm... Look left... Hmmm. I do not know what you are doing here...sir...taking up a valuable bed. Have him discharged, Sister." The flotilla moved to the next bed.

"Nurse, do so," came a second order, and without further preamble, Brendan found himself with his clothes on, his wallet—containing the pound note, five shillings and six pence—in his pocket and his necessary eye patch, standing at the exit to the David Lewis Hospital in Old Hall Street with instruction to turn left for Bootle.

Deserted streets greeted him as he made his way back to Bootle. On the dock road, he recognised a few buildings and found himself, an hour or so later and somewhat exhausted and cold, at the door of his temporary accommodation.

"It's only me, June. Are you there?" he called out as he stepped into the small hallway, immediately assailed by the stale smell of cooked food. Not receiving an answer, he looked into the uninviting kitchen with its deal table, assorted wall cupboards and gas oven. There were a couple of saucepans balanced on the cooker, probably something for the evening meal. "Hiya, Ginger," he greeted the green eyes of the cat looking out from under the table as it moved silently out of its bed, watching him suspiciously.

"Don't worry, old boy. I'm just going to make a cup of tea. Your mother must be out, probably gone to church. Should be back soon...it's gone midday." *God, what am I doing talking to a cat? It's about time the miserable thing got used to me. I've been here a while now.*

Suffering from a light headache and exhausted from the restless night and long walk back to his digs, Brendan made himself a couple of thick slices of toast and scraped some slivers off the solid pat of butter from the fridge. He was about to head upstairs when he heard footsteps approach from outside, and turned to see the glass in the front door darkening and hear the key turning in the lock.

"Come in, then, Sheila..." June invited as she stepped into the hallway, looking over her shoulder at her companion, unaware of Brendan standing in the hallway. "I dunno where he got to. He wasn't in before I left for ch—well, well, look who it is!"

"Hello, June." Brendan grinned foolishly. "Just on my way upstairs. Would you like a cup of tea? I've just brewed a pot. Hello, Sheila, did you have a good evening? Mine turned out rather badly. Tell you both later." With that, Brendan turned on his heel and made his way up to his room.

***

"God, it's cold." Brendan hugged himself in his brown duffel coat—the same one that had helped keep out the cold when on watch on board the tanker ship taking oil to the various small ports on the Norwegian coast.

Ah, those were the days. Now, here I am, catching the train on a dark, cold winter morning to take me to my exalted position as assistant store man. I could so easily have been in the tropics enjoying the sunshine and foreign lands but for that accident. Still, I could have been killed, there is that.

Brendan mused to himself as he boarded the scruffy train to take him the short distance into the city centre, where he clocked into the Lewis's staff entrance, joining the other morose and uncommunicative workers as they had their time cards stamped, registering their entry to the store.

He descended into the depths of the labyrinth, the elaborate structure designed and built to hold the minotaur without escape. It was now the early weeks of December, cold and damp, no snow, but with a bitter east wind seeking out the uncovered skin. Brendan continued down the narrow staircase into the cold, uninviting storeroom with its hushed atmosphere and voiceless toys all awaiting their entry onto the toy department, to be examined by excited children and resigned parents.

Donning his brown work coat—now his new uniform—Brendan took the dull and battered kettle to the kitchen, nodding to the other faceless brown-coated shapes as they filled their kettles from the noisy tap.

There's the guy from Carpets, Kitchen Ware, the Gardening floor. Now, wait, there's a change, a new face, a girl—I recognise that ponytail and that swing of the hips.

In high heels, dressed in a tight dress and warm cardigan, it was young Mary from the ballroom. Brendan's day brightened up.

"Hiya, Mary, remember me?" he called out to the advancing figure.

She stopped abruptly and looked up, warily examining Brendan, who must've looked a sight in his brown coat with sleeves too short and a silly grin topped by a head of untidy brown hair.

"Yes, I know you from somewhere. Why should I know you?"

"Reece's ballroom. June introduced us. You left early with Paul."

"Oh, yes, I remember. I thought you were a sailor. What are you doing here?"

"Didn't have time to explain—you left so quickly with Paul. Look, what break are you on, and I can tell you all?"

"Oh! Paul..." she acknowledged with a disdainful shrug of her shoulders. "He's history. Gone to the other side of the world... I dunno... maybe...see you around." Giving Brendan a seemingly apologetic smile, the slim figure in high heels continued on her way into the warehouse.

Well, that puts me in my place, thought Brendan to himself as he took the boiling kettle of the hob and kicked the cooker in frustration.

"Come on, Bren, are you going to be all day. I'm gaspin'!" The shout came from behind the stacks of boxes.

"OK, Maureen girl, hold yer hosses, I'll just be a minute," Brendan answered in his marked Dublin drawl as he spooned three teaspoonfuls of loose tea into the cracked ceramic teapot—one each plus one for the pot—followed by the boiling water from the hissing kettle. Giving the pot of tea a brisk stir, he took the unopened bottle of milk, gave it a good shake to mix the cream with the rest of the pint, took the cap off and poured some into the awaiting stoneware mugs. He poured the thick brew on top of the milk, put two teaspoonfuls of sugar into each, stirred them clockwise (anticlockwise in the Southern Hemisphere) and proudly took the two mugs, with the opened package of Marietta biscuits, to the dimly lit rear of the storeroom.

"There you are, Maureen," said Brendan to the brown-coated woman perched on an unsteady stool with her elbows resting on a small wooden desk covered in papers. "Still doing the paperwork? Now don't be lettin' the tea go cold."

"We've a lot on today, Brendan me boyo, so let's get this tea down us an' get stuck in. Do anything special over the weekend?" Maureen spun on the stool. "Oh! God, I'm falling!" She toppled over, dropping her mug of tea and sending her Marietta biscuit into orbit.

Startled, Brendan also dropped his mug, stuffed his biscuit in his mouth and reached out to stop the falling body. In an intimate hug of arms and legs, they both fell to the floor. Brendan cushioned the body on top of him, quite enjoying the intimacy, and started laughing as Maureen, trying to unwrap herself, fell against him, her protective cloth cap falling off and her long hair spreading across his face.

"We should do this more often, Maureen," Brendan exclaimed as Maureen again tried to disentangle herself, once more falling against him.

Giggling somewhat uncontrollably, the two of them stood up, their faces close together. His arm still around the relaxed body, Brendan looked Maureen in the eye, and in a deep resounding voice, said, "Me Tarzan, you Jane." Surprising himself and Maureen, he kissed her on the lips and then immediately jumped back in horror, apologising for what he had done.

Maureen stood her ground. "Me Jane, you Tarzan," she said huskily. "Let's do it properly this time." She stepped forward with her arms outstretched. Brendan didn't need any further bidding and complied with her wishes.

"Wow, Maureen, we gotta do that again."

"Maybe, Bren, but there's work to be done. Now, go away and make another cup of tea. I spilled mine, an' the biscuits are all broken. Go on, while I sort myself out." Maureen, in a bit of a fluster and with a confused grin on her face, shooed Brendan away and tried to settle down with her paperwork.

The rest of the morning was spent in a joyful haze, with Brendan grinning mightily as he trundled the boxes of toys up to the toy floor greeting Mr. Jones 'the manager' like a long lost friend and giving Noel Danster—the assistant manager—a good-morning wave.

"You're in an excellent mood this morning, young man," declared Danster in his marked southern-English accent and smoothing his shiny moustache with his customary flourish. It was unusual for Danster to even acknowledge the presence of storeroom staff. However, the relaxed tone of voice soon reverted to the usual disdainful tone. "Would you please ensure all outer wrappings are taken away immediately? There are some across there, behind the doll stand. Standards must be kept, young man. Sloppiness cannot be accepted."

Touching his forehead with his forefinger in mock deference, Brendan collected the errant sole piece of cardboard, patting the demonstration Sindy doll on the head as he passed it, muttering, "Sit up, Sindy girl, we can't have any sloppiness here. Now give us a smile."

"That OK, Mr. Danster?" Brendan asked as he passed the slight figure with dark suit, shiny shoes and oiled hair. Danster's whole being was concentrated on a poorly dressed, nervous female customer with a large shopping bag. "All tidied up and shipshape. Not many in today, I see." Brendan wasn't expecting an answer as he danced across the floor to the staff lift. He was inviolate, on top of the world! Nothing could dampen this newfound euphoric feeling; he was in love.

Returning to the basement with its smells of cardboard and dust, Brendan rounded the stack of large boxes—*lots of Meccano there needs to be shifted*—to see Maureen sitting at the small makeshift office table with her head in her hands, deep in thought. Seemingly conscious of Brendan's presence, she turned, dropping her pen and, in what appeared as slow motion, rose from her seat. Placing her spectacles on the cardboard box in a deliberate movement, she stepped forward.

This was the telling moment; would they both react as both wished?

"Oh, Bren!" Maureen cried as she came towards him with arms outstretched.

"Holy moley!" Brendan gasped. "Come here, Maureen, me beauty." Throwing caution to the wind, Brendan rushed forward raising his arms, unfortunately catching the edge of the high stack of boxes of Meccano as the brown-coated pair became one in their passionate kiss while boxes of Meccano crashed down around them. Clark Gable had met his Maureen O'Hara.

***

"You live with your mum in a house in West Derby? That's the posh side of Liverpool isn't it?"

Still adjusting to their newfound awareness of each other, Brendan and Maureen were sitting on the cracked-leather-covered bench seat in the dimly lit basement restaurant bar of a typical Liverpool pub in a small side street off Dale Street. The smell of stale tobacco smoke, mixed with the sweet smell of frying fat, filled the air. There were very few customers at lunchtime on a weekday.

"Yes. I live off Green Lane. Not very posh at all, a terraced house in West Derby—or is it Tuebrook? I have a sister who's older than me. She's married with a young daughter, lives in Warrington. Thanks, love."

Maureen interrupted her flow to thank the waitress for the plates of egg and chips she placed on the table for herself and Brendan.

"Yer pot of char is comin', den, an' yer butties. Won't be a minit," the waitress said and flicked a damp cloth over the tabletop.

"OK, love," Maureen acknowledged.

The waitress stepped away from the table, having difficulty keeping upright in her extravagant high heels and showing a lot of leg in her miniskirt.

Both watched the retreating waitress and laughed in agreement. Earlier, when they had entered the bar, both wearing overcoats due to the light fall of rain, Maureen had thrown her coat over the adjoining seat, and Brendan, adjusting his black eye patch, had involuntarily stopped in admiration of her appearance. Maureen was wearing a tight cream sweater that accentuated her body shape, over a red minidress with high-heeled knee-high black leather boots, and Brendan had exclaimed somewhat in awe, "Wow!" Notably pleased with the reaction, Maureen had shuffled along the bench seat, the short skirt exposing an attractive pair of knees and thighs.

Now, she threw her long hair over her shoulder and settled down to eat her egg and chips. "Do you like my new skirt, then?" she asked coyly.

Brendan nodded his head enthusiastically at the transformation of the dowdy brown-coated flat-shoed woman in the storeroom to this startling woman.

The lunch hour flew by, and as a breathless pair clocked in and reached the storeroom hand in hand—some minutes over the allotted lunch hour—who should be awaiting them in the dusty interior but an accusing assistant manager Noel Danster.

Standing to his full five foot six inches, he started to lecture them in his clipped London accent with its upper-class undertones and laughter-inducing squeak. He prattled on about time-keeping, and the importance of being available all the time, and may they take this as a warning to behave or Mr. Jones, the manager, would have the next word.

With this final squeaky tirade, Mr. Danster swung around and, unfortunately for him, minced down a blind alley of cardboard boxes. Undaunted, he swung on his heel and, with an admonishing finger wag, made his haughty way back towards the lift, leaving Brendan and Maureen arm in arm and having difficulty controlling their laughter.

***

Over the next weeks, Brendan revelled in this newfound euphoric state. He was in love, had reasonable digs, and a job of sorts. Was it time to start looking for employment with career prospects, or, at least, something that would provide some more money? He was now on eight pounds a week, which just about paid for his rent, meals and clothes.

Inwardly ambitious, Brendan had aspirations for management. Management, in his view, was an acceptance of his ability to lead from the front, as well as reaping the presupposed greater financial rewards. What were the opportunities in his present employ?

I'll see if I can make an appointment with the personnel manager. Now, what's his name? I remember he was an unpleasant guy. Yeah, John Marsden, that's his name. I'll wait until the Christmas rush is over—no, I'll go up now and see his secretary and try for an appointment.

During his next coffee break, Brendan divested himself of his brown coat, donned his suit jacket, and took the lift to the fifth floor. Knocking on the door marked 'Personnel', after some long seconds he heard a distant female voice call out, "Come in."

Pushing the door open, Brendan stepped forward into a room with a wooden desk in the centre and a multitude of grey filing cabinets with papers everywhere, the owner of the female voice somewhere behind them. There was a door to the right of the room, slightly ajar.

"Hello, Miss. Oh! I see it's Mary. How are you?" Not hearing a reply, he continued, "You may remember me? Brendan Harris…storeroom… toys?" Receiving a quizzical look from the young female behind the large desk he again continued, "I would like to make an appointment to speak with Mr. Marsden."

"Oh! Mr. Harris. Yes, you are part of the temporary staff. What do you wish to see him for? He is very busy, you know, especially with it coming so close to Christmas."

"Is he in? Perhaps I could see him now? If he's not too busy," Brendan suggested, raising his voice at the sound of a muffled cough from behind the linking door.

"No Mr. Marsden is—"

"That's all right, Mary," Marsden called. "I've got a few minutes. Send the lad in and bring me his file."

With a resigned glance at Brendan, Mary tottered over to a large grey filing cabinet. Brendan straightened his tie, smoothed his jacket and unconsciously patted his hair into place. He took the proffered file from Mary and pushed open the door.

Unbeknown to Brendan, only that morning, Marsden had the unwelcome and surprising resignation of the under-manager in the carpet department, and had thought, come the New Year, he would need to replace the missing manager. Perhaps he could promote one of the sales staff, and Harris, he remembered, had voiced ambitions for management. Perhaps he could put him in Carpets and place him on the permanent staff with a view to seeing his management capability.

"Right, Harris," Marsden welcomed, leaning forward to receive the file from Brendan. What can I do for you? Do sit." He pointed to the vacant chair in front of his desk. "I have about five minutes."

Brendan took the offered seat and began to answer Marsden, only to be cautioned by a waved hand as Marsden opened the file folder and began reading its contents.

"Ah, I see…well…well…" he muttered to himself, scanning the contents of the file, then raised his head. "Yes, Mr. Harris, you were saying?"

"Yes, Mr. Marsden, I have been in your employ for two months now, and am…looking towards the future…I consider myself to be management material."

"You do, do you?" Marsden peered at him over the top of his glasses. "And what makes you think you're management…material, Mr. Harris?"

"I gather you have my CV in that folder and will have seen over the past four years I've been at sea as a trainee ship's officer. You may be aware of the extensive training and preparation for both ship and crew management I have undergone."

"Why aren't you sailing the high seas now, Mr. Harris?" Marsden leaned back in his large cushioned swivel chair and emphasised the question with a wave of his hand.

"Oh, that I were, Mr. Marsden," Brendan replied with a resigned smile. "The accident I had two years ago put an end to that adventure. I am now quite recovered, however, still suffer from diplopia, hence the eye patch." He pointed to the black patch over his right eye.

"Right," said Marsden. "Thank you, Mr. Harris. We may be in need of an under-manager in the New Year. Are you suitable? Well, we'll see. Now, away with you, and let me get on with my day's work." Marsden replaced his reading glasses with a dismissive wave.

Thinking what an unpleasant man Marsden was, Brendan returned to the sub-basement and an anxious Maureen, who was awaiting the outcome of his foray up to the fourth floor.

"He hinted at a permanent post in the New Year with a view to management, Maureen, but then, I'm not too keen to follow in the footsteps of men like Jones and Danster. I want the wide open road…"

Standing back from Maureen, Brendan went into poetic mode, spreading his arms wide. "Do you want to come with me? Do you want the open road? Shall we make our way together and conquer the world? We could emigrate to Australia or Canada. What do you think?" He leaned forward enthusiastically.

Maureen, caught up in the flow, replied with gusto, "Yes! Let's… Ah!" She hesitated. "But wait a minute. We need to do some thinking. You're talking about leaving England, our relatives, our friends. I barely know you. Sounds exciting, though. What would Mum say? Oh! I'm in a dither. You would really do that, up sticks?"

Catching Brendan's hand, Maureen stepped closer, gave him a kiss on the cheek and then stood back. "Bren, my love, I'm all for it, for the excitement, but let's stop and think. If we feel like this in the New Year, let's do it. We could do some reading before then. There must be books about emigrating…in the library… Oh, God, you haven't even met my mother yet."

"Yes, Maureen," interrupted Brendan, somewhat startled by his decision and her surprising agreement. It had been a spur-of-the-moment thought, but the idea was growing on him. "Right, we have a lot of planning to do. Let's keep it a secret until we finally decide. I know when I tell my mother she'll hate the idea."

"OK, Bren. Enough of that. We have a job to do. There's a few skip-loads of toys to be taken up to the floor. You grab that one—it's the heaviest. Australia…kangaroos…sunshine…" she mused. "Would you ever!"

5

Driving Test

It was now early January 1964, and Brendan was still working in the sub-basement with Maureen. He was no longer too bothered whether he got a call from Personnel to get on the management ladder as over the Christmas he'd been in conversation with one of the sales representatives calling to see Mr. Jones the Toy Manager. Brendan was quite envious of the smart relaxed approach of the salesman in his dark suit and polished shoes. When he heard that same salesman was provided with a company car, he decided that was the career for him. Of course, he had to acquire a driving licence as his Irish licence was not recognised in the UK, and he was quite apprehensive, but pretty confident in his driving skills to pass the forthcoming test.

Having driven quite extensively in Ireland, however, he needed to gain experience on the UK roads and learn the many rules and buy a provisional driving licence. Maureen had agreed he could get some experience using her car. So Brendan bought the necessary licence, which only allowed him to drive provided he was accompanied by a qualified driver. Whenever they could, the pair of them drove around Bootle and sometimes out to Formby on the north coast, with Brendan learning the Highway Code and doing emergency stops.

The day for the test arrived. Maureen collected Brendan from his digs in Bootle in the Ford Anglia. Extremely proud of her car, was Maureen, a blue two-door saloon with stylised rear wings, raked windscreen and hooded headlights. Brendan drove very cautiously to the corner of Renshaw Street and Bold Street and parked alongside the bombed remains of St. Luke's Church, which was kept in its ruined state to remind everyone of the futility of war.

Maureen gave him a kiss, wished him all the best and said she expected to have a set of L-plates to sell. "You've still got the log book and insurance cover note I gave you?" she anxiously enquired.

"Stop worrying, Maureen. They're safe here." Brendan smiled, patting his jacket pocket. "Now, don't worry. You go and enjoy your shopping. Here's the tester."

A smart Ford Consul had pulled in behind the Anglia, and a large male dressed in a tweed overcoat and cloth cap clambered out. He nodded to Brendan and, without a word, the tester—who looked like one of the farmers from deep in the country in Ireland—shook hands and squeezed into the passenger seat of the Anglia.

"Right, Mr. Harris. My name is Bennett, Richard Bennett, and over the next hour or so, I shall determine whether you can sell your L-plates or not. Ha-ha." He grinned, clearing his throat and spitting into a grubby handkerchief before continuing in a throaty voice, "Let me see your licence and insurance policy. I'm just at the beginning of a cold. Is there a heater in this damn thing? An' what's with the eye patch, Paddy?"

Brendan was quite surprised with the relaxed attitude of Mr. Bennett, who examined the paperwork and handed it back. Brendan replaced it in its folder while commiserating with him for his cold and explaining the reason for the patch.

"Just so long as you can drive, Paddy. Right, let's git going. Excuse me a mo. I'm…atishoo. Ah! That's better." Replacing his handkerchief in his pocket, he ordered, "Straight up the road ahead an' turn left into Upper Parliament Street."

Brendan looked in the rear-view mirror, checked handbrake, gears in neutral, started the engine, and gave it a congratulatory touch on the accelerator as it started to purr. Glancing over his right shoulder—he had previously switched the eye patch to his left eye—he indicated he was pulling out from the kerb, went into first gear and smoothly moved away.

On their way to the first corner, Mr. Bennett questioned Brendan on his road-sign knowledge, ticking off his answers in a notebook, in between long sniffs, sneezes and throat clearing. Continuing along Smithdown Road, a busy shop-lined road, Bennett advised Brendan he would, "At any time—at any time, Paddy," strike the dashboard with this notebook as a signal for an emergency stop. Brendan acknowledged this information and, negotiating a large van parked some feet from the kerb, braked sharply to allow a little old lady to continue her stuttered passage across the road. Not prepared for the sudden braking, Mr. Bennett was propelled forward, catching his nose on the dashboard, notebook and pencil flying into the air.

Brendan waved in reply to the woman's startled glare of indignation as she continued on her way across the busy street and, smiling to himself, apologised to Mr. Bennett for the abrupt stop and asked if his nose was all right.

Bennett settled back in his seat, gathered his pencil and notebook and once again dabbed his nose with what must have been a very soggy handkerchief, sniffing loudly. "We'll call that the emergency stop, Paddy. Right, continue on to the next right turn and pull in to the side when I tell you. God, this cold will kill me!"

"Park between those two cars. Good, well done. Not perfect…" He sniffed loudly again. "That's a good fella, I'll only be a minit."

With that, Mr. Bennett fell out of the car and, sheltering his hair from the driving rain with a raised arm, produced a set of keys from his overcoat pocket. He unlocked the door of one of the whitewashed houses lining the street.

Brendan settled back into the seat and briefly pondered the strange state of affairs before starting to read the previous night's *Liverpool Echo*. Always on the lookout for employment opportunities, he noticed an ad from a large food manufacturer in Aintree—Broons Foods—were seeking a sales representative, driving licence required.

I'm halfway there for the licence, provided Mr. Sniffy returns, Brendan thought. *A strange business, this test. Oh! There he is.*

Bennett emerged from the house and waved farewell to the open door before quickly depositing himself in the passenger seat.

"Apologies, Paddy, I had an important message to pass on. Right, let's continue. Where's my notebook?" He patted the side pocket of his overcoat. "Jaysus! I'd forget my head, only it's screwed on—" sniff "—here it is. Right, where were we?"

The test continued, with the windscreen wipers fighting a losing battle with the driving rain and making a loud clunking noise on every visit to the left of the windscreen. The interior of the car fogged up, and Bennett continued sniffing, sneezing and constantly clearing his throat.

With some relief, they returned to the starting point and parked. Bennett sniffed, gave a loud cough, scribbled on a piece of paper, and announced, "Right, Mr. Harris—" sniff, cough "—you may sell your L-plates. Well done. Here, sign this piece of paper. I'll keep the copy." Sniff. "I'm off home to my bed."

That evening, Brendan settled down to complete his CV and wrote to a few companies, including Broons Biscuits of Aintree.

6

Brendan Meets Mother!

"Hi, are you there, Mum?"

"Won't be a minit, love," was the reply from the back of the terraced house. It was a cold, miserable Sunday afternoon in January, and Maureen had come to introduce her beau to her mother. Brendan had prepared for this very important moment, instructed by Maureen as to what her mother expected.

"She will make an entrance, Bren. She's in her mid-fifties and comes straight to the point. She's a good mum; she's had a hard few years. Enough of that, Bren, I'm sure she'll love you." Maureen laughed in embarrassment as she parked her car outside the lop-sided gate and low wall in front of the two-up-two-down pre-war terraced house.

Brendan followed Maureen through the wooden gate, making sure it was closed behind him on Maureen's instruction, carefully stepping over the cracked and uneven flags. Maureen, who had walked ahead, was leaning over and patting an exuberant red setter whose large sweeping tail seemed to be trying to spin the dog around. Maureen turned and introduced the large bundle of quivering excitement as 'Bandit'. Bandit wasted no time in greeting Brendan, the dog's slobbering jaw leaving a smear of froth on Brendan's trouser leg before turning in one bound to continue his effusive greeting of Maureen.

"Down, Bandit," Maureen commanded, glancing back at Brendan. Her face showed slight concern at the mark on his trousers. Bandit turned towards the open door, his tail drooping and his head dipping in response to the severe female voice coming from the entrance.

"In, boy," said a tall thin woman wearing her hair in a tight bun. She wore a pair of loose grey slacks topped by a warm red jersey, and her face was as thin as the bare arm pointing to the back of the house. Bandit slid past, looking apologetically at the terrifying human.

After a further pointed command to the poor dog, Mrs. Byrne turned to welcome her visitor with a smile that would have frozen a snowman.

"These animals must know their place," she volunteered in a refined Scouse accent. She looked suspiciously at Brendan, who expected to be told to sit at any moment. He stepped forward, remembering his father's words: always allow the lady to offer her hand first.

"Hello, Mrs. Byrne."

"Introduce me, dear," she ordered, looking directly at Maureen. "I take it this is your young man?"

Maureen, somewhat embarrassed by her mother's attitude, apologised. "Oh, sorry, Mum, this is Brendan Harris." She pointed towards Brendan. "Brendan, this is my mum." Maureen looked at Brendan, hoping he would understand her mother's unwelcoming attitude.

Brendan stepped forward with one of his biggest and friendliest smiles and gave a short bow, almost clicking his heels.

"Hello, again, Mrs. Byrne. Yes, I like to think I am Maureen's young man." Brendan's right hand itched to offer to shake hands. He was surprised to receive a semblance of a smile from the thin face, with a long limp hand rising from the voluminous slacks like a white snake, ready to bite. *Does she want me to shake it or kiss it?*

Brendan again bowed, leaning forward and taking the proffered snake by the head, squeezing it gently before returning it to its owner and stepping back. His episode of gallantry was somewhat spoiled as his left foot missed the edge of the cracked paving stone and he stumbled backward and, trying to regain his footing, collapsed against the privet hedge. Undaunted, he regained his footing and laughingly stated his next trick would be to stand on his hands singing 'Old Man River'.

Mrs. Byrne gave something like a smile and turned to Maureen. "Maureen, my dear, I think your young man needs some support. Do bring him into the house for a cup of tea, as I look forward to his rendition of *'Ol'* Man River'—not *'Old* Man River', as you suggest. Is it the Paul Robeson classic, you mean, Brendan?" The offer was surprisingly welcoming from the thawing icicle.

Maureen rushed over to Brendan as he regained his footing, wondering whether to laugh or sympathise with him as he straightened his suit jacket, picking the pieces of hedge from the cloth. "Oh, Bren, you haven't hurt yourself, have you?" She caught his hand.

"No, no, I'm OK, just feel a right eejit," Brendan replied as nonchalantly as possible. "It must have been very funny, seeing me staggering around, and I don't even know the words of 'Ol' Man

River'. What possessed me to say such a stupid thing? Your mother must think I'm a right fool."

"No, Brendan, don't you worry. She's in there tut-tutting to herself, wondering what sort of…eejit—" she laughed "—eejit, what a lovely word—I've got mixed up with. Now, take a deep breath and let's get through this together."

Together? Hey, hold on a minute, where is this leading? Am I getting a wee bit involved, here? She's a lovely girl. Am I being a bit selfish? I'm hoping to start a new career in sales… Anyway, let's see how things go. I've got the challenge of Mother ahead of me.

"Yes, Mrs. Byrne, I spent four years at sea." The threesome sat in the front room of the house. Mrs. Byrne was enthroned in her single armchair to the right of the tiled fireplace. Maureen and Brendan sat on the double settee with its sagging arms and body. The two pieces were of an indifferent brown colour, probably bought in the 1930s. Maureen poured tea from the ceramic pot and handed round very delicate teacups that probably hadn't seen the light of day for a decade. The whole room gave the impression of pre-war Britain and austerity.

What surprised Brendan was that both women, on entering the room, had turned to the right to face a small grotto in the corner. A blue light shone down on a statue of the Virgin Mary, and both bowed slightly, making the sign of the cross. Brendan was used to seeing such religious statues in Ireland but hadn't considered religion. *I suppose Maureen assumes I am Catholic,* Brendan thought, *as I come from Ireland. Wonder how Mrs. Byrne and Maureen will react when they discover I'm a Prod? I'll leave that question alone for the moment.*

Faded watercolour landscapes hung on the walls and a bushy, weary-looking plant sat in the corner behind Brendan.

"Brendan's from Ireland, Mum. Remember, I told you, and you wondered if he might know Uncle Declan."

"Don't be silly, Maureen. He won't know your Uncle Declan." Mrs. Byrne crossed her legs. "Declan is in the Maynooth Seminary; he's a resident seminarian there." She threw her hands up in disgust at such a ridiculous suggestion. "You're named after St. Brendan, aren't you, Mr. Harris—Brendan? Brendan… 'The Navigator', 'the Voyager'. Wasn't he one of the Twelve Apostles of Ireland, renowned for his legendary quest to the Isle of the Blessed?"

Brendan, who wasn't aware that his namesake had been a saint, and an apostle at that, was intrigued to hear he was known as The Navigator. To save face, he pretended he knew and nodded wisely.

He wondered if he was now a danger to this lady and her present life. Did she fear he was going to take her daughter away? His perhaps selfish thoughts of marrying a woman like Maureen receded into the background at the thought of becoming involved with this severe woman who lived in the past, apparently devoted to her religion. He shuddered. *Play it cool, Brendan, and lighten the atmosphere a bit. Come on, where's the one-liner. Yes, where's the dog? What was its name? Banjo, was it?*

"Before I bore you with my life story, Mrs. Byrne," Brendan laughed self consciously, "we had a red setter at home in Ireland. He was as crazy as Banjo. By the way, where is he now?"

"I'll answer that, Mum," Maureen interjected, giving Brendan a relieved glance. "Bandit, Brendan, not Banjo...you eejit." Maureen laughed nervously. "He's in the back yard. We got him as a puppy. Didn't we, Mum? He was mad then and used to take anything that wasn't bolted down."

"A lovely dog but certainly quite scatty." Brendan laughed, moving into a more comfortable position on the sofa, away from a loose metal spring. "Well, Mrs. Byrne, you asked me about my seafaring exploits." He took a deep breath, wanting to impress this lady, and started. "I was reared in Ireland, had a grammar school education. When I left school at sixteen, I went to sea in the Merchant Navy."

Seeing his listener's head raise in interest, he continued.

"Yes, Mrs. Byrne, with a company called the Calvex Tanker Company, as a trainee navigating deck officer. I was at home in Ireland, to take my finals, when I had a rather severe road accident, which led to the end of my career. I am now, hopefully—" he offered a disarming smile "—recovered, and, as you know, working in the department store with Maureen." Touching the black eye patch that covered his right eye, he continued, "This helps overcome a problem I have with my eyes as a result of the accident."

"How interesting," Mrs. Byrne said. "Especially your seagoing exploits. My Rupert, Maureen's father... Oh! What am I saying? I mean Peter! He was in the army. Lord only knows what he is doing now." Brendan noticed Mrs. Byrne slip a faded sepia-tinted photo of a man to the back of the well-thumbed photo album on the sideboard.

After a short uncomfortable silence, Mrs. Byrne slowly rose with difficulty. Brendan went to help her but was dismissed with a cursory wave.

"I have managed on my own for many years, so please go away, young man."

Mrs. Byrne made her feet and said in a severe, tight-lipped tone, "Please excuse me...Mr. Harris...I must leave you." She turned to address her daughter. "Maureen, will you see Mr. Harris out?" And with this abrupt farewell and instruction, the lady of the house, making a point of taking the photo album with her, left the room, leaving Brendan rather surprised and Maureen dismayed and apologetic.

"That's my mum, Bren," excused Maureen. "She blows hot and cold, but I'm sure she likes you. I'm sorry…I hope you understand."

"I don't, really," replied Brendan. "Don't worry, she's probably not feeling too well. Should I leave?"

"Oh, I'm so sorry, Bren, but I did warn you."

"Shush," whispered Brendan, putting his forefinger up to his lips and pointing with his free hand to the door which he had noticed had moved slightly. "Look, Maureen, shall we leave?" Brendan felt the urge to laugh at the ridiculous situation. "What do you want to do?"

"Let's go for a drive somewhere. You could drive… Oh, I know." Putting her finger to her mouth and looking anxiously to the doorway, she daringly whispered, "Let's go to the pictures. It's still only four o'clock. We could go to the Abbey in Wavertree—it has that picture, you know, the Walt Disney one. *The Lady and the Tramp*. My friend Jill told me it's lovely."

Brendan, thinking *I've got a ten-bob note, could afford it*, stepped closer to Maureen, delighted with the idea, and gave her a welcomed hug, looking to see if there was any movement of the door.

"Right, Maureen," he raised his voice, "let's do that, then. Would your mum be around that I might say goodbye?"

Glancing at Brendan in some surprise, she turned to the open doorway and, catching Brendan's hand and moving forward, called, "Mum, Bren and I are going now."

Stepping out into the small hallway, they were met by Mrs. Byrne, who just happened to be coming down the stairway.

"What was that you said, dear? You're not going out, are you? What about your tea? What about evening Mass?"

"That's all right, Mum," answered a slightly exasperated Maureen. "I'll be back later, you go ahead without me." Turning to link her arm with Brendan in an apparent show of independence Maureen shut the front door behind them.

"Oh, what have I done, Brendan?" she cried, gripping his arm tightly. "I've never stood up to her before."

"Right, come on, then, Mo. Let's go an' enjoy ourselves. She'll get over it. Now, where's the Rolls Royce?" He laughed, catching Maureen's hand. "We'll get some popcorn and a drink of lemonade, and then after the picture go to a chippy. What more could you want?" Feeling a hesitation in Maureen's response, he turned around and realised his big evening out was no more.

"Can't do it, Bren. I can't leave her on her own. She's…"

"Don't worry, Maureen. I understand. *So much for our evening out.* "Look—you go back on in. I'll walk home. It'll do me good. I'd better not come back in with you."

"Oh, Brendan, I'm so sorry. I'll make it up to you. Thanks for being so understanding. I'll work on it. No…" She hesitated. "No, I'll run you back. It will only take a few minutes. It's the least I can do." Wiping a tear from her cheek, she produced her car keys, got into the car and motioned Brendan to board as she leaned over in the driver's seat to unlock the passenger door.

In the dark early evening, with the mournful moans of the shipping in the background and the everlasting rain, they drove to Bootle. Brendan wondered what next. He liked Maureen a lot, and she obviously felt bad for ruining their evening, but her mother was a bit of a drawback. Then there was the religion angle.

The drive back was as unhappy as the weather, what with the noisy wipers, the complaining engine and the crash of the gears indicating the driver's lack of concentration and the uncomfortable cramped sitting position. It was with some relief that they arrived outside Brendan's digs. Maureen pulled over to the driver's side of the road and parked on the slope. Brendan noticed the handbrake sounded a bit loose, but he was ready to leap out and let Maureen get back to her mother. It was a surprise when she put a restraining hand on his arm and said, "Let's talk."

"Yes, let's," agreed Brendan, resignedly awaiting Maureen's next move as he shifted his position on the narrow car seat.

"You don't get on with my Mum."

Well, I'll be honest here, thought Brendan to himself, *Mum is afraid I'll take her daughter away from her.* "No, Maureen I don't. It was obvious she didn't like me. She's very religious, isn't she?" Brendan wondered if Maureen would refer to her own proclivity to the religion angle.

"Yes, she is. I do what she wants for some peace. She's driving me mad. You don't know the half of it." She turned to Brendan, looking to be consoled. In the dim illumination from the broken streetlight, he could see the reflection of the tears on her cheeks. Feeling so sorry for the poor girl, Brendan leaned over to kiss the tears away, getting a stabbing pain in his groin from the gear leaver. Maureen put her hand behind Brendan's head and pulled him forward as she kissed him hungrily. The pain of the gear lever and now the handbrake didn't help Brendan's response, but he manfully returned the kiss, pulling the willing body towards him.

Brendan liked the taste of the lipstick and salty tears. Wondering where to put his hands, he was beginning to enjoy the experience when Maureen suddenly drew back.

"God, you must think of me as a right tart, Bren, but give me more." She pulled him close again.

Delighted by the response, and relieved to find one of the irritating obstructions had disappeared, Brendan put his arms around the eager body and returned the hungry kiss.

By now, the windows had all steamed up, and they felt isolated in their own little world. Drawing back for a breath of air, Brendan sensed movement in the car and leaned forward to clear the window over Maureen's shoulder.

God, the car was moving! "Maureen! Pull back…the handbrake…let me at it. Quick, the car is moving backward down the hill."

Just as he got to pull up the handbrake, there was a crunch at the rear of the car and it stopped moving. Looking at Maureen in trepidation, Brendan opened the car door and stepped out into the rain, more than relieved to find the car had mounted the low pavement and had come to rest against a tree. There was no damage to the car, but the tree, only a light sapling, was bent over some thirty degrees.

"All clear, Maureen. Start the engine and go forward onto the road," he suggested. As she did so, the sapling sprang back to its upright position.

Rather than get back into the car now that he was dripping wet, Brendan signalled to open the driver's window and, seeing the anxious face of a girl torn between two people, gave her a peck on the cheek, said, "Maureen, I'm going in, hopefully to have a bath and see you at work tomorrow. Good luck with your mum."

She acknowledged his comment with a weepy smile, and he waved goodnight as she started the engine, activated the inefficient nearside unlit indicator and pulled away in a small cloud of wet smelly exhaust.

7

Promotion from Sub-basement

"Looks like I'm losing you, Bren," Maureen greeted him the next morning. "They're expecting you up in Personnel—better hurry. Don't put your overalls on—I think they want you for the spring sales. Let's meet over lunch, tell you about Mum."

Brendan had just arrived in the sub-basement after a cold and uncomfortable train trip from Bootle into Liverpool, followed by a hurried walk in a light snow shower. He was not looking forward to another day trundling toys up and down in the lifts and wondered what was in store for him. He had been hired on a temporary basis for the Christmas rush. It was now into January, and nobody had been in touch to tell him his future. He had tried to get an interview with John Marsden of Personnel without any success so it was some relief to hear the message. Maybe they were going to offer the trainee management post to him or maybe…just offer an employment contract.

"Thanks, Maureen. I'll let you know what they want me for, but sure, I'll meet you at lunchtime—dying to hear how you got on with your mum. Must get going."

Striding towards the lift, Brendan looked back into the gloom of the sub-basement, with its distempered walls and metal frames with their plethora of many sized cardboard containers. All he could see through the ever-constant clouds of dust was Maureen in her flat shoes, brown overalls and hair in that dreadful hairnet, with her hand raised in farewell.

***

"Hello, Mary, nice to see you again. Brendan Harris—Mr. Marsden wished to see me urgently."

Swinging around from the ever-demanding typewriter and endeavouring to pull her minidress to cover the exposure of flesh, Mary sought the telephone with her free hand.

"Mr. Harris to see you… Yes…five minutes." Turning to Brendan, she motioned to the vacant chair beside a small table with a newspaper on it and turned back to her typewriter. 'Train Robbers on Trial' was the stand-out headline. *I remember,* thought Brendan, *this was late last year… 'The train robbers stopped the Glasgow to London express and got away with two and a half million'—reads like a crime novel. Look at the names of some of the accused—'Buster Edwards, Ronnie Biggs, Bruce Reynolds and sixteen others were all accused of the robbery'—must keep my eye on this…*

"Mr. Marsden will see me now? Good," acknowledged Brendan. "Oh! Thanks, Mary."

Replacing the newspaper on the table, Brendan ran his fingers through his hair, straightened his jacket, took a deep breath and gave a tap on the closed door—the door which, when opened, could determine his future. Some career prospect was on offer, he was sure, as if he were to be sacked, to put it bluntly, a lesser mortal than the all-powerful Marsden would be involved.

Marsden kept his head down, examining the papers on his desk, sniffed and, without looking up, pointed to a vacant chair. The offered seat, a tubular bendy model cowering against the acres of polished timber, was most uninviting. Balancing uncomfortably on it, Brendan awaited Marsden's first move.

After a minute, Marsden sat up and pointed his fountain pen at Brendan, gave his expected sniff, and said, "So we meet again, Mr. Harris."

Brendan nodded in agreement, and added a smile.

"I see you have been working on Toys for the past few months. There have been a few changes in personnel over that time, and we have considered your request to work for the company in a more permanent role."

This should be interesting, thought Brendan. *What's he going to offer?*

"What are your ambitions for the future, Mr. Harris?" Marsden emphasised his question by again pointing sharply forward with the fountain pen. Brendan instinctively ducked as a small blob of bright-blue ink ejected from the pen nib, landing fortunately on the desk in front of him. Marsden kept the pen pointing at Brendan awaiting his reply.

"Success through endeavour, Mr. Marsden," announced Brendan, rising to the challenge. "My ambitions are to obtain from employment sufficient funds to lead a comfortable life. To attain this, I need employment with a company offering a future to an ambitious man—a man willing to learn his trade, a man who will put in the hours required to prove his value." Stopping in his flow, Brendan, surprised with his own rhetoric, awaited a response from Marsden, having hopefully thrown the question back to him.

Lowering the pointing missile very slowly, Marsden pondered.

"OK, Mr. Harris, you've proved your worth. I won't beat around the bush. Would you be interested in a trainee manager's role with the company?"

"I'll certainly consider it, Mr. Marsden. I would appreciate some more information."

"Excellent. I shall put together a new contract for you. However, I have arranged for you to transfer to Mr. Goodblood on menswear. Due to the after-Christmas sales, they require an additional salesman. Miss Byrne will be sorry to lose you—Ha! Ha!—I'm sure. She has been informed. You will, over the next few months, be allocated to different departments. Now, go report to Mr. Goodblood on the first floor."

A bit sketchy, the information—the new contract will be worth looking at, thought Brendan as he bid farewell to Marsden and gave the blonde secretary Mary a wink. *Right. Mr. Goodblood…what a name… Wait, I'll nip down to tell Maureen… No, I'll wait till lunch. What shall I do about her?*

Arriving on the first floor, he made his way to menswear and stood behind a high counter, unobserved, to have a look at his workplace for the next few months. The silence was overwhelming, not a customer in sight. Of course, it was a cold morning and it was snowing.

Rows of counters dominated the floor, suits and overcoats to one side, with underwear alongside the many rows of men's shirts, all in their cellophane see-through packages. The predominant colour was white, with handwritten notices displaying the collar sizes. Dominating the scene was the cash register—a wonderful-looking edifice with bright price keys displayed on the front, buttons to press, levers to pull. At the base of this large monument to modern retailing were four drawers, mahogany in colour with brass edges, merged into the overall outstanding lighter coloured unit.

A male figure dressed in a sombre business suit moved between the counters of shirts and underwear, making minute alterations to the display. *That's probably a salesman,* thought Brendan. *He looks the part.*

Oh! Who's this? A further male figure materialised from a side curtained wall—a fussy-looking man in an ill-fitting suit with bulging waistline, receding hairline and an air of pomposity.

The salesman, one could see, sensed this and increased his shirt-squaring task, turning when he heard the surprisingly squeaky voice from the intruder and looked with raised eyebrow.

"Carter, where is this relief salesman? Look, I'm away to a meeting." These two sentences were thrown out through a bushy wet nicotine-stained moustache in an explosion of annoyance.

Carter the salesman, with an air of amusement, replied, in a well manicured voice, "I have no idea whatsoever, Mr. Goodblood. You go along to your—" Carter wafted a limp right hand "—meeting, and I shall look after things. If you will excuse me, I shall look after this customer."

Mr. Goodblood, who did not like this superior air, swelled up and muttered his way towards the escalator in a ball of spluttering indignation.

Brendan, dressed in his rather beaten business suit, wondered who the supposed customer was, but before Carter could say anything, he strode forward with outstretched hand.

"Mr. Carter, I'm Harris—the new man. Sorry to see I have just missed Mr. Goodblood."

Offering his right hand with an air of haughty indifference, Carter replied, "I saw you hiding behind the men's suits. I had guessed you were 'the new salesman'." Stepping back, Carter's indifferent attitude relaxed and, hitting Brendan gently on the shoulder, he said, "Not a bad-lookin' beast, either."

Brendan was quite startled with the reception. *Reminds me of that steward I knew on one of the ships—he was a homosexual...wonder if Carter is, too?* Stepping back, Brendan smiled, recovered his hand and asked when Mr. Goodblood was expected to return.

"Have no idea, friend. Mr. Bloody Goody disappears for an hour or so during the day. I'm leaving the end of the week—just serving my notice. What's your name, duck? I'm called Curtis—Curtis Carter, at your service." With a big smile, Curtis danced a few steps away from Brendan. "Looks like we are getting a bit busier. 'Bloody Good' should be back about twelve. Oh, the smell of the man. Yes! Madam, neck size fifteen and a half, how sensible, our most popular size..." Curtis surprised the lady customer by taking her hand and encouraging her to dance with him towards the respective counter.

What a nice guy. Pity he's leaving. Now, who's this? Brendan wondered as a small, well-dressed man appeared on the floor, unconsciously picking his teeth, walking purposefully towards menswear. Passing Brendan, he acknowledged him with an apologetic glance, apparently thinking Brendan was a customer.

"Hello there," Brendan called out as the toothpicker disappeared behind the screen. Following his target, Brendan pulled aside the screen to be met with a sharp retort.

"Customers are not—"

Before the target could finish, Brendan interrupted in exasperation, "I'm not a customer. I have been sent by Personnel. I'm your new salesman."

"Oh, I see!" replied the toothpicker as he balanced on a small stool to change his shoes. "Well, you must be Harris. Many welcomes, kid. Thank God, we were getting a bit short of sales staff. 'Tony' Curtis is leaving the end of the week. Been in sales long? Of course, what am I thinking? My name's Sean Coyle—me dad's from Wicklow." He spat out the well chewed toothpick and caught it in his left hand as his right hand was offered in greeting. "I gather yer from Ireland with that accent. Whereabouts?"

"I'm a Dublin man and, by the way, I'm not a salesman. I've been sent by Personnel and I'm looking for someone to tell me what to do."

"Have you not seen Goodblood? What's that, Tony?" Coyle called out in reply to a call for help from Curtis Carter. "Ye need me? Gotta go...what's yer first name, then?" asked Sean as he hopped across the enclosed space adjusting his shoe.

"Brendan."

"A good saint's name. Better wait until Goodblood returns. Come out on the floor anyway an' look on. Comin' Tony. Speak of the devil, here he comes. Your new salesman, Mr. Goodblood," called Sean as he exited the enclosure.

"Coyle, see to your customer!" Goodblood hollered as he stopped and looked indignantly at his new recruit. "Harris, is it? Where have you been?"

Brendan was taken aback by the abrupt introduction, but before he had time to answer, Goodblood went into a spasm of a hacking cough. The phlegm could be heard trying to escape through the white handkerchief he hid his reddening face behind.

With his rotund body dressed in a bulging black waistcoat and straining jacket shaking in its seemingly uncontrollable cough, Goodblood stumbled into the curtained enclosure and could be heard coughing up the phlegm.

Leaving Goodblood coughing up his innards, Brendan looked around the sales floor. 'Tony' was engrossed with an attractive-looking woman who was looking at him quizzically as he displayed his wares with some flamboyance. The Scouser Sean was ringing up sales on the mountainous cash register. His customer, another woman, was dressed in a loose jacket over a pair of voluminous trousers with plimsolls peeking out beneath the cloth.

There were a few other customers on the floor, some looking positively at the wares on the counters, but one particularly tall woman who looked familiar to Brendan was making her way towards him. Trying to remember who she was, it suddenly came to him. It was Maureen's mother!

She doesn't look at all well. Yes! How could I have not recognised that disdainful stare? What does she want?

"Mr. Harris, you remember me—Mrs. Byrne?" she started, steadying herself with one hand on the shirt counter. Without waiting for a reply, she continued in a trembling voice, "I am requesting you…to leave my daughter alone. We have no wish to see you again." Without waiting for any reply from the dumfounded Brendan, Mrs. Byrne turned on her heel and, with effort, made her way back to the escalator.

Quite taken aback by the sudden confrontation, Brendan stood still for a moment, looking around to find a few customers staring at him, the males with a smile and the women with knowing looks and nodding heads. Curtis Carter passed him, with customers' purchases, gave him a smile and in a loud whisper and suggestive grin asked, "And what have you been up to, nice boy?"

Looking around, he was relieved to find there was no sign of Goodblood. Sean gave him a short wave.

Before Brendan had time to recover, Goodblood reappeared, looking somewhat more composed after his coughing fit, and called him over. "Harris, I see from my notes you should be up in the training room for eleven o'clock. You had better get up there quickly as it is now ten past."

Brendan held back from remonstrating with Goodblood for being so late with this information, but gave him a scornful look, and replied, "Thank you, Mr. Goodblood. I gather the training room is on the next floor?"

Getting a cursory nod, he hurriedly made his way to the lifts, his mind in turmoil, what with the order given by Maureen's mother and the expected no doubt caustic remark from Marsden when he arrived late.

"Hello, Mary. I'm here for sales training where…?"

"Through that door," replied Mary, looking guilty as she dropped her novel in a basket on the floor and pointed towards a closed door to her right.

Knocking on the door, Brendan pushed it open to be greeted by sudden silence and three men sitting at a long table, staring at him, with a further man in a dark suit—not Marsden—who walked towards him looking at his watch and commented in a sarcastic voice, "You must be Harris. You are rather late."

"So sorry, yes. My name is Brendan Harris. Mr. Goodblood kept me."

With a shrug of his shoulders, the dark suit, aged about thirty, pointed to a chair alongside the other staff members. "Sit there, Mr.

Harris. Gentlemen, if you will excuse me, I shall repeat what this meeting will consist of for Mr. Harris's benefit." In a bored monotone, the instructor outlined the standards and procedures expected from sales staff, advising each salesman they would be given a small daily float of money from accounts and allocated a drawer on the multi-till where, at the end of the day, the salesman would total monies received and place them in a sealed bag to be collected by Accounts.

"Any errors are questioned thoroughly, gentlemen, *thoroughly*. Your respective floor managers will have your quotas, and after some training on customer approach, product knowledge and till awareness, you will be let loose on the public. You may go for your lunch." This last comment was made with an unpleasant smirk.

God, look, it's one o'clock. Maureen will be waiting in the canteen. What do I do? I wonder if she knows what her mother is up to. The woman did not look at all well.

Acknowledging the last comment from the trainer with a smile, Brendan nodded to the other men in the room and left to make his way to the training room and the canteen.

Looking over the heads of the hungry herd of store staff, enabled due to his greater height, he could see no sign of Maureen with the usual group.

Time's passing, must get some food into myself. It's going to be a busy afternoon. There's an empty table, got a copy of the Daily Post on the way into work, won't join the group. Give them a hi with a raised hand and point to the paper, and when Maureen comes, she can join me...if her mum allows it.

Settling down as best he could on the mass-produced seat amidst the background noise and the odd burst of laughter, he began to enjoy his shepherd's pie and the newspaper. *Well, well, well,* he mused, *they captured some of the train robbers...* His readings were interrupted by a sudden tap on the shoulder.

"Are you Bren? Been looking for you everywhere. Maureen Byrne asked me to give you a message—I was down in the storeroom. Looks like some problem with her mother. Maureen's in a right state."

"Thanks, pal. Wonder what's happened?" asked Brendan with a resigned shrug. *Mother is certainly making a nuisance of herself.*

"They've called for an ambulance. She was lying on the floor. That's all I know. See you."

Gulping down the remains of his shepherd's pie, Brendan made his way down quickly to the cellar to see two uniformed men carrying a still body on a stretcher with Maureen stumbling alongside, trying to hold her mother's hand.

Seeing Brendan hurrying towards her, she stopped for a moment, and with an anguished face explained in a rush, "Mum came to see me—how she found me I have no idea. She looked terrible, I sat her in my chair. He helped—" pointing towards a delivery man waiting impatiently "—and she told me she had seen you and then she collapsed in pain. Oh, it was awful, and then she stopped breathing. Oh, Bren, I tried to help her breathe, but she died. Oh, poor Mum... But why did she go to see you?"

"Come on, lass," called an anxious ambulance attendant, "we'd better get the old lady to hospital as quickly as possible."

"See you at the house later, Bren. Tell me then," cried Maureen as the attendants bundled her into the ambulance.

"I need a signature for those toys over there." A brown-coated man waiting impatiently by the entrance pointed towards a small stack of cardboard boxes. "Yep! She just keeled over. Helped the lass to make her mum as comfy as I could. Now give me a signature, mister. I'm falling behind."

"Sorry, friend, don't work... Ah, there's the supervisor—coming over the hill, yes Mr. Sullivan," said Brendan, noting the name card attached to the suited supervisor. "Miss Byrne has gone with her mother in the ambulance. Apparently, she had a heart attack. I must go as I should be on Shirts."

"You're Harris, aren't you? You've been on Toy Stores. Good, good. There's another delivery... Look, you stay here, I'll settle with Mr. Goodblood," said Sullivan. "All right by you, Harris? Miss Byrne should be back shortly."

Brendan was surprised and pleased and gave Sullivan an affirmative nod, thinking, *we won't see wee Maureen this side of tomorrow.*

As Sullivan rushed away, Brendan turned to the impatient driver, checked boxes, signed the delivery note with a flourish and repeated the process for the five boxes of Meccano delivered by the second driver.

"Yes, Toy Stores, Harris speaking..."

"What are you doing there, Harris? Where's Miss Byrne?"

"Tell you all about it, Mr. Danster. Now, how may I help you?"

"Three boxes Scalextric and whatever Meccano there is."

"Okey dokey, Mr. Danster, up to you in a jiffy. Just had a delivery of five boxes of Meccano—you want the lot?"

"No, just the first three."

Humming to himself, Brendan took the goods to the Toys floor to see Sullivan heading towards the lift, leaving the two managers, Danster and Jones, in close discussion. On Brendan's appearance, they looked at him resignedly. Jones raised his hands, dismissing the whole business and Danster over to tell Brendan to look after the stores until Miss Byrne returned.

***

That evening, Brendan took the bus over to Maureen's to find he wasn't terribly welcome, no reason given. He had knocked at the small terraced house expecting Maureen to open the door with a grateful smile and to be brought into the kitchen, offered a cup of tea and brought up to date about Mother. Nothing of the sort. A rather severe woman in her early thirties with a most unwelcoming attitude opened the door, silently looked Brendan up and down and resignedly enquired his business with a cursory, "Yes, what is it?"

Brendan, quite taken aback, stammered, "Brendan Harris. Is Maureen here?"

"Oh. It's you, is it? Into the parlour, please."

This is ominous, thought Brendan. *The parlour—only visitors are sent to the parlour. Where's Maureen? Have I done something wrong?*

"Mr. Harris, no need to sit. I will be blunt. I am Miss Byrnes's sister Mary. Our mother, Mrs. Byrne, has unfortunately passed away, and Miss Byrne has gone into mourning, so your presence is no longer welcome."

Before Brendan could reply, the forbidding female made a gesture of dismissal and ushered him out of the house again.

With the door shutting with a farewell bang, Brendan stepped back, bamboozled. *What's going on? Poor Maureen…wonder will she turn up at the store tomorrow? Is it something to do with the church?*

8

Maureen Disappears

The following morning, assuming he was to continue working in the storeroom, Brendan donned his brown coat, only to be interrupted the moment he arrived by a telephone call from Mary of Personnel: he was to report to Mr. Marsden at ten o'clock.

"And so we meet again, Mr. Harris. What is it this time?" Marsden asked rhetorically and continued in his cynical manner, "Miss Byrne, I see, has phoned in to say she will not be available for work for the next few weeks. I understand her mother has suddenly died. I also hear there was some disturbance on the men's department when you started there yesterday?" Not receiving a reply to his leading question, Marsden prompted, "Was it Miss Byrne's mother, Harris?"

"Yes, Mr. Marsden. Mrs. Byrne did have a few words with me yesterday. Mrs. Byrne, I must point out, was not very well and was very protective towards her daughter. I was invited for tea by Miss Byrne a while back—"

"For tea, Mr. Harris? For tea? How very quaint and old-fashioned."

Where are we going here? Is he going to reprimand me or sack me? Maybe he's going to leave me in charge of stores…

"Yes, for tea, Mr. Marsden," agreed Brendan, putting what he hoped was a final comment on the situation.

"Why was, may I ask, Miss Byrne introducing you to her mother?" Marsden gave a sarcastic laugh.

None of your business, thought Brendan, *but I'll give you a reason you can't dispute.*

"Mr. Marsden, by the way, you are aware I am an Irishman?" Receiving a sceptical nod of agreement from Marsden, Brendan said, "In Ireland—and I must tell you, Mrs. Byrne had Irish connections and was a very religious lady, may God rest her soul… In Ireland, there is an expression, widely used: 'do-lally'. Mrs. Byrne was *very* protective of her daughter and *very* old-fashioned in her attitude and a bit, as I have already said, do-lally."

"Do-lally, Mr. Harris?"

"An expression, Mr. Marsden." Brendan stopped to take a deep breath and bowed his head. "So sad to feel I have to use it, but Mrs. Byrne was somewhat *non compos mentis*, or a bit…do-lally."

"Enough, enough, Mr. Harris. I have heard enough." Marsden sighed in resignation. "I have spoken with Mr. Jones, manager of Toys, and we have agreed you are on the edge of dismissal. However…" Marsden stopped, looked Brendan in the eye, and in a very serious tone, continued, "However, we propose to give you a second chance and ask you continue in Toy Stores until the return of Miss Byrne."

Wow! That was a near one.

"Thanks, Mr. Marsden." Relieved, Brendan rose and offered his hand to consolidate the offer. "I won't let you down. I have a few ideas which could improve reception of goods. Oh! Will I have a salary upgrade for my new responsibilities?"

"All contained in this letter, Mr. Harris—your offered contract for trainee manager. Sign the copy and return it to me within the week. Now you are dismissed, go—please go."

9

Game of Hockey

It was now well into January 1964, and Brendan was still running Toy Stores for the departmental store. The trainee manager contract he had been offered was most unattractive, full of promises of training and movement between departments, with examinations on progress, two weeks' holiday a year and a pension scheme. He was passed a manual, all glossy, showing serious-minded young men posing as trainee managers and outlining the various stages to management. The starting salary was £624 a year.

The extra two pounds would come in handy, so Brendan signed the contract and awaited further instruction on his management career. So far, it looked as if he would be in the stores for ever.

He was beginning to get somewhat jaded and tired of the dust in the basement, the pettiness of the staff and the boring travel to work each morning. Maureen never reappeared—Brendan even tried the sister's house in Warrington—but there was no sign.

He had, at long last, bought some transport: a second-hand upright metal box on wheels. The Ford Popular 100E was not built for comfort. With its shiny leather seats and basic amenities, a very loud engine, two noisy screen wipers, two doors and a three-foot gear lever that vibrated noisily when the car was moving, it was a bargain for £50, with a low recorded mileage and—as with so many cars built in the 'fifties—nothing as helpful as a heater.

As a way of expending some energy and to make friends, Brendan joined one of the many sports clubs in Liverpool area: the Merseybeats Cricket and Hockey Club. In spite of his eye patch and gammy leg, Brendan had a short turn of speed and was one of the younger fitter players. He played centre forward in the fourth team, with Eric Denmark, who was a retired businessman and a moderately fit pensioner carrying a bit of extra weight, as middle defence. Colin Brown accompanied Brendan in attack. Colin was a young doctor/consultant based in the renowned children's hospital Alder Hey.

Then there was Arthur Smith, a tall, gangly, middle-aged grocer and quite short-sighted. Arthur, who refused to wear his glasses when playing, which was quite understandable, played on left wing. He was surprisingly fast and had a devastating reverse stick which, with his lack of perfect sight, meant the ball would come at furious speed from the left wing whether there was any one to receive it or not.

Another notable player was Brian Bell, the goalkeeper. As a builder's labourer and fitness fanatic, he came in at eighteen stones, five foot six. The extra weight for his height came from his developed muscles. He had muscles everywhere and was quite entertaining in the shower. Due to his body weight, he could only move fast in short bursts, and due to his width, he fitted in the goal mouth quite nicely. Lastly, there were Jim and Bob, right wing and half backs respectively. Eric was the captain, being the eldest.

It was a particularly cold and miserable February day, but the fourth team had had an extremely good winter. They had won most of their games and were looking forward to the match against Crewe Vagrants. Crewe Vagrants were renowned for their aggressive playing and invariably won their matches by sheer intimidation. This year, things were going to be different, Merseybeats were out to win—aggressively if necessary.

At one o'clock on a cold winter's afternoon, they set off for their annual match against Crew Vagrants. Brendan, who hadn't been to the Crewe away match before, said he would follow Jim in his Hillman Imp, with Bob, who didn't know the way, driving his souped-up Ford Anglia at the rear. Eric, in his confident smiling manner, volunteered that he had been before and could take over directions where necessary.

"Should make the trip in an hour and a bit, lads. It's close on fifty miles, just follow me," offered a confident Jim with a pat on the back for Brendan. "By the way, Bren, could you take Brian's goalkeeper pads? You've got plenty of room in that big wagon of yours."

"I'll take your hockey sticks as well, Jim. You'll have a job to fit yourself and three others in that dinky toy you call a car," he joked then followed in a concerned tone, "Are we wise to go, though, Jim? It's beginning to get a lot colder an' the roads are slippery after the ice last night."

"Nothing to fear there, me old son. It's main roads all the way, and they're a grand social bunch, the Crewe lads. You agree with me there, Bob?" he called over to the crowded Ford Anglia.

Bob turned as he was just going to board. "It is a bit parky, Jim," he called, "but we've done it before—when it was snowing. Remember a few years ago? Now that was weather. They beat us six-nil as well. We've gotta good team this time, so let...wagons roll."

In convoy, the three cars left the car park and headed towards Runcorn to take the new bridge over the River Mersey. With a clear sky and some silver remains of ice on the roadside from the previous evening's freeze, and the temperature in the mid-thirties Fahrenheit, all looked fine providing they were careful. Brendan drove cautiously, concentrating on the road, and fearful of hitting an unsuspected icy patch; he was conscious of the bald rear tyre. Well, not completely bald. More like the shaved head of a trooper. Eric, sitting alongside Brendan, regaled him with stories. He was a busy man, active in the local council as an unpaid councillor. When he was done telling those stories, he wanted to know how things were going for Brendan in Lewis's, and congratulated him on his trainee manager's job.

Closely following the first car, they crossed the new Runcorn Bridge and shortly afterwards, passed through a town called Frodsham, then Tarporley, and after fifty miles of open roads, they reached their destination.

Relieved to get there in one piece, but concerned there was no sign of Bob and the Anglia, Brendan drew alongside the Imp on the rough, rock-hard parking lot and looked over at Jim, who shrugged his shoulders as much as to say 'wonder where Bob's got to?' The immediate surroundings were a bit dismal, the pavilion being a wartime, prefabricated, long, low-lying, green building. When rounding the 'pavilion' to gain entrance, they could see two hockey pitches lying side by side with the important netted goals at each end. The ground looked rock solid and glistened in parts where ice had formed. The clear skies which had heralded the group's departure were beginning to cloud over with a low bank of grey, miserable cloud, and the temperature had risen slightly, which foretold the possibility of snow.

"Is this all there is? Eight of you? You missin' some?" was the slightly indignant question from the burly player, already changed into his shorts, shirt and boots. "The name's Mike. I'm the captain."

"Why, hello, Mike. I'm Eric. How do you do? Time's getting on. One of our group got left behind—should be with us shortly. Is there a game? The ground looks pretty hard."

"Played many a game on harder pitches than this, Eric. We're willin' if you guys are. We're short of one player—we could give you Tony to even up a bit. Seems a shame not to have a game now yer here." Mike hitched his shorts up, exposing the two massive tree trunks he probably referred to as legs.

"What do you say, lads?" Eric called out. "Do we give them a game?"

Receiving the affirmative, Eric led the others into the cold uninviting changing room, some looking with concern at the gathering cloud cover.

With the disparity in team numbers, Eric gave a short team talk and a cautionary comment. "We're going to be two short if Bob doesn't turn up, so we defend. Maybe make a break for goal—that's up to you, Bren, as centre forward, and you, Colin, as inside forward. Don't suppose this Tony... Oh, hello. You must be Tony—kind of you to come and join the better team, ha-ha! What position do you play?"

"Nowhere really, sir. This is only my second game ever. Mr. Clarke asked me to come along an' make up the numbers, sir. Hope that's all right."

"That's fine, Tony, and enough of the sirs. I'm Eric—old enough to be your granddad, I know. You know what to do with the stick?"

"Oh, don't you be worrying. I know what to do with the stick, sir... Eric."

"Here, Tony, grab a hold of this," encouraged Eric, throwing a hockey stick to the young lad, as the way he gripped it could give some idea of his competence. Unfortunately, Tony grabbed the hockey stick incorrectly, left hand under right.

"See you haven't played before, laddie. Still, you're a willing body, and we are sure short of them. Everyone ready?" Eric called, his words forming a white cloud of freezing air in front of him.

What are we doing? Brendan wondered as he looked around the sparsely furnished changing room with the icicles around the dirty windowpane beginning to drip from the heat generated by the eight bodies. Apart from Brian the goalie, all dressed up in sweaters and knitted cap, the remaining team members were all in their white shorts, blue knee-length stockings and blue shirts. Each one wore studded boots, fine for a soft underfoot but not much use on the freezing surface to be encountered. Short of three men, young Tony wasn't much of an asset. Hopefully, Bob and the other players would turn up.

With a clatter of boots on the wooden decking around the building, the eight frozen stalwarts, plus Tony, ran out onto the frozen hockey field. The home team was already out hitting a couple of white balls, no thought given about colour here, with the ground rapidly turning silvery white in the hardening frost.

"Just look at them, Bren. They're huge and there's ten of them," Colin muttered. "Bet the ref is from Crewe as well—where is the ref, anyway?"

With that, a small, coated figure broke away from the menacing opponents and trotted gingerly up to the centre line. He stood shivering but patiently awaiting the two captains to join him.

Eric looked rather ungainly in his large, long white shorts and brown socks, his much worn blue shirt straining to stay over his belly, and his bald head surmounting the remarkable sight. He walked gingerly over the hard, slippery surface, his arms spread to hold his balance. Nearly over-balancing a few times, he arrived alongside the ref in the centre of the frozen field.

Eric won the toss and decided to defend the goal where he stood. The Crewe team, in the gathering gloom in the end furthest from the pavilion, were waiting impatiently. Brendan took his position as centre forward and prepared for the 'bully-off'; Colin, as centre half, with Tony and the rest of the team, took up defensive positions. This brought all of the team, apart from the goalkeeper and one defender, up forward.

"We're going to slaughter you lot today," the centre forward from the Crewe team muttered threateningly at Brendan as the two positioned the rounded ends of their hockey sticks each side of the frozen white cannon ball on the centre line.

Brendan, at his six-foot height, overshadowed his opponent and ignored the threat.

When the ref blew his whistle to start play, each player raised their stick to touch their opponent's and returned it to the ground, this to be done three times, and then each player made to take control of the ball.

On the third step in the bully-off, Brendan was slightly quicker than the other guy and took control of the ball, brought it towards himself by curling the head of the stick around the ball and made to pass it to Colin, who had run—carefully on the ice—forward to take the ball. The Crewe centre half moved on the frozen surface to Brendan's left to intercept the expected pass to Colin, leaving a clear path to goal. Brendan, renowned for his ability to hit the ball hard and direct, took the opportunity. Noticing the goalkeeper was at the side of the goal mouth speaking to someone, he struck as hard as he could. His stick met the ball perfectly, lifting it about four feet off the ground and, like a bullet, it sped over the ice, catching the goalkeeper unawares, and ended up in the back of the goal, surprising everyone, especially Brendan.

Returning to his match position to bully off again, and quite delighted with the surprise goal, Brendan could not help grinning at his opponent who muttered ungraciously, "Just a lucky shot."

This time, after the start, Crewe got the ball from the bully, and four of the team advanced, passing the ball between them. Tony, God rest his soul, went to tackle the player with the ball, only to be shouldered off and left in a heap on the frozen ground.

Fortunately for the visitors, the ball player lost his balance after the encounter and crashed to the ground. Arthur, the indomitable left wing player, gathered the loose ball and pushed it towards Colin, who was in the centre of the field. He collected the fast-moving ball and started a hesitant run, with Brendan running, or trotting carefully, down the centre of the frozen waste, careful to avoid the various dangerous polar bears wielding sticks. Colin used the reverse side of his hockey stick to successfully pass the ball to Brendan, who couldn't stop to collect it and narrowly missed a polar bear who stole the ball and hit it hard towards the visitor goal. Another polar bear collected the fast-moving ball and redirected it towards the goal mouth. The immobile Brian, who was unable to move fast enough to his left, saw the white cannon ball hit the back of the net.

By now, the weather had closed in a worrying amount, with low, snow-laden grey clouds gathering. The players were beginning to find it impossible to keep their footing, and it was becoming somewhat dangerous to life and limb. Catching Eric's eye in the lessening light, Colin pointed his stick towards the pavilion to say *let's call it a day*. The others, noticing the gesture, all agreed. Eric called over to the ref and Mike, the opposing captain, who both agreed to stop play as it was too dangerous. A draw was declared, and all slid back to the welcoming shelter of the pavilion.

As they were leaving the field, who should arrive but Bob and the rest of the team. Bob and fellow passengers were full of the drive down, what with losing their way and sliding into the back of another car, sustaining some damage to the front of Bob's pride and joy.

The Crewe captain came forward to thank Eric and team for making the effort, agreeing a draw as a satisfactory result. The lads stripped off, ready for the accustomed hot shower, and were disappointed to find the water pipes had frozen. There was not even enough water for a cup of tea. It was decided to pile into the cars and start the long drive home as it had now, to add to their difficulties, begun to snow.

Three hours later, they gratefully arrived at the Jolly Miller in the swirling blizzard. The three cars, encrusted with frozen snow, and ten tired, cold men made their way home.

10

Job Hunting

"Hello, June," called out a weary Brendan as he pushed open the door of the terraced house in Bootle and made his way up to his uninviting room. *What's this, a couple of letters, looks like one from Ma, the other is a bit business looking.* He was still acting manager for Toy Stores—*is this part of my trainee manager contract?* he wondered. He was getting bored with the monotony and the claustrophobic conditions.

Sitting on the side of his bed, he eagerly tore open the envelope to find an invitation to attend interview with Broons Biscuits of Aintree, Liverpool, for the post of salesman. His endeavours had born fruit: an interview on Tuesday 18th February. *I'll write to confirm and phone. Make sure they know I'm coming. Mustn't forget I've got one with the Gas Board on the Monday for wages clerk.*

His social life at present had dried up. He'd called around to the house in West Derby to see Maureen, but there was no sign of her. The neighbours were none the wiser.

"Strange woman, that Mrs. Byrne," was the comment. "Sad she died, but she always wanted to meet her maker. Her daughter went away in a big car—not seen her for ages."

I'll have to start looking around for some female company, thought Brendan. *Quite fancy the landlady, dangerous ground. Wonder when the husband is due home? He never arrived for Christmas.*

Must go dancing again—go a bit farther afield now I've got the car. I've heard there are some good spots in Southport. Next day off, I'll drive out there. Haven't been to the hockey club for a few weeks... Eric offered a place on the team for a home game next Saturday against a team from Wigan. Must get out and do some exercise. These thoughts crossed Brendan's mind as he changed out of his work clothes, had a wash, and made his way down to the kitchen where June was preparing tea.

"Ah, there you are, Bren. Was just goin' to give you a call. Your tea's ready." June turned from the kitchen stove with a frying pan in her hand and scooped a couple of fried eggs onto fried bread on a plate. There were already a couple of pork sausages and some fried tomato, all swimming in a pool of grease on the large dinner plate.

"That'll put hairs on yer chest, Bren. I know you like a fry-up." June placed the laden plate before Brendan on the small Formica table and turned back to the stove.

"I'll join you in a minute—just do a couple of eggs for myself. How did yer day go? I did a bit of shoppin'—the prices of things now! Still, we've gotta eat. Sheila was over—remember you met her at the dance? You know her husband is with Bibbys. Due home in a couple of weeks."

"When's John due home, June?" asked Brendan between mouthfuls. "He's been away some time now. You expected him back at Christmas."

"Yes," answered June over the sizzling frying pan. "As I told you, he's been transferred to another ship. Now headin' for the East Indies an' due home in June. What's it now, beginning of Feb? God, how the time flies. It's my birthday tomorrow, would you believe? He's bin away more than eight months now. Eight months..." she repeated in a wistful voice.

Placing her plate on the table facing Brendan, June settled herself on the wooden kitchen chair and somehow accidentally kicked Brendan under the table. As she withdrew her foot without apology, Brendan's senses went into red alert. *Is that a message? God, what's she up to? Was that deliberate?* Raising his head from his half-cleared plate, he noticed June looking at him over her teacup.

"Bren, you never told me how your day went. Here am I, gabbin' away, not givin' you time to say a word—are you still workin' in Lewis's?"

"That's OK, June, it was a long day. Yep, still working in the basement as a store man, but listen to this..."

June's attention perked up on this command as she forked a mouthful of egg white into her mouth.

"I've been offered an interview for sales with Broons Biscuits of Aintree. Do you know them?"

"Not too well. I think I've seen them in Irwins. Remember...fancied their chocolate biscuits."

"Well, will you do me a favour, June? When you're out shopping next, please have a look for Broons biscuits and buy a couple of packets." Brendan smiled as he placed his knife and fork parallel to each other on the empty plate. "That was great, June. I did enjoy it. Any more tea?"

"Yes." June lifted the large, heavy ornate ceramic teapot—a present given by her long, dead grandmother. "I'll be going for a shop on Thursday, Now, where's my list? Ah, there we are. What was the name again, Bren?"

Having written it down, June rose from her kitchen chair and started removing the dirty dishes.

"Allow me to help, June. I've nothing on for the night—would it be OK if I watch a bit of telly in the front room?"

"Of course, Bren." June turned from the sink, tossing her hair back and smoothing down her dress. "You have no need to ask. I've got the fire lit and *Emergency Ward Ten* will be on in a quarter of an hour. Look, you take your cup into the front room and get the TV warmed up. I'll be in, in a minit."

"OK, June." A satisfied Brendan rose from his kitchen chair, picked up his half-full cup with its fancy designs and went to squeeze past June in the small kitchen.

Not realising Brendan was behind her, June turned quickly to say something and knocked against his hand, sending the cup, saucer and spoon into the air.

Both of them frantically made a lunge to save the crockery. Brendan caught the cup, June caught the saucer, the tea hit the ceiling, and both ended up on the floor laughing uproariously. Rising to their feet, Brendan was very tempted to kiss the attractive, flushed face, but thought better. *What would be the consequences? Have I read the messages right? Oh, God, what do I do? Let's wait and see.*

A rather flustered June prepared the dishes to clean. "Won't be long, Bren," she called as he made his way into the front room. "Have a whiskey if you like. You'll find a bottle and glasses in the cabinet. If you're havin' one, pour me out one as well. I'll bring in some water if you want it."

Television, a nice warm room, an attractive woman…things are looking up. Now, where's that cabinet? Well, would you believe it? A bottle of John Power. With the TV switched on and the whiskeys poured, Brendan took off his jersey and shoes and settled himself on the sofa. The flickering screen settled down to show that Goodyear tyres gave extra skid resistance, Kellogg's cornflakes needed 120 days of sunshine, and that Surf gave you 18% more powder for your money.

"Yes," agreed June as she came into the room, having made a rapid change into a fresh skirt and blouse and dabbed a powerful perfume behind her ears. "Yes, get Square Deal Surf and you get eighteen percent more from your washing machine," she misquoted deliberately. "My machine is on its last legs." She laughed as she settled herself beside Brendan on the comfortable sofa.

"Now for a session at Oxbridge Hospital…"

June lay back on the sofa with her left leg touching Brendan's right. "Oh, good. I do like him," she exclaimed when Doctor Don Nolan, the rugged Australian Ray Barrett, entered the ward and gave nurse Young, or Jill Browne, a meaningful glance as she was talking to a very young John Alderton playing the part of Doctor Moone.

"This is cosy, June," Brendan murmured. "How come you had a bottle of John Power in the cabinet?" He gave her a knowing smile.

"Just drink the stuff," June said. "Here, put a drop of water in mine. Now let me watch the TV."

Settling down to watch the flickering screen where the black-and-white images sometimes went out of shape and the voices reduced in volume, Brendan let an adventurous hand stray onto June's leg. Not being repelled, he squeezed gently. *Wow, where do we go from here? There's another twenty minutes to go before the programme is over.*

June snuggled up a little closer and rested her head on his shoulder, intently watching the flickering screen.

Ah, the adverts are due now. Brendan turned his head to the right, and for a moment, June's face was in profile as she watched the screen, then she turned her head to face him, and they went to kiss. Unfortunately, Brendan's aim was poor, and he kissed her nose.

Making another attempt, trying not to laugh, he was more successful, and they had a long, satisfying kiss with hands searching out hidden parts. Doctor Nolan's harsh Australian accent dominated the room with his orders to pass the scalpel. With a nod of agreement, Brendan untangled himself and rushed over to turn off the TV.

He was ready to leap on his captive deer when the doorbell rang. *Ring...ring...ring...come on, answer me, stop whatever you're doing... ring...ring...*

"I'd better answer it, Bren," said a disappointed June, adjusting her dress and patting her hair into place with a glance into the large mirror over the mantelpiece. "You'd better put your shoes on, switch on the telly. Right, I wonder who it is..."

"Why, hello, Sheila. Do come in. What a lovely surprise."

"Well, as it's your birthday tomorrow, June, the girls and I—they're in the car outside—thought you'd like an evening out. Do say you can come, we've arranged a surprise for you."

"What a lovely thought, Sheila. That's a great idea. Brendan just came down to watch *Emergency Ward Ten*. He's a big fan. You remember Brendan?"

"Yes, I do," Sheila replied as the two women entered the front room to be met by the welcome heat from the fire. "Hello, Brendan. No, stay put," she said as Brendan began to rise from the settee.

"Hello, Sheila," Brendan greeted the intruder. "There, I knew he would do it," he said, referring to the TV. "How are you keeping? Not seen you for a long time."

"Give me a minute an' I'll throw something on," June said and dashed from the room, leaving Sheila in the doorway. Brendan wasn't entirely sure who Sheila was or what was happening on the TV.

"You must remember me, Brendan. We met at the dance in Reece's…"

"Of course. Reece's—remember it well. Have you been since?"

Before Sheila could answer, June's voice came from the hall. "All right Sheila I'm ready. There's some supper for you in the kitchen, Bren. I'll lock up. Probably be late. Nighty night."

"Night, June," Brendan called. "Goodnight, Sheila. Lovely to see you again."

As the front door slammed shut, Brendan, standing in his shirt sleeves in the cold hallway, kicked the hall stand and cursed. He hadn't put his shoes on.

11

The Landlady Gets Drunk

Brendan went to bed around eleven and was woken at one o'clock by June clattering about downstairs. After one particularly loud bang—she must have walked into the kitchen table and knocked it over—he heard a curse and a sigh and then tears. *Must be a bit drunk,* thought Brendan. *She's coming up the stairs… Oh, God, no, she's coming in. I'll pretend I'm asleep.*

"Oh, Bren, I'm so, so solly," cried June as she sat on the edge of the narrow bed. "Where's my John? It's been munts an' munts. Are you listenin', Bren?" She poked Brendan in the ribs. "Yer only pretendin'. Come on, move over, I wan' a cuddle." With her endeavour to get into the bed, she lost her balance and fell on the floor. She began to snore.

Now what do I do? Brendan turned in the bed and leaned over the side to see the landlady lying on her back, her dress above her knees showing bare leg and suspender. One of her very high-heeled shoes—with broken heel—was lying on the floor beside her. Her handbag was lying open just under the bed. She slobbered a bit and retched as if she wanted to be sick and then subsided into a sleep with odd whistling sounds as she breathed out.

I've got to get her out of here. "Can you hear me, June?" he called loudly, not expecting a coherent reply. He gave the collapsed body a vigorous shake, with little response. *Maybe I could lift her—God, she might vomit—*"Right, woman, can you hear me? I'm going to lift you now."

Surprisingly enough, there was some assistance given as the legs pushed her upright, and he heard her mutter, "Mus' help luvly Bren… Oh, John, where are you?"

Yes! Could do with your help, John. But you're probably entertaining the mademoiselles in Bangkok.

With June half upright under his right arm, and her head pressed hard against his chest, Brendan peered down to find June looking up at him with glassy eyes and hair all over the place. She grinned, and in a drunken voice, said, "Shall we dance?" then threw up half-digested chicken curry over Brendan's pyjama jacket.

Half dragging, half carrying the body, Brendan turned her face to the floor, to avoid her choking on the vomit, and eventually got her through the door into her bedroom, where she heaved again and deposited a bucketful of badly digested curry and rice over her carpet. It was definitely a woman's bedroom—thankfully—as the perfume smell overrode that of the vomit.

At last, Brendan got her onto the bed. *Can I leave her? She might get sick again. What's the time? Two o'clock—must get some sleep…got to be at work for eight…I'm playing a game of hockey at three—God, I smell. Right, I'll settle her on her side—better pull some clothes over her keep her warm. I think she's got rid of the curry. Poor woman. She'll feel a right fool in the morning. Goodnight, June, or should I say…good morning.*

At seven o'clock, a weary Brendan rose to the alarm and dressed hurriedly in the cold room, and on his way downstairs he knocked gently on June's door. Getting no answer, he cautiously opened the door and peered in. It was with relief he saw her still in the position he had left her, snoring gently.

Glad all appeared well, he closed the door and continued down to the kitchen. *I wonder what she will remember. Now, this is the second time this has happened, maybe I had better move. She's a lonely woman. Come home quick, husband.*

With a bowl of cornflakes and a boiled egg with toast inside him, he made his way to work at the department store, wondering how much longer he'd be there. The trainee course in management seemed to have been forgotten, and the most immediate prospect was the van sales post with Broons Foods. There were other sales opportunities on the market: Pet Foods down south were looking for a sales rep to cover the Midlands area, and a firm called Kelly's were looking for people to sell sales space in their business telephone books. There was an offer for interview in Manchester with Kelly's the week after next, and one with Broons—which was Brendan's favoured job—on the following Tuesday at four-thirty.

So, with a fairly contented mind, Brendan turned in for the five hours he was expected to do at the store. However, he wondered what June would remember from the previous night. *I won't say anything unless she asks* he thought.

***

"Hi, June, what a cold miserable day. You know I'm going for a game of hockey—any chance of a bite to eat? I'm starving."

"Can do egg and chips, OK? And, by the way…" she continued in a carefree tone, gathering her ingredients, "I found my handbag in your room…an' my shoe. God, what were they doing in your room, Bren?" Becoming more serious she said, "There was an awful smell of sick, too. I've spent the morning cleaning up my room. It was me, wasn't it? The smell was in your room as well… An' why was my handbag in your room an' my shoe?"

I've got to be a bit careful here, thought Brendan, *spare the poor woman's feelings.*

"Well…" Brendan answered, "there I was, fast asleep, dreaming of beautiful girls on a lovely beach, when I felt a shake of my shoulder. When I opened my eyes, there was this beautiful woman leaning over me, breathing whiskey fumes—was it Johnnie Walker?" he asked with a smile.

June shook her head, looking terribly confused.

"Then you said, 'Goodnight, Bren,' hiccupped and stumbled back to your room. I was returning to my dream when I heard a call from a distressed swimmer out on the landing and got up to find her sitting on the floor looking quite ill. I got her to her feet, and whilst she was getting into bed, she was violently sick over me and the floor. Then she apologised and fell asleep."

"Oh, Bren!" June looked mortified. "Oh, I am so sorry. Don't tell John when he comes home. Oh, God, I feel a fool…here's your dinner. Sorry again, Bren," she apologised, breathing a mix of fresh-smelling toothpaste and sour whiskey over him.

"Thanks, June, that's lovely," he answered as he turned his head away and looked at the overcooked chips and solid fried egg on the plate before him. "And don't worry. I won't say a word to John. It'll just be between you an' me. Now let's make a cup of tea."

He was feeling quite subdued on his way to the station to catch the train for the hockey match. It was a wet, dark and smelly afternoon with smoke belching from the factories and many ships in port.

What's the future? Should I look for new digs? Maybe find a new job first. I'm better than the job I have, trudging in each morning, donning my brown coat and running around for self-important little men. Wonder how the match will go? My leg's a bit painful today…God, that was a long time ago…three years since the accident. Boyo, doesn't time fly? And the double vision is still there—I'm fed up with this eye patch, although it's a bit dashing.

God, the smoke in this train carriage would kill you. Ha, who am I to talk? I'm adding to it with my Rothmans King Size tipped…look, everyone is puffing away. Must give up, can't be good for me, an' the price—five bob a pack. Right, here we are.

Through crystal roofs the sunlight fell, and pencilled beams the gloss renewed...

The poem, describing the dramatic sweeping dust holders of Liverpool Lime Street, came to mind every time he passed through the station, always impressed at the flow of passengers—some as local as Brendan, others with their suitcases, heading north or south...

The next train on platform eight is...

Brendan smiled, remembering eight years ago, when he took the train to Newcastle to join his first ship... *Ah! Those were the days.*

12

Back to Sub-basement

Down into the depths of hell again. Today was the day for the stock check—Brendan's first. Mr. Danster—he of the squeaky shoes—was expected in the storeroom at eleven to check Brendan's work before the administrators descended. Brendan was quite happy with his figures, starting from the day he took responsibility for the storeroom. Donning his dusty brown coat and brewing up a cuppa, he put his feet up to have a read of the *Telegraph*.

Hidden in the depths of the sub-basement, amongst the many cardboard boxes piled high and hidden passages amongst them, Brendan felt immune to the outside world. This world consisted of a table with one drawer he could lock, a kettle, two cups and saucers—*never know when I might have a visitor for tea*—a Tetley tin of tea leaves with spoon—*must try those new teabags*—with a tin for sugar. To the right of the table were two trays filled with receipts and correspondence—an organised jumble with the stock book and a photo of Maureen Byrne and her attractive smile, surmounting it all.

I thought we were going somewhere...she was nice. Wonder what happened after the mother died? Why did Maureen just disappear? Anyway, let's have a quick look at the headlines. What's this...a guy called Beeching in the government has called for a huge cut in the railway network. Wonder if that'll come off...Beatles have released another record—'Please Please Me'. They certainly play some catchy tunes...I wonder if they'll last?

There's the phone ringing, contact with the outside world...

"Toy Stores, Harris speaking. Yes, Mr. Danster, Sindy dolls are expected today. As soon as they arrive they will be taken up. Yes... Dinky cars and the Barbies are on the trolley ready for delivery to the floor... The passageways need sweeping? Done immediately, Mr. Danster... Up in ten minutes... All ready for your call to the basement at eleven hundred—do you take sugar in your tea?… No time for tea. That's OK. See you in ten."

Must ease off a bit on him, though he is a twit. Anyway, wagons roll.

Rising to his feet, Brendan replaced the *Telegraph* on the table and limped over to the laden trolley; his right leg was still playing up a bit. He noticed a shift in the air pressure—having been so long in the dungeon, he was becoming accustomed to movements in his domain—and braced, expecting the squeaky-shoed approach of Mr. Danster.

God, I'm becoming institutionalised—must get out of here. He pushed the trolley towards the lifts. *I recognise that figure… God, it's Maureen.*

Stepping out from behind the trolley, Brendan called out, "Would you be lookin' for an Irishman, then?"

"Oh! Bren. Thank goodness you're still here!" Maureen stepped forward hesitantly with her arms at her sides, awaiting Brendan's next move.

Delighted to see her again, Brendan stepped forward, and they gave each other a mighty hug. Leaning back in each other's arms, they laughed in delight and kissed.

"Oh, I have waited so long for this," Maureen said. "I've been afraid you wouldn't want to see me."

"Thought about you a lot, Maureen, but Danster is expecting me within minutes, so you'd better get out of here. By the way, how did you get in?"

"Old George on the gate let me in without a second thought."

"So much for security… Ah, well, what of it? Look, let's meet at the coffee shop on the ground floor at twelve. I've got a stock check with Danster at eleven… No, make it twelve-thirty."

"That'll be fine, Bren. Oh, I'm so looking forward to hearing all your news."

"Me, too. Now let me get on with my important work." Kissing her again, Brendan waved to Maureen as he swept the heavy lift door shut with a celebratory crash.

***

Having delivered and displayed the toys on the trolley—under Danster's supervision—and swept the floor—again, under Danster's eagle eye—Brendan returned to the sub-basement seething because of Danster's interference.

He checked in the delivery of the Sindy dolls and had barely sat down for a well-earned cup of tea when the peace was broken by the sound of Squeaky Shoes approaching—ten minutes early.

Better look as if I'm busy. I'll get a couple of delivery notes out.

"Good morning, Mr. Danster," Brendan welcomed cheerily, as if he hadn't already spent half the morning with the man breathing down his neck.

"Mr. Harris, your stock records, please, and I would appreciate it if you were to direct me to the various—"

"Perhaps this could help," interrupted Brendan apologetically. "The paper on the top of the stock sheets gives a plan of the toys' whereabouts."

"Thank you, Mr. Harris. That is most helpful. Now, perhaps you might continue with your work whilst I continue with mine," Danster instructed in his *I am your boss* voice.

Oh, God. Get me out of here. All this for eight pound a week. Still, I'm going to see Maureen later. Wonder what she's been up to for the past couple of months? Oh, and I'm off for the interview with the Gas Board—got to be there for six-thirty. Of course, I've got that other one with Broons Biscuits tomorrow, which—my goodness, what's that crash?

"Everything is all right, Mr. Harris," Danster called from somewhere within the corridors of boxes. Brendan found him in a matter of seconds. "Just misstepped on the stepladder and pulled a couple of boxes off the stack. Could you perhaps replace them whilst I continue?" Squeaky Shoes started to limp away.

"Wait a moment there, Mr. Danster. That was a loud crash. I'm hoping there's nothing broken, as these cartons hold very pricey toy Wedgewood tea sets."

Danster stopped in his tracks and looked back at Brendan.

"Don't worry, Mr. Danster," mollified Brendan. "You continue with your stock check. I'll examine the sets."

With a nod from Danster, Brendan got his penknife from his pocket, lifted the first large carton in both hands and shook it. Nothing rattled. However, the second carton was a different matter.

When Danster returned looking rather hot and flustered, Brendan showed him the result of his accident—a teapot with its spout snapped off—and had him sign an accident report.

Danster then had Brendan co-sign his stock report, stating the first stage of the stock check balanced, and hurried away, leaving Brendan to dispose of the broken tea set.

Glad that's out of the way—just a quarter past. Oh, God, now what?

"There's two deliveries waiting for you, Bren," one of the warehouse men called. "Can you come an' get 'em? They're blockin' up the delivery bay."

"OK, OK, I'm coming." Brendan arrived and looked over the boxes. He was going to be late. "Look, Tom, I'll just leave them at the side here. I've checked them. Got an important meeting at half past."

"OK, Bren. I'll keep me eye on them—though I knock off at half one."

"Don't worry, I'll be back. Thanks, Tom."

Depositing his brown coat behind the toy boxes, Brendan dusted off his clothes, ran his fingers through his hair and raced for the coffee shop on the ground floor.

Where is she? Gosh, it's pretty busy. Ah! There she is, looking a bit anxious. Don't worry, Mo, I'm a-coming.

"Hello, Maureen," greeted Brendan, leaning forward as he pulled out the light plastic chair. He noticed the coffee and roll on his side of the Formica table. "That's great, thanks. Well, that was a surprise this morning. Where have you been? Sorry, must shut up." He sat down on the hard seat and took a bite from the crusty roll.

"Hello, Bren, lovely to see you again. I need to apologise for disappearing. You know my mum died. Sorry, Oh, sorry. Must stop apologising." She dabbed the tears from her face, stretching her left hand tentatively across the small table.

"Yes, Maureen, I did know. I am so sorry." Brendan put the half-eaten roll back on the plastic plate and took Maureen's hand in both of his, giving it a comforting squeeze.

"Ouch! That hurt," cried Maureen. "No, no, keep a hold of it, but not so bloody tight." She grinned through her tears. "I went to stay with my sister in Warrington—to get away from the church," she continued, putting the damp hanky up the sleeve under her overcoat. "Boy, did they chase me."

"What are your feelings now?" enquired Brendan tentatively as this was important.

"Oh, I still believe, I think, but I'm putting all the religious business aside—bastards—excuse me, Bren. Oh, how I've missed you, you big gorilla." She squeezed Brendan's hand tightly.

"Go on, you big ape, tell her how much you missed her," someone called from a nearby table.

Brendan looked over to see a middle-aged couple smiling at them. He smiled back and turned back to Maureen, leaning forward to say, "I missed you, too, Maureen. Oh, how I did," and found himself blushing. He gathered himself for a few moments, receiving an acknowledging squeeze and smile from Maureen. "You don't mind if I miss my roll and coffee, do you? I've got to get back to the loading bay in five minutes. When can we meet again? Tonight's out as I have an interview with the Gas Board. Tomorrow, I'm here in wonderland, and another interview at four-thirty…"

"Have you still got the car, Bren? You could come over to the house after the interview and tell me all about it. I'll give you your tea."

"That would be great. I hope I get the job with Broons Biscuits—"

"Broons Biscuits? Oh, I do love their chocolate creams and chocolate wafers," interrupted Maureen. "I know of a Jim Corrigan, who works there. Haven't seen him for yonks."

"I really must go, Maureen. See you tomorrow, then." Brendan rose from the tubular chair, somehow sending it crashing to the floor.

"Don't worry, son. I'll pick it up for you," offered the man at next table. "Go on, give her a kiss. She won't say no."

Brendan looked at Maureen, who nodded her head, and Brendan leaned over and gave her a long kiss to the accompaniment of spontaneous applause from the surrounding tables.

That evening, Brendan signed out from Lewis's at five-thirty and found he had an hour to spend before the meeting at the Gas Board in Bold Street just around the corner from the store. He joined the emptying street and wandered around; everywhere was shutting down for the night. There were no cafés open where he could get a cup of tea, and he was getting wetter and wetter in his duffel coat as the drizzle increased.

Wandering along Bold Street, he noticed the café called The Odd Spot where Maureen once told him she'd met Paul McCartney—one of the lads in that band called The Beatles. They seemed to be popping up everywhere.

It's quarter past…I'll go knock on the Gas Board door now, at least get in from the rain, but I feel I'm only wasting my time. My leg's aching and I'm getting a headache.

***

"Hello, Mr. Harris, do come in. I'm Mr. Wilde, manager of the Gas Board here in Reliant House. My, you do look wet. Here, let me take your coat…would you like a cup of tea—"

"Mr. Wilde," interrupted Brendan.

"Just follow me, Mr. Harris. Into my office. Isn't it grand? Do sit down—"

"Mr. Wilde," interrupted Brendan again. His trouser legs had been drenched by the rain, as had the back of his suit, so sitting down was most uncomfortable.

"Yes, Mr. Harris, just one moment whilst I make your tea—do you take milk and sugar?"

"Both, please," Brendan said, adjusting his position on the leather armchair.

"Here we are, Mr. Harris, a nice hot cup of tea with a few biscuits. Now, tell me all about yourself, Mr. Harris. I must say, the eye patch looks most dashing."

"Thank you." Brendan smiled at the diminutive man balanced on the edge of his large leather armchair. "I was surprised by your offer of interview and feel—looking at the grand surroundings and probable staff you control—my experience as a wages clerk with Paintwell, with a staff of ten, is a bit pathetic."

"Mr. Harris, I have considered your CV and the varied posts you have held since you left school, and I'm very interested in the person it painted. We have, I must admit, shortlisted two persons for the post advertised. Both would be most capable. However, what I am now seeking is a back-up man—someone to supervise my drivers and fitters with, of course, some office work. Does that interest you?"

"Thank you, Mr. Wilde. I'll be frank. From my CV, you may recall I had a serious accident three years ago, and I'm still getting over it. I don't feel I am ready for such a position."

"That's fine, Mr. Harris. I understand. It has been a pleasure meeting you."

"And you, Mr. Wilde," Brendan said, rising to shake the offered hand.

13

Interview for Sales Post

"Brendan Harris for interview with Mr. Hawkes."

"Take a seat, Mr. Harris. I shall let Mr. Hawkes know you are here. You found the place OK, then?" So asked the motherly secretary as she lifted the telephone, smiling at Brendan with his dated grey suit and wayward hair.

Brendan was very nervous; he had done some research into the company, Broons Biscuits, whose slogan—'Make it a Biscuit'—was not the most inspiring. The Liverpool office, where he was now, was the main office and factory, with three other sales offices: one in Glasgow, one in Birmingham, and the third in Bristol. Their main product was a range of biscuits called Chunky Ginger, Chocolate Wafer and Chocolate Digestive, to name just a few. However, the top of the range—the biscuit which apparently outsold the rest throughout the British Isles—was the Blue Ace: *'a crisp wafer biscuit covered in real milk chocolate with a feathery taste—an ace taste for all'*. The Blue Ace dominated the sales picture.

They also made and delivered bread and bread rolls and had been in business since 1840; they were given a Royal Warrant by Queen Victoria.

The office was obviously part of the main factory building as there was a very strong sweet smell of biscuit pervading the room and the sound of machinery in the background. The office itself was untidy with loose biscuit wrappers and papers everywhere but in the waste basket. The motherly secretary was obviously a bad shot. Brendan could not help but notice some sales brochures proclaiming a new range offered by Broons.

"Right, Mr. Harris, follow me, please. Mr. Hawkes will see you now." Motherly Secretary raised her ample body from the creaking chair and walked towards a door into the factory.

Over the increased noise of the machinery, she directed Brendan to a door on the other side of the large building, alongside it a lighted window looking into the factory. The sweet biscuit smell increased, and Brendan got some inquisitive glances from the coated and head-covered staff as he made his way over.

Giving the office door a positive rap, Brendan heard a gruff voice bidding him enter. With a cursory nod from the bowed, noticeably balding head and a flailing hand directing he sit in a chair opposite, Brendan awaited the next step. Mr. Hawkes did not give the impression of a successful entrepreneur, a man on top of things.

Just then, the phone rang. Hawkes muttered under his breath, lifted his head and grunted in a marked Scots accent, "Harris, is it?" Getting a nod from Brendan, Hawkes gestured at the phone and said, "Take that, will you? An' tell them to bugger off."

Brendan picked up the receiver. "Good afternoon, Broons Biscuits. How may I help."

"Oh, hello, Mr. Harris! This is Vera the secretary. Will you please tell Mr. Hawkes it's Joe Kelly calling for him."

"Sorry, Vera—" *to hell with it* "—please tell Mr. Kelly to call back in an hour or so. Mr. Hawkes is pretty busy at the moment." Brendan glanced at the harassed Hawkes and got a nod of agreement.

I'm going to take over here. This guy needs help, thought Brendan as he replaced the phone.

"Afternoon, Mr. Hawkes, my name is Brendan Harris, here to join your company and start as a van salesman and help promote your new range." With a smile, Brendan leaned over the desk to shake the surprised sales manager's hand. "You seem to be a very busy man."

"Yes! I am that, Harris. I don't know if I can gie ye an hour, though. What's this about a new range?"

Brendan looked at Hawkes and smiled. "That's fine, Mr. Hawkes. It will take as long as it will. I noticed your brochures in the office and just wondered what the new range might be."

Silence. It was in Hawkes' hands now to start the interview.

"It's been a hard day, Harris," he admitted, sitting back in his swivel chair and taking out a pack of cigarettes. "The new range is pretty secretive at the moment. Do you smoke?"

"Yes, thanks." Brendan took one of the proffered cigarettes and produced his silver lighter. Hawkes leaned forward to light his cigarette and sat back blowing out a plume of smoke in satisfaction.

"Right, Harris, tell me why I should gie you the job? I gie ye ten minutes."

Here we go, thought Brendan, taking off his watch and placing it on the edge of the desk. "Ten minutes, you say..." He proceeded to disclose his knowledge of the company, and he'd done a lot of research—building his knowledge of the area on offer and his abilities to negotiate and close. "Ten minutes are up, Mr. Hawkes. Will you give me the job?"

"I like your style, Harris. Will Rangers win the cup this year?"

"They have every chance, Mr. Hawkes. If you support them."

Hawkes shuffled his body in the narrow swivel chair, looking quite tired with his uncombed hair, another cigarette dangling from his thick lips, and his weary off-white shirt. Taking the cigarette in his left hand, he cleared his throat and leaned forward, stretching out his right hand, and offered Brendan a beaming smile that took years off his florid appearance.

"Right, Harris, you've got the job. Now, I've got a lot to do and it's getting late."

"Thanks, Mr. Hawkes, that's great. But before I leave you, I should like to confirm a few details. I understand that a starting salary of twelve pounds a week is what you offer?"

"Yes, of course, my apologies," Hawkes grunted as he stubbed out the cigarette. "Yes, twelve a week will do. Wait a minute," Hawkes instructed as he lifted the phone. "Vera, will you tell Jim Corrigan Mr. Harris is joining us and he'll need to give him the lowdown... Oh, good, he's with you. And will you get Joe Kelly for me...another Irishman...they're surrounding me," Hawkes exclaimed in a bout of benign exasperation, replacing the receiver.

"Right, Harris. Jim Corrigan—my under-manager—and Vera will answer your many questions and get a contract in the post. Good luck, glad you're joining us. Give us your hand, oh, we have already done that. Still no harm..." Hawkes stood up and came around the desk, showing a large stomach.

Brendan, towering above him, took Hawkes' hand firmly in his own. "Thanks, Mr. Hawkes. I'm sure looking forward to the future with Broons."

Nearly jumping with joy, Brendan made his way back to the office. He was very pleased with himself and eager to tell Maureen of his success. *Of course, I'm to meet Jim Corrigan. Wonder how Maureen knows him? Should know in a few minutes, anyway.*

"Hello again, Vera. Great news, isn't it?"

"Yes, Mr. Harris. Congratulations. I'm just typing out your contract. That reprobate over there is Jim Corrigan." Vera pointed to a heavy, middle-aged man dressed in slacks and tweed jacket.

"Hello," greeted Jim in an educated Scots accent. Passing one hand through a shock of red hair, he walked forward and offered his free hand. "Delighted to see you are joining us, Brendan. We are certainly in need of a good hard worker to cover the North Liverpool and South Lancashire areas. Oh, good! Vera has your contract ready. I'll just give it the once-over and you can take it away to study."

Whilst Jim checked over the contract, Brendan collected a few sales brochures detailing the various biscuit ranges. The bread loaves and bread rolls were mentioned, but Brendan would only be involved in the biscuit side.

"Right, that's fine," Jim said, placing the contract in an envelope.

"Mr. Corrigan, do you mind if I have a look over it now? You could answer any questions and I could maybe give you a decision now?"

"Of course, Brendan, and do call me Jim. We're all very friendly here—just like a big family, aren't we, Vera?"

Due to the lack of seating, Brendan went to the side of the small office and had a look over the offer.

Position, Van Salesman, Merchandiser. To promote the expansion of Broons products in the North Liverpool and South Lancashire area. Two weeks paid holiday. Salary twelve pounds a week with expenses.

Twelve pounds a week—that's a fortune…and expenses. Start two weeks time. Six months probation. That's enough for me. Wonder what the new range is.

"That looks fine, Jim, but I'll take the contract home and study it some more. Shall I give you a call in a day or two?"

"That's quite all right, Brendan. Do come back quick as you can. Vera—a bag of Broons Biscuits for the man. There you are, Brendan, my good chap. Look forward to seeing you again."

"Thanks, Jim—oh, by the way, Jim, I have been asked by a close friend of mine to pass on her good wishes—Maureen Byrne?" Brendan was interested to discover Corrigan's reaction.

There was a short pause followed by a sudden spark of recognition. "Maureen Byrne, mother Marjorie died recently?"

At Brendan's nod and smile in agreement, Jim continued, "Mid-twenties, red hair, quite a character—I know her sister Mary. Well, well, small world, eh, Brendan? How do you know Maureen?"

"We worked together in Lewis's."

"Do pass on my best wishes. I must tell Pat, my wife—they were good friends."

"Shall do, Jim. See you, Vera. Thanks for the biscuits."

With his bag of goodies and new contract, a gleeful Brendan shook hands with Jim, bidding him all the best, gave Vera a beaming smile and wave and tripped over the doormat on his way through the open door. As he stumbled forward, the bag of biscuits left his grasp and went sailing into the twilight. Recovering manfully, Brendan acknowledged Jim and Vera's offers of help but waved them away with a smile, and collected the bag of now broken biscuits. The ever kindly Jim came forward with a fresh bag and wished him, "A safe trip home."

14

Moving House & Leaving the Department Store

"Yes, Maureen, twelve quid a week, start in two weeks, must look over the contract. Oh, and Jim Corrigan wishes you all the best and will mention your name to Pat, his wife."

With the sheet of paper in his hand, Brendan danced a jig around the delighted Maureen and collapsed in a heap in an armchair.

"Sorry, Maureen…but how did your day go?"

"Pat Corrigan," mused Maureen. "So she's still around, then, his wife… Tea's nearly ready, Bren. You read your paper and I'll tell you over the table."

Six hundred and twenty four pounds a year that's nearly three hundred more than I'm getting now. I'm quids in…and join the pension scheme after a year with them. I'll give my week's notice in tomorrow and have a few days off before I start with Broons.

"Tea's ready, Brendan love. Come on, now, or your eggs will get cold."

"A fry-up, smells gorgeous. I'll have to come here more often."

Maureen raised her head, considering the hint offered and continued, "How are things going with your digs in Bootle? You said you were lodging with a seaman's wife. Sounds very dodgy if I may say so."

"Too right, Maureen," Brendan replied, loading his fork with sausage and egg. "I'm intending to move nearer Broons in Aintree anyway."

"Well, I have a suggestion, Brendan. Why not lodge here? I've got a spare room you can use. You can help me pay for food and expenses. It would suit me to have a man around."

Brendan stopped eating and looked Maureen in the eye, somewhat startled by the offer. "What a wonderful idea. But what would the neighbours say, Maureen?"

"I can say you're an Irish cousin or something, and what about them, anyway?"

"Yes! Well, if you really mean it."

"Yes, you big lump, I do."

"Do I shake your hand or give you a kiss to seal the deal?"

"Well, I...yes..." Maureen considered. "Yes, here's my hand. You may shake it and kiss it."

Brendan shook her hand, and then clicked his heels and stood to attention before bringing her hand up to his lips to lightly caress it with his lips.

Maureen giggled and retracted her hand. "Give me a couple of days, Bren, and I'll get your room ready. I'm getting all excited at the thought of having you here. Oh, yes, I must talk to you about my sister Mary. Come on, sit down." She directed Brendan back to his chair, where he sat with chin cupped in palms, giving her all of his attention.

"Mary is older than me—she must be twenty-nine now...five years difference in May... Yes, that's right. I see very little of her since she married this guy." She hesitated. "Cecil Weeks, a shady character." She laughed. One daughter, Beatrice whose nearly ten. Anyway, Mary and I don't get on at all, because of the religion thing, you know." Maureen stopped for a moment. "I don't know what to believe. Mum's belief was absolute, no questions asked—the priests really had her under their thumb—and all her money went to them.

"She left me the house and a few quid, thank God, but it has a mortgage on it. Mary got nothing. Cecil was most annoyed...serves them right. Poor Beatrice, though. She's a nice kid—I haven't seen her for a couple of years. So there you are, Brendan. Do you still want to know me?"

"Why, yes, of course, Maureen. We've all got our nasty relatives. I have an uncle called Horace—never met him—he's in a jail somewhere in Australia. I'd say that equals things out." After a short pause while they ate the food Brendan raised his head. "You appear to have a story to tell about Pat Corrigan."

"Yes! Pat Corrigan! As you can probably guess, she's Irish, from somewhere in the south. She was—what am I saying—she is a Roman Catholic. She and others used to come to the house to meet with my mother and myself. We'd go together to Our Lady's and be battered with religious dogma for a few hours. Afterwards, we'd come back to our house and pray over a cup of tea. Pat Corrigan was a good-looking woman, about ten years older than I. I thought she was wonderful, I did so want to be like her." Maureen stopped talking for a moment as she brushed a stray hair from her forehead.

"Being the youngest in the group—there were eight of us—I used to be the skivvy, making the tea, arranging the chairs, getting the prayer books out—having the bottle of whiskey available when Father Murphy called. To cut a long story short, I began to rebel and had a row with Pat. Then Mum died, and the meetings stopped. I haven't seen Pat since. I met her husband once—a nice man—gave me a packet of biscuits." She laughed. "I can see why now."

Brendan laughed sympathetically. "Would you like to meet her again, as it looks quite possible?"

"Let's take it as it comes, Bren, love. It all depends."

"OK, Mo," Brendan gave her a comforting kiss and sat back in his chair. "Now, let's work on some rules—especially the costs of running the house…"

Better not mention the sex side, though I bet Maureen is as aware of it as I am. The temptations are so great. Oh, what do I do? Why not get married? I'm on my own she's on her own. That's the answer…or is it?

But what else is there to do? Get a flat in a high rise block? No thanks. Don't want any more temporary accommodation.

Yep! That's the answer. Get married. But will Maureen want to marry me? Or even get married at all? What if she says no? What do I do then? I could offer to pay half the mortgage.

Do I want to marry her with her recent ties to the Roman Catholic Church? Would she expect me to become an RC?

Oh, what of it? She's lovely. When we're apart, I can't wait to see her. When she disappeared, I felt I had lost something special. Is it love? She came back looking for me…possibly she feels the same?

"Maureen, I have something to say." He adjusted the cutlery on his plate and took a deep breath. *Yep, 'nothing ventured nothing gained', as Chaucer used to say.* Leaning across the small table, Brendan took Maureen's hand in his and started to ask, "Maureen, will you—" when his right elbow hit his half-full teacup—hidden from his sight due to the eye patch—and spilt its contents over the tablecloth.

Maureen startled but remained seated, awaiting the end of the request.

Glancing at the widening stain, Brendan returned his gaze to the girl in front of him and repeated the question. "Maureen, will you marry me?"

"Yes. Yes, I will, you big messer, only if you get a cloth and mop that up. Oh! What have I let myself in for?" She laughed. "Yes, Bren, my love, I'll marry you. Oh, how lovely. Come on, give me a kiss… Oh, God, mind the tablecloth… Whew, that was a near one." She gasped as Brendan deftly caught the teacup and its remaining contents, which had rolled off the tabletop due to Brendan's weight as he leaned on it in his haste to comply with the welcome summons.

**

The following morning, Brendan told his landlady he was moving out in a couple of days as his circumstances had changed, and thanked her. June was just as pleased—and relieved, as her husband was due home on leave by the weekend.

Turning in for work, and donning his brown coat, it was with some pleasure that Brendan made his way to the toy floor. Even the large lift seemed to smile at him as he opened the sliding door.

"Oh, good morning, Mr. Danster. Is Mr. Jones in today?"

"No, Harris, not at the moment. What is it you wish?" Danster asked in his distant, *I would rather not speak with someone in a brown coat* voice.

"Just to give him a week's notice, Mr. Danster. I shall leave my written resignation on his desk. Now, is there anything needed on the floor today, Mr. Danster?"

"Well, Harris, we shall be sorry to see you go," replied Danster, stepping back in surprise but continuing without hesitation, "The Dinky and small toys counter needs replenishing—would you please see to that?"

Brendan nodded—*shall be glad to see the back of him*—and left, detouring to leave the envelope containing his written resignation on the tiny desk in the manager's office before he examined the small toys counter to follow Danster's wishes.

Next step: I must tell Marsden of Personnel I'm leaving. Returning to the friendly lift—it was company policy for brown-coated staff to use the goods lifts rather than the escalator—he gleefully went upstairs to Personnel and handed his resignation letter to Mary for her to pass on to Marsden.

Returning to the sub-basement, his next step was to call Broons Biscuits. As the phone in the basement was only tuned to internal calls, he nipped out to a local street telephone box. The motherly Vera took the message that he would hand in the signed contract before the day was out. Floating on air, Brendan let the heavy door on the red telephone box shut with a crash behind him and wished the small queue waiting to use the phone a good day.

The rest of the week passed by very slowly; a sullen and distant Danster was sent down from the toy floor to take over from Brendan. Jones the manager ignored Brendan whenever he visited, and the floor staff expressed their envy. Marsden didn't acknowledge Brendan's letter but must have acted upon it as, when Brendan collected his wage packet on the Friday, he found his P45 and final payslip enclosed.

Part Two

15

Broons Biscuits

Brendan had served his week's notice with the store, moved his few belongings into the spare room at Maureen's, and was preparing himself for the first day at Broons Biscuits. He had given Maureen's address to Vera and had received a copy of his contract, subject to references, with a six-month probationary period. References, he felt, from Lewis's should be favourable, as with Calvex.

He had come up in the world. Expenses and a company car... *And all the biscuits I can eat. What more could a fellow want? Wait a moment, I'm also going to get married*, he thought as he adjusted the eye patch on his right eye. *Must do something about this double vision. More importantly when and where will we get married?*

"Maureen?" he called from the cosy front room with its log fire and radio tuned into family favourites. "Maureen?" he called again, stretching out on the sofa, sniffing the spicy tang of roast lamb and humming along with the mellow voice of Bing Crosby crooning 'Till the End of Time'.

May this continue to the end of time.

"Come on, you lazy sod, get off your backside," were the laughed orders from the kitchen.

"OK, I'm coming."

"Turn up the radio, Bren. Is that Perry Como? You're doing the washing up, you know."

"Boy, that looks good. Sure, I'll do the dishes. Don't I always?" Brendan feigned astonishment. Maureen gave him a playful shove towards the table, and they sat down to eat Sunday roast.

"The big day tomorrow," Brendan mused around a mouthful of lamb. "Must develop a Scots accent...though this Irish one I've got has done me proud over the years. This lamb is very tasty, Maureen.

Oh, by the way, I met a guy a couple of days ago—he's a butcher, lives up in Maghull. Offered me half a lamb for twenty quid, all butchered. Could be an idea. We could go mad and buy a freezer. Of course—" he wondered "—do we have the room?"

"Look, Bren..." Maureen looked pensive. "Bren...you're the lodger here, for the moment. Your ideas are fine, but let's talk about gettin' wed first." She stopped eating with her knife poised over the leg of lamb. "Are you still interested in getting wed? We haven't spoken about it for the last few days."

"Oh! I am so sorry, Maureen. I've been so wrapped up in Broons. Now listen to me, young lady, I love you and want to live with you for the rest of my life. I want to bring a couple of little Brendans and Maureens into this world—with your agreement, of course—and live happily ever after. What do you think?"

"Ooh, Brendan, I think that's lovely. Yes, we could buy a freezer and put it in the bedroom and get a whole herd of half sheep. Come over here, you big lummock, and give me a kiss—careful! Those mugs cost a lot of money," Maureen warned as Brendan squeezed his way out from behind the table, making sure he didn't pull the cloth with him.

Reaching his goal, Brendan leaned forward and, holding eye contact, in his deep melodious voice, whispered, "For my beautiful redheaded lady, I traverse mountains, ford raging rivers and hack my way through the steaming jungle to kiss her on her welcoming lips."

With a smile in her eyes, Maureen dropped her gaze and replied, "Does my gallant troubadour know he has a large pimple on the end of his nose?" Standing up and holding onto Brendan's arms, she continued, "However, I shall welcome a kiss from him as he traversed such a dangerous and man-eating table without accident."

Laughing out loud, they put their arms around each other, kissed and hugged.

"Here, Bren, give me your hanky an' I'll pop that bloody pimple—been dying to do it all day. You'll have to do something with these pimples you get. They must be pretty painful."

"You're correct there, Mo. They are very painful, especially the ones on my back—enough, enough!" exclaimed Brendan. "I was planning to make this a romantic evening, and here we are talking about pimples. I'll make an appointment with the doc and see if he can prescribe anything. Now, let me get at those dishes."

"Whatever turns you on, dear," remarked Maureen as she patted her red hair into place and tossed her apron aside with a flourish, revealing her short dress and long legs.

Concentrate on the washing, Bren boyo, remember you're only the lodger.

She called back on her way to the living room, "Must watch *Sunday Night at the Palladium*. Who's on tonight? Where's the *Radio Review*, Bren?"

"Probably under the cushion on the sofa. Be with you in a minute. I'm up to me eyes in soapsuds."

"Frank Ifield is on—you know, the Australian singer? And Jimmy Tarbuck. Guess who's compere?"

"Not Bruce Forsyth again, I hope. He drives you nuts with his poses and inane actions."

"Yep, your evening is made, Bren. The lovely Bruce Forsyth. Come on in when you've finished the dishes, and let's cuddle up on the sofa."

Now, there's an offer no lodger could refuse—I'll leave the lot to dry on the draining board.

"Coming, dear, just drying my hands."

The first of Brendan's dreams had seemingly been fulfilled.

***

"Better get up, Bren, it's eight, and you've to be at Broons, spick-and-span, for nine. And I can't be seen to have Roger the Lodger in bed with me. Come on, wake up!" Maureen leaned over in the bed, giving Brendan a severe shaking.

"God…yep…eight o'clock…right…" stuttered Brendan as he rolled out of the bed. "Where's me suit? Oh, it's the 'landlady'. What are you doing there? No, don't, please put them away. Now look what you've done," Brendan complained, standing naked beside the bed. "No, please, Mo, pull those covers back. No, I mustn't. Get down, Rover," he instructed, laughing, as he turned for the bathroom.

After a quick wash and a bowl of cornflakes, Brendan donned his suit jacket, adjusted his Broons tie—making sure the italicised prominent letter 'B' stood out—and called out goodbye to a probably somnolent 'landlady'.

***

"Good morning, Vera, Brendan Harris reporting for duty." He leaned forward to give Vera a peck on the cheek.

"Hello, Brendan, welcome. I'll just give Bas a ring to tell him you're here. Patrick has your car ready out… Send him down to you? OK! Brendan, Bas, wants to see you. Yes, Patrick Cooney has your car ready outside to pick up, and Jim Corrigan wants to see you later."

Feeling quite important, Brendan made his way down through the factory, waving to a couple of the packing staff. He reached Basil Hawkes' office door and took a moment to hitch his trousers up, straighten his suit jacket and run his fingers through his hair and then knocked and entered when told.

"Good to see you again, Brendan. Now, I'll be brief," smiled Basil Hawkes, placing the burning cigarette in the ashtray before him as he came out from behind his desk to shake hands. The smell of burning tobacco and the smoke cloud were very noticeable in the small office, and Brendan held back the urge to cough.

"Jim is sorry he's not here to take you through the area you'll be covering—he's gone to meet Nolan's Teas to discuss opening an account. Nolan's are on your patch. However, Vera will have the customer cards in the office. Oh, and head office would like you up in Glasgow for a three-day assimilation course this Wednesday. OK?"

Hawkes re-seated himself on his comfortable chair behind his well-used desk. "Vera has all the necessary paperwork, and Patrick will show you some of the ropes this morning. Later, Jim will tell you what's happening on your patch. You'll be out for a half-day with Patrick on Tuesday and then take the train to Glasgow and come back on the Saturday. A busy time for you, Brendan. The sooner you get out selling the better."

Before Brendan had time to reply, the phone rang and with a dismissive wave and nod of the head from Basil, the meeting was closed.

"Hiya, Patrick, I'm Brendan Harris. Thanks for taking the time out to help me. Mr. Hawkes has—"

"That's OK, Brendan," interrupted Patrick, holding out his hand. He was a small man, with a rounded body and a pleasant chubby face, aged around the late-forties. His accent was certainly not an Irish one, more a relaxed Scouse accent.

They were standing in the small car park adjoining the factory, where there were six vehicles parked: a sleek and sporty Aston Martin saloon, alongside it a new model Ford Cortina. There were two vans with Broons Biscuits stencilled on the side panels, a well-used two-door Morris Minor, and, of course, Brendan's own overworked and tired Ford Popular.

Patrick stood back and pointed at the Morris Minor. "That red shiny one is your transport for the immediate future: your company car. Your keys, sir, and may you have many miles of enjoyment." He grinned and passed a small bunch of keys to Brendan.

Brendan moved closer to get a good look at his company car. "One up on the Ford Popular, Patrick—by the way, what do you like to be called? Patrick, Pat, Paddy…?"

"Call me Patrick…Bren?"

"Yep! Bren will do fine, Patrick."

And so a relaxed friendship was formed with the seasoned salesman in his late-forties, happy to pass his knowledge to a much younger man.

The rest of the morning was spent looking over a large-scale map of Liverpool and South Lancashire, pinpointing the area Brendan was to cover and giving the lowdown regarding competition.

"The main competition is United Biscuits in Liverpool. Two firms—McVitie & Price and MacFarlane Lang—joined together in 1948. They took over the shortbread firm William Crawford a couple of years ago, and there are rumours they are looking at Broons.

"Jim will run over the call cards for the outlets and any special deals—wonder how he's getting on with Nolan's Teas? There's some fifteen shops around the north. Be quite a scoop if he gets them. Would certainly do you no harm, Bren, as it would be credited to your area sales as the head office of Nolan's, is on your patch. Oh, there's Jim, right now, pulling into the park."

Brendan was up on his feet already.

"Wait a mo, Bren, the news might be bad."

"He's looking our way, Patrick. Is that a thumbs up?"

"All set up for you, Brendan."

A short while later when the three men met up in the canteen, Jim outlined his morning's work with Nolan's. "They've ordered fifteen cases of Blue Ace, and they're open for discussion on others in our range. When the order is delivered, they would like a small display made, promoting Blue Ace. I'll help Brendan on this, Patrick. I'm sure you're biting at the bit to get back to your own area."

"I will indeed—oh, I didn't tell you, Jim, did I? I'm sure you'll be interested to hear, Midas confectionary of Speke, quite close to the airport, have been taken over by Maurice Fitzgibbon—a fellow countryman of yours, Bren. That's our first call tomorrow."

"So, Maurice rears his Irish head again, eh? I'm sure I've no need to offer a word of caution about Maurice, Patrick, but wasn't he involved in that bit of jiggery-pokery with the Fitzgibbon chain a couple of years ago?"

"Nothing proven, Jim. Don't worry, I'll be careful. Anyway, credit control will check his recent history. He's looking to open a head office account as he has four shops now. Right, Brendan, let's get to work. There's a lot to cover, and we need to sort out your rail tickets for Glasgow…"

***

After a very busy afternoon planning calls, learning the Broons sales procedures and meeting Norman Byrne—the other salesman—Brendan returned to his digs, exhausted, with a briefcase full of papers, a boxful of calling cards and a Morris Minor full of marketing material and biscuit samples.

"What a day, Mo, I'm up to my eyes with paperwork already, I'm away up to Glasgow tomorrow, back on Saturday, and I've got an ancient Morris Minor parked out on the road behind your Anglia. I've left the Popular in Broons' car park." He paused for a moment, realising Maureen was eager to say something. "What sort of day did you have?"

"Wait until you hear this, Bren. Remember I told you I was going for an interview with Armitts Do-It-Yourself? Well, they've gone and offered me a job! It's a new idea, display everything on what they call self-service shelves and pay at the till on your way out. No, let me finish," Maureen interrupted Brendan before he could congratulate her. "You remember when you went to buy some screws the other day—the bathroom cabinet still wants fixing, by the way—an' you were muttering about old Arkwright and how slow he is, saying how much better it would've been if you had been able to see a variety of screws and pick the ones you wanted? Well, that's just exactly what Armitts are doing. I've been offered a job on the ordering and display. Denzil Armitt reckons this is the future for retailing. All very exciting."

"Oh, well done, Mo—fingers crossed he can make it. Probably just a fad. How much has he offered you?"

"Ten pound a week!"

"Ten pound a week? That's over a thousand a year between us. When do you start?"

"Denzil wants me to come over to the shop on West Derby Road to work on the layout and then start ordering the stock. He's looking to a grand opening in a month's time. So, put your mind to it, Bren, as a do-it-yourself expert—" Maureen laughed "—and give me a list of the tools and other things you can think of."

Must meet this Denzil, thought Brendan, *he could be dangerous.*

"Well, let's go through the alphabet, Mo, start with an A now there's…an awl."

"What's an awl?"

"A pointy thing for boring holes in wood or leather. Then there's an anvil."

"Oops, I'd better get a pen and paper. I've got a lot to learn. Right, the pointy awl then an anvil—anything under B?

"Brush and pan set, and a bucket."

"Keep going, Bren. What about C?"

"Chisel all sizes, claw hammer, clamps… D…is there such a thing as a dowel, Mo? Look that one up. Anyway enough of that for the moment. Anything for tea?

"I thought we could have a treat of fish and chips, as we're in the money now."

***

It was a cold and wet winter's morning when Patrick and Brendan arrived at the shop in a windswept narrow road close to Liverpool Airport. The name above the white distempered window read Midas Café/Shop. There was an open-topped lorry with wooden frames and other assorted builder's knick-knacks parked outside.

Parking behind the lorry, Patrick looked ruefully at Brendan and suggested he try the shop door, which was bedaubed with stickers and the important information that Midas Café/Shop never closed.

As Brendan tried to open the shop door, without success, a dungaree-clad male alighted from the lorry, tossed his cigarette butt into the gutter and called out, "Is it Mr. Gibbon there?" Upon receiving the negative, the dungarees made a point of examining its watch and cursing under its breath.

Noticing a small, worn-out Ford van with the name 'Sirius Shopfitters of Speke' pull up behind him, Brendan climbed back into the Morris Minor, receiving a resigned frown from Patrick. The driver of the van, dressed in faded torn jeans, got out, looked at the closed shop door, ran his fingers through his hair, shivered slightly and tried the door without success. With that, he approached the Morris Minor and leaned over to speak with Brendan, who had opened the car window.

"I know it's a waste of time asking you, but you never know," the van driver said. "Would it be Mr. Fitz—you are?" Again receiving the negative, he stepped back, shrugged his shoulders, returned to the van and shouted something to the occupant. Slamming the van door with some venom, he then marched up to the lorry. The lorry driver, who had already dismounted, strode towards the van driver. They approached each other like two cowboys in the movies, and Brendan was expecting a fight, but then the two men suddenly decided they knew each other and offered each other a cigarette.

By now a good quarter hour had passed; the rain had ceased, and the wind had lessened, but Patrick was becoming restless. He had other calls to make.

"We'll give him another five," he said, adding to the smoke-filled car interior by lighting another cigarette, "and then we say goodbye to Mr. Gibbon. This is one of those cases, Bren—do we cut our losses, that is, valuable time, or wait for the sod to turn up? There again, maybe we shouldn't have bothered with the man in the first place, but a new outlet with three shops sounded very promising. Oh, what's this? Looks like our man…"

A rather dirty old Jaguar car roared into place behind the van and, with a hiss and exhalation of steam, settled down on its haunches. A moustachioed, brown-coated figure unfolded through the open door, preceded by a ridiculously long cigar, placed a soft hat on its bald head and stood to its full height of five feet two inches. Without acknowledging either of the two workmen or Patrick, Maurice Fitzgibbon produced a bunch of keys, opened the shop door and stepped aside, indicating the two workmen to enter.

Patrick and Brendan, by this time, had taken the opportunity to position themselves between Fitzgibbon and the open door. Patrick offered his hand and introduced himself in a loud voice, "Patrick Cooney, Mr. Fitzgibbon, and my associate Brendan Harris, from Broons Biscuits."

Fitzgibbon took the cigar from his mouth, blew a stream of fragrant smoke into the air and looked up at the two tall figures in front of him. He spat a gob of tobacco juice into the wall and said in an unintelligible North Dublin accent, "Yes, now there, I see they've sent out the heavy mob to meet me. What is it you want with me, den, boys? I'm a busy man."

Aware of Patrick's momentary hesitation, Brendan stepped forward and, accentuating his Dublin accent, said, "We're sorry, Mr. Fitz, but from one Dublin man to another, give us a break. Patrick made an appointment to meet you here to talk about an account with Broons. What do you want?"

Fitzgibbon put the cigar back in his mouth and scratched his head. "If you wait ten minutes…"

Brendan looked at Patrick and shook his head slightly. "No can do, Mr. Fitzgibbon we're running out of time…"

"Here, give me a ring on this number later in the day." Fitzgibbon passed a business card to Brendan. "Now let me get on with me business." With that, he pushed past the two salesmen and made his way into the dark interior of the unlit shop.

"Hope you didn't mind me stepping in there, Patrick. Will you phone him?" Brendan asked as they walked back to their car, which looked tiny compared to the large Jaguar.

Before Patrick could answer, Brendan walked over to the larger car and peered through the closed driver window. "He's got a car phone, Patrick. He must be doing well. Sorry again for butting in."

"What's your thoughts about Fitzgibbon, Brendan, he being a fellow country man?"

"We may have been born in the same country, but I think he's a lot of trouble. But really, who am I to offer advice on Broons customers? I've only been here a couple of days." *Wouldn't touch the guy with a barge pole… Come on, Patrick, forget Fitzgibbon. I want to meet real customers.*

"Time's getting on. You know I'm taking the train to Glasgow this afternoon."

"Of course. I'd forgotten. Let's see what's the time…close to ten. I call in once a week to Sharps Cash and Carry. They do a good trade in our chocolate biscuits, especially the popular Blue Ace. We'll go there, see what they need and have a cup of tea in the canteen. What do you say?"

Brendan, very disappointed with Patrick's plans, knew he wasn't going to learn much from such a casual attitude. He clambered into the Morris. "Right, Patrick, let's go. Let's get some action."

And so, the next two hours passed, going into a dusty and busy cash-and-carry where Patrick was greeted like a friend by the staff and left to his own devices to check what stock was on the shelves. In his element, Patrick, followed by Brendan, made his way to the biscuit section where there were mountains of assorted biscuit brands with Broons three packs of Blue Ace hidden by McVitie's assorted-biscuit packs.

Annoyed, Patrick pushed some of the McVitie packs aside and pulled the Blue Ace packs forward. "Right, there were seven cases here last week, so five have gone. I've tried to get them to stock the Choc Wafer, Bren, but no go. I'll have Liz sign the order and let's have that cup of tea."

Is that it? Who is Liz? Is she the boss? I thought Blue Ace was a top seller. Five cases? That's five customers at the most. Look at the mountains of other brands. God, let me get away to Glasgow…

"Yes, Liz is a nice woman, Patrick. Of interest, how long have you been with Broons?" enquired Brendan as they sipped their tea in the small canteen with—of all things—a free McVitie digestive.

"Let's see…1951…that's thirteen years. Boy, have I sold a lot of biscuits in that time. Liz is a great girl, isn't she? She's the boss's daughter. She and her father Phillip started Sharp's Cash and Carry about three years ago, serving the small retail trade—you know, the newsagents, sweet shops—I've got a great understanding with them, have helped Liz a great deal."

Half listening to Patrick prattle on, Brendan considered: *if there's a confectionery shop in every square mile of my area, and the area is twenty square miles, that's at least twenty potential customers. Wonder how much profit the store makes on each case?* With these and other thoughts running through his mind, he returned to the car with Patrick, thanking him for the insight into how a Broons salesman worked when Patrick dropped him off at the factory.

Thinking he would pop into the office before heading for Glasgow, Brendan was greeted by a flustered Vera.

"Thank God you called in, Brendan. Your course at head office has been cancelled. Is Patrick with you? Can you go get him, quick?"

Turning on his heel, Brendan dashed out to see Patrick's car pulling out into the road. Hoping to be seen, he waved furiously, but the car continued its journey.

"Sorry, Vera, just missed him."

"Do you by any chance know where he's going on his next call?" Before Brendan could get a word in, the hot and flustered secretary snatched up the ringing phone. "That you, Norman? An emergency meeting at two o'clock. What for? Jim will tell you when you get here."

16

Visiting the Cavern – Marriage in the Air

"To be brief, everyone," offered Jim in his most earnest manner, "Broons Biscuits has been taken over by Aldertree Confections. And everything here closes down from today at five o'clock. Your cars, gentlemen, I am sorry to say, will be impounded. I have a letter for each of you, outlining your terms of dismissal. Bas is up at head office today and offers his sympathies to each of you and wishes you all the best for the future, as I do myself. So there we are, everybody, it's goodbye."

Brendan's immediate reaction was relief that he hadn't sold his Ford Popular; it was still in the car park. Opening his envelope, he found the enclosed letter offered the usual platitudes and informed him that he would be paid to the end of the month. However, Mr. John Alderton, recruitment manager, would be in the Adelphi Hotel to discuss his position the following Friday at ten o'clock.

Glancing up from his letter, he noticed Patrick was looking somewhat crestfallen. No doubt, it was a big shock; as he'd just told Brendan, he'd spent many years with Broons. Vera was crying on Jim's shoulder, and Norman appeared somewhat shaken. There was a sudden, startling cessation of noise, silence—the factory had shut down after close on a hundred years, and it brought a fresh bout of tears from Vera and Patrick called out, "Why, Jim, why? I'm sacked after all these years I've given to Broons. Why me? What about you, Norman? You've been with Broons as long as I?"

"Yep, Patrick, I'm out on my ear, too. I've found another job—thought this was going to happen. What's with you, Bren?"

"I've been offered an interview by Aldertree, 'to discuss my position', which looks positive enough."

"An' you've only been here a minute, Brendan. It's not fair, after the years I've given," complained Patrick. "And I suppose you've got yourself a big manager's job with Aldertree, Jim?"

"No, Patrick. I'm going to retire. Now there, Vera," consoled Jim, patting her on the shoulder, "calm down. Do you think a cup of tea would go down well?"

"All right, everyone—" *sniff* "—what'll you all have?" *sniff* "Forty years... Please excuse me, everyone." Vera stood back from Jim, patted him on the shoulder and shouted, *"The bastards!"* She hesitated with a smile. "Now I feel better. Tea all round?"

Everyone else, some grinning, some grimacing, stood tall and shouted out in unison, *"The bastards!"*

***

"But why did they employ you, knowing this would happen, Bren? What do you think they want to see you on Friday for?"

"Yes, very strange, Maureen. Must be just what big business does—treat their employees like shit. At least I have the chance on Friday of being employed by Aldertree—must look them up in the library before then. The other guys look like they got the push. Anyway, how did your day go, Maureen? You look a bit glum."

"Brendan, do I look like a tart? "Maureen asked. "Wait a moment—I'll put my heels on... There...now how do I look?"

Looking at the tall, striking figure in front of him, Brendan took a deep breath to compose himself. Dressed in a dark silk blouse over a black miniskirt, with her long legs encased in nylon, and her red hair accentuating her striking features, all balanced on a pair of silver high heels, the vision was certainly eye catching.

"What do you mean, Maureen? You look pretty OK to me. Why! What's happened?"

"Denzil Armitt—remember he was my boss. One of the things about him I never liked, he has a squeaky voice—"

"Sorry to interrupt, Mo, but you said *was* my boss—what do you mean?"

"The little shit came into the office, earlier today. I was just adjusting my suspender, with one leg on the desk. He was supposed to be away, an' he went into his office, slammed the door and then called me on the intercom. When I went into the office, there he was, the little moron, doing his nails—doing his nails, would you believe? 'Miss Byrne,' he says in his squeaky voice...ugh horrible... 'I don't think you are suitable, I have changed my mind. Please collect your things and leave the premises. I have no room for a tart in my employ.'

"I looked at the little fart," she continued, beginning to laugh, "and I leaned over his desk, and I told him to keep his poxy job and stick his nail file up his arse. And in one dramatic move—I repeat, Bren—in one dramatic move—" she laughed "—I swept all the papers off his desk onto the floor and left the office, slamming the door behind me.

"So there you are, Bren my love. I am now unemployed. But he said I was a tart."

Stepping forward and putting his arms around the alluring body, Brendan gave a short laugh, exclaiming, "Wish I'd been there to see my Maureen sort out that little creep. What do you think he meant by calling you a tart?"

"You don't think I'm a tart, do you, Bren? I'd die if you did."

Boy, I'm in a right pickle here, thought Brendan. *She looks like she should be front page of Playboy, with her high heels and short skirt. Not the girl I first met in Lewis's, that's for sure. How do I put it to her that she's not dressed for the part?*

"Maureen, my love..." commenced Brendan, taking a deep breath. "You are gorgeous, attractive, alluring, intelligent, and sexy, but you look like you're going to a party. Your Mr. Armpit doesn't know what he's talking about. You're not a tart. I think, from what you say about him, Armpit maybe wishes he looked like you. Now, please, get changed into something less attractive as my hormones are working overtime."

After a comfortable evening and an early night, the couple decided the next day they would have a day in Liverpool, call in to the central library in the city and look up Aldertree Confections. Brendan intended to buy a couple of shirts and get measured for a new business suit.

"Here we are, Liverpool Central, Maureen. Let's go into Lewis's for the shirts. I'd like to wallow in the thought that I don't have to line up any more shirts and try to look busy when there's nothing to do. Brendan shivered at the thought. *Wonder if Sean is still there and Goodblood? What a man, yuck. Wonder if he's still alive? With that awful cough.*

"I wonder where the yellow went," laughed Maureen. "That ad I saw for toothpaste on ITV—can't get that line out of my mind. Ah, here's the main entrance..."

Maureen was looking very smart in a three-quarter-length brown tweed coat with fur collar, her red hair topped by a smart red woollen cap. She turned to Brendan, saying, "Isn't it grand not to have to use the staff entrance? You're looking very nautical in your white roll-neck jersey. Come on, isn't it fun?" Maureen caught his hand. "Let's go up and wreck the toy department. Then we'll go and tear up a few shirts. Remember Danster? 'Miss Byrne, will you please be careful with that trolley!'" she mimicked. "And Mr. Jones, the Welshman. Oh, this should be fun."

"Now ease down a bit, Mo. It wouldn't be wise to wreck the toy department—maybe break the necks of a few Sindy dolls—Oh! Hello, Mr. Marsden, fancy meeting you here!" Brendan interrupted his suggestions as Marsden of Personnel came towards them, dressed in his outdoor clothes.

"It's Harris, isn't it? Well, well, hello, and I must say goodbye," were his few words as he strode by.

"That was my friend Mr. Marsden from Personnel," laughed Brendan sarcastically.

"Yes, I know him, a bit of a creep," Maureen said as they both stepped onto the escalator, Brendan on the step behind.

"Stop that, Brendan Harris, or I'll swipe you with my handbag," remonstrated Maureen to Brendan for patting her on the backside.

"Right, shirts, here we come. Rows and rows of white shirts, size fourteen to eighteen neck, all in order. Not a soul around... Shop?" called Brendan. "Wonder who will appear... Shop!" he called out again. Still no response. "Dreadful service, not like in my day, Mo." Brendan was ready to replace the two shirt packages he had taken from the row.

"Would sir be liking a bit of the service now, then?" asked a soft Irish male voice from behind the counter.

"You took your time, Sean Coyle. What were you doing hiding in there?"

"I was just thinkin'...there now, what a fine couple you make. Is it Maureen from Toys you are, then? I was thinkin'...I know that girl..."

"How are things going with you, Sean?" Brendan asked, passing the two cellophane wrapped shirts to him. "Maureen, this is Sean Coyle—another Irishman."

Sean acknowledged Maureen with a nod and answered Brendan's question. "We're in turmoil here. Goodblood is off sick, and I'm here on me own, apart from a junior who's on break. You wouldn't like to come back, would you? Be with you in a moment, den, sir," Coyle called over to another potential customer. "Sorry, Bren, haven't got time to chat. Are you buying them shirts or just admiring them?"

Brendan handed over his money in exchange for the shirts and left Sean to his work.

"He's a nice guy, Bren," Maureen said as they headed towards the escalator to bring them to the toy department.

"He is. It's a bit nostalgic, this, Mo. It seems like years ago when Jones in his singsong Welsh voice, said, 'Miss Byrne will look after young Mr. Harris?' and pointed to you—the brown-coated female with a dust cap hiding her red hair, and clumping around in her flat boots, pushing a shelved trolley stacked high with Meccano boxes."

"I must have looked dreadful, Bren. God, whatever did you see in me?"

Giving a sympathetic shrug of his shoulders, Brendan caught her hand, squeezed it, and together, they joined the other customers as they stepped onto the moving escalator.

"Good morning, Mr. Harris, and is it Miss Byrne? How pleasant it is to meet you again. You are both looking very well. Please accept my sympathies for your bereavement, Miss Byrne."

"Thank you, Mr. Danster. How kind of you to remember us," Maureen responded, somewhat startled that Danster would even acknowledge her presence, let alone remember her name and Brendan's.

"We do hope you are keeping well," said Brendan. "Would Mr. Jones be around at the moment?"

"At one of his time-consuming meetings, Mr. Harris. Now, I must leave you, a customer awaits. I shall tell Mr. Jones you called," offered Danster as he backed away, bowing in jerky movements.

"Well, that was a surprise, Maureen, Danster recognising me. We'll certainly buy the kids' toys here…I like that Scalextric set." Brendan pointed to a large layout of track and petrol stations with racing cars, all lined up at the grid. "Always wanted one. Let's buy it now."

"God, we could have some fun with it," agreed Maureen, "although we don't have the room. The house is too small."

"OK, Maureen… Let's get married when I get my next job. You could find work easily and we could buy a larger house in…now where would you think? Southport? Crosby? Or even Formby—or across the water on the Wirral. We could then buy two sets of Scalextric for the twin boys. Problem solved."

"'Thought you had forgotten, Bren. Yes, let's get married—could we buy a house in Formby? They must be really expensive, though. Give us a kiss, you big lump. Aw, to hell with Danster, give me a decent kiss. No, better not. I remember my mother saying girls who kiss in public always have twins, and along with the boys you have arranged—really do you want to get married?"

Brendan struck a pose, ready to draw his six guns, and spoke in an American drawl. "You betchum, Red Ryder, but maybe I better have a chinwag with Gabby Hayes first. Do you wanna hitch yer waggin to mine, Daisy?"

"What on earth are you up to, Brendan Harris? Who's this Red Ryder and Gabby who? And what's the pose?"

"Maureen Byrne, you haven't lived!" exclaimed Brendan, standing back in mock astonishment. "The Red Ryder cowboy pictures on a Saturday morning at the Adelphi cinema, with Gabby Hayes, sidekick to Hopalong Cassidy and Roy Rogers. Oh, those were the days…an empty jam jar—washed, mind you—got you into the front seats. The price for the balcony was a jar and thruppence. Marry me, Miss Byrne and I can extol you with tales about my heroes and their adventures in the *Vigilantes of Dodge City* and *The Cheyenne Kid*."

"I cannot wait, Gabby. Now let's get out of here before we're thrown out. Yes, Mrs. Brownlee, it is Maureen, used to do stores. Thank you." Catching Brendan's hand, Maureen waved to a startled Mrs. Brownlee, and the happy couple made their way from the department store.

"Central Library next stop, Maureen, to find anything about Aldertree Confections."

***

"Founded in 1862…factories in York…many brands of sweets—I can see why they took over Broons. The Blue Ace biscuit would merge in nicely with their other brands. Wonder what they may offer me tomorrow? Come on, Mo, let's go and have a wander over to Mathew Street and visit the Cavern."

"Yes, let's. Will they be open, though, during the day? Isn't it a nightclub?"

"We might as well take a look, anyway. I paid it a visit years ago. It was a right dump then, but it may have improved. I saw the Beatles when they called themselves the Quarrymen."

"They're on a world tour at the present. Wonder if there's anyone famous on today? It's gone midday—look, there's a queue going down that…hole in the wall."

That was an apt way to describe the entrance to the now famous Cavern, although the crowd looking to be mainly office girls having a quick lunch break.

Brendan and Maureen paid their shilling entrance fee and were immediately assailed by the smell of stale perspiration and cigarette smoke. There was also a definite smell of drains. Amongst the hubbub of voices could be heard accents from around the world.

Taller than most, Brendan and Maureen stood at the side of the cave with the small stage in front of them. Pressed up against each other, with the 'cave' getting hotter and the white distemper peeling off the roof and falling on the crowd below, they looked at each other and agreed they wouldn't stay too long.

"Can you see what's written on the side of the drum, Mo? Something like Herman—can't make out the other name."

"Herman's Hermits, mate," said a short male figure alongside them. "Used to be Herman and the Hermits. Peter Noone is the leader—used to be on Corrie."

"Oh, did he?" Brendan was none the wiser. "What time do they come on stage…mate?" he asked, beginning to wish they hadn't come down into this rank dungeon.

"The Clayton Squares or the Four Pennies are on first—or Herman and his lads may even come on first. Dunno, mate. Right, Sean, comin'—ta-rah, mate." The source of information dissolved into the growing throng.

"See, Bren, there's movement on the stage. Look, there's four of them," exclaimed Maureen. "They're only kids. Maybe they're the Four Pennies. It seems they all come in fours."

"Yes, miss!" another knowledgeable Scouser advised. "They're the Four Pennies. They used to be called The Lionel Morton Four. There's Lionel there, look, second from the right with the rhythm guitar. Hiya, Lionel!" shouted the admirer, getting a wave from the man himself. "He's the singer, is Lionel. Me sister is married to a friend of his. Hope they play 'Juliet'. Lionel's friend's mother is called Juliet—"

"Thanks, mate" Brendan interrupted with a smile. "Let's listen to the music."

With a roll of drums and screeching guitars, the Four Pennies went into their routine with various rock 'n' roll numbers. However, they finished off with a soppy rendering of their recent hit 'Juliet'. The crowd went into raptures, and another layer of white distemper dislodged from the ceiling.

In the relative silence after Lionel and his buddies disappeared from the stage, Maureen indicated she'd had enough of standing, of the smell, the noise and the intermittent shower of white distemper. "Let's give Herman a miss this time, Bren. I could do with a breath of fresh air."

Brendan agreed readily and started to move out of the cave— "Excuse me, excuse me, sorry was that your foot? Sorry, mate."

With a sigh of relief, glad to get out of the claustrophobic atmosphere, the two made their away to the nearest café for a bite to eat. While they were in there, it began to rain quite heavily, so they decided to call it a day and took the train back to the house.

17

Look to the Future – Another Job Offer

That evening, with a nice warm glow from the coal fire, and after the twice-weekly dose of Corrie, Maureen rose and declared, "Bren, I'm away for a bath. Could we talk about the future when I come down? You know a girl likes to know these things."

"Yes, sure, Mo. I'll turn the TV off—there's only that *Doctor Kildare* series and that guy Harry Worth on. I'll read the paper." Turning around on the sofa, Brendan called out hopefully, "You wouldn't like me to scrub your back, by any chance?"

"You go on, read the paper. I can do my own back thank you," was the gentle put down by Maureen as she left the room.

"Bren, wake up, here's a cup of tea," called out Maureen as she shook Brendan. "It's nine o'clock."

"Oh! Yes! Nine o'clock. What day is it?" muttered Brendan as he sat up stretching himself. Catching the sight of a pink dressing gown and a shining face surrounded by red hair, he stood up, took the proffered cup, placed it on the side table and wrapped himself around the warm bundle of pink, saying in a deep voice, "My! Oh! My! You smell like a woman in a pink dressing gown should smell—of pink carnations and shining red roses."

Slightly startled by this sudden burst of affection, Maureen pushed him away and indicated the cooling cup of tea. "Get that down you—we can do a bit of smooching later."

Brendan picked up the cup and downed the contents in a couple of gulps. "Right, I'm away for a quick bath. Oh, hold on—is there enough water in the tank, do you think?"

"Sorry, Bren, love, I think I used it all. There could be enough for a wash, though…"

"Not to worry, Mo. I'll suffer. Is this what married life will be like? I wonder…" he called over his shoulder as he left the warm room.

"Yes, I wonder," Maureen said.

Brendan returned to the sight of Maureen showing some cleavage, her dressing gown parting above her knees as she perched on the edge of the sofa. The record player was going—Frank Sinatra's 'My Way'.

"There you are, then, Bren. Come here and give me a kiss."

Brendan's reactions below the midriff were very obvious.

"Oh, dear me, Brendan what's going on down there? Oh, God, what do we do now?"

"Leave it to Brendan the Bold—I've come prepared. Now lie back there and enjoy yourself, Maureen."

Over the clatter of the records falling on the turntable could be heard the satisfied *ohs* and *ahs* and *wows* of two bodies doing it 'Their Way'.

***

Lying back on the sofa, feeling relaxed and enjoying the Black and White Minstrels on *The Andy Stewart Show*, Brendan was startled to hear Maureen say, "Bren, you spoke about us getting married…"

Has she changed her mind? Have I done something? "Yes, I did, and you promised me twin boys. Joking apart, Maureen—" Brendan sat up "—you haven't changed your mind, have you?"

"No, no, Bren, I'm still all for it."

"Thank God for that."

"Kiss me again and let's talk—only a kiss, Bren! Oh dear, not again. No…I want to talk. I'm adamant. *I want to talk.*"

"I'll try hard, Maureen, I promise. Now, don't laugh. It's not funny…" and both went into uncontrollable giggling.

"What money have we got together?" Maureen asked. "I have £100 in the bank and, of course, the value of the house—maybe worth a thousand. That's £1,100. Quite a lot."

"I've got £50 in the bank and £900 in shares, so…a further £950—£2,050 in all. We could buy a house in Formby for that, I'm sure. Or maybe get a mortgage."

"We would need money to buy new furniture and things, but to get a mortgage you need a job."

"Yes, there is that…small matter. Ha-ha. OK, say I get the job with Aldertree tomorrow, and they offer £700 a year. The bank will probably give twice my salary as a mortgage—that's £1,400, and we put the £2,000 in. We could look for a house priced in the £3,000 range.

"Look, when I go for the interview tomorrow, I'll call in to the bank in Castle Street and see what they might offer. This is getting quite exciting. Jobwise, I have a few other feelers out. That razor blade company down in London is one—"

"I know what I'll do," interrupted Maureen. "I'll come into town with you tomorrow and have a look around in Castle Street or Dale Street for a building society and see what they may offer. What time's your meeting?"

"Ten-thirty. Should be out by eleven-thirty. Meet you in the Mercantile Café about a quarter to twelve. You know the one where you go down the steps under the office buildings. Hopefully, I'll have some good news."

"Yep, and at the weekend, we could drive out to Formby or Southport, see what houses there are for sale and make a day of it. What do you say, Bren? On, and there's another thing—where and when are we goin' to get married?"

"Let's hold on a minute there, girl," cautioned Brendan. "Look for a new job, look for a house, get a mortgage, get married…have twins." He stopped talking; Maureen drew back on the sofa, eyeing him suspiciously.

"Can't do it all in one week, Maureen, especially the twins, but we can try. After we're married, of course. Come on, don't look so worried." He laughed. "We are going to have fun! Yippee!" he shouted, leaping up from the sofa and dancing a jig in front of Maureen.

"OK, Brendan, sit down and stop acting the fool. I have a serious question to ask. Do you want to get married in a church?"

"Do you?"

"You answer. I asked first."

"Not really. I don't mind, but a registry office would be less complicated. Of course, you're a Catholic, so you tell me."

"I'll probably be consigned to hell and damnation, but yes, a registry office would be best, I think. Mustn't let the priests know."

"Well, Mo, we've got a busy future ahead of us. Oh—one last thing. I'd better let my parents and brothers know I'm getting married. Would you like to meet them? We could fly over to Dublin and stay a couple of days."

"'I'd love to meet them all, Bren, love," agreed Maureen as they snuggled up together. "But let's see what happens tomorrow."

***

"Yes, Mr. Harris, we are Pioneer Consultants recruiting for Aldertree. The company, as you are no doubt aware, is one of the leading companies in the UK. They are expanding their sales force, particularly here in the North West. I understand you were an officer in the Navy?"

Over the next hour, Brendan parried and offered questions about himself and the post in question, and was quite surprised to be offered, there and then, an opportunity to join Aldertree.

"Yes, Mr. Harris, we are happy to offer you the post as a salesman/merchandiser at the salary of £650 per annum. After training at the company's head offices in York, and subject to references, there will be a company car supplied with all the necessary expenses of running same reimbursed. What do you say to that, Mr. Harris?"

Rather disappointed with the salary offered, but the attraction of the company car could override that, Brendan took a deep breath and thought *nothing ventured*... "Thank you for your offer, Mr. Birch. I would just like to confirm as I understand it. Training will be for two weeks whilst resident in York. At the end of the course, I will be supplied with a Vauxhall Viva with essential expenses paid. Were I to successfully complete the training course and Aldertree are satisfied with my approach, I would ask if the company could then increase my salary by another £100 per year to £750 per annum?"

"Mr. Harris," replied Birch, sitting back in the hotel chair, "I think I have been very generous in my initial offer of employment to you. However—" he leaned forward, hands palms upwards, and smiled "—I shall meet you half way. Will you accept £702 starting from now?"

"Certainly, Mr. Birch. That's great. I accept and look forward to working with Aldertree."

"Ideal, very satisfactory, Mr. Harris. Now, there will be a fresh training course starting in three weeks' time—Monday the first of June. Shall I put you down for that date? The company will be in touch with you very shortly."

Rising from his chair, Birch rounded the desk and, after shaking Brendan's hand, ushered him to the hotel room door.

"Goodbye, Mr. Harris—offered contract will be in the post."

***

"Yes, Maureen, I've got that one in the bag. Nearly double the money I was getting in Lewis's and a car—a Vauxhall Viva—all expenses paid. I start in three weeks. Go on a training course. What about yourself, Mo? any news?"

With a big grin, Maureen produced a small pile of papers from the table behind her and declared, "Houses for sale in Southport and Formby. There's lots of them, so after tea, maybe we could look at them. And I found some building societies." Maureen continued in a snooty voice, "'Young lady, our society would consider up to two and a half times the main earner's income. What did you say the company offered you?"

"Seven hundred and—"

"Seven hundred? Wow! That's...one thousand seven hundred and fifty pounds. We could easily bump that up with another two thousand..." Looking anxiously at Brendan, Maureen stopped. "What do you think? Have I jumped the gun? Are you annoyed?"

"No! No! Mo, I'm not annoyed—far from it. We've got so many things happening it's a job to keep up. Look, let's just stop for a moment. We've got three weeks before I start with Aldertree, then I shall be away for a few weeks on training courses. The most important thing before anything else is—" he halted for a moment for emphasis and donning a mock serious face "—when do we get married?"

"Ahead of you there, Bren. Not for another two months at least, I'm afraid. There's a waiting list at the registry office. I called in to our local one. They said waiting time up to eight weeks."

"Now I shall put something to you, Mo. Let's book the marriage for eight weeks. I'll be well back from the course by then. Put the house up for sale immediately. Find a house from this lot—" Brendan pointed to the sheaf of papers "—and everything should be done and dusted by the end of the year. What do you think?"

"Sounds very exciting, Bren, but to afford a mortgage, I'll need to get a job, and what about our visit to Ireland? You forgot that."

"Oh, no I didn't. I called in to a travel agent and found we can take an Aer Lingus plane from Liverpool Airport to Dublin. Take the bus from the airport, or even get my brother to pick us up in Dublin and stay in Laurel Cottage—that's where my parents live. Where I was brought up. Maybe we could even hire a car from the airport. So, do we register to get married in eight weeks' time? Please say yes." Brendan caught hold of Maureen's hand and looked her in the eye.

"Yes, of course, you big softie. We'll register tomorrow and get the paperwork going. Target: Monday, 8th of August. We'll need a witness or two. Leave that nearer to the day. Right, next: the trip to Ireland."

"I'll look after that, Mo. Let's keep quiet about the religion side. My mother is an active Protestant churchgoer. Not too keen on her favourite boy marrying an RC, even a lapsed one, but we can work on her. My father will love you. He likes tall good-looking girls. My brother Jono—who's older than me, he's twenty-eight—is engaged to a Catholic girl. Billy is single, working somewhere in Dublin he's three years younger than me. I'm sure they will organise a small party when we get over there. Have you ever been to Ireland?"

Before Maureen could answer, the doorbell rang. "Eight o'clock in the evening? Wonder who it could be?"

"I'll go, Mo," offered Brendan groping around with his right foot for his slippers. "OK, I'm coming," he growled as the bell rang again.

Opening the door, he could see in the light from the street lamps two adults and a child. The woman looked faintly familiar; she was slightly taller than her male companion, who had an aggressive pose. The female stood forward and informed in a Liverpool accent, "I'm Mary Wells, Maureen's sister," and started to push forward.

"Now, hold on a minute! Maureen?" he called back over his shoulder. "It's your sister Mary, and…is it Cecil?" He directed the question to the male, who also stepped forward and in an aggressive voice tinged with a Caribbean drawl said, "Come on, man, it's raining out here. Isn't it, Bea?" He looked down at the small girl in a pink mackintosh.

"Oh, it is you, Mary. I see you have Cecil and Bea. What do you want, Mary?" These questions and greeting were delivered in a cold impersonal voice from Maureen as she peered over Brendan's shoulder.

"Come on, Maureen, let us in. We want to talk."

Grudgingly, Maureen pulled Brendan's arm to let their visitors in and stood back as they shook the rainwater from their clothes.

"Hello, Bea." Maureen bent down to help take off the small girl's mackintosh.

"Hello, Auntie Mau…reen," Bea answered hesitantly. "Look at Teddy. He's all wet."

"We'll put him beside the fire to dry off, shall we?" Maureen looked up from the child. "Hello, Cecil. I'll give you ten minutes to say what you have to say. Brendan, this is Cecil, Mary's husband. Cecil, my fiancé Brendan Harris. Now, come into the living room and state your piece."

"No need to be like that, Maureen," Mary beseeched. "We're sure you will be interested in what we have to say. Cecil has changed his ways, haven't you, Cec?"

"That I have, Mo. I am a new man and pleased to meet you again, and your fiancé. Is it Brendan?" Cecil asked in a booming voice.

"Any chance of a drop of lemonade for Bea, Mo?" asked Mary, settling down in the sofa and adjusting her dress under her thighs and tugging down her tight brown sweater. Cecil was dressed in a dark, two-piece suit with tie and polished black shoes, and was obviously very aware of the effect his melodious voice and flashing white teeth had on his company.

"Sorry, Bea," said Maureen, "but we don't have any lemonade. Will a drop of water do?"

Before Bea could answer, Mary, whose accent was broader than Maureen's, asked, "Any chance of a cup of tea, Mo, and a whiskey for Cec? We've come a long way!"

"Look, Mary," Maureen began through clenched teeth, "you have been a nasty sister over the years. You've ignored me since Mum's funeral and created a fuss at the reading of the will. I haven't spoken to you for months. Now, what do you want?"

"You are a worried lady there, Miss Maureen. Calm down, and let the girl say her piece," Cecil boomed. "I can see we're not welcome here."

Mary carried on as if Cecil hadn't said anything at all. "All right, Maureen. I'll agree I haven't been much of a sister to you. I'll come to the point. I felt Mum should have left me more in the will, especially where this house is concerned, but be that as it is, we want to make an offer to buy. What do you say?"

"Well, well, that is something I didn't think of. What do you say, Bren?"

"What's it got to do with him?" Mary demanded.

What a setup, Brendan thought. *Let's see if we can squeeze them for £1,500 or more.* "What an interesting idea, Mo. Makes you think. I'm quite happy here as the lodger. We intend getting married soon and we've been looking forward to living here. Do you want to talk about it?" Brendan asked, pointing towards the kitchen.

Getting the nod from Maureen, they both rose and went to the kitchen, where they stood in shock. What an opportunity, but they needed to be careful.

"Can we trust them?" Brendan asked.

"I don't know, Bren."

"OK. Let's try them out. How much to go for? The market price is around the £1,600 mark. If they bought, we would save the estate agency fees. What about going for £1,800 and let them beat you down to the £1,600 if necessary? Of course, there's the mortgage of £315 still owing."

Maureen nodded. "Let's do it," she said.

Coming back into the living room and trying hard not to smile, they sat down on the dining room chairs alongside each other.

"Well, this is a turn-up for the books, I must say, Mary. There's always a price for everything. What's yours?"

"Well, Maureen, we were looking at similar houses and would offer you £1,200—in cash, of course.

"You know, Mum was still paying off the mortgage, and there's something like £400 still owing. We'd have to buy another house to live in as well."

"What do you think, Cec?" Mary turned to face him.

"Up to you, though we could afford to make it £1,200 plus no more than the £400 mortgage."

"Here's what we might consider, Mary, Cecil," Maureen said. "Round the total to £1,800 and we'll let you know when we've talked it over." For a final flourish, she crossed her legs in a flash of nylon.

"What about the furniture, then, Maureen? We'd want the furniture."

Maureen looked around her, obviously doing a bit of quick thinking. "OK, if you are of your word, we'll let you know if we want to sell, and if so, I think the furniture should be shared equally."

Cecil nodded. "A lot here to think about, Miss Maureen and Brendan. It is all right if we have a look around…just in case you decide to sell?" He rose from the sofa. "Look, Bea has gone asleep. Don't she look lovely?"

"No need to show me, Mo, I used to live here. Remember?" Mary retorted sharply.

"Just hold on a minute there, Cecil. I'll just go and tidy a bit and give you a call. Bren, will you show them the kitchen."

"God, there's not much change here," criticised Mary, standing in the kitchen doorway. "Still the same old sink—that'll have to be changed, Cec. Is that a fridge? Well I never. I see the old Ascot is still there. Could do with a lick of paint. What do you think, Cec?"

"Looks OK to me, Mary. We'll see what the survey comes up with. Get George to have a look-see."

Over the next twenty minutes, the couple scoured the building from top to bottom, asked a few questions and took a few notes, with a parting comment from Cecil—emphasised with his flashing teeth—that he would be paying cash.

After the front door shut, Brendan and Maureen looked at each other, still reeling.

"Did that really happen, Mo?"

"Do you think they'll come back, Bren? Do you think we may have asked too much? I don't think they'll return. Oh! If they bought, it would save so much trouble. Can we trust them?"

"I think what we do is forget about them, and if they don't come back within the week, we put the house up for sale. We'd better start looking around for somewhere to buy. Let's get in touch with a couple of estate agents in Formby and arrange a few visits over the weekend."

18

House Hunting

"Go through Crosby out onto the Formby Bypass, turn left at the lighthouse roundabout, and you're then into Formby. A nice quiet residential village just north of Liverpool on the railway line between the Pool and Southport. I wouldn't be surprised if within a couple of years the prices will rocket." So said the smart, well-dressed salesman from the estate agent's. "There are some good choices here—detached three-bed going for £6,000, detached bungalows for £5,000, semi-detached three-bed in Victoria Park for £4,000, and, perhaps, a starter house for a young married couple such as yourselves in a quiet residential area called Formby Fields. Shall I arrange some viewings for the weekend?"

"Say Saturday for those two," suggested Brendan, pointing to the semi-detached properties. "And the more expensive ones on Sunday. Oh, yes—we may have sold our house in Tuebrook. But if that falls through, your firm could arrange to put it on your books. Here's our telephone number—let us know what you arrange."

On the Saturday, the house seekers drove through Crosby town out into Ince woods and entered the dual carriageway—the Formby Bypass.

"There's Formby, Bren. Turn left at the roundabout. Where's the lighthouse? Oh! There it is," Maureen thought aloud as they approached a turn in the roadway where a mock lighthouse on the roof of a low lying building. "It's only a restaurant called The Lighthouse. What a shame… Into Formby Fields on the right. Look, Bren, they're all bungalows, oh, and there's some semis—that's our one. See, it's got the estate agent sign in the garden. A bit disappointing…looks like a little box."

"Good morning, the agent has—"

"Hi, you must be Mr. and Mrs. Harris," interrupted the house owner, a man in his early twenties. "Are you coming in?" The young unshaven man called out to the back of the house, "It's them all right. Come in, down, Butcher, down. Pay no attention to Butcher, he's just a friendly old chap. Aren't you, Butch?"

Smiling at his visitors, the man patted Butch the bull mastiff on the line of spittle on its grey jowls rather than on the back of the head. He wiped his wet hand on the side of his trousers whilst holding back the hound which lunged menacingly on its strong leather lead.

Moving forward into the small porch—and keeping his eye on Butch and trying to ignore the overpowering smell of dog and sterilising nappies in the air—Brendan ushered Maureen through a side door of the small porch into the main living room. The room stretched the length of the house and was carpeted in a cheap broadloom. There was a pram positioned at the rear window, which looked out onto a small, unkempt garden with houses looming on all sides.

"You've come to look over the house, have you? I'm Barbara Sidell, this is Rob, my husband. Can I leave you to Rob who will show you around? Sorry for the smell. I've just got a little job on with Paul the baby." With that, Barbara stepped back into what must have been the kitchen.

"Can you take Butch, Babs?" Rob called after her. "You know you don't like him upstairs." Rob further shortened the lead on the dog in an effort to stop it lurching forward to sniff the intruders.

"I'm up to my eyes in poo. Put him out in the back. You'll just have to take the chance he doesn't escape… That's a good boy, Paul, no need to cry. Daddy-waddy will dig a big hole and put Butchy-wutchy in it forever."

Rob quickly dashed out with the dog. "Right," he said when he returned, "come on upstairs with me, and I'll show you the bedrooms."

On the way up the narrow staircase, Maureen whispered to Brendan, "Let's get out of here as quick as we can."

They took a cursory look at the untidy bedrooms and messy bathroom.

"Want to see the garage?" Rob asked.

"That's a good idea, Bren," Maureen said. "You go out with Rob and have a look at the garage, and I'll have a word with Barbara and have a look at the kitchen while I'm at it."

Shortly afterwards, as Brendan backed out of the junk-filled garage, Maureen came out the front door and waved to Barbara, who waved back with her free arm, the baby cradled in the other.

"Thanks, Rob, we'll let your agent know when we decide," Brendan said. "Come on, Mo, on to the next." Once they were back in the car, he asked, "What did Mother have to say?"

"I'll tell you after the next—it's just down the road in a cul-de-sac. What does the sale sheet say? £3,700—can't be any worse a state than the one we've just been to."

They got a pleasant welcome from the next home owners, along with the offer of coffee, and with the noticeable smell of flowers and well-tended garden front and rear, Brendan and Maureen left feeling they could move in tomorrow. The owners, unfortunately, were in no hurry to move.

"Well, what do you think, Bren? What a contrast. Both houses only ten years old and look at them."

"Let's call them A and B. A wants £3,500, and B is looking for £3,700. I get the impression A would accept less, as they look pretty hard up, and B would stick at the price asked but might take months to move. I think A is a no-go—what a mess."

"Thought you'd say that, Bren, but consider this: I had a word with Babs, poor girl—she's only eighteen. They're desperate to move and would take £2,900. We could get house A looking like house B for a couple of hundred pound or we could buy B for £800 more and move in without any immediate work. We could put all our savings into a deposit and get a mortgage for £1,750 on your salary with Aldertree, and I could start working again. Though I'm enjoying being an idle woman. Of course, there's Mary and Cecil—we would be well in, if they buy."

"I'm thinking we would be very stretched were we to buy B, so maybe A. God, they'd have to clean up the place. If Mary comes up trumps, we could buy the place outright, but we're depending on two dodgy facts. I think the best thing to do is sleep on it—is there any point in looking at one of the pricier houses tomorrow?"

"We could go and have a look at it now. It's in a Victoria Park down by the squirrels, they say. We could drive down there and have a look see. Look there's ours, Bren—acres of space in front of it and a double garage…going at £6,250. There's a guy in the garden. Draw up, Bren. Hello, there, we're down to view your house tomorrow any chance—"

"Well, well," the guy in the garden interrupted. "We've just phoned the agent to cancel as we have a definite buyer. It's Mrs. Harris, isn't it?"

***

"OK, onto the next one, Mo."

"Let's not bother, Bren. There's a phone box over there—cancel the other visit and let's have a little drive around Formby. The village looks nice and compact." Maureen hesitated. "If we bought the first one and did it up, we could sell it at a profit and buy a bigger one. That's what we'll do."

"No, wait a moment, Mo, I think there's something fishy about the young couple. How were they able to buy in the first place?"

"That's your trouble, Bren," snorted Mo in mild derision. "Overcautious."

"Better the devil you've looked in the face rather than the gift horse up the arse, as my Granda used to say. OK, let's drive around the village and see if there are any further semis for sale and take a note and then go home. It's nearly time for tea. What's that I smell—fish and chips? Let's get a packet each with a bottle of lemonade, Mo."

"Look, Bren, over the railway crossing, a chip shop. Five bob should do it. It's called Whites—must remember if we buy a house here."

***

"Boy, I did enjoy those fish and chips," Brendan said as they arrived back at the house. "We should watch *The Palladium* and have an early night. And I'm going to look out for a few more jobs—the *Telegraph*'s full of them, looking for sales reps countrywide." He followed Maureen through the front door. "What's this? Post on a Sunday? Oh! It's an envelope from June…my old landlady."

"Yes, I remember," Mo said with a toss of her head. "What does she want?"

"It's a telegram—June's forwarded it on." With increasing excitement mixed with trepidation, Brendan opened the envelope. "It's from Sceptre Sword Edge—gosh, they want me in the Midland Hotel in Manchester at nine o'clock tomorrow… Ask for Mr. Anthony Palmer, sales manager, Sceptre Sword Edge. Well, I've got to go for this, Mo."

"I've never heard of them," she said.

"They're a UK firm, based in London. They produce razor blades—I sent my CV to them a while ago." Brendan was already thinking ahead to getting to their office for nine a.m. "I'll drive there—get onto the East Lancs road…leave about seven in the morning—should be there shortly after eight…wonder if there'll be a parking meter free around that time? This could be the one, Mo. This could be the one."

"Why don't I drive you in, Bren? I've nothing on tomorrow. I could drop you off at the Midland and find a car park and maybe we could do some window shopping. I haven't been in Manchester for years. Come on, let's make a day of it. I can wait for you in the foyer."

"Great idea—whatever the result, I've got Aldertree as a backup. Wonder what they're offering?"

"That's agreed, then. Now, you put your feet up and watch *The Palladium*, and I'll make a cup of tea."

***

The following morning, Maureen pulled up outside the Midland Hotel at ten to nine and waved to a smartly dressed Brendan in his new business suit and polished shoes as she drove away to park her car.

Somehow I feel this is going to be different. Sword Edge, the double-edged blade… Right, Mr. Palmer, I'm your man.

Upon entering the grandeur of the hotel foyer with its large patterned flooring and high ceilings, Brendan made his way to the wide expanse of the reception desk, looking around to see if there was any reference to any of the business rooms allocated to Sword Edge, but there was no mention of them anywhere. He thought he heard his name being called from one of the elaborate leather sofas to the side of the foyer. Turning around, he saw a tall man in a business suit pushing himself off the low seat and looking towards him. *This must be Palmer.*

"Mr. Harris?" was the question awaiting confirmation with hand outstretched. Brendan shook the man's hand. "There's a small table to the side there—better than sitting on that dead elephant. I'm Tony Palmer, sales manager for Sabre Sword Edge. Please excuse the informality of the meeting, but time is not on my side. I have to leave you in the next five minutes. I've read your CV, and we've made some enquiries about you. To all appearances, you fit the part to fulfil the role required. I am so, so sorry to be so abrupt, but there's my call." Palmer raised his hand to acknowledge the signal from the uniformed concierge.

"I have a broadsheet on the company. There—read it after I've gone and then give my secretary a call with your decision. All things being equal, joining us will be the best thing you do."

"I'm quite taken aback, Mr. Palmer, but subject to the salary offered, I am sure I will accept.

"Salary?" Palmer was already moving away from the table. "I forgot. How much do you want?"

"Twenty a week will suit me as a starter, Mr. Palmer."

"Done, Mr. Harris. Here's my card—call my secretary, Natalie. Porter—" he signalled to the nearby attendant "—give Mr. Harris a coffee if he wishes and a telephone. Charge to my account. Goodbye. Hope to see you again soon. Sorry for the rush."

"Yes, goodbye, Mr. Palmer," a pleased and surprised Brendan bade farewell to the retreating figure. A *thousand a year...twenty pound a week. Should I have asked for more?*

As Palmer exited through the revolving doors, Maureen made her entrance, looking very attractive in her tweed skirt and high heels. Noticing Brendan on his own, she apparently surmised he had been let down and came to give him a hug and commiserated with him. "Better luck next time. What happened? He not turn up?"

Finding it hard to keep a straight face, Brendan pointed to the vacant chair and signalled the porter. "Tea or coffee, Maureen?"

"Coffee...why? What are we doing?"

"Yes, sir?" the porter asked.

"Coffee for two and a plate of biscuits and a telephone, please."

With a nod, the porter departed.

"What are you up to, Bren? You're up to some devilment. Come on, tell me."

"Just wait a minute, Miss Byrne. Allow the magic to happen."

Taking the proffered telephone from the grinning porter, Brendan dialled the London number on the card, winked at a bemused Maureen, and then answered in his seductive Irish accent, "Good morning, Natalie. Brendan Harris from the Midland Hotel... Oh, good... Yes... Please tell Mr. Palmer I accept... In the post... Yes... That's very important. Thank you, goodbye."

"Bren..."

"Wait until I tell you, Mo. I've been offered a salesmen's job with Sabre Sword Edge on—wait for it—the magic twenty pound a week. Over a thousand a year! I'll have to go down to London for a week's course. They've been making swords for hundreds of years—it's only two years ago they brought out a stainless steel razor blade—and they want me to join a team here in the North West. Twenty pound a week, Mo! That will get us the house we want. What do you think?"

Brimming over with excitement, it was only then that Brendan noticed Maureen was a bit withdrawn and not showing the enthusiasm he'd expected.

"Bren..." she answered. "Whilst I am more than happy with your good fortune, I'm rather put out that you didn't think it worthwhile to discuss it with me before you decided. Let's get it straight, Bren. There are two of us in this together. I'm not your chauffeur and tea maker. And, by the way—" she gestured to the large plate of chocolate biscuits on the table "—these coffees and biscuits must be costing a fortune."

Brendan realised he had been thinking only of himself and the great bit of fortune which had fallen his way. "I'm so sorry, Mo. I got a bit carried away there." She was, of course, now unemployed and must have been feeling somewhat low, especially when everything seemed to be centred around Brendan and his activities.

"Just thought I'd make the point," she said. "Now, where do we go from here?"

"How about we finish these lovely biscuits, and there's another coffee in the pot—don't worry, the company is paying. All I do is sign for it. Is the car in a multistorey?"

"Yes."

"Good, Let's go window shopping, and as a treat why not buy that dress or the shoes you wanted? I could do with a pair of new shoes myself. Let's spend a bit of money. We can pay by credit card."

Calling the porter over, Brendan signed for the coffee and they left the grandeur of the Midland Hotel behind them, arm in arm, prepared for the world ahead.

19

Job Offer – Who is Maureen's Father?

Can't let this fella leave me behind in the success stakes. Must get a job, thought Maureen to herself as they drove back from Manchester down the crowded East Lancs road. *He's certainly not holding back on his ambitions. Let's hope Mary buys the house. He wants to go to Ireland as well, and there was even talk of going to Australia.* With all these thoughts coursing through her mind, she looked to her side to examine this man—a man who, only a few months ago, she did not even know existed, and here she was, beside a long, underweight, pimple-faced, tousled-haired, Irishman wearing size eleven shoes. He was a likeable sort who needed a lot of training in the needs of a woman. *You'll do, Bren, lad.* She patted him on the knee, getting a pat and a smile in response.

"Look, Bren, there's a note with the post—it's from Mary. They want to see us—says they're dropping in at seven tonight."

"It's just gone five. Are they going to buy? How much? We've got to look at the figures again. It's all go. Remember house B going for £3,700? Better than the doss house with the dog. If… Shall I nip down the road to the chippy, before they come and we can talk over what to decide on? That's if they still want to buy?

"OK, I'll get the table ready." *Everything is happening. Now, if I could get a job… Must really give it a try.*

***

"Come in, Cecil, Mary. Hello, Bea. We got your note—give me your coats and sit down. Would you like a coffee?" Maureen fussed her sister into the house and called, "Bren, they're here. Could you make up a couple of coffees and an orange juice for Bea? Would you bring me in one as well?"

"Coming, Mo, won't be a minute."

"Sugar and milk on the tray, help yourselves," offered Brendan. "Here's your orange juice, Bea."

"Thank you, Uncle Brendan," the little girl said, looking coyly over the edge of the glass tumbler.

"That's a good girl, Bea," Mary praised. "Hello, Brendan. Have you decided yet?"

"Decided what, exactly, Mary? I think you should be directing your questions to Maureen if it's the house you are talking about."

"You know it's the house we're here about. Do you want to sell, Maureen? Mary asked tetchily, glancing in annoyance at Brendan.

"You certainly left us to think, Mary," said Maureen. "Selling was the furthest thing from our minds, as we are quite happy here."

"As I said, Mary," came the deep voice from behind the flashing teeth, "I don't think they want to sell. Perhaps we just drink our coffees and leave. But, wait a minute—is it the price you're bothered about?"

"Go on, Cecil, try us," answered Maureen with a grin.

"We'll give you £1,500 for the house and contents, and that's it."

"£1,500 and us with a mortgage on it and we'd have to furnish another house? No way."

"How much is the mortgage? About £400, if I remember?" With a confirmatory nod from Maureen, he continued, "We'll meet you in the middle and give you £1,700, and no more."

"What do you think, Bren? Is it worth the hassle?"

"Another £100 and we agreed we would consider a move, didn't we, Mo? So there you are, Cecil, Mary—the house, *half* its contents, apart, of course, from our own possessions, and mortgage free, is yours." Brendan held out his hand to Cecil.

Cecil looked from the proffered hand to Mary, who gave the faintest of nods. With a beaming smile, Cecil said, "Put it there, Brendan, sir. We have a deal."

"£1,800 it is, then, Mary," Maureen confirmed. "This merits a celebratory drop of the hard stuff. Whiskey all round while we talk about the next steps. You know where the special whiskey is kept, Bren, and another drop of orange for this grand girl Bea."

***

God, everything is happening all at once. The house is sold with the furniture. I've got a new job at £20 a week and a company car. Only a few months ago, I was on £8 without even a bike. Even if we have nowhere to move to, we can always stay in a hotel or a B&B for a few months. If we could get house B to move on the price, all would be perfect. I'm looking forward to seeing the Sabre Sword Edge contract…

"To a successful house sale, Cecil, Mary, and may all go smoothly without any complications."

After a congratulatory clinking of whiskey glasses, Brendan passed a piece of paper to Cecil. "Here's our solicitor's address. I shall tell him to expect a contact from your solicitor with a deposit of, shall we say, ten percent? Have you got their address with you, Cecil?"

"Who shall we use?" Cecil asked Mary. "Manny Freedman is usually the best. Yes, Manny Freedman—you'll find him in Hackins Hey Liverpool. Here, I've got his address and telephone number. That is a nice drop of whiskey, Miss Maureen. Is there, by any chance, any more going?"

"Certainly, Cecil, a drop all round—we have something to celebrate now."

Brendan leaned over to fill the small whiskey glasses. *Better go easy on this stuff, I still have some reservations about this pair.* "So, what are your plans, Mary? We want to work closely together."

"We're in a flat in Warrington at the moment. As you have already noticed, Mo, I'm pregnant, and we thought we'd love to come home to the old house. We deal in house purchase, doing them up and renting out. Cecil is a lay preacher with Evangelical Fellowship. We are so glad you decided to sell—you've no doubt gathered we're ready to move in anytime."

"Well," Maureen said, "as we're starting from scratch, and Brendan is starting a new job—and we're getting married in six weeks—there's a lot happening."

"Yes, you are a busy pair. One question we will need to consider: in five weeks, our rental agreement runs out, and, of course, we would not wish to renew."

"Don't worry, Mary, we'll move out to a hotel or B&B and put whatever bits and pieces we agree to take into storage."

"That looks great, doesn't it, Cecil? Let's go. Bea is looking very tired and she has school tomorrow. So very, very glad things are working out so well. We are both very pleased with the outcome so far. Goodnight and God bless you both."

***

"Well, Maureen, lass, there's a turn up for the books." Brendan caught Maureen's arm as they stepped inside the front door, having bid goodnight to their buyers. "Couldn't have worked out much better. Are you happy with things going as they are?"

"Just wondering if we're possibly taking too much on. Sell this, buy another, you start a new job. I suppose it's goodbye to Ireland for the moment, and what about us getting married? And I must get a job. Exciting, though, isn't it? So much depends on Mary and Cecil. I'm still not a hundred percent happy with them. An', of course, you haven't seen the contract yet from Sabre Sword Edge. Wonder what sort of car you'll get? Bet it's another Morris Minor—you'd love that, wouldn't you?" Maureen chuckled. "You did hate the other one. Still, we will probably know tomorrow. Let's have a cup of tea an' away to bed."

**

"Is that the postman, Mo?"

"No, you eejit, it's Santa Clause. Go on see what he's got for you."

"It's a large brown one. Look, it's got Sabre Sword Edge on it—it's lovely an' thick," grinned Brendan, playing the fool.

"Go on, open the bloody thing…what does it say?"

"Offer of a contract as salesman to promote et cetera, on £1,040 per annum, two weeks hols, company car a Ford Cortina 1600, all expenses paid…short introductory course in London…subject to references et cetera—give me that biro and let's get it in the post tonight. It's all happening to us at the moment. What house will we go for? Let's see if we can get house B to accept £3,500. We could get the agent to ask them or we could see what else there is on the market."

"About the house, Bren, I think we'd better wait until my lovely sister puts down a deposit and shows her real intention. There's something going on there, I feel. The bold Cecil was too agreeable. Nothing like the Cecil I knew of old."

"Yeah! Maybe you're right, Mo. It's only been a couple of days since they agreed to buy. We'll give them until Wednesday next, OK? Did the registry office in Crosby agree a date for the wedding?"

"God, I forgot to tell you. Saturday 15th August at 11 a.m. Here—the confirmation came in the post a couple of days ago. Meant to tell you…" Maureen produced a typed sheet from her writing pad. "Doesn't cost much. Who will we ask? Who will we tell? Will we have a reception? Do we go away for a honeymoon? We could drive away into the sunset in your Ford Cortina. That's another thing—when do you go to London?"

"Monday 8th June—that's only two weeks away. Are we trying to do too much all in one go? I'm thinking…could you hold back on getting work until we get a few of the things out of the way? Ireland is a no-no for the moment, but I'll let them all know we're getting wed and leave it up to them. You've got Mary and Cecil and others. We could stay in Liverpool for the weekend—I'm sure to be back to work on the Monday. By then, let's hope we are somewhere ahead with the sale and purchase. Hey, why don't we pop around to the estate agent and tell them we're interested—see if they could give us a possible programme."

"Right, I'll do that, Bren. I'm still going to keep my eye out for a job along the way…I'd love to get a bit of dancing in one night. What do you think?"

"We could drop into Reece's some evening…but not at the moment please Mo."

"OK, OK, just a thought."

"Ah, its Saturday, to hell with it—let's go to Reece's, have a few drinks, dance the night away and talk about wedding plans and a honeymoon in the Caribbean."

"That's a deal, Bren—let's wow them. I'm sure there will be a few from Lewis's there. We could tell them about the wedding. Maybe not mention the Caribbean, though it's a lovely thought. There's always the possibility of preparing for those twins you mentioned a while back, when you were out to seduce me."

Brendan grinned and picked up the phone to call his mother. "That's another bonus we have to look forward to. Let's keep practising. No, not now—oh! There's Humperdinck at it again. Come on, what's keeping you?"

"Lines to Dublin exchange are engaged, please try later…"

"There is a three-hour delay on lines to Dublin. Do you wish to reserve a call?"

"No thanks, operator." Brendan replaced the receiver. "I'll write to them, Mo—wonder what Jono's address is now? Billy's probably still living at Laurel Cottage. I'll write to them both there, and Ma will let them know. It'll be a bit of a shock for them. We should get a photo of us together. Anyway, let's go dancing."

***

"Is that the doorbell, Bren? Can you answer it?"

"OK, Mo, I'll get it."

Opening the front door in the reducing early evening light, all Brendan could see was a large shadow of a male filling the doorway, wearing a cloth cap and with a large haversack on the doormat beside him.

"Yes?" enquired Brendan tentatively.

"Hi," came a booming voice with a southern hemisphere twang. "My name is Pete Byrne—does Marjorie Byrne or Mary Byrne live here now, cobber?"

Brendan's immediate reaction, to what felt like an invasion, was to shut the door and hope the intruder would go away.

"No, but there is a Maureen Byrne here," he admitted grudgingly.

"I am looking for a Marjorie Byrne with a daughter Mary. Does—who did you say, Maureen Byrne? Does she have a sister called Mary?"

"Look, buster…" Brendan began.

"Who is it, Bren? Did I hear right—someone asking for me?"

"Yes, Mo—oh, there you are." Maureen came alongside him in the porch way. "This gentleman is looking for Mary—a Peter Byrne."

"Sorry, sir, I don't recognise you."

"I'm Peter Byrne—married to Marjorie Byrne with a daughter named Mary."

"Are you the Peter Byrne who broke my mother's heart so many years ago? The Peter Byrne that went away to the war and never came back? Are you?" Maureen glared accusingly.

"Mary, my daughter, was born in 1938 before I went to war. Who are you, Maureen? And this guy here?" He pointed at Brendan.

"I am getting confused here. You say you were married to Mum but only know about Mary? I think you had better come in, Mr. Byrne, and explain yourself."

Getting the nod from Maureen, Brendan stepped aside to allow the large interloper with the strange accent to enter the hallway.

Doffing his cap, Mr. Byrne passed it to Brendan and stepped inside, leaving his haversack on the step. The unwelcome visitor, showing a striking hairless head which accentuated a luxuriant moustache, looked most out of place in his heavy brown anorak and tight blue trousers.

"Thank you, miss," the intruder continued in his loud—Brendan thought it was Australian—drawl. "I wonder if your man could bring my bag in?"

"Let me stop you there, Mr. Byrne," interrupted Brendan, beginning to get a bit annoyed with this brash and badly mannered visitor. "Your bag is staying right where it is until you explain yourself. Now, into the front room and git talking, buster."

"Ease off a bit, Bren, the man looks exhausted. Would you like a cup of tea, Mr. Byrne or perhaps a whiskey. Oh, what am I thinking? All Americans drink coffee. Would you like a coffee?"

"Sure, miss, as it comes. Hold on a sec. I don't know where you got the American from. I'm an English man born in Blackburn, here in England."

"It's a black coffee, then," agreed Maureen, slightly confused with the strange accent. "Now, Mr. Byrne, tell us what you want."

"Miss Byrne—may I call you Maureen?" Getting the affirmative nod, Byrne asked, "And you, sir, may I call you Bren?"

"Just continue, Mr. Byrne," ordered Brendan, sitting forward on the settee alongside Maureen. "What are you here for?"

"Firstly, please excuse my unannounced arrival, but may I enquire if you know the whereabouts of my wife Marjorie Byrne?"

"My mother, Marjorie Byrne, died a short while ago, Mr. Byrne," answered Maureen abruptly.

"I am sorry for your distress, Maureen, and my lovely Marjorie. Back in 1936, when I was a youngster, I came back to England to visit a dear old uncle. I should explain. As I said, I was born in Blackburn, and my parents emigrated to Australia when I was a baby. I met Marjorie. We fell in love and got married in 1937.

"Your mother was a beautiful woman and quite wilful. We ran away to that place in Scotland called Greeta Green—or is it Grate Green? I know the word green is in the place name somewhere? Anyway, we rented a two-room apartment with Uncle Robert, and in 1938, Mary was born.

"I was, I must admit, a scared young man, and the responsibility of marriage and a child caused me to drop my responsibilities. I enlisted in the army as a recruit in February 1939. I won't go into detail how I did this, but apart from changing my name, it was quite easy. I am ashamed of what I did and would very much like to meet Mary and ask her forgiveness. I have a small photograph, which I have always treasured—a picture of Marjorie and Mary with myself. Are there any photos around that I may see?"

"No! My mother destroyed all photographs and any possessions of Peter Byrne, seeing as he left her without anything apart from two baby girls and a lot of debt. But—wait a minute! I was born in November 1940... When did you last see my mum?"

"January 1939. I am so ashamed," cried the Australian.

"So you should be, you waster," accused Brendan. "Now look what you've done, turning up here unannounced."

"Bren, who's my father, then? What's my real name? Oh, Bren what are we to do? Why did you have to come here, you dreadful man..." Maureen directed her anger and distress at Peter. "Right, what are you going to do now, Mr. Byrne?"

"Ask for your forgiveness, and then I'll be on my way."

"What do you think, Bren?"

"Really up to you, Mo, but I would certainly ask for some identification before we go any further."

"Of course, of course," Peter agreed without hesitation. "I have my passport here, somewhere, in one of these pockets. Ah, here it is." He produced a small, worn booklet, opening it to show a photograph.

"Just wait a moment, mister," Brendan warned as 'Pete' stepped forward. "See what it says, Mo."

"It looks OK to me, Bren—Peter Byrne born 13th March 1915, in Blackburn, England. What was your mum's maiden name?"

"Something like festivity—I could never pronounce it, but it began with an 'F'. Maureen, you must believe me. I know your mother's maiden name was Robinson. Look, please could I be excused to go to the lavatory?" Pete rose from the easy chair.

"Up the stairs first door at the top," said Brendan. He watched the man leave and turned back to Maureen. "What a mystery... We could put him up in the spare room. After all, there are lots of questions he might be able to answer about your mother. She certainly kept quiet about all this."

"Hadn't we better get Mary and Cecil over—not now, maybe tomorrow? I bet Mary will have a few questions to ask. Who am I, though, Brendan? Who's my father?"

"I'm sure we'll find out one way or another, Maureen. Let me give you a hug. Now, don't cry—I know it must be a great shock. But your Mum. What has she been up to? When Byrne comes back downstairs, we'll give him something to eat. It's only eight in the evening; I could give Mary a ring and have them come over in an hour's time—oh, there you are now, Mr. Byrne. Have you arranged accommodation for yourself for the night?"

"No. I came straight here from the airport. I know it's a lot to ask, but if you could allow me to stay for the night, I'll be away first thing in the morning. And if you have a contact number for Mary, I would be most grateful."

"All right, Mr. Byrne, sit yourself down and we'll get you a meal," Brendan said as Maureen was already bustling away to the kitchen. "We'll get in touch with Mary and arrange for her and her family to come over tomorrow. As I'm sure you can understand, your sudden appearance has come as a shock to Maureen. You were always in the background. Now here you are, and she's preparing a meal for a stranger. I don't know whether to throw you out on your ear or to sympathise with you."

"I understand," Peter said. "Thank you for not throwing me out."

"Don't thank me yet. You may be of some use to us. Do you know who Maureen's father is? No—hold on a minute. Let's wait until Maureen returns."

"Egg and chips be all right, Mr. Byrne? Bren, could you bring in the pot of tea. Let's turn the telly on for a bit while I gather my thoughts." Maureen placed the meal on the table.

"Thank you both for your hospitality, and please, I apologise for this disruption to your evening." Byrne raised his large body from the sofa to sit at the table. "That food smells wonderful." He sniffed deeply and tucked in. "I may have some clues for the many questions which must be on your mind, Maureen."

Brendan pondered. "Maureen, remember when you introduced me to your mum—seems an awful long time ago. She had a small photo album, and she deliberately hid a couple of photographs."

"Yes, I remember, Bren." Reinvigorated, Maureen sat up on the sofa, knocking Brendan's arm away. "I think Mary has that album. Oh, I wonder… Did she and Cecil take it when they were here?" Jumping to her feet, Maureen started rummaging in the shelves to the side of the fireplace.

"Everything all right, Mr. Byrne?" asked Brendan, noticing Byrne had already finished his meal. "I'll go get your bag from the porch. Turn the telly off, Mo, will you? This is important."

Brendan left, taking the opportunity to get what Byrne had told them straight in his mind. He returned with Peter's bag. "Right, let's get the dates right. You married Marjorie in 1937, Mary was born in 1938, you disappeared in late 1939, and Maureen was born in November 1940. Where were you early 1940, Mr. Byrne? Apparently not in Liverpool…"

"I was just another lonely frightened young man away from my country, with no friends, and afraid of dying. I joined the Second Battalion Cheshire Fusiliers and was sent overseas in October 1939, to join the BEF. We fought against the Germans in Belgium and France until we were forced to retreat to Dunkirk and then evacuated back to the UK.

"I remember the day—28th May 1940. It was a Tuesday. I came back to Liverpool to see Marjorie, to find her in this house with a four-year-old child, Mary. Marjorie was pregnant and didn't want to know me. She was very bitter with the world—said she'd met your father, Maureen, at a dance. He was posted shortly afterwards. She showed me a photo of him, a good-looking guy, all out to win the war.

"I went back to the regiment and fought in North Africa and Italy, and when it was over…" Byrne, getting a bit emotional now, took a deep breath. "I should have been dead a thousand times. I tried again to see Marjorie, but by then, the church had got her. I went back to Australia." Byrne held his arms up against his face and started to cry softly.

"That's one hell of a story, Peter," said Brendan. "One hell of a story." He squeezed Maureen's hand as she started to cry. "Thank you for telling us. We must find that photo album, Mo—it might have the answer we want. Where could it be?"

Wiping her eyes, Maureen got up and, giving Peter a brief hug on the way past, started to pull books and magazines from the shelf in the glass cabinet. "It must be here, Bren. Can you lift the cabinet away from the wall? It could be hidden underneath it. Yes, that's right, give him a hand, Peter."

With the tall cabinet away from the wall all there was to see was a dusty mark on the wallpaper and four very marked indentations of the cabinet's feet in the carpet, along with a couple of discarded matches and sweet wrapping paper. No sign of the album.

"Just put it back, Bren. I'll give it a dusting tomorrow. What a disappointment. Careful, Bren, Oh, well caught, Peter!" exclaimed Maureen as Brendan, lifting the cabinet, found it falling away from him and Peter caught hold.

"Wait! What's that?" Maureen crouched low. "Something stuck under the base. Is it… Yes! It's the album."

Attached to the base of the wooden unit by an elastic band was the small blue album, about four inches square and about half an inch thick. Maureen removed it carefully and stood with the unopened album in her hands, full of anticipation and fear. What might be disclosed when she opened the pages?

She looked at Brendan with tears still on her cheeks. *Go on, Mo*, willed Brendan, *open it, please.*

Realising she was gripping the album tightly, she loosened her hold, and a small black-and-white photograph dropped out onto the floor. Brendan stooped to pick it up; it was a photo of a very young Peter Byrne in shorts, fishing with a long pole. On the back was written *PB Melbourne 1927*.

In the album, there was a group of very faded photos of females with long dresses, posing beside large flower pots. A couple of snaps were of the front of the house, Marjorie posing with what would have been Mary in a pram as the date recorded was April 1939. There was a photo of a very serious Pete, in a pinstripe suit, standing beside a very demure Marjorie outside a red building, dated April 1937.

"Where is it?" cried Maureen, rifling through the pages. "Wait, here's an envelope. There's something in it."

There were two photos in it, both of the same male in an officer's uniform: a smiling captain in the Cheshire Fusiliers. One was a posed picture with the words *To my darling Marjorie from her Captain Rupert. Shall remember 9th Jan 1940 for the rest of my life* written on the back and signed. The other photo was of the same Rupert in sports clothes playing tennis on a clay court with the inscription on the back stating *Rupert 1937*.

"There's a newspaper clipping, too," Maureen said and then sagged in disappointment. "Oh, no, Rupert died in battle in Belgium. Rupert Walker. Do you know anything about him, Peter? You were in the same regiment." An excited Maureen was now beginning to put two and two together hopefully resulting in the expected four.

"Captain Rupert Walker," announced Peter. "I knew him—not very well. He was an officer, and us squaddies were only gun fodder to him. He joined early February, I think—I didn't hear anything about him until later, when we were in Belgium. We were preparing for an attack, and he was wishing us all the best. He gave me a searching kind of look that day…I remember wondering why. Now I know. He died later that day, blown to bits by a mortar round."

"Oh, how awful, the poor man. Oh, Bren, could he have been my father? It looks like he and Mum were together before he was sent to Belgium. What do we do?" She squeezed Brendan's hand tight.

"Look, it's getting late," Brendan said. "Let's have a night cap and relax. Do you want us to get in touch with Mary, Pete, or will you give her a call yourself? There's the phone. The number's in the book there, under Mary Wells. Maureen and I will make the tea—coffee for you, Peter?"

Once they were in the kitchen, Maureen said, "I'm getting all excited, Bren. Could Rupert be my dad? He sounds like he was a bit posh. I have certainly seen things about Mum that are hard to believe. The dates work out all right, and I can see why Mum had my birth certificate with Peter listed as my father. Perhaps we could do some research and find out more about Captain Rupert Walker. Where did he live?"

They returned to the living room as Peter finished up on the phone. Mary and Cecil will be over tomorrow morning," he announced.

"Is she all excited?"

"No, Maureen, I think a bit shocked and dubious."

The three of them drank their drinks in subdued silence and then went to bed, with Pete once again expressing his thanks for the hospitality and apologising for the great disturbance he had caused.

***

The following morning, there was a ring on the doorbell.

"That must be Mary and Cecil," Brendan guessed. "Are you there, Peter? Do you want to answer the door? It's a big moment for both of you."

"Thanks, Brendan. God, I feel so nervous." Pete—in a changed shirt, tight trousers and a pair of brown suede shoes—took a deep breath and stepped towards the front door.

"Hello, Mary, how lovely to see you," he greeted the unprepossessing woman standing on the doorstep. Dressed in a large pair of trousers tapering to a pair of high heels, Mary was keeping her balance by holding tightly to Cecil's arm. Her hair was somewhat askew, framing her round rouge-dabbed cheeks. Cecil appeared the opposite to Mary with his slight body dressed in a loose business suit, a wilted white carnation with drooping head ready to drop its tentative hold on the safety pin catching the eye. Beatrice, half his height, dressed in a light summer dress and wearing pigtails over an attractive but apprehensive dark face, was being pushed forward by Cecil.

"Go on, Bea, give your grandpa a kiss."

Peter and Mary were eyeing each other up, Peter with his arms tentatively outreached to embrace the daughter he hadn't seen for more than twenty years, Mary no doubt wondering who this stranger was and how to address him. With a noncommittal, "Hello," she raised her head for a peck on the cheek and accepted the embrace Peter offered.

Peter immediately was suffused in tears and stepped back into the hallway to let the smaller figure of Mary enter. Offering his hand somewhat grudgingly to Cecil, he leaned down to kiss Beatrice, who immediately stepped behind Cecil and clung tightly to his trouser leg, saying, "I want to go away, Daddy."

Catching Maureen's eye, Bren nodded and ushered the four of them into the front room and, whilst shutting the door, offered tea all round. Wondering whether to laugh or cry, he followed Maureen to the kitchen. She caught his arm and began to giggle.

"Did you see the look on Mary's face when she saw the wild Australian in his tight trousers and bald head? I don't think Peter likes Cecil. I don't think he was expecting him to be black. Right…tea for two with a coffee, 'as it comes, miss,'" she finished, putting on an Australian drawl. "Wonder what Peter's going to do? It's funny—I always thought he was my father, always somewhere around in my thoughts, but now all he is, is a stranger. I do hope it works out for Mary, though, but I don't think she's too bothered, anyway. When they're done, Bren, do we remind them about the house?"

"We said we'd wait a week and if nothing happened, we'd start advertising. Of course, it's only another seven days to my stay in London with Sabre Sword Edge. I'll have to see about selling the Popular."

"Never a dull moment," declared Maureen, giving Brendan a kiss as she poured out the tea. "And only another three months and we'll be married—Mrs. Maureen Harris sounds right. Maybe I should be Lady Maureen Walker from Cheshire. All very exciting."

Back in the living room, things did not appear to be going too well. Cecil was standing close to the window with Bea still hanging onto his leg. Mary and Pete were sitting opposite each other, with Pete looking somewhat distressed.

"Right, everyone, here's the tea," Maureen announced loudly. "A glass of orange juice for you, Bea, and your coffee, Pete. How are things going?"

"Thank you, Maureen," offered Pete, seemingly relieved at the break.

"Thanks, Mo," Mary said sharply, "but I don't think we will be staying any longer. My father—or this man who professes to be my father—is criticising my choice of husband and child." Mary stood up and beckoned to Cecil. "I cannot forgive him for the way he treated our mother, and to think—he believes he can come here and expect our forgiveness. Come on, Cecil."

"I am very surprised, Mary," interrupted Maureen. "I thought it was the boast of a Christian that forgiveness overcame everything."

"Not this time, Mo dear. Goodbye, Father."

Ushering Cecil and Bea ahead of her, Mary left a perplexed and bewildered Peter, who must surely have realised he was losing his family, yet the shock of the knowledge that his grandchild was black appeared to have overcome this devastating fact.

Silence reigned in the room after they had gone. Peter stared into space, and Brendan and Mo left him on his own to work out his options.

"Well that's that," Maureen declared. "Wonder if they're still buying? Do we chase them?"

"Give them until tomorrow morning," Brendan advised, "and if no joy, put the house up for sale. Let's give the agent a call and find out the position on house B, make them an offer. What do you want to do about Rupert, Mo? Proving anything is going to be very hard, but I'm sure you'd love to know. We could get in touch with the regiment and see if they give any clues. Make your thoughts known to the family when we find out who they are and send the photo of Rupert to them."

A downcast Peter appeared in the kitchen. "I was devastated to find Mary had married a black and my granddaughter was one as well. How can I make it up to them, Maureen? I think I'd better head back to Aussie. I have a family there and a business. Here's my business card with my contact address. Look, do you think money could help? Don't they wanna buy this house? What if I bought it for them? Say $4,000? The British pound's about two Aussie dollars. I think Marjorie would like that. What do you think, Maureen, Brendan?"

"A lovely idea, Peter," Brendan said. "You gotta talk to them, though I see from the paper the exchange rate is now two and a half dollars to the pound."

"So $4,500 should cover it?"

"Are you sure, Peter? It's an awful lot of money."

"Don't worry. I've got the money. Mary seems a proud woman. Do you think she'll she agree?"

"Maybe if you say you want to help in the upbringing of Beatrice and apologise for the misunderstanding, it would help," suggested Brendan, thinking that if she were to agree it would certainly solve a lot of problems.

"Yep!" a happier Peter bounced on his feet. "I can get our lawyers to work on it. Now to convince Mary. Could you give me the room to make the call, you pair? Give me her number again, please. Oh, thanks."

Some ten minutes later, after some raised voices and long silences, Peter opened the sitting room door and gave the thumbs up success signal.

"She's agreed. All to be for the benefit of Beatrice. Right, I must get on to the lawyers. Would it be all right if I stay another night and arrange to fly back tomorrow?" At Maureen's nod, he said, "Good, thank you. I'll make another phone call, thanks," and closed the sitting room door again.

"That's wonderful, Bren. We can re-do our sums and maybe make an offer for house B. I did like it. Hate to lose it."

"It's early enough. We'll go to Southport and speak to the agents and maybe get a further one or two sales leaflets. See if B is still on the market.

When Peter was finished on the phone to his lawyers, they invited him to accompany them to Southport, and Maureen hugged him. "Oh, thank you so much, Pete. You've solved so many problems."

After their visit to the agents, they called to the property for sale and made a more comprehensive examination.

"Yes, I love it, Bren—a big garage, three beds, and I do like the back garden. It borders the school playing fields. It's so big and roomy compared to where we are. Let's make an offer."

"I agree with you, Mo," said Brendan. "We'll make them an offer and see what happens. They said they've found the house they want to buy. Great news."

20

Buying and Selling

"Afternoon…Brendan Harris…interested in house B… Yes! We'd like to make an offer… But…but…sorry, are you refusing to make an offer on my behalf?… You are aware of our interest… Good…good. Right, yes, we've sold our house and will be ready to move very promptly… Yes, we offer £3,550. Will you please put this to Mr. Jones immediately? It is now three-thirty… Mr. Jones is in the property and awaiting your call. Perhaps, on second thoughts, I should have bypassed you altogether and rung Mr. Jones directly. Look forward to your call."

Within ten minutes, the agent rang back. "Mr. Jones will accept £3,650, Mr. Harris."

"That's fine. Accept and get the ball rolling, thank you. Message time three forty-five, and you are?… Nicol. Well done, Nicol, goodbye."

"Now to start the mortgage application, Bren. I suppose we'd better do a bit of life insurance as well. There was an insurance salesman from the Pru used to call my mum. Maybe he could help."

"There was a guy in Southport was mentioned to me. Meggerty or Mitchell was his name, and he did deals with building societies. Maybe he could help. Yep, he's in Yellow Pages. Not too keen on the guy with the Pru, a bit scruffy."

This is another world—life insurance. Wonder if there's a future in it? I'll look into it another day—five days to London and the Cortina. Yippee.

***

"Hello, Mr. Mitchell, you've got my details?"

"Yes, Mr. Harris," replied the tall, pleasant-looking, middle-aged man in his dark suit with white handkerchief showing in his top pocket. With his dark hair falling over his bright blue eyes and his engaging smile, Mr.

Mitchell was a winner in appearance. The following requests were made in such a smooth velvety, educated voice the recipient could only agree.

"Do please sit down, Mr. Harris. Cream with your coffee? Good, good, a most beautiful day. Do tell me about yourself and how I may help."

Half an hour later, Brendan came out from the interview feeling he had got the best arrangement on the market and Mr. Mitchell would be working day and night to look after his interests. A mortgage for the amount he required was there waiting for him.

Now to find out about Captain Walker. This was the most important quest on Brendan's calendar. Upon phoning the Cheshire Fusiliers in Chester, Brendan was advised to put his request in writing and post it to the barracks and they would look into it.

"What do you think, Maureen? We could write to the barracks and give them your details and a copy of the photo and what's written on it with a photo of yourself. They said they will look into your claim…"

"Bren, it's not a claim I'm making. I'm not a gold digger…"

"Sorry, Mo, perhaps you could say you are searching for your father's identity and could they help to eliminate Captain Walker from your search. We could, of course, look in a Cheshire directory and trace him that way. Maybe his dad was an officer in the first war. There must be lots of things we could do."

"That's great, Bren. Let's put together a letter to the regiment first and see what happens. It would be lovely to find out, so glad Roy Rogers is not my Dad." She laughed; she meant Peter Byrne. "Isn't he way out?"

"Quite a guy, Mo. Glad we said our goodbyes last evening. I do hope he abides by his promises. You know, we are going to be a mite strapped for cash if we don't get the mortgage, but Mitchell seems quite sure of it. Whatever, Mo, we could always move into a furnished flat…"

"Stop worrying, Bren, stop worrying…" Maureen pleaded in exasperation. "It will all work out. Now, let's go to a Berni Inns restaurant this evening and have a lovely meal cooked by someone else. To hell with the cost."

***

The following day, there was a phone call from Mitchell to see if Bren and Maureen could come into his office in Southport.

"Lovely to meet you, Miss Byrne. Please take a seat, and hello again, Mr. Harris." Resplendent in his expensive business suit with folded handkerchief, Mitchell pulled his chair closer to the low table between them.

Brendan was feeling very comfortable in his cavalry twill trousers with brown sports jacket and open-necked shirt and, of course—his trademark—the black eye patch. Maureen was wearing a light flowered summer dress showing a lot of bare knee and shoulder. Both were very eager to hear Mitchell's news.

"Before we start, would either of you care for a coffee? I am sorry; my secretary has…left for the day. Would you very much mind helping yourselves? The kettle has just boiled." With a smile, Mitchell pointed towards a table at the side of the small room.

Maureen rose from her seat beside Brendan and, grudgingly, poured out three cups and passed them around with the plate of Jacobs assortment, while Mitchell started to explain he had acquired a mortgage, in principle, for £2,600. This would, however, require an endowment policy and survey fee and the need for a solicitor. Brendan, with so much else on his mind, had left Maureen to do the homework.

Going over the income and savings situation, Mitchell showed surprising interest in the fact that Maureen was not working. A second income, he emphasised, would have been of great assistance in his seeking a mortgage for them. "Store control in Lewis's—how interesting, Miss Byrne. How conversant are you with—"

"Excuse me, Mr. Mitchell," interrupted Brendan, "but have you or have you not acquired a loan for us?"

"Of course, of course, Mr. Harris, my apologies. Yes, I have, with the Ofcone Building Society, a small private society. I am very keen to find out if Miss Byrne could be interested in working for me. Would you, Miss Byrne?"

"That's most unethical, Mr. Mitchell. Perhaps, do you agree, Maureen, we should leave that until we have the mortgage question decided."

"Don't be so pompous, Bren," Maureen chided. "Of course I would be interested, and if it helps Mr. Mitchell get the mortgage question resolved, I am very willing to talk."

Realising how well things were turning out, Brendan leaned back in his chair and, smiling at Mitchell and Maureen, held up both arms in surrender.

Mitchell acknowledged the signal from Brendan that he carry on. "I know what we'll do, Mr. Byrne…" He hesitated. "Sorry, my mistake—Mr. Harris. I shall pass the society papers to you and Miss Byrne to complete, along with a life policy application for each of you and, if I may be so bold, include a job application sheet for you, Miss Byrne. Salary may be discussed; Miss Daly was on £700 per annum. Do please excuse me, the phone, I believe, is ringing. I must take it."

Running his fingers through his mop of hair, Mitchell endeavoured to offer his hand to shake, pick up the phone at the same time and pass over the forms to be taken.

Taking the offered papers, Brendan and Maureen bowed their exit, gaining a cursory wave from Mitchell, and danced out into the street.

***

"There was a call from Peter earlier, Bren. He just wanted to thank us for putting him up and said he's glad that things worked out so well. Didn't they do just that, Bren? I'm just waiting for the drawback—something we won't like is bound to happen."

"Let's just keep our fingers crossed, Mo, that the good fortune continues. The next big step is the Sabre Sword Edge course tomorrow. Any news from Mitchell about the mortgage?"

"Give it time, Bren. He only got the papers yesterday," laughed Maureen. "I've completed the application for the job as secretary—my typing skills are not up to much, but I can hold my own on the telephone. Wonder if he'll take me on? I'm reading up about life insurance and mortgages, especially these endowment mortgages. All very interesting. And look at this, Bren; remember I wrote to the Cheshire Fusiliers? They replied and are forwarding my letter to Rupert's parents. I wonder what they'll decide? It would be wonderful to know who my father is…or was. Oh! Shut up, Maureen, you'll have yourself crying."

"That's OK, Maureen, have a wee weep if you wish," offered Brendan, putting his arm around her shoulders. "I do hope it works out for you."

"Yes, I do hope so, Bren. I'm a bit frightened—what if they don't want to know?"

"Let's worry about that in time. Look at it this way: at the moment, there is an elderly couple looking at the letter and wondering if it can be true that they have a granddaughter. Surely they are going to leap at the chance of meeting you."

"Right, of course they are." Sniff. Sniff. "I'll just go have a little wash and we had better get stuck into those forms from Mr. Mitchell. Didn't he look—" Maureen gave a weepy grin "—funny, Bren, scratching his head, answering the phone and waving to us all at the same time. Isn't he a cutie? I do hope he offers me a job. I'm sure I can sort him out. Wonder why Miss Daly left?"

"Let's get the life insurance forms filled in first. God, there are pages of them, and here's a book on mortgage endowments. Must do the figures again for the mortgage, especially if we'll both be earning. Let's fill in what we can and get to bed early—I don't want to oversleep and miss my train."

"It will be strange without you, but I'm sure we'll manage." Maureen grinned mischievously. "There are three things pending," she continued. "One, the mortgage on house B, two, chase up about my dad, and three, getting a job with Mitchell Insurance Services. That should keep me busy whilst you are away living it up in London. Look, it's still early enough—why don't we go for a dance at the Grafton? We could practice the cha-cha, we were getting quite good at that."

***

"Don't worry, Bren, I'll look after things. Give me a ring when you arrive at the hotel. Look forward to seeing you Wednesday in your lovely Ford Cortina. There's the guard waving his red flag, bye-bye, love."

"Bye-bye, love you, Maureen," called Brendan, stepping back into the carriage as the guard slammed the door shut.

As the train pulled away, Maureen gave a last look at Brendan's waving arm and returned to her car parked in the street alongside the station.

What a whirlwind of events, she thought. *Buying a house, getting married, new job... I know, I'll give Mary a ring, haven't spoken with her for a while, there's been so much going on. There's always something happening when Brendan Harris is around.*

"Yes, everything's going well this end, Mary. There's no problem with you is there?... Solicitors are talking that's good to hear... Yes, as soon as we can, Mary. We have had our offer accepted on our new house... You have three weeks... OK, I'll work on that... Oh! He's on a week's course down in London... OK, how's Cecil and lovely Bea... Good...good. Speak with you soon. Byee."

Replacing the receiver after the call to Mary, Maureen stretched out on the settee and got as far as thinking—*I've got the whole week, now what shall I do?*—when the phone started ringing again.

"Hello? Maureen Byrne speaking. Oh, hello, Mr. Mitchell... Tomorrow morning, nine-thirty. Why, that's excellent... Look forward to meeting you as well. Goodbye."

Well, would you believe it? He's keen. Right, what do I take with me? My exam certificates—pity I didn't finish the degree in business studies... References from Lewis's... How much money to ask for? £15 per week seems fair to start with. Do I need any exams to sell life insurance? Must do some real reading about mortgages. The info required for our own should help. Can't wait to hear from Bren when he gets into the hotel... Mitchell must be keen, calling on a Sunday. He looked like a lonely sod... Keep him at arm's length. Now, where's that application form...

The following morning, Maureen dressed in a plain grey pencil skirt and white blouse with grey short-sleeved jacket and moderate high heels—she figured Mitchell to be only slightly taller than herself. With her hair in a businesslike bun, Maureen knocked on Mitchell's office door at exactly nine-thirty and awaited the summons to enter.

"Come in," was the call in Mitchell's well-educated accent followed by a throat-clearing cough. "Hello, Miss Byrne, do sit down," he invited, rising from his chair behind his desk and motioning towards the single soft-back armchair—one of two, with a small low coffee table between them.

"Coffee with one milk and no sugar, if I recall, Miss Byrne? So glad you could come so promptly. While I get our coffees, could you please tell me what you think working for Mitchell Insurance Services would entail?"

Maureen placed her papers on the table and leaned forward, pulling her tight dress to cover her knees. She noticed Mitchell was not looking the dapper, smart, smooth operator she had met previously with Brendan. He looked as if he had slept in the office chair all night. "I think the first thing I would take over," laughed Maureen," is the making of coffee. Seriously, Mr. M, I believe I would, I am sure, be expected to provide a competent and pleasant introduction to current and prospective customers. I would possibly be expected to make appointments for you and, of course, to answer the phone and educate myself in the products you sell."

"A fair answer, Miss Byrne," agreed Mitchell, depositing himself in the soft armchair and nearly upsetting the coffees he had just made. "What are your shorthand and typing speeds?"

With Mitchell subsiding slowly into the chair, and Maureen quickly realising the man needed a personal assistant rather than a secretary, or even both, the two found themselves in relaxed conversation. The tone of the interview changed to where Mitchell began telling her his life story and the many problems one can find when selling insurance. Realising there was an attractive future here for a person willing to work some twelve hours a day, she thought, *lets go for it—maybe there could be a job here for Bren some day.*

By ten-thirty, Mitchell, after examining Maureen's references and examination results and impressed she had gone as far as she had with the business studies degree, realised he had the opportunity of hiring someone who could be of great value and offered her the job.

"Thank you, Mr. Mitchell. I am indeed flattered that you should offer me the post of secretary, but before giving an answer, please tell me where Mitchell Insurance Services are going and whether you can afford me."

Fighting his way out of the unyielding chair, and realising his trousers had slipped from under his belt whilst also showing a great expanse of very hairy leg, Mitchell heaved himself to the edge of the seat and unfortunately began to cough.

What with coughing, trying to cover his mouth and endeavouring to hold his balance and adjust his trousers, Mitchell went very red in the face, and when the phone on the desk began to ring, he threw his hands in the air and accepted Maureen's offer to answer it.

Regaining his composure, or what was left of it, Mitchell rose from the grasping armchair and went and sat behind the safety of the impressive office desk.

"A Mr. Dene Floyd from the Ofcone Building Society would appreciate a call back when convenient, Mr. Mitchell," Maureen informed him.

"Thank you, Miss Byrne, my apologies. I applaud you on your positive attitude. However can I afford you? Miss Byrne, there is an offer of £780 per annum for you to consider for the post of secretary. Where your ambitions lie beyond that depends upon whether your abilities match your forceful attitude."

"Noted, Mr. Mitchell. I shall return to you shortly with my decision. Now, I should like to talk about our mortgage application. Have you any further news?"

"Of course. I'll give Dene a call back. Mr. Floyd, please… Yes, Dene… No… No… Possibly. Yes! Ha-ha. Yes, she is sitting before me… Main earner two and a half times salary and secondary earner half salary to be added to main earner with same multiple. Good, thank you, Dene… The Driscoll case? I'll call you back on that."

Replacing the receiver, Mitchell sat back in his plush office chair and, with a beaming smile, declared, "Miss Byrne, were you to be on a salary of £780 per annum, and Mr. Harris, as we know, is on £1,040, the Ofcone Building Society are prepared to consider a mortgage advance of up to £3,575."

"Excellent, Mr. Mitchell. Perhaps I could come back to you with our decision?"

"That's quite all right, Miss Byrne. The offer stays open for a further seven days. Now, if you will excuse me…" Mitchell shuffled papers on his desk, hand hovering over the phone. He looked as if he wished to curl up in his big office chair and go to sleep.

"Thank you, Mr. Mitchell, I'll see myself out," said Maureen, thinking to herself, *Boy, does this guy need some lessons on approach. Do I bother coming back? I'll have a word with Brendan tonight when he rings.*

21

Area Sales, Sabre Sword Edge

"Good morning, Mr. Harris, a pleasant trip down from the North, I hope? Good… Good…"

It was readily seen that Mr. Stafford had welcomed many salesmen over the portals of Sabre Sword House as the important man did not look once at Brendan but continued talking to his cup of coffee.

Feeling somewhat redundant of the one-way conversation, Brendan thanked the uniformed lady for his cup of indifferent coffee whilst Mr. Stafford mumbled on in his marked London accent about the Sabre expansion in the barren north. Brendan examined the many papers passed to him about pensions, life insurance and expenses, and was surprised to hear that storage space at his home would be needed to house his razor blade samples—up to ten cartons, in fact—and display material.

"Your programme has been altered slightly, Mr. Harris. Miss Arkwright—oh, there you are—Miss Arkwright will take you into administration and introduce you to your contacts there. When you return—" Stafford hesitated and, glancing up at Brendan with apparent sympathy, muttered the words "—to the North. After a short lunch, you will be returning on the early afternoon train from Euston. Yes, thank you, Miss Arkwright."

Miss Arkwright—a youngster in her late teens and seeming somewhat afraid of Stafford—placed a brown envelope on the desk. Stafford, with a *the world is against me* sigh and lift of his shoulders, opened it and remarked, "Miss Arkwright is from…the North as well, Mr. Harris. Where from exactly, Miss Arkwright?"

The young girl, startled to be addressed directly by His Eminence, stuttered, "Wigan," in reply, blushing furiously.

With a knowing smile, Stafford nodded at the coffee cup. "Is that near the pier, Miss Arkwright? Ha-ha." Sitting back in his office chair.

he pushed the contents of the brown envelope towards Brendan. "Your revised train ticket and a note to say you will be staying in the hotel listed—The Hazeldene, I see, in Berry Road, Berry—somewhere near Manchester. Mr. Kenneth Shanks, your sales trainer, will collect you from your hotel tomorrow, and may I wish you all the best. Over to you, Miss Arkwright."

Rising on the dismissal, Brendan thanked Stafford, who was already reading one of the many papers on his desk, and followed Miss Arkwright out of the room.

The rest of the morning was spent with introductions to the various persons involved in the Sabre Sword Sales operation, and after a quick lunch, Brendan was driven back to the hotel and thence on to Euston station.

After some hours travelling, Brendan eventually arrived at his hotel in Bury Road—not Berry Road, as the Londoner had advised—and rang Maureen to bring her up to date with happenings.

"Maureen, I'm not in London but Manchester. What a day! I feel I've been travelling for days. Anyway, I should be home Thursday or Friday—how, I don't know, but I'm sure something has been arranged. Anyway, how did your day go?"

"Quite exciting, really. Mitchell, the broker, believe it or not, has offered me the job as secretary on £780 a year and us a possible mortgage advance of up to £3,575. What do I do, Bren? Help! What do I do?"

"You're amazing, Mo. Firstly, what do you think?"

"I think Mitchell would drive me mad."

"Interesting, but do you think you could control him?"

"Like falling off a log. No, he would be difficult. He is a bit pompous."

"If you think you could manage it. I think you're already looking forward to the challenge. Give him a ring and say you accept, subject to a few points you would like to discuss. Maybe get some more salary. I'll do my best to get back early Friday. If you think it's worth it, go for it, Mo. Everything else OK? Mary and Cecil still keen?"

"All quiet there… God, I'm tired. I'll give you a call tomorrow night."

The following morning, after a full Irish breakfast, Brendan took himself and his papers downstairs to be ready for the sales trainer who was due at eight-thirty. Sitting in the lounge, he noticed a lot of activity in the car park; a truck with cars tied down on a trailer had reversed into the park and the brown-coated driver had descended from the cab, stretching his limbs. Then, surveying the scene and checking the papers from his top pocket, he tossed a smouldering cigarette from his lips onto the gravel and crunched his way into the hotel foyer.

"Have a delivery for a Mr. Harris, miss."

"That's all right, I'm Harris," Brendan called out, having anticipated the request.

"Right. I've got a delivery of a car for you, mister," was the gruff statement from the weary-looking driver. "I'll go get it off the trailer an' then get the papers signed."

Brendan followed the driver outside into the bright sunlight, but before he could savour the thought of this brand new blue Ford Cortina, delivered especially for himself, he noticed the arrival of his sales trainer.

With quick introductions, Brendan signed for the delivery of his car and gave the engine a turnover, savouring the smell of his brand new plaything, before he and Ken Shanks repaired to the lounge to discuss the days ahead.

"Right, Brendan, my name is Ken Shanks—for the past twelve months, area sales manager for Sabre Sword Edge in the North West. The company is now starting a marketing campaign to increase distribution in the UK."

Ken appeared a confident man, dressed in a smart two-piece grey suit with a company tie—blue with a silver sabre sword highlighted on it—and very businesslike in his attitude. He continued the discussion with a quick demonstration of the blade display: a plastic holder to take the grey dispenser holding twenty individual packs of five stainless steel razor blades. There were added clamps to position the display on shop tills or shelves along with Sabre Sword Edge banners and posters.

The rest of the morning went by in a flurry of calls to local retail shops, chemists and barbers to encourage them to stock and display the blade dispensers. When the retailer agreed to purchase and display, Ken provided, from the boot of his car, the required products and invoiced the retailer through his wholesaler.

The next step was to call upon the respective wholesalers to encourage them to take in stock to satisfy the increased demand hopefully realised by the new displays.

The first evening, after a meal and drink with Ken, Brendan rang Maureen, who was full of news. She had had a further word with Mitchell and had made an appointment to meet him on the Friday but, more importantly, the Cheshire Fusiliers had been in touch and invited her to meet them at their offices in Chester.

"Oh, Bren, I'm all excited. I'll wait until you're back home before I arrange a time to go to Chester, as I would like you to come with me. It's great you will be home on Thursday evening—when we can talk about the offer from Mitchell. How are things with the new job? I'm dying to hear the news."

"Before I mention that, I meant to tell you, a van is going to deliver some marketing material and boxes of Sabre Sword blades in the next few days. We could put them in the spare room…OK? I've got the new car. Have only had time to drive it a couple of yards, but I'm looking forward to driving home Thursday night… Must get rid of the old one. About the job. Well, it's the old story, Mo—my day's been spent endeavouring to get people to buy from me something they had no intention of buying before I told them they were idiots if they didn't—in the nicest possible way, of course. I get weary of it at times, but it helps to keep the strawberry jam on the dining room table."

"But you don't like strawberry jam, Bren," laughed Maureen. "I know what you mean. Oh! By the way, Mary has rung to say the money has been received from Peter Byrne's solicitor, so all systems are go for the sale."

"Lovely to hear. Now, I'm away to bed must get my shuteye, it's going to be a long day tomorrow. Goodnight, my love."

***

The next few days were spent under the instruction of Ken, learning company procedures and calling upon regular customers to replenish stock or encourage them to call their wholesaler. To gain new customers, they called in to every retail shop or service outlet that might promote Sabre Sword Edge and encouraged them to buy. Each evening, Brendan was instructed on the many administrative steps of new accounts, report forms, call planning, sales targets and numerous other demands to get the North West to notice Sabre Sword Edge razor blades.

On the Thursday morning, Brendan and Ken competed with each other to see how many outlets they could get to buy and display the presentation pack. Brendan decided he would approach the buyer in a newsagent's and stopped outside to prepare for his encounter.

Who is the buyer? One obvious clue was the words painted over the shop window: Woodsides, P. Sullivan. *Maybe an Irishman…or woman—possibly that tall blonde behind the shop counter. Throw the smile over there be on the safe side. The smart youngster filling the birthday card rack is certainly not the buyer.*

Brendan entered the shop and made his way over to the counter, which, he was pleased to notice, had a flat top which would take the clamp on the base of the display unit, putting the blade dispenser with the picture side facing the customer.

"Good morning, miss. Could I have a word with Mr. Sullivan, please?"

"Peter?" was the immediate response in an obvious Irish accent as she called to the open side door. "Peter, yer wanten in the shop."

Brendan smiled his thanks as she then looked enquiringly towards Ken, standing behind, alongside the ice-lolly fridge. Ken conveyed that he was with Brendan as the draped strings on the doorway swished aside, and a flustered, medium-sized, overweight, balding man in a crumpled green and yellow jersey emerged from the hidden depths. He took a quick glance around, decided it was Brendan—standing six foot tall in his grey suit and shiny shoes—who wanted his attention, and stopped with his hands on his hips and a resigned smile on his lips. Brendan stepped forward with his presentation pack on the crook of his left arm and stretched out his right hand.

Better go easy here. It's ten o'clock and the man has probably been up since the crack of dawn getting the newspapers ready for delivery.

"Good morning, Mr. Sullivan, I'll not take too much of your time as no doubt you have been—like many of my other customers—up very early, is that so?"

"Yes, yes," agreed Sullivan accepting the handshake grudgingly. "Now what is it that you want?"

Recognising the accent was definitely a Dublin one, Brendan relaxed to a degree and launched into his pitch, making the comment that outlets such as Sullivan's shop were essential to the community, and there were so many male beards needed shaving—"In Sabre SE, we have designed a means for the smaller shop to help his customer and make a small profit..."

Whilst he was talking, he positioned the display unit on the till top with a flourish, and with his other hand he slid out a package of blades from the dispenser and declared, in his Dublin accent, looking directly at Sullivan, "There's twenty percent profit for you." Alas, his triumph was somewhat short-lived as his grip on the badly balanced dispenser loosened, and the top-heavy unit crashed to the floor with razor blade packages disappearing under the fridge and card display and skidding amongst the feet of a few customers.

Sullivan laughed. Brendan stood in shock, and Ken looked as though he didn't want anything to do with the episode, whilst the two customers and the girl assistant started a game, collecting the errant packs. Within a couple of minutes, well over three-quarters of the packages had been retrieved, and Brendan, recovering his aplomb, looked at Sullivan. He mimed the replacement of the display unit on the till.

Getting a resigned nod of agreement, Brendan delved in his pocket for the few blade packets necessary for the full quota and produced his order book, requesting the wholesaler's name to invoice through.

"You sign for it Pat, please, and use Hendersons. Now, Mr. Sword, allow me to get back to my coffee." With a farewell grunt, Sullivan disappeared behind the swishing curtains.

"One of our double-sided display stickers would go well at the side of the entrance door, Ken, what do you think?"

"Perhaps not this time, Bren. I'll put a note for next call."

This was an example of the types of call to get the Sabre Sword Edge product on display in as many outlets as possible—newsagents, hairdressers, even greengrocers and pubs. There were sales competitions for the exercise. The plan was to get as many unsuspecting retailers to display Sabre as possible, pushing the main competitor aside. When the retailer sold out, they were encouraged to replenish their stock by buying from the wholesaler.

Prices were keen, especially in the cash-and-carries—the newer wholesale outlet style—where, as the name implied, instead of delivering orders, the retailer went to the warehouse to choose their purchases, paid there and then, and took the goods, relieving the wholesaler from delivering. This meant there were many cut-price deals on the market, and Brendan had a fair idea of what was required from him.

By Thursday lunchtime, Brendan and Ken had sold out of packs and decided to have a late lunch, over which they had a good talk and a lot of laughter, recalling some of the instances over the past few days.

22

New Family Development

It was with great anticipation that Brendan, after his farewells to Ken over a last evening meal at the hotel, set out from Bury Road in the brand new, blue, four-door Cortina with a head full of ideas. For all of that, it was an uncomfortable journey home through the rain, the traffic and the many roadworks for the new motorway system under construction.

"Isn't she a beaut, Mo? Taxed, insured and petrol paid for. Apart from private use, of course." He laughed. "It's got an alarm system as I'll be carrying valuable blade samples." Standing back with his arm around Maureen, both admired the new possession and laughed at their good fortune. "Missed you, Mo, I'm glad to be home. Now, let's get inside, out of this rain, and you can tell me the news. Did you say you arranged a meeting with Mitchell tomorrow?"

"Yes, Bren, ten o'clock. I've done a bit of homework and know a lot more on insurance than I did. I now know what a mortgage endowment is. Maybe we'll do one when we buy the new house. Have to work out if we can do a joint endowment if we're not married—insurable interest, you know," laughed Maureen, touching the side of her nose to convey she was wise to these secrets. "I'll have a go at looking for more salary—I'm quite excited. If we agree a deal, maybe start Monday the 22nd June."

"Sounds OK with me. Maybe we could get to see the regiment sometime next week about your dad? Oh! Yes, must go and have a look at the stuff delivered while I was away."

"A real nice guy delivered it a couple of days ago and took it all up to the spare room. What's it all about, Bren?"

"A lot of hard work. I'll have a look at what they sent." Brendan went up to the spare room, Maureen a step behind. "I've got a box of calling cards—they're in the car—to sort out tomorrow and get them all in order and work out how I'm going to make the many targets they want me to reach. Still, it all looks very interesting. After we've seen Mitchell tomorrow, let's go for a drive to Formby and have a look at the house. What do you think?"

"Great idea. The survey's done—should get the result of that within the week. The solicitor is difficult to get hold of, but I'll soon sort them out."

"Doesn't leave much room for the twins." Brendan gestured to the spare room, now filled with large boxes and banners proclaiming Sabre Sword Edge were the best. "I'll sort out that lot tomorrow. Shall we go and put our feet up?"

"Why not treat ourselves and have a meal in the Berni Inns down the road? Come on, Bren, let's live it up. I've been living on scraps whilst you were away."

***

Over the meal in the restaurant—steak and chips for both, with ice cream for dessert—Brendan suggested they have a recap of all their activities and expectations.

"When you've sorted out Mitchell, Mo, between us, we will be grossing close to two thousand a year, which is very satisfying, but we should be bringing in more. We're well on the way to moving into our new house in Formby, and we've got a wedding and honeymoon to pay for. I've had a letter from Jono—he's getting married on the Saturday 18th July, and we're invited to that, and, of course, at some point, I'd like to seriously consider going to live in Australia. There you are—just a few things to discuss—"

"Bren, sorry to interrupt your flow, but there's the matter of my father. We've got to arrange to meet the Cheshire Regiment. Hopefully, they will see us on a Saturday or Sunday."

"Yes, that is most important. God! We are leading a busy life. It's going to be difficult fitting in work amongst all these things we're doing." He laughed. "Will you give them a ring on Monday?"

"Shall do, though I'm a bit scared as to the possible outcome. If they accept me, what will be expected? Anyway, let's wait and see. Your brother's getting married, did you say?"

"Yes—we're going to the wedding, aren't we?" Brendan received an affirmative nod. "I'll introduce you to my parents and brothers then. We could fly over from Liverpool to Dublin on the Friday and come back on the Sunday. We'll be able to stay in Laurel Cottage."

After a short silence while they ate their ice cream, Brendan laid his eye patch on the table and made the following statement: "You know what, Mo, I'm going to see how I get on without this eye patch. It's a bit of a nuisance. The problem is, when I have both eyes open and look forward, I see two of everything, one above the other. There, just looking at you now, I know which is the real Maureen, as the other Maureen has her head in her ice cream, but…when I gradually turn my head to the right, still looking at you, both heads come together. Now, if instead of turning my head to the right I cock my head to the right and readjust my focus, hey presto! The world is single again. I can, of course, shut either eye and again see a single object."

Maureen, listening intently, commiserated with Brendan by giving him a pat on the hand. "Yes, I notice you haven't been using the patch every now and then and cocking your head to the right. I would be sorry to see the patch go—it gives you a devilish look and it's a great talking point. What about driving, though, if you're seeing two of everything?"

"Easy-peasy, Mo, I drive between them. Ha-ha. No, joking apart, I have tried it already, and all is fine provided I angle my head to the right or shut one eye. I had an operation in 1961, shortly after my accident, which was unsuccessful, and my doctor suggested I leave well alone. Maybe one day I'll pay for a specialist to give another opinion."

***

Over the next week, Brendan spent most of his time finding his way around his area and familiarising himself with the sales procedures and introducing himself to the wholesalers. Ken Shanks joined him for a couple of days to help him settle in. With many hundreds of possible outlets, an ordered call pattern was certainly required, with protocols to follow. You didn't get your chemist to buy and display Sabre blades and go in next door to the newsagent and do the same. Chemists and hairdressers apparently felt they should be the only outlets to sell razor blades. Brendan called in to one of the large cash-and-carry wholesalers in Liverpool where, from the record card, they had bought a carton of ten packs two months previously. *A minimal amount,* thought Brendan, *it will be interesting to see what's there now.*

"Brendan Harris, salesman Sabre Sword Edge," he said, holding up a display brochure with the Sabre name and picture of his product to the face on the other side of the protective glass.

"Wait a minit while I get the manager," was the instruction with the face then calling over the intercom, "Mr. Carroll, you're wanted at the office."

Some five minutes later, a man in his mid-twenties, wearing the customary brown overall, was seen through the glass, directing Brendan to progress through the turnstile. "Sabre Sword Edge? I see from the records we stock your blades, Mr…?"

"Harris," informed Brendan, passing his business card to Carroll.

"Do we have any packs of Sabre razor blades in the office here, Mavis?" Carroll asked.

"Nothing here, Mr. Carroll."

"Let's go into the warehouse, down to the toiletries section, Mr. Harris. I know your competitor... Yes, here we are."

Having passed some mountainous metal frames with packs of soaps, toothpaste and various other bathroom essentials, there stood three cartons of Sabre's competitor's blades, one carton open, but no sign of any Sabre Sword Edge.

Mr. Carroll immediately reacted by asking, "What's the carton size and cost price?" Brendan, prepared for this question, turned to the page in his display manual, showing the prices as asked. Carroll ran a quick calculation in his head. "Let's have a carton as soon as possible."

"Mr. Carroll, perhaps I may suggest something? Sabre Sword Edge is starting an advertising campaign in the very near future, and for this one-off opportunity, I can drop you a carton in from the car. This will mean immediate sales, and we can have the other carton you ordered for delivery in perhaps two weeks?"

"God loves a tryer, Mr. Harris. The one carton will be enough. Get Mavis to sign for it. Now, I must go on. Right, Bill, coming," Carroll called out, acknowledging another brown-overall-garbed inhabitant.

***

Maureen thought she would prepare for the imminent move to the new house in Formby and had listed what she considered should be hers and Brendan's share of the furniture in the house.

Better get Mary over — she certainly has mellowed in the last few weeks — and work out what she wants. Now...cup of coffee and then ring the army. Where's that number and name...

"My partner, Mr. Brendan Harris, and I shall come down to the offices in Chester, ten-thirty on Saturday next... Ask for Captain O'Keefe? OK, thank you... Goodbye."

Now I'll ring the building society and find out how things are going on the house we're buying. What's his name...I know it's an odd one...Dene. That's it. The Ofcone Building Society.

"Yes, hello, Mrs. Byrne."

"Miss Byrne, if you would, please, Mr. Floyd."

"My apologies, Miss Byrne. All is progressing smoothly. You have a copy of the surveyor's report on the property? Nothing untoward on this. It is, however, recommended you have the outside woodwork re-treated and painted. But yes, an advance of £2,600 is granted for a term of twenty-five years. Your insurance policies are still being underwritten, and, of course, are in your insurance adviser's hands, which I see is Mitchell Insurance. We look forward to your further instruction. Is there anything else, Miss Byrne?"

"No, thank you, Mr. Floyd. Goodbye." *Better ring Mitchell.*

"Mr. Mitchell? Maureen Byrne. No need to call Floyd at the Ofcone. He's cleared the £2,600 advance for a twenty-five-year term. Now, about insurance policies…?"

"Yes, Miss Byrne. The insurance company has advised me they wish your…boyfriend…Mr. Harris to take a precautionary medical examination. *Your* application, I am pleased to say, has been accepted. I am just putting the paperwork in an envelope for you. How are you keeping, Miss Byrne? Well, I hope. I'm looking forward to seeing you on the twenty-second."

"As with myself, Mr. Mitchell. Could you give me the name and number of the doctor that I can get a medical arranged for Brendan? We want to get this all tidied up as quickly as possible."

Now that's done, must get on with a bit of reading about the Cheshire Fusiliers. If we meet my grandparents, it would be nice to impress. There's Bren, she noticed as the Cortina drew up outside. *Must do something about the old Popular. It's getting like a car park out there, what with my Anglia and the other two cars.*

"What is it, Bren? What have you forgotten this time?" Maureen called as Brendan stepped into the hallway.

"Ran out of stock, Mo—need a couple more cartons of blades. Any news?" Brendan asked as he bounded up the staircase.

"Yes—Saturday next in Chester for half ten, and the insurance company want you to go for a medical," she shouted after the retreating Brendan. "There's a doctor in Liverpool or one in Southport."

"Could you do that for me—the one in Southport will do. I suppose they're cautious about me and the result of the accident. Gotta go, Mo. Have an appointment with a cash-and-carry in Huyton in half an hour." The from door slammed shut.

"Yes, sir, anything you say, sir," Maureen muttered to herself. Even so, she made an appointment for Brendan for the following Friday at ten.

What'll he do when I'm working full-time? Still, what am I moaning about? He's all go—nothing boring about him. Right, must get down to the library and find out what I can about the Cheshire Fusiliers and endowment policies.

***

There we are, Bren, Cheshire Fusiliers Recruitment Office."

"Right, where can I park? Down this side street should do."

"Did I not tell you, Bren? I'm joining up—thought I'd look good in a captain's uniform."

"What a good idea, Mo. Captain Maureen Byrne—or even Harris sounds good. Ah, there's a car pulling out. Now, to reverse this monster in…"

The Saturday morning had arrived, and they had prepared themselves. Brendan was wearing brown slacks and sports jacket and shiny shoes;

Maureen was looking very smart and comfortable in a summer dress and blouse with her red hair framing her now lightly suntanned face.

"This is the big day, Bren," Maureen anticipated, holding tightly onto Brendan's arm. "I hope—what's his name—Oh, yes, Captain O'Keefe will let us meet the grandparents. Oh, shut up, Maureen. Pay no attention, Bren. I'm all worried."

"No need to worry. He'll think you're the cat's whiskers, Maureen. The photo will be the clincher. You do have it with you?" Brendan asked with a grin; he'd seen her put it in her handbag.

"Oh! The photos! Have I? Did I?" She frantically started rummaging through said bag. "Of course I did, you bastard," she exclaimed, discovering the photo of Rupert. "Oh, God, I hope this Captain O'Keefe is not another Irishman. They would drive you mad. Here we are, Bren. Look at the window display—it's full of models of young men sunbathing—'Join the army and see the world'. Where's the guns?"

"Don't worry, Mo, we're not expected to join up." Brendan pushed open the glass door for Maureen to enter first. There were two desks in the room, both displaying encouragement for the reader to join up—*Now Start a Career in the Army.* The desk to the right had a young man, dressed in khaki, interviewing a prospective recruit. A couple of feet away, the other desk had an older male soldier, again in camouflage dress, looking as if he had just come off parade with a welcoming smile on a weather-beaten face.

Stepping out from behind his desk, this picture of the perfect model of an active soldier shook hands with each of his visitors, welcomed them in a polished accent, and guided them to sit on arranged wooden chairs placed in an alcove behind the desk. "Miss Byrne, Mr. Harris. My name is Captain Rory O'Keefe, and as you well understand, we are very protective of our members and their relatives. Now, Miss Byrne, tell me why you are here." The soldier was suddenly serious looking: *thwart me or waste my time and you will be put up against the wall and shot.*

But nothing daunted Maureen, who sat forward on her hard chair and, looking straight at the soldier, said in her most polished demure voice, "How do I address you? Is it Captain or Captain O'Keefe?"

"Captain O'Keefe will do fine, Miss Byrne," replied the captain with a slight smile.

"Thank you, Captain O'Keefe. I and my friend Brendan Harris—" she smiled towards Brendan "—are here to discover if Captain Rupert Walker and I may be related. In brief, for all my life, I was led to believe by my mother, who died a short while ago, that a certain Peter Byrne was my father. He deserted my mother in wartime, and I had no contact with that man until only a few weeks ago. He told me at this meeting he had no knowledge of my existence." Feeling somewhat emotional, Maureen took Brendan's hand and a deep breath before continuing. "It was at this time we were going through my mother's possessions—she was very secretive, was my mother—and we came across the photographs already in your possession. Here are copies. From the message on the back, I hope you can understand my anticipation."

"Yes, I agree, Miss Byrne. This is certainly a picture of Captain Walker, and the writing would appear very similar to our records of the captain's script. Do you have, by any chance, a copy of your birth certificate?"

"Yes, of course, Captain O'Keefe." Maureen handed the creased flimsy piece of paper to the captain.

Maureen Marjorie Byrne, born Liverpool, the Woman's Hospital, 5th September 1940. With Marjorie Byrne as mother, formerly Richardson, and Peter Byrne, soldier, as father. Signed by SA Lecky, Registrar, and witnessed by DH Hetherington, who was present at the birth. Certificate dated 25th September 1940.

"Very interesting, Miss Byrne, but from this, your father is proclaimed to be a Mr. Peter Byrne. Why should we doubt this?"

"Every reason, Captain O'Keefe. Peter Byrne was a private in the British Army in Belgium, ten, eleven months prior to my birth in September 1940, whilst Captain Rupert Walker, apparently, was intimate with my mother in January 1940—as the message on the photo implies. Please would you read the message, Brendan? I can't." She dabbed her eyes.

Brendan consoled Maureen with a quick hug and read out the message. "To my darling Marjorie from her Captain Rupert. Shall remember 9th Jan 1940 for the rest of my life."

The Captain looked quite uncomfortable at this juncture and shifted in his seat whilst Brendan continued.

"Yes, Captain. All dates prove Private Peter Byrne was nowhere near Maureen's mother in January 1940 whilst the good Captain Walker was, as this message reveals. Now, where is this Peter Byrne at the moment, you may ask, Captain O'Keefe." Receiving an affirmative nod, he continued, "He has returned to Australia, and here is his contact address," said Brendan somewhat triumphantly. "The million-dollar question is where was Private Peter Byrne on the 9th January 1940? If you look in your regiment's archives, you will, I am sure, find Private Peter Byrne of the second battalion Cheshire Fusiliers was in Belgium at this time."

Captain O'Keefe was taken aback with this surprising development. He sat back in his chair and scanned the paper with the Australian address, unconsciously crossed his legs and cleared his throat. "Miss Byrne, Mr. Harris, you put a compelling case, and I am sure everything you have told me is correct. However, before an introduction to Captain Walker's parents, we would wish to make some further enquiries."

"Can we not help you, Captain O'Keefe?" said an anxious Maureen. "We are both respectable people. Brendan has a sales position with a reputable British company, and I am starting work next Monday as secretary to a firm of insurance brokers. Neither of us have broken the law in our lives. All I wish to do is ascertain if Rupert Walker is my father."

"Give me a week, Miss Byrne, and call me on this number if you haven't heard from me by then," replied O'Keefe, rising from his chair with his right hand outstretched.

"Before we leave, Captain O'Keefe," Brendan said as he took the captain's hand, "have the Walkers been advised of Miss Byrne's request?"

"Yes, I have spoken with Mrs. Walker, and she is naturally very curious."

Brendan released the captain's hand. "May we ask, as you have now met us, why the reticence? What is holding you back from arranging a meeting?"

"Mrs. Walker has asked us to report back to her the outcome of our meeting today, and it will be her decision as to the next step. I will advise, Major Walker is quite ill at the present, and Mrs. Walker is anxious to avoid any emotional upset which may have a damaging effect on his health."

"Thank you, Captain O'Keefe," offered Maureen. "We are very grateful for the time you have given us. As you can understand, the answer to this question is very important to me."

"Yes, Miss Byrne, I understand. It has been a pleasure meeting both of you, and I shall be in touch."

***

Over the following week, Brendan acclimatised himself to the requirements of his new job with a target of twenty calls a day, all to be recorded. A definition of a call was where the salesman spoke with the relevant buyer. A successful call was where he sold at least one display pack of blades and had it put on display in the shop. Bonus points were gained where the shop put a display in the window using the banners and cards available.

Maureen started at Mitchell Insurance Services and spent the first days finding her way around the system, as used by Mitchell. She was given a desk in the outer office and found the salesmen from the insurance companies far exceeded the number of customers calling either in person or on the phone. The vast majority of the insurance salesmen were male, and word had been passed there was a good-looking female working for Mitchell. Maureen had been told what to expect and became quite proficient at fending them off. New customers were few and far between, and over the days, Maureen began to weed out who were time wasters and who genuine cases.

Mitchell was like a little boy with a new toy and kept phoning through on the intercom for Maureen to take dictation and make cups of tea. For the first few days, he never stopped smiling at his good fortune.

***

Returning from a day's hard work, Brendan, quite exhausted, found Mary with Cecil and Beatrice on the doorstep.

"Hello, how nice to meet you all again. Hello, Beatrice," welcomed Brendan, rather dismayed at their presence.

"Hello, Brendan. I don't see Maureen's car—is she away?" Mary asked, following Brendan into the hallway as he picked up the post from the floor.

"She's working in Southport and should be in at any moment. How can I help, Mary?"

"Time's passing quickly, Brendan. We've called to see how things are progressin' as we're to be out of the flat within the next ten days."

"Look, can this wait until Maureen comes in? She should have the up-to-date info on the house we're buying. She's just started work with an insurance broker in Southport, you know."

"Well, good for her, but be that as it may, Brendan, we are intending to move in here in ten days."

"Yes, and we are doing everything we can to help this happen. Why don't you and Cecil go into the front room? I'll make a cup of tea—wait! Sounds like the front door. Yes, hiya, Mo."

A tired-looking Maureen, carrying a briefcase under her arm, closed the front door with a resounding bang behind her and then, noticing Cecil and Mary, stood back and exclaimed, "Hello, Mary. Cecil. Brendan looking after you? I'll be down in a minute." Leaving the papers on the hall stand, she hurriedly made her way upstairs.

"Right, tea for two. What would you like, Bea? Lemonade? That all right by you, Mary? Good, good. Now, make yourselves comfortable in the front room and I'll bring in the drinks in a minute."

As he ushered the small party into the front room, he was aware of Maureen sneaking in behind him into the kitchen.

"A busy day, Mo?" he asked as he came up behind her and gave her a hug. "Let's get the kettle on first. As you no doubt gathered, they were waiting on the doorstep. Mary says they need to move in in ten days' time."

"One hell of a day, Bren. The most important thing, though, is the mortgage. Everything seems to be running OK, but the insurance company hasn't come back yet with the underwriting decision on your insurance, and the Mortimers reckon they will give vacant possession on the 13th July. That's two weeks from now."

"So what do we do for those four days?" wondered Brendan as he poured out the tea. "Do we stay at a B&B or tell Mary to do that—"

"No, Bren," Mo interrupted. "We promised. I think we go to a B&B, and over the next ten days move the furniture we've agreed to take into storage and give them possession on the 9th of July. Save a lot of messin'."

"We'd had better get into them and put their minds at rest."

Over the next hour, it was agreed that Maureen and Bren would move out on the 9th of July. Surprisingly, Cecil made an offer of £200 to buy out Maureen and Brendan's share of the furniture and produced the money there and then. Maureen and Bren agreed wholeheartedly with this arrangement and pocketed the money.

23

Meet the Grandparents

Later in the week, when they returned home from work, there was a phone call offering them the opportunity to meet Major and Mrs. Walker at the Pied Bull Hotel in Chester city centre, at eleven o'clock on the following Saturday morning.

"Oh, Bren, I'm scared. What do I do if she agrees she is my grandmother? What would she want from me? There again, she might want nothing to do with me. But whatever the outcome, it will hopefully put my mind at rest. It constantly surprises me to think that my mum kept such secrets from me, and here was I thinking she wouldn't say boo to a goose."

"Yes, Mo, what a girl. Right, I've got that in my diary. I certainly understand your worries. If she agrees you're her granddaughter, what then? Hopefully, we'll get some answers on Saturday."

"I don't think there are any siblings, but Saturday hopefully will come up with some answers. And I've booked us into a B&B in Southport for a week, as by then, we could get a bed and a few other essentials to live with. That £200 from Cecil will come in very handy. We'll have to arrange with the B&B to allow you to keep your Sabre packs in our room."

"Yes. Things are going quite well—the chemists are tough to break down. Some of them want bribes. I have one presentation pack of twenty-five blade dispensers to give away, which doesn't go very far. Still, early days. How are you getting on with Mitchell?"

"I'm finding my way around and learning a lot. It's one hell of a way to make money. The insurance companies are falling over themselves to get concerns like Mitchell to use them. I'm seriously looking at the prospect of becoming an adviser, and maybe, in time, you might look at the idea, Bren."

"I'll keep it in mind, Mo. I've got other news. I've been back to the doc today, who's referred me to the specialist in the eye clinic in Walton

Hospital. The doc reckons there's a waiting list of three months. He doesn't offer much hope, but I'll go for it. That could be September, which would fit in with our programme."

"Right, Bren," interrupted Maureen, I'm off for a bath. I'll leave the water on for you.

She returned a short while later in her dressing gown and settled on the settee, with TV on, to await Brendan. With a cup of tea each, they relaxed and watched *Come Dancing*, organised by Mecca Dancing, with Peter West and Alan Weeks introducing the various amateurs. With their feet tapping to the rhythm of the Ray MacVay Orchestra, Maureen said, "Let's go dancing this Saturday—go to Reece's and meet some of the old gang. What do you think?"

"Yeah, that's a great idea, Mo. We haven't had a break for a few months. I'll look forward to that, and hopefully, Mrs. Walker will welcome you with open arms and accept you into her family."

"Oh, yes, Bren, wouldn't that be lovely?" she cried leaning forward to give Brendan a kiss. "I'll be happy just to have that knowledge. Hey, stop that. Keep your hands to yourself," she admonished with a laugh. "But I do like it."

That Saturday, they dressed in their best and drove into Liverpool, taking the Mersey Tunnel to Birkenhead and thence onto Chester. They parked close to Northgate Street and walked through the old romantic buildings, steeped in history, and approached the Pied Bull Hotel.

"See the plaque on the wall, Mo? It says the premises were built in 1535 and this is the oldest coaching house in Chester."

"Come on, Bren, I don't care how old it is. Just let's get this over with. It's five to eleven—we mustn't keep her waiting."

Entering the foyer, the world and its noise seemed to stop; all that could be heard was the light clinks of spoons in cups and quiet conversations. Looking around, there was no sign of an old lady waiting for them. A middle-aged man in a two-piece suit sitting on his own in one of the foyer chairs looked up enquiringly, seemed to make his mind up, came across and, in a broad northern accent, asked, "Miss Byrne?" Gaining Maureen's positive if surprised reaction, and looking at Brendan, he introduced himself as Reginald Wilmslow, butler and driver to the Major.

"Major Walker and Mrs. Walker are here and looking forward to meeting you. They are in a side room. Would you care for refreshment, sir, madam? You have had a long drive."

"Coffee for both of us would be excellent. Thank you, Mr. Wilmslow," Maureen replied as Wilmslow stopped a passing waiter and placed the order.

"You are aware, I understand, that the major is not terribly well. He's a bit forgetful and repeats himself regularly," said Wilmslow as they approached a side door in the foyer.

Brendan stepped back to let Maureen enter first, whispering, "You're the star of the show. I'll stay in the background. You look lovely and, by the way, I think you should address Wilmslow as Wilmslow without the 'Mister'."

Taking a deep breath. Maureen passed through the door into a smallish room with a very high ceiling and embossed wallpaper overshadowing the space. There was a large fireplace and mantel of dark oak, with a three-seater settee facing it. Two single armchairs were placed near a coffee table, which had a paper folder on it. Facing the door, with his back to the fireplace, was a large male in a wheelchair. He was dressed in a sports jacket and had a light blanket over his knees. He was looking forward intently and raised a shaking arm to greet Maureen.

Mrs. Walker, a tall angular lady with a severe face and greying curly hair, was dressed in a grey skirt and black brogues, and was sitting in one of the single chairs. She looked up, giving Maureen, who looked fresh and young and full of vitality in comparison, a long look and directed her to sit on the settee. Brendan slid in beside her, trying to remain inconspicuous. Wilmslow stood protectively behind the major.

Maureen was sitting all tense on the edge of the settee with her small satchel containing the important photograph clasped tightly in her right hand.

Mrs. Walker cleared her throat in the immediate silence, and in a surprisingly mellow and pleasant tone which belied her severe appearance, asked, "Miss Byrne, we would find it helpful if you were to outline your reasons for your claim that my son Rupert Walker is your father."

"Major Walker—" Maureen addressed the person in the wheelchair, who sat up to attention and garbled a few unintelligible words "—Mrs. Walker, I never saw my father, or the man my mother, Marjorie Byrne, implied was my father—a Peter Byrne—until a few weeks ago when he arrived on a short visit from Australia. He was not aware of my mother's death, nor of my existence, but wished to see my sister Mary, some five years older than I. Peter told me he was in Belgium when I was conceived, and when we looked at the dates, we discovered he was correct."

"Belgium...A-ha...Flanders..." spluttered Major Walker, trying to rise from the wheelchair. "Must get back. Where's Clements?" With his eyes wide open, he looked around the room, then directly at Maureen and smiled, shutting his eyes and lapsing again into semi-consciousness.

"It's all right, James," comforted Mrs. Walker, standing up to adjust the blanket around the major's knees. "Do continue, Miss Byrne," she instructed as she returned to her seat.

"Thank you, Mrs. Walker." Maureen could feel the tears coming. "It's when we looked more thoroughly through my mother's things that we found some photographs hidden behind a cupboard in the drawing room. You have had a copy of the relevant photo, I believe, Mrs. Walker?" Receiving a nod of agreement, Maureen continued, "As you can well understand, I was quite startled, particularly that my mother had kept this secret for so many years, and very interested to find out more about Captain Rupert Walker." Maureen stopped talking and took Brendan's hand for support. *How is Mrs. Walker going to answer?*

After a short silence which seemed to last for hours, Mrs. Walker went to her husband's side, took his hand and turned to Maureen.

"Miss Byrne, our lovely Rupert went to war and died fighting for his country, and we are very proud of his achievements. Over the years since his death, we have had nothing to remember him by but his letters and a few photographs. The major—" Mrs. Walker turned to face her husband "—found it very hard to accept his death and is now declining rapidly. However, before I go any further, Miss Byrne, may I show you and Mr. Harris—" she gave Brendan a gracious smile "—a photograph we found shortly after Rupert's death? It is a photo of Rupert with a young lady. There is no detail written on the back. Please, tell us, if you can, who the lady is."

Maureen stepped forward as Mrs. Walker lifted the folder from the small table, opened it and rummaged inside, giving Maureen an apologetic smile. From amongst the letters and various photographs, she produced a small, faded photo, beginning to brown at the edges, and passed it to Maureen.

Taking it in her hand, Maureen looked at it, stood perfectly still for a moment, and then started to weep. Brendan immediately jumped to his feet and put his arm around her shoulders.

"What is it, Mo, what's wrong?" he asked gently.

"Just look at the photo, Bren," she cried. "It's Mum. Doesn't she look so happy, smiling at my—" she looked across at Mrs. Walker anxiously "—father?"

"It's like a photo of you. The image of you, Mo."

Mrs. Walker was gripping her husband's hand so tightly he was trying to break free. "James, James…" she cried out. "I do believe this lovely young lady is our granddaughter. Oh, Maureen, do let me welcome you home. Please excuse the tears. Oh, I am so happy," cried Mrs. Walker, stepping forward to embrace Maureen. James looked up, and in a loud voice, called out, "Let's all have a cup of tea," and subsided into his own world again.

Brendan, delighted at the outcome and very pleased Maureen had found what she was looking for, wondered what the future would now bring as she hugged Mrs. Walker and leaned over to give her grandfather a kiss. Stepping back from the embrace of her new grandmother, she caught Brendan's hand and pulled him into the family group. "Grandma, Granddad—it is so lovely to say those words—this is Brendan Harris.

Brendan is the love of my life and we love each other so much we are engaged and getting married in August." With a fresh rush of tears from both women, Maureen held out her right arm and, with her left around Brendan's waist, gently encouraged him to step forward, saying, "Bren, may I introduce my grandparents."

Brendan stepped forward as bid and noticed that Grandma's arms were beginning to reach forward. He accepted the embrace and gave the slim body a warm hug, bouncing his nose on her forehead. Blushing furiously, with this old woman in his arms, he leaned back, looked at Mrs. Walker, and said, "What do I call you? Granny?" With a broad grin, he continued, "I am so pleased Maureen has met you."

Inwardly, he was wondering what the Walkers' intentions were. Did they want a close relationship with their newfound granddaughter? How far did Maureen wish the relationship to go? He was pleased with Maureen's enthusiastic introduction and their instant close bond, but wondered how Mrs. Walker would—as she seemed quite old-fashioned—introduce their son's illegitimate granddaughter to their friends and relations.

Wilmslow coughed discreetly and interrupted the tear-strewn introductions.

"Mrs. Walker, if I may interrupt," he stated quite firmly, "I do feel the major is in need of attention. May I take him to the bathroom?" Receiving Mrs. Walker's nod of agreement, he walked the wheelchair from the room.

On his exit, Mrs. Walker took a deep breath and turned to Maureen and Brendan. "My poor, poor James. In his younger days, he was such a leader of men, vibrant and commanding, and look at him now." Wiping her eyes and gripping Maureen's hand, she reached out to Brendan, took his hand, too, and said, "Enough, enough, my lovely pair. Let us not spoil this wonderful day. It is so lovely to be addressed as Grandma. What plans—" Before she could finish her sentence the door swung open, and Wilmslow without hesitation, approached her.

"Madam, I would request your immediate attention," he announced in his well-modulated voice. "The major has unfortunately collapsed, and I have ordered an ambulance. Could you please come quickly?"

"Maureen, Brendan, my apologies. The major gets these attacks fairly often. We must meet again soon. However, I must accompany James to the hospital. Wilmslow, do please give Mr. Harris a calling card, and Brendan, do give Wilmslow yours. Now, I must go." Mrs. Walker gave Brendan a peck on the cheek and Maureen a brief hug and kiss, and hurried out to care for the major.

"Come on, Bren, we'll say goodbye."

As they left, they were just in time to see the unconscious major being stretchered out to the waiting ambulance. They waved to Mrs. Walker as she followed him into the ambulance. Wilmslow approached the couple, and they exchanged calling cards. Brendan's was the card issued by Sabre Blades, giving him the title of 'Area Manager, Sales'.

"God I hope he'll be OK, Mo," said Brendan as the ambulance departed. "Let's have a pot of tea and a few biscuits. We can talk about the last hectic hour."

"It's all I dreamed of, Bren. But poor…Granddad. He's not at all well. I do hope Grandma will get in touch. It is so strange to address them so intimately. What does the card say, Bren?"

"Major and Mrs. J. Walker, River View, Dee Banks, Great Boughton, Cheshire. I'd say they are pretty well off. What do you think will happen now, Mo? Or, really, what I should ask, is what would you like to happen?"

"You know, Bren, this has got me thinking. I want to know more about my father and really, not much else. The major and his wife have lived for many years not knowing I was around, and it's all a big surprise to me as well. Socially, we are miles apart. Here we are, delighted to be able to afford a semi-detached house in Formby whilst they probably live in, from that address, a riverbank mansion. Let's leave it to Grandma to make the first move. If we haven't heard anything in the next couple of days, we'll give them a ring to find out how the maj—or should I say Granddad is?"

"I agree with you, Mo. We have enough on our plate at the moment, but you must be pleased to know for sure who your father was."

"Yes, I feel more secure, but, of course, how would they introduce me to their friends?" Imitating Mrs. Walker's well-refined voice, Maureen leaned forward and said, "Hello, Archibald, do please allow me to introduce my granddaughter—Rupert's bastard daughter—Maureen Byrne."

"That's a bit ruthless, Mo. I see what you mean—'Why is your name Byrne?' 'Where have you been for these past twenty-four years?'—but would these friends be as critical as that? They're a bit priggish, the upper class, I know, but when we're married, you will be Mrs. Maureen Harris, so there should be no problem then about names." Taking Maureen's hand, Brendan tried to console her fears by saying, "She'll come back, Mo. She was bowled over by you."

24

What Does Grandma Want?

Later in the week, after Brendan returned home from his many calls to retailers to encourage them to stock Sabre blades, he was pleased to find Maureen was already there preparing the tea.

"This is a nice change, Mo—business easing off?" he asked because, over the last few days, Maureen had not returned home before seven in the evening.

"No, busy as ever, but I told Mr. Mitchell I had a life outside the business and was leaving at five. He got a bit narky. Enough of that—the immediate news is Mary rang to tell us they want the house on Monday next. I've rung the B&B in Southport, and all is well there. Now, how will Sabre react to that? Oh! Yes, the good news is the house in Formby should be ready the following week, and your life policy has been accepted on standard terms."

"'That is good news," Brendan said with relief in his voice. "How about the Walkers—any news there?"

"I've rung a few times without an answer. Hope there's nothing serious, but the major—still hard to call him Granddad—looked pretty far gone. I'll give them a ring now. Would you fry a couple of eggs, Bren? The sausages are done, and put the kettle on." After a brief hug, Maureen went into the front room, and Brendan continued preparing the tea. Some minutes passed, and he could hear Maureen's muffled voice and long silences. With the meal prepared and placed on the table, Maureen returned looking quite pale and worried.

"Bren, what do we do? Grandma apologised for not calling us earlier, but apparently, the major is not at all well. He's back home, but Grandma believes he could be dying."

"What do you want to do, Mo?"

"I think I should go, for Grandma's sake. Could you come?" she pleaded.

"Absolutely. I'll tell Ken I'm taking the day off tomorrow. I'm sure he'll agree. He'll play annoyed, but my sales over the last few weeks have been pretty good. What about your boss?"

"He's probably working away in the office. I'll give him a ring and explain what's happened. Here we go, onto the next thing, my bold Irishman. To think of it, before I met you, I was living a peaceful, if a bit boring, life. Now look at me—getting married, working for an insurance broker, part of a family I had no idea were alive, and buying a house in Formby."

Looking at Brendan's slightly crestfallen face, she said with a wide smile, "But I wouldn't change it for the world, so give me a kiss, and I'll ring my grandmother and tell her we'll be down tomorrow."

"Same goes for me, Mo. I was on my own, leading an uneventful life, and you came along, but as you say, I wouldn't change a thing. Just one more little visit to add to your list—my brother's wedding."

"Oh, yes. I can't wait to meet your family and visit Ireland."

"Right, we'll book a flight on the Friday night, stay with my parents in Dunlaoghaire and come back on the Sunday. After you've rung Grandma, I'll give Ireland a ring." Stopping in his flow, Brendan suddenly thought, "Then there's a wedding present… Oh, I know—" he sighed in relief "—I'll get my ma to get something. It'll save us carrying a set of crockery or something else on the plane. I'll book a call now."

"Good idea," Maureen said as Brendan picked up the phone and dialled out.

"Hello, operator? May I book a call to Dublin, please?"

"There's a two-hour delay, sir."

"That's OK, just book me in." Brendan hung up. "That'll be eleven o'clock tonight. Hope they call us back. Now I'm off for a bath. What's on telly tonight?"

***

"Wake up, Bren. There's the phone—it's eleven."

"What's that, Mo? The phone… Oh! Dublin.

"Hiya, Ma, hope you weren't in bed. Bren here… I know, I should have called you before now, but anyway, we will be over for Jono's wedding. Is it the same girl?… What's her name?… You've got to be joking, Ma! The wedding's off? Well, I'm glad I rang—we were just going to buy the tickets… They've split up…just today… Wonder what went wrong? Yes, Maureen and I are definitely getting wed the 15th of August… I do hope you and Pop can come—hope you all can. There's the pips again, they're only giving me six minutes. See you in a month. Aggh, there we've been cut off."

"Maybe just as well the wedding is off, Bren. We were being a bit pushed for time. Come on to bed. We've got a busy day ahead of us tomorrow."

***

The following morning, after the planned telephone calls that left a couple of disgruntled employers, they set off for Chester to Major and Mrs. J. Walker. Arriving at Dee Banks, with its imposing houses alongside the River Dee, they pulled up behind the lines of rather expensive cars on the driveway leading up to the large, double-fronted house with a well-tended garden. The door was answered by a uniformed housemaid, who directed the couple into a side room off the hallway, past oil paintings on walls lit by a large sparkling chandelier.

"Oh, look, Bren," exclaimed Maureen as they made their way across the expensive Axminster. "There's paintings of the major and…my dad. Both in uniform—don't they look handsome? Wasn't he good-looking, Bren? Oh, how I would've loved to have met him."

"We're in another league here, Maureen. We've got to act the part. You look stunning in your summer outfit. I'm glad I wore my blazer with the Calvex badge. Now, where's Grandma?"

"Here I am, dears." Mrs. Walker entered the room looking very smart in a cream morning suit with a big welcoming smile on her face. Giving both of them a hug, she took each by the hand, relaxing her reserve, and led them out into the hallway.

"Both of my men," she exclaimed pointing to the two portraits. "Maureen, you've seen Rupert. Didn't he look impressive? And now the poor major—what a man he has been. Come on, into the drawing room, and I'll introduce you to a few of my friends."

"Before you do, Grandma, we must know—how is Granddad?"

"I am so pleased to say he has improved greatly. Much improved."

Upon entering the room, there was a sudden hush as all in unison turned to look at the entrants. The room was very large and dwarfed the five persons—some sitting on a long settee—three mature men and two grown-up women, all with drinks in their hands. James, looking more alert than usual, was in his wheelchair, as expected, with his back to the large ornate marble fireplace and his ever-present aide Wilmslow standing erect behind him. Above the mantelpiece was a posed portrait of he and Mrs. Mitchell in their younger days. There was a large dining table to the right.

"Everybody," called Mrs. Walker, "allow me to introduce James's and my granddaughter and her fiancé, Brendan Harris." There was a halting attempt at applause which quickly subsided into embarrassed laughter. The nearest male, in sports jacket and slacks, in his late-sixties with a severe haircut, stepped forward with his hand outstretched.

"Hello, Maureen, how lovely to meet you. I'm Norman, Norman Hardy—Pauline's brother and your great-uncle—and hello to you, Brendan. It is a wonderful surprise to meet you both. How lovely to meet Rupert's daughter. Where have you been all these years, Maureen?"

Before Maureen could reply, she was introduced to Norman's wife, Joyce, and she and Brendan then spent the next while shaking hands, trying to memorise names and relationships.

Catching Brendan's eye between introductions, Maureen whispered, "I'm getting fed up with this, Bren. Let's go and say hello to Granddad. Hopefully, he's better than he was last time."

"Hello, Mr. Wilmslow, are you well?" Maureen asked the butler as she approached the fireplace.

"Very well, Miss Byrne," was the stiff reply.

Taking the major's limp hand in both of hers, she squeezed it and said slowly, "Hello, Granddad. How are you? Remember me? I'm Maureen, your granddaughter."

The major, hearing her voice, looked up with both eyes wide open and said in a loud voice, "I know you. We have met before. Is that Clements with you? Do get my horse ready, Clements, will you?" Off he went, back to his own world.

With a tear in her eye, Maureen squeezed the major's hand again, receiving a consoling hug from Grandma, who had just come up behind her.

"Clements was James's batman over the years," she explained. "Did he recognise your voice? I wonder. Oh, my poor James."

"Grandma, is there any chance we could have a chat about my father. I am dying to know more about him."

"I would love to tell you, Maureen—perhaps over the weekend? You could call down and spend the day with me."

"Yes, that would be lovely. I'll come down on my own. I'm sure Brendan will agree. I'm afraid we must leave at midday, as we both work."

"Oh! You do? What at, may I ask, Maureen dear?"

Taking a deep breath, Maureen answered the question elaborating somewhat: "I am secretary…investment analyst…for a small insurance and investment brokerage in Southport."

"My, oh, my, that sounds very exacting and interesting. How about you, Brendan?"

"Brendan is area and distribution manager for Sabre Sword Edge. He is responsible for the North West area. Aren't you, Brendan?"

Receiving an affirmative nod from Brendan, Mrs. Walker touched the badge on his blazer, "I am interested in this badge, Brendan. It seems to have a maritime connection, and—please excuse the question—why the eye patch?"

Brendan was surprised at the direct question, thinking it was rather bad manners by his hostess. Now becoming the centre of attention, he looked around the sea of faces awaiting a reply. "The badge, ladies and gentlemen, is of the Calvex Tanker Company. I was a ship's officer and travelled the world. Unfortunately, a short while ago, whilst on shore leave, I was involved in a road accident and damaged my left eye. Hence the Long John Silver eye patch."

Casting his glance around the enquiring group, he gave a disarming smile, patted his left shoulder and said, "Normally, I have a talking parrot, to compensate, but he's not too well at the moment."

There was a momentary silence as the audience assimilated the information, and then Norman Hardy started to laugh. "Where's your peg leg, Long John? Touché, Pauline."

There was a hesitant attempt at laughter by the others, and Mrs. Walker, slightly shamefaced, signalled her apology for asking the personal question.

The party began to break up, with each bidding adieu to Maureen and Brendan, all delighted to welcome them both into the family. Maureen agreed to drive down the following Saturday, to have a long chat with Pauline—her grandma.

***

Back home, Brendan got on the phone immediately to the house agents to find everything on the purchase of the house in Formby had progressed satisfactorily. Would he be interested in buying a few of the pieces of furniture the Mortimers didn't want to take with them? Brendan leapt at the chance and said he would be over to have a look at what was on offer. They confirmed they were moving out on the Saturday week, giving 'vacant possession' for the Monday.

Maureen drove out to Southport to speak with Mitchell about taking time off. She pleaded her case: grandfather close to dying and their house move had come earlier than expected. Mitchell agreed grudgingly but said he wouldn't pay her for the time off.

Brendan called upon a few wholesalers to have something on his weekly log sheet for Sabre and confirmed with the B&B everything was ready for them moving in on the Monday.

The following two weeks flew by, with Cecil and Mary arriving on the Monday with a van load of clothes and personal possessions. Fortunately, Brendan and Maureen had moved what they were taking with them into the B&B. The rent for the rooms had taken some negotiation as, being the summer months, bed-and-breakfast establishments were at a premium. Brendan had to plead with Ken Shanks for time off, which, again, was grudgingly given.

But everything resolved itself. The big day arrived when they collected the key for the new purchase: number six in a small close in a relatively new estate in Formby, the semi-detached house had small gardens to the front and the rear. The garden in the front sloped down from the road, and every springtide, it flooded, as it was found the house was built on sand below sea level. The house had a one-car garage built alongside the main wall with a doorway into the main building, two bedrooms and small office upstairs with a large through room downstairs. The main room was tiled in a chocolate brown with underfloor electric heating.

There was a kitchen/dining area off the main room. Brendan was relieved to see the gas cooker and table and chairs were still remaining as he had bought them from the Mortimers, along with the curtains. There were no carpets or bed. A bed was pretty essential. A hectic week passed by, and at the weekend, they had a bed delivered by a supplier in Southport and bought a few essentials at a general goods auction in the same town.

Maureen's visit to Chester for the chat with her grandmother resulted in her finding that Captain Rupert Mitchell had been quite a lad. His parents were aware of his assignation with Maureen's mother, but had no idea that this had culminated in a granddaughter. Maureen got the impression that Grandma was a lonely woman and was very eager to cultivate the relationship. While she was there, James had a relapse and had to be rushed to hospital again.

"Bren, I'm in a bit of a quandary now with my new grandparents. I seem to have become responsible for their well-being. With Granddad being so ill, Grandma is wishing to share the responsibility of his health. She even suggested I move in with them. I told her we were a pair—that you and I go together. I don't know why—" she laughed "—you do drive me mad at times, but I can't consider life without you. So there you are. God, where did all that come from?" She shook her head in embarrassment.

"Wow, Maureen, that's lovely to hear. I feel the same—we are in this together. You are a bit bossy at times—" he laughed "—but I look forward to our life together and a couple of sets of twins. But about your grandparents. I can understand your concern as suddenly you have this new responsibility. They are relatives, so no matter what, you support them. Or do you? What do you do? Any ideas?"

"Well, you come first, whatever happens. Get that straight, Bren lad, this is a problem we share together. Granddad has no brothers or sisters, and Grandma only has the one brother—Norman, who we met at the house. They have a few friends. Grandma laid it on a bit thick, and I agree with her—we've got to keep in touch, maybe a visit each weekend—but we've got our own lives to lead."

"That we have, Mo. We both have jobs, or did have a couple of weeks ago," grimaced Brendan. "They take a lot of our time. Did Grandma talk about money, by any chance?"

"Yes. She really emphasised how comfortable they were. Granddad has a good pension from the army, and they have a broker who looks after their investments."

Brendan's immediate thoughts were: *If we get involved with the grandparents, Maureen could be asked to run the house, and a lot of her time would be spent in Chester. Especially if Granddad were to die...* Their cosy relationship would be broken up, with Brendan left housekeeping in Formby while Maureen looked after Grandma in Chester. *Enough Bren, stop. This is ridiculous.*

"What do you think Grandma really wants, Mo?"

"To be frank, I'm not too sure. I get the feeling she wants to use me as a reminder of my father…still feels strange. She said she was in a number of clubs and was quite honest about wishing to show me off. She wants that, and to revel in having a younger female in the house to run things."

"This must be quite wonderful for her, finding a granddaughter she didn't know existed. I suppose we must give her as much of our time as we can without ruining our own plans, Mo. I feel she's had a comfortable life, and it must be difficult for her to adjust with her husband being so ill. But we've got a lot on, with getting the house ready to live in and preparing for the wedding—it'll be upon us before we know it."

"Not to mention two employers waiting impatiently for our return," Maureen added. "I feel quite guilty about poor Mitchell. Must give him a ring and thank him for his patience. He was a bit annoyed when I told him I wanted the time off. Hope he hasn't found someone else."

25

Moving House

"Well, Maureen, let's pat ourselves on the back. There's Number Six, The Close, Formby Fields—our home for the future."

The two lovebirds were standing on the pavement, admiring their possession: their new house. They'd had a hectic week arranging the tradesmen and deliveries, but now they had the basics for living. The double bed was in situ in the front bedroom; the TV was in the front room, with a second-hand dining table and sofa both bought for a song at the general auction in Southport. Money was becoming a bit short, and it was now time to concentrate on their work. They both had a lot to do to make up with their employers. Maureen had called Mitchell, who said the post was still open, whilst Brendan was ordered to make himself available for interview with Ken Shanks the sales manager.

If they were going to sack me, there would have been a dismissal in the post, but I'm going to have to fight my case when I see Shanks, thought Brendan. *I'm lucky to still have a job with a car and all the free razor blades I could ever use. Pity I use an electric.*

Brendan got a severe warning from the dapper Ken Shanks. He was told he had better start producing high sales figures to make up for time lost, as Ken was aiming to have his team in the top three for the annual sales conference at the end of the year. Meanwhile, Maureen slotted straight back into her role of secretary, confidante and sales woman, without any trouble.

The next big event was the wedding, still booked at the registry office for Saturday, the 15th August, at eleven o'clock. The honeymoon was going to be restricted to the Sunday as it was back to work on the Monday. The wedding reception was to be held in the Blundellsands Hotel, with accommodation for the newly married on the Saturday and Sunday.

Brendan's referral for the eye consultant arrived, for which he was glad. Having somewhat tired of wearing the black eye patch, Brendan had discovered if he tilted his head to the right, he could refocus his eyes to reduce the two images to one. Alas, he now found, with his head constantly leaning to the right, he got neck ache, and his appointment wasn't until September.

"Oh, God, Bren, we never sent out wedding invitations. There's been so much happening."

"Well, get on the telephone to all. Wait—I'll nip down to Smiths. They'll have some suitable cards. Who's going to be my best man? Wonder if Grandma will come? They're all coming over from Ireland—should be about twenty, all told. This is going to be a right shambles. Ah, what of it, Mo? We'll have some fun. You're going to meet my mother…I wonder how that will work out? I know you'll win her over. You'll love my Pop—he's a smashing guy. What about yourself, Mo?"

Maureen laughed in embarrassment. "I'm afraid the Byrne family is going to be overrun by the Harris lot. But I'm certainly looking forward to it. I've got Mary, Cecil and Bea, maybe Grandma and Granddad. I have a few friends I haven't seen for a while. Must dig out their addresses…"

"What about your boss?"

"I'll leave him for a while, get to know him a bit better. Now I've got to do a bit of reading and brush up on my mortgage lore. When married, we'll be known as Mr. and Mrs. Brendan Harris—sounds OK. But why not Mr. and Mrs. Maureen Byrne or even Mr. and Mrs. Harris-Byrne?" Stepping away, with her back to the fireplace, Maureen put on her announcer voice and said, "And next to take the floor in the World Dance Championship final are—" clearing her throat, she raised her voice "—Mr. and Mrs. Harris-Byrne representing County Dublin, Ireland. Your applause, please." With both of them laughing, Maureen continued, "Yes, when we're married, we can do a joint endowment on our mortgage, and we'll then be complete. So there you are," she declared in a final flourish, dancing to the swinging music on the radio.

"There's the phone, Mo. Wonder who it is on a Sunday night? Hello, Harris speaking."

"Hello, Brendan, your ma here," was the reply. "How are you?"

"Why, hello, Ma. How lovely to hear you."

"Just confirming, Bren—Pop and I will be over for the wedding. Thanks for the address. We're coming over with Jono and the girl he's going out with at the moment. I lose track of the names. Billy will be bringing a girl called Mavis. A nice girl. Glad to say she's a Protestant."

"That's great, Ma. We're holding the reception in the Blundellsands Hotel, near Liverpool. Getting married in the registry office down the road from the hotel."

"A registry office, Bren? It would have been nicer if you had come over home and got married in the parish church. Maureen's RC, is she?"

"Yes, Ma. You'll love her. She's looking forward to meeting you and Pop."

Maureen, listening in to the conversation, gestured to Brendan to give her the phone. "Hello, Mrs. Harris, Maureen Byrne here. We're both so glad you and Mr. Harris are coming over. I'm especially looking forward to meeting you. Brendan has told me so much about you."

"Well, Maureen dear, so nice to speak with you. We must have a long chat when we meet."

"Lovely to speak with you, Mrs. Harris. I'll give you back to Bren. Goodbye, see you soon." She handed the phone back to Brendan.

"She sounds nice," Ma said. "Is that a Liverpool accent she's got? There's the pips, gotta go, Brendan, see you soon."

"Bye, Ma. All the best to Pop." *Brrrr* "That was quick, Mo. She said you sounded nice."

"That's the first step, Bren. Looking forward to meeting your Pop—he sounds like a nice guy—and your brothers... What is it? Jono's the eldest—what a strange name—and Billy's the youngest? He sounds a real handful."

"Yes, that's right. Jono—his name is really Jonathan—he's the good looker of the family, has the dark features of an Italian from Naples. Needs to shave twice a day. At the moment, he's running his own business, dealing in office equipment. Travels the country—has a girl in every port, as the saying goes. Billy is the bright one of the three of us—tall, brainy and a natural at sport. Not quite six foot with a head of brown wavy hair. They're both bringing their girlfriends for the wedding, Ma says. It'll be interesting to see them.

"Right, Maureen love, it's time for bed. We've both got jobs to do. Hope your day works out with Mitchell. I'll continue my job getting the retail industry to stock and display Sabre razor blades, but I think what you're doing is more interesting. Wonder if Mitchell would take me on part-time to sell some mortgage endowments? I reckon from what you say they would be quite easy to sell. What do you think?"

"Let's look at that another day," Maureen suggested. "You've got plenty to do with Sabre blades. Now, come on. I'll race you to the lav."

***

For the next two weeks, the two of them knuckled down to their work. Maureen expanded her knowledge of the insurance industry, specialising in mortgage provision and insurance protection. When she saw the commissions Mitchell could earn placing a mortgage, she thought maybe it would be worth getting in on the selling side herself.

Brendan was settling into the daily rota of twenty calls encouraging retailers to stock Sabre razor blades. "Things are pretty OK in Sabre, Mo. I'm getting on top of targets—in line for a bonus this Christmas. The only drawback is carrying stock and display material. Have you seen the garage recently? There's close on a thousand pounds' worth of razor blades in there."

"Yes, Bren, does Sabre insure us against break-ins?"

"Interesting you should say that, Mo. There's two stories going around—one about a salesman who reported a break-in into his garage, through the roof apparently, and a lot of blades were stolen. However, it was proved he had done the supposed break-in himself and was given the sack.

"The other tale is the salesman who sold the contents of five boxes—around a thousand pounds retail—and filled the empty cartons with bricks. The sales manager, on a stock check, gave them a kick, not suspecting anything amiss, and nearly broke his toe. That was the end of another salesman's career. Yes, Mo, we are insured against break-ins and told never to accost a thief, just report it to the police and Sabre office and stay watching telly."

Later that evening, over a nighttime cup of tea, Maureen brought up the question of the risk they were taking holding so many cartons of razor blades for Sabre and the money he was making.

"You know, Bren, I was working out how much Mitchell is earning. In the last year, he averaged three thousand pounds a month in commissions. That's thirty-six times what you make flogging yourself with Sabre, and he doesn't have a garage full of valuable razor blades worth pinching."

"Yeah, that's worth thinking about, Mo. That is worth considering. Could you give me some idea what Mitchell does, and—"

"Do you know how much he will get when he gets cover for our mortgage using the insurance policy he has recommended? Go on, guess.

"Fifty quid?"

"No."

"A hundred?"

"No."

"Go on, tell—not a hundred and fifty?"

"Not a hundred and fifty, Bren, and not two hundred, either. Five weeks' wages—two hundred and fifty pounds."

"God, Maureen, we've got to look at this seriously. Look, I'll start doing some positive reading up on insurance, and when we're ready, we could put an arrangement to Mitchell. I could… No, wait, how does Mitchell get his customers?"

"He's starting a mailshot campaign, sending out letters to householders on the voters' list. You know you can buy those for a few quid. The letter is an invitation to a householder to use insurance to pay off his mortgage."

"Right, we'll start tomorrow. I'm quite excited about it, Mo. Between us, we'd make a bomb. That aside, you remember we're getting married in ten days' time?"

"Haven't forgotten, Bren. Cecil and Mary are definitely coming. There are three of my pals coming as well, and Grandma said she will do her best with Granddad. I don't think she likes the thought of the registry office. Let's hope she can make it."

"Isn't it strange, Mo? We now accept her and Granddad as family. Only a few months ago, we didn't even know they were around. I hope he's all right, poor man. I complain about my problems with my eyes but must consider myself pretty lucky. I can't wait for that appointment with the eye specialist…"

26

The Wedding

Following the custom that the future bride should not see the groom on the eve of the wedding, Brendan made arrangements to stay with a friend he and Maureen had met whilst dancing in the Floral Hall in Southport. Peter Mane and his wife Elizabeth had offered to put him up on the wedding eve. Peter was a top sales inspector in one of the leading Scottish life offices and was always suggesting Brendan come into insurance sales. Both in their early thirties, Elizabeth was the motherly type while Peter was a bit of a go-getter, always ready to pick up the next sale. He'd suggested they were made for insurance sales.

"You're a natural, Bren, and with Maureen in the business, the two of you could certainly make some money. Get yourself clued up on the insurance jargon and a bit of product info, and you're quids in. I deal with the brokers—or, should I say, insurance advisers—in the North West. Some of them are making big money, and I mean big money."

With this advice ringing in his ears, Brendan had started reading up on life insurance, investments and, of course, pensions. On his calls to the many small independent retailers, encouraging them to buy Sabre razor blades, he made enquiries on the success of the business and the retailers' personal circumstances, building up a picture of a growing client base.

On wedding eve, Maureen was quite excited. The girlfriends were coming to have a party on the Friday night. There were a few old school and business friends, plus Mary—her sister. The contingent from Ireland was expected the morning of the wedding. It was going to be a tight schedule, with the ceremony arranged in the registry office for eleven o'clock and the plane expected to arrive at Speke Airport—a distance of close on twenty-five miles—at nine forty-five. As there were six of them, they had hired a minibus and hoped to get to the registry office by a quarter to eleven. It was a big day in more ways than one, especially for Maureen. Apart from tying the knot, she was to meet Brendan's family.

That Friday evening, Brendan went to Peter's house in Southport—a palatial detached five-bedroom mansion—straight from work, quite exhausted after a successful day.

"And a very good evening to you, my Irish friend," welcomed Peter in a dreadful pretend Irish accent. "Your last night of freedom, boyo. Now, what do you want to do with it? We could perhaps go down to the local."

"Let me have a wash first, Pete—Oh, hello, Elizabeth. Thanks for putting me up for the night."

"Hello, Brendan," said Elizabeth in her London accent. "You're very welcome. Looking forward to tomorrow? I am."

Brendan smiled in reply. "Not really. It's going to be quite hectic, but I have my best man here to look after me. Haven't I just that, Peter?" laughed Brendan, giving Elizabeth a hug and patting Peter on the shoulder.

"Peter friend, I'm bushed, and tomorrow is going to be one hell of a busy day. Do you mind if we don't go drinking? I'd rather watch a bit of telly and get an early night."

"That's fine, Bren. Get a meal into you and see how you feel afterwards," Peter suggested.

***

The following morning was bright and sunny, temperature in the mid-seventies. Brendan, adorned in his freshly cleaned dark suit with a white carnation in the buttonhole, climbed into his Cortina while Peter boarded the Volvo estate with Elizabeth in the front. Peter, due to his small stature, had a cushion on the driver's seat.

"'It's pretty early. We should be in Crosby about a quarter to eleven. What a lovely day to get married. This is your last chance, Brendan." Peter grinned, leaning out the car window. "You can always change your mind."

"Enough of that, Peter Mane, just concentrate on your driving," admonished Elizabeth. "The poor guy has enough to think about without you putting silly ideas in his head."

"OK, dear," replied Peter and started to sing 'I'm Getting Married in the Morning'.

"Pay no attention to the daft fool," laughed Elizabeth, turning to look at Brendan. "You've got a wonderful—oh, shut up, Peter—girl there in Maureen. Come on, Peter, get moving."

Brendan had turned down Peter's offer to drive him to the registry office, as the newlyweds would be staying overnight in the hotel and would need to have the car available to get to work on the Monday.

After parking the cars, the three of them made their way to the office to find Maureen outside with her friends.

"Look, there's Maureen, Bren. Still not too late to change your mind, old chap. Though, looking at her, I wouldn't mind marrying her myself." Peter laughed and Elizabeth hit him on the shoulder.

"Pay no attention to him, Brendan. I'm sure you will both be very happy. Now, come in, you randy devil, and make sure everything is laid on for the wedding."

Maureen, looking very elegant in a green sheath dress, with white flowers in the glorious red hair that framed her lovely face, smiled and waved to Brendan, who thought to himself, *haven't I done well for myself? Doesn't she look gorgeous? Am I glad I worked in the department store in Liverpool. How long ago was that? Was it only six months ago?*

He strolled over to Maureen, acknowledged the introductions to the group of women surrounding her, gave Mary a peck on the cheek and asked was Cecil with her.

"Hello, Brendan," greeted Mary. "Cecil has gone inside with Bea—my congratulations to the pair of you. Good Lord, what's this?" Mary exclaimed as an impressive Daimler car silently pulled up alongside the pavement.

"Maureen, it's the grandparents. Would you believe it?"

"No, it's only Grandma," Mo said as he opened the car door for the elegantly dressed Mrs. Walker as she stepped out onto the pavement.

"I am so sorry, but Granddad..." She hesitated until Maureen took her free hand. "He's not with me. He sends his love. I wouldn't have missed this day for anything, Maureen dear. This is the day that you and our lovely Brendan become part of my family. Now, introduce me to all your friends."

"Hey, Bren," Peter called as he hurried out of the office "It's getting close to eleven. Have the Irish lot turned up yet?"

"Not yet, Pete. I'm getting a bit anxious," Brendan answered, looking along the main road. "What if I stay here and keep an eye out for them and you run in and ask the registrar to wait?

"No," Peter argued. "You get on into the waiting room with Maureen. Go on, the lot of you. I'll hang on here."

"OK, Peter. Wait, look, there's a minibus at the traffic lights flashing its lights. My brother said he was hiring a bus at the airport. It must be them. Leave you to sort them out. Come on, the lot of you," Brendan repeated with a laugh, receiving an acknowledging flash of headlights to his wave.

***

Within the minute, with a screech of brakes, the minibus pulled up, and a smiling curly headed Irishman leaned out the side window and asked in a marked Dublin accent, "Would this be where the wedding is taking place, young fella?"

Peter laughed in reply. "They're all waiting for you—we're running late. There's a car park around the corner, driver. I'll get them to wait a bit longer. God, you're all huge!" he said as Harris men, all over six foot, and the three women, all over the five and a half foot, piled out of the bus.

"My name's Peter. I take it you're all here for the wedding?" he joked. "The reception room is on the right on the ground floor—Bren had to get in to calm down the registrar. The toilets are on the left as you go in. See you in a few minutes, driver."

"Thanks, Pete," said Brendan's older brother—Peter assumed—as he pulled out from the kerb.

***

The reception room was now becoming quite full with a lot of laughter. Billy, with his turn of wit, was introducing himself to everyone. The porter who had just entered the room had to shout over the noise. "Will the Harris group please repair to the ceremony room?" Gaining everyone's attention, he turned on his heel and strode from the room with all dutifully following. They passed through the badly lit hallway and dusty atmosphere to the staircase. There was an overriding atmosphere of gloom and old-fashioned splendour due to sombre paintings of past mayors and the standard picture of Queen Elizabeth II on the walls. Following the porter in his black uniform, they ascended the ornate wooden staircase with its shiny handrail polished from the many hands supporting themselves as they climbed the wide stairs with their worn Axminster.

Peter was taking his duties very seriously and had ensured he was first into the ceremony room to apologise to the registrar. The porter held the door open for the guests, who filed in, exclaiming how impressive the room was with its dark wooden desk and heavy curtains. However, the room, which had obviously been created for some other purpose, was let down by the lines of hideously coloured kitchen chairs lined up in ordered rows.

Behind the mahogany desk sat two officials moving papers on the desktop and paying no attention to the rapidly filling room as the guests chose which of the yellow plastic seats to sit on. The registrar was a serious-looking woman wearing a grey blouse with long sleeves. Her grey hair was severely clasped close to her head, and she was wearing a pair of National Health glasses on the end of her nose. The junior official, a young girl with her blonde hair tied in a sober bun, looked somewhat scared of her compatriot; she sat forward at the desk, nodding her head repeatedly to the whispered instructions from the registrar.

As the hubbub of noise reduced, the severe-looking woman rapped her desk with a wooden gavel and said in a startlingly high voice, "Good morning, everybody. Do settle down, please, time is very precious. My name is Miss Simpson; my assistant is Miss Murphy."

The guests sat paying rapt attention to this formidable woman with her strange high-pitched voice.

She continued, "We are here to conduct the marriage of Miss Maureen Byrne and Mr. Brendan Harris. Will both parties step forward?"

Brendan rose from his kitchen chair and took Maureen's hand. Both stood in front of the seated registrar. They smiled at each other as the registrar stood up to conduct the ceremony. However, before she had begun speaking, there as a knock on the entry door, and Jono's head appeared from behind the half-opened door.

Miss Simpson signalled to the porter, calling out in her squeaky voice, "Yes, sir, what is your business?"

Jono opened the door, checking it was the right room. "Sorry, miss, just parking the bus," he excused and sat on one of the kitchen chairs.

"It's all right, Miss Simpson," Brendan explained. "He's my big brother."

With a resigned sigh, Miss Simpson nodded to the porter to return to the side of the room and, after clearing her throat, continued the ceremony. "The purpose of marriage is that you may always love, care for and support each other through all the joys and sorrows of life, and that love may be fulfilled in a relationship of permanent and continuing commitment."

She paused for a moment, looked up and continued with her irritating voice, "If there is any person here who knows of any legal reason why these two people should not be joined in matrimony, then they should declare it now."

Brendan squeezed Maureen's hand in the ensuing silence and turned to look at the sea of faces behind them. He was not expecting any response but was startled to hear Billy call out with a laugh in his voice, "Don't worry, Bren, I'll keep your secret."

There was a stunned silence as everyone turned to look at Billy.

"What's he on about? Maureen whispered. "What's he mean, Bren?"

Miss Simpson looked at Brendan in surprise and demanded in a raised tone, "Would sir like to explain that statement?"

Billy, realising his faux pas as the crowd all looked around to see who could make such a damning interruption, was abject in his apology and replied, "Sorry, Your Honour, I was just being funny."

"Not funny, at all, sir. Any more comments from you and you will be expelled from the service. Now, let us continue."

Looking at Brendan, the registrar, in a lowered voice, asked him with the trace of a smile, "Do you know that young man, Mr. Harris?"

"At the moment, Miss Simpson, I wish I didn't. But he's my little brother."

"I see, Mr. Harris. I do hope there won't be any more interruptions. Now, quiet, please, everyone."

The ceremony continued with Brendan, followed by Maureen, declaring there was no lawful impediment why they shouldn't be joined in matrimony. Nobody uttered anything this time. The guests were then called upon to witness that Brendan Harris would "...*take thee, Maureen Byrne, to be my lawful wedded wife,*" and Maureen Byrne would "...*take thee, Brendan Harris, to be my wedded husband.*"

Peter, who had been fidgeting with the wedding ring, dropped it on the floor. There was laughter from the guests as he knocked over his yellow chair in his haste to recover the ring. He passed it to Brendan, who then, looking directly at Maureen, both smiling broadly, repeated the registrar's words at the same time sliding the gold band onto Maureen's finger. "I give you this ring as a token of our marriage and the sharing of our lives together."

A big cheer went up from the guests, led by the Irish, with Miss Simpson calling them to quieten down. In the ensuing silence, she wished the smiling couple a happy and rich life together and finished with the following: "I now pronounce you both legally married. You may now kiss."

A further cheer arose from the guests as the newly married couple kissed each other with great enthusiasm.

With a great deal of noise and laughter, everyone trooped out of the ceremony room. The newly married couple stopped to thank the registrar and Miss Murphy. Brendan apologised for the disruption caused and, tongue-in-cheek, excused his relatives, stating they had just come over from Ireland. Miss Simpson frowned and said, "From Ireland…I thought so. Goodbye, Mr. Harris, and good luck to you, Miss Byrne. Now, Miss Murphy," glancing at her young assistant, "who's next?"

As the happy couple exited the room, they could hear the noise from the floor below and the porter calling out, "Ladies and gentlemen, please will you be after leaving the premises—and don't be after throwing the confetti. Stop it, sir." The porter, obviously another Irishman, was trying to clear the path from the waiting room for the next couple and their friends.

Peter came across to the grinning couple. "Come on, Bren, get outside or the porter will have a heart attack."

"OK, Pete. Hi, Ma, Pop—see you outside. Hello, Grandma, these are my parents. You are coming to the hotel?"

"Yes, Brendan. Congratulations, Maureen, I am so happy," cried Grandma. "Oh, if only James could be here."

With Maureen and Brendan leading, they all eventually made their way onto the pavement where the Daimler pulled up alongside and Wilmslow came around ready to open the car door.

"Would you care to join me, Mr. Harris, Mrs. Harris?" Mrs. Walker asked Brendan's parents. "I'm Pauline—as Brendan said, Maureen's grandmother."

"Hello, Pauline, do call me Alice," replied Brendan's mother in her newly purchased summer outfit from the department store, looking in envy at the car and the aura presented by the expensively dressed Pauline.

"Hello, Pauline, I'm Henry," greeted Brendan's father in his grey slacks and brown-speckled tweed jacket with leather elbow pads. "That would be great," he continued in his deep Dublin accent, overshadowing the two women with his six-foot-plus stature. "All right if I sit in the front with the driver?"

As the two women climbed into the spacious back seat adjusting the embossed cushions, Henry settled himself into the passenger seat. Wilmslow acknowledged Henry's presence with a smile and short greeting, and with a whisper, the Daimler sped away.

"Wonder if we could have a go in that beauty, Maureen," Billy said as Peter arrived with the Volvo, followed by Jono with the minibus."

"We'll have a word with Grandma when we get to the hotel," answered Maureen, climbing into the Volvo along with Elizabeth and Brendan. The rest of the party piled into the minibus and one of Maureen's girlfriends' cars.

***

Within the hour, all guests were helping themselves to sandwiches and cooked chicken and a glass of wine at the buffet lunch.

"We're all staying in a B&B in a place called Bootle, Bren," said Jono. "And flying back tomorrow on the three o'clock plane. I'd better ring the B&B to say we'll be at their place at...how late do you think?"

"I don't know, Jono. After this meal, we've got a room booked from eight tonight until midnight. Isn't that right, Peter?"

"Yes, Bren, and a disc jockey for those four hours. A pal of mine is doing it for us. There's a bar in the hotel and a piano for your mother. I hear she's good on the old-time singsong. You can sing a bit as well, Bren, can't you?"

"Bing Crosby isn't in it, Peter."

"So we can look forward to a good evening?" Peter laughed. "You singing, Bren, young Billy on the geetar and Mother Harris on the honky-tonk. What are you going to do, Henry?"

"I'll be the compere, and the star will be Jono on the harmonica."

"Don't forget me, Pop," called out Maureen. "I can render a good likeness to Alma Cogan. You should hear me singing 'The Tennessee Waltz'."

"Wait, everybody," called Mary, who was sitting at the next table. "Some of you may be able to play your banjos and mouth organs and even sing, but you haven't heard Cecil and 'Ol' Man River'. Come on, Cec, give us a couple of notes."

Cecil, looking somewhat abashed, wearing a white T-shirt which emphasised his black skin and flashing white teeth, stood up at the table and put the half-eaten chicken leg on the paper plate. "I'll just give you white folks a few words from the chorus of 'Ol' Man River'." He commenced to sing in a strikingly attractive, deep and melodious voice, "Ol' man river, that ol' man river…" Finishing in a particularly enviable deep note, Cecil bowed to the applause, sat down and picked up his half-eaten chicken leg.

Ma Harris and Grandma Walker were now deep in conversation as they had surprisingly found a common theme. Ma had a first glass of wine inside her and was mellowing slightly. Grandma wanted to know more about her new grandson-in-law, and Ma wanted to know more about her daughter-in-law. The next couple of hours were spent with Henry joining the two women's conversation, then Ma and he got Maureen and Brendan aside to find out more about Maureen firsthand.

Meanwhile, Billy seemed to have forgotten the girl he had come with and was flirting with one of Maureen's girlfriends. Peter told everybody the rest of the day was up to themselves, until eight o'clock when there would be a party with a disc jockey and a buffet meal at nine o'clock. He and Elizabeth left in the Volvo and said they would be back for the party at eight. Jono was, as ever, recounting his experiences in war-torn Cyprus to anyone who would listen. With the wine flowing, the sun shining and the conversation pleasantly rolling along, Brendan and Maureen, unnoticed, slipped away to their room.

Ma, whilst talking with Grandma, found out she was staying overnight in the hotel, so on the spur of the moment decided she and Henry should do the same and had him book a room and told Jono to cancel the B&B. It was a big move for Ma, as she had found it difficult enough to find the money for the B&B, but she wanted to impress the newfound grandma. Alice had always believed she had been born for greater things in life. Anyone who dressed well and spoke posh would get the full extent of Ma's attempt at poshness. She would raise her voice, round her vowels, lengthen her words and throw a limp hand around. Poor Henry just stood behind her like a big protective bear.

That evening, the disc jockey arrived with his record players, tapes and speakers. He was a man in his early forties who was accosted by Ma Harris and instructed to play background music and keep the volume down.

"Are you Mrs. Mane, by any chance?" the disc jockey asked. "Mr. Mane said there was going to be a party of youngsters in their twenties, and wished a lively evening."

"No, my good man," answered Alice, who, by now had had a fair amount of wine. "I am not Mrs. Mane." Stepping back to focus on the disc jockey, she asked in a loud voice, "Who in the name of God is Mr. Mane? Mister dis' jockey, I am the groom's mother…Alice Harris. Mother of three fine strapping lads. Now, do what I tell you, my good man." Having given her orders, Alice turned away from Jack the smiling disc jockey, noticed the upright piano with its gleaming white keyboard waiting for someone to make it sing, and turned back to Jack.

"Jack—may I call you Jack? I see from that card your name is Jack… I'm going to entertain you all with a medley with the piana, so put all your bits away, Jack, an' go an' have a cup of tea with your Mr. Mane. Come on, Jono, Billy, let's make some music," shouted Alice, catching everyone's attention with a ripple of her fingers on the keyboard."

"God, Bren," exclaimed Jono, "what's in the wine? Though I think she's had a few whiskeys as well. But she's great on the ould piano. There's Billy with his guitar. Next we'll have Pop with his spoons. I know she's been practising some of the Beatles songs. Bet she gets the crowd singing."

"What's she going to play, Bren?" asked Maureen. "Is she a bit drunk?"

"Well, Mo, I am sure she's had a few, but wait, she's sitting down… flexing the fingers…now taking a drink… Bang, away she goes—'If You Knew Susie'—it's like she has a musical machine gun. Look at her fingers go."

Heads in the room turned to hear 'Knees Up Mother Brown' followed by 'Swanee River'. Everyone was grinning, their feet tapping; some, especially the older people, were singing the words of the well-known tunes pouring out from the piano which had suddenly come alive.

As Ma Harris was nearing the end of her current number, Billy strolled over to the piano, nodded to his Ma, who, with a final flourish on the white keys, turned to the room. There was a great expectant round of applause as Alice took her bows.

Billy nodded to her and held his hand out for silence. "That was my mum—isn't she good?" He clapped his hands, prompting a response from the crowd. "Now, listen to this. Ma and I are going to play that great new song by Louis Armstrong, 'Hello Dolly', followed by a Beatles medley, so let's rock the night away, but before you get on the floor, I'll introduce you to my big brud Jono. Some of you will have heard of a Larry Adler, he plays the harmonica. Well, here's Jono to make the harmonica sing."

With Ma filling in with the piano, and Jono playing the tune on the mouth organ, Billy started singing and strumming the guitar. The party really got into gear with the youngsters rock 'n' rolling. Cecil was dancing with Elizabeth, and Henry was endeavouring to keep up with a very flexible Pauline. Peter was clearing away for the evening buffet. Brendan was dancing in his ballroom mode with an impressed Mary, and Maureen was talking to one of her girlfriends, both swaying slightly and not in time to the music.

The poor disc jockey, Jack, was getting more and more bemused. Here he was, being entertained by his employers, instead of he entertaining them. Where was Mr. Mane? He approached Henry, Brendan's dad, and was directed to Peter.

"Mr. Mane," Jack called out over the sound of the piano, the harmonica, the singers and laughter. "What the hell is going on?"

"Haven't a clue, Jack. I'll find out from Mr. Harris. Look, just have a drink and enjoy yourself. Consider it a night off with pay, though, I'm sure we'll be using you before the night's out."

"Fine, Mr. Mane, you're the boss."

"Hi, Peter." Brendan and Maureen, who had been dancing to the Beatles songs had noticed the conversation.

"What's going on, Bren?" Peter asked, looking around at the happy crowd.

"Yes, Peter," said Bren with a grin. "I am as surprised as you, but I had forgotten to tell you about my family. They are a bit spontaneous in their actions. But I say let 'em get on with it. I'm enjoying myself. Best we keep our eye on young Jack. We will probably need him later as Ma won't be able to keep up the Winifred all night."

Noticing Peter's questioning look, Brendan explained, "You know Winifred the piano player? Winifred Atwell who plays boogie-woogie and ragtime? No, you don't. Aw, come on, Pete. Join the twentieth century."

"Bet you haven't heard of my hero, Bren—Charlie Kunz?" replied Peter in a triumphant voice.

"Got ya there, Pete. You mean my old pal Charlie, played lovely background piano. He was an American, died in 'fifty-eight. Must go find Grandma."

"OK, Bren, I surrender," said Peter with a laugh, downing his drink. "Bren, you mean your grandma-in-law—her with the posh accent. She looks like she's enjoying herself, dancing with your new brother-in-law—his name's Cecil, isn't it? He really has a nice voice, Bren, maybe we could get your mum to play and get him to sing 'Mammy' or one of Al Jolson's hits."

And so, the evening progressed, the buffet table was cleared, and Jack was invited to start his disc-jockeying. By now, he'd had a few drinks and was slurring his words slightly. The first song he announced he was going to play was the introductory hit of the Rolling Stones, 'It's All Over Now'. Unfortunately, Billy called out in his inimical way, 'It's all over for you now, Jack lad."

Instead of Jack ignoring the interruption, feeling a bit sensitive he retorted, "No! Mr. Irishman. There seems to be dozens of you lot here, maybe this will please you. I have got the latest from those countrymen of yours…the…the…Bachelors on tape. Now, if you don't mind…I've got the tape here somewhere… Ah, here it is."

Standing upright with some difficulty, balancing with his hand resting on one of the large loud speakers beside him, Jack pushed the buttons and switched the switches needed to start the music to find the volume was on full blast. Con Cluskey—or was it the other Bachelor brother Dec Cluskey?—in his tuneful celebrated roar blasted out the first line of the hit song 'Diane' before Jack could find the volume control.

With the music bellowing, Jack apparently remembered the essential piece of the disc jockey repertoire: the revolving flashing coloured lights. Leaning over unsteadily, he found the correct switch, starting the yellow, blue and white lights revolving and flashing. Grinning in triumph, he stepped back, admiring his handiwork. Unfortunately, his right foot caught in the tangle of electric flex. Trying to regain his balance, with absolute fear on his face, he fell back against the fortunately empty buffet table and slumped in a broken heap on the floor. The lights had stopped revolving but were still flashing on and off on his relaxed face. He had fallen asleep.

Everyone stopped what they were doing and looked on in astonishment.

Henry, who was closest to the badly behaved apparatus, switched off the lights and stopped the tape. Peter ran over to Jack, caught his legs and pulled him out from under the table. This disturbed the sleeping disc jockey, who sat up slowly and was immediately sick over his trousers. Henry and Jono, one at each end, took the sorrowful body out of the room, and Brendan called out, "Let's have some music, Ma. What about a singsong?"

"OK, Bren, the poor guy—hic—can't hold his likker. What's the world comin' to? C'mon, Bren, let's have a try at your fave'rit, the fence song."

"You mean 'Don't Fence Me In'—the Bing Crosby number? Give us a twiddle on the keys, Ma, an' I'll just have a sip of my drink." Settling himself in front of his audience, Brendan started his story: "Well, folks, there he was, this cowboy standing in the courtroom in Dodge City, out of place amongst all the bewigged and pompous city dwellers. Are you all listening, folk? He had got himself on the wrong side of the law, riding his horse the wrong way up a one-way street. Now, his name was Wild Cat Kelly, remember that, folks. He had his old geetar slung over his shoulder with him, an' when the judge said in his grand voice, 'Why shouldn't we put you in gaol, Mr. Kelly?' Wild Cat replied with his head hung low, 'If Yer Honour don't mind, I'll sing it for you an' these gracious folk in the jury.' Unslinging his geetar from over his shoulder he—" Brendan went through the motion of positioning a guitar, tipped his Stetson onto the back of his head and started to sing in an attractive conversational tone. With his Ma playing in a slow background rhythm, Brendan began to sing the words; after a couple of verses, Billy joined in with his geetar, and the partygoers, all swaying to the rhythm of the tune, ended each verse with a spontaneous rendering of 'Don't Fence Me In'.

When he finished, Brendan took a bow, replaced the imaginary guitar over his shoulder, raised his imaginary Stetson to the crowd, mounted his make-believe horse and rode away into the sunset to the applause of the crowd.

It was now getting quite late in the evening, and Cecil and Mary excused themselves as Bea was getting—as Ma said—a bit nouty. The Harris group spent the next half hour saying goodnight to Brendan and Maureen, so it was close on one o'clock on the Sunday morning that everyone retired to their homes, lodgings and beds.

27

Interesting Offer

Grandma was feeling quite pleased with herself. She had met Brendan's parents—a bit raucous, she felt. *Henry seemed a nice gentle man, while Alice—a gifted lady on the piano—is rather loud and common. What a night! I did enjoy myself. Hopefully, everything is all right with James. Wilmslow said he would ring the hotel if there was any problem. Yes, that man Henry was very nice. Brendan and Maureen seem devoted to each other. I wonder if there is a way I can make their life easier.* With these thoughts going through her mind, Grandma Walker happened to look at the wall clock.

"Two o'clock?" she exclaimed under her breath. "Haven't been up this late for years." Smiling to herself, she snuggled down under the bed covers.

***

Further down the hotel corridor, Alice and Henry were settling down ready for bed and talking about the evening.

"I think Bren has done all right for himself there, Henry. The girl Maureen is lovely and seems to love him—pity she's a Roman Catholic. The Pauline one seems to be a bit of a snob, her with her chauffeur, but she's all right, I suppose," stated Ma grudgingly. "What do you think, Hen?"

Climbing into the bed alongside Alice, Henry said, "Yes. I agree with you, Alice. I think Bren is on a winner with Maureen. She's attractive and sensible. Pauline is very nice, I thought. You know her husband James is very ill. Seems he's on his last legs."

"Anyway, Hen, I'm going asleep. Come on, give me a goodnight kiss, or, should I say, a good mornin' one. Glad we came over."

***

Everybody had settled down in the hotel. The night watchman was dozing on and off in his little office, picking out the winners at Kempton races, when the phone rang in reception. Looking at the clock on the wall, he exclaimed, "All right, I'm comin'," and muttered his way to the phone. "Blundellsands Hotel here."

"Hello, my good man. My name is Wilmslow, chauffeur and butler employed by Mrs. Pauline Walker. I have some very important news for her. Please put me through to her room immediately."

"Who's that again…Mrs. Walker? She's not goin' to like to be woken at this hour in the mornin'. Do you know what room she's in, mister?"

"Room ten, my good man. Now hurry up, please."

"OK! OK! Keep yer hair on, sir."

After a minute, or so, Grandma answered the phone expecting bad news. "Yes! Hello?"

"Hello, lady. There's a Mr. Williams on the phone for you, do you wanna take it?"

"Do you mean Wilmslow?"

"That's right, lady."

"Put him on quickly."

"Wilmslow here, madam. I am afraid to say the major is declining rapidly. Perhaps I may suggest you come quickly. I shall stay with the major if that is your wish, madam?"

"Yes, Wilmslow, I shall be down promptly. Do tell him I love him and will be as quick as I can."

"Certainly, madam."

Now, where are Maureen and Brendan? Maybe they could take me home. Oh, God, I hope he is all right, thought Grandma to herself as she started to dress. *I remember Maureen said room twelve if I needed her…*

"Maureen dear, wake up, wake up."

"Oh! It's you, Grandma. What's wrong?"

It's your grandfather, dear. Wilmslow says he is…fading fast."

"Bren, wake up. Grandma needs us."

"What's the problem?

Within twenty minutes, both had dressed and were in the car heading into Liverpool through the Mersey Tunnel, and within the hour were drawing up outside the house in Chester. Grandma was out of the car immediately, closely followed by Maureen. Wilmslow met them at the door, dressed immaculately as ever, looking quite distraught.

"Madam, I have called for an ambulance as the major is quite unwell. Hello, Miss Byrne, and hello to you, Mr. Harris. Shall I make a pot of tea before the ambulance arrives?"

"That is an excellent idea, Wilmslow," agreed Brendan as the two women raced up the staircase to the major's bedroom.

"Will sir take milk and sugar, and what shall we prepare for Miss Byrne?" Hearing the doorbell ring, Wilmslow walked briskly to the door and admitted the two ambulance men, each carrying his bag of medical equipment.

"Follow me, gentlemen," instructed Wilmslow as the two men entered the hallway and, followed by Brendan, they hurried into the bedroom to see the two women sitting at the bedside, the major lying on his back.

"Looks like this one's a goner, Bill," suggested one of the ambulance men out of the side of his mouth. "Allow me, ladies, while I take the patient's pulse…

"As we thought. Sorry, ladies and sirs, but I am afraid the poor man is deceased."

"You mean… You mean my husband is dead?"

"Yes, missus," agreed Bill, placing the major's hand back on the bed. "I am afraid there is nothing we can do."

Wilmslow, who had been standing quietly in the background, fully dressed as if it were daytime, stepped forward. "Thank you, gentlemen, for coming so quickly. Perhaps before you go, you might care for a small refreshment?"

"Yep, Bill?" Getting the nod of agreement from the other ambulance man, he said, "OK, mister, that would be great. A cup of coffee would go down well." Then, turning to Grandma, he said, "Sorry, lady. I suggest your next step is—"

"That's all right, my good man. We shall call a doctor," interrupted Wilmslow. "Now, everybody, may I suggest we all leave madam with the major?"

"Maureen, please can you stay?" pleaded Grandma, stretching her hand out.

"Of course, Grandma," agreed Maureen, glancing at Brendan who nodded his approval.

Brendan followed the others from the room, leaving the two women comforting each other. After the two ambulance men had drunk their coffee, they went on their next call, and Brendan had a talk with Wilmslow.

Aware of Wilmslow's position, and standing in the Walker household, he was careful to ask Wilmslow his opinion on the next steps to take.

"Don't you worry, sir. I shall take care of everything," was the positive reply from Wilmslow, much to Brendan's relief.

"Brendan?" called Maureen as she and Grandma came down the stairs. "I'm going to stay with Grandma for the day. Will you tell your family what's happened and tell them I'd better stay with here?"

"I understand, Mo. I had better get back to Liverpool. They'll all be up in a couple of hours wondering where we've got to. Grandma, I am so very, very sorry about Granddad. I would have loved to have known him better."

"It is such a shame, Brendan. He would have loved to know you both. I thank God I have met you and lovely Maureen. Oh! Here I go, crying again." Taking a deep breath, she regained her composure. "What about you having a bit of breakfast, Brendan? It's a long drive back, and you've had little sleep. Would you mind, Wilmslow?"

"Not at all, madam. Would sir like an Irish breakfast?" Wilmslow asked with what looked like the suspicion of a smile. "What about you, madam, and Miss Byrne?"

Brendan and Maureen both agreed to a breakfast, but Grandma decided a slice of toast and a coffee would be enough.

"I'll ring the Blundellsands, if it's all right to use your phone, Grandma, and ask them to pass a message to my parents."

"Of course, Brendan. There's no need to ask."

After a short silence, Brendan, concerned about his parents and his and Maureen's absence suggested, "Maureen, Grandma… My parents are going to be very disappointed if they don't see you again before they return to Ireland, Mo. Could I ask you to change your mind and come with me to Liverpool to say goodbye? I'll get you back here by eleven o'clock."

"Of course, Brendan," said Grandma. "Of course. They have come a long way to see you, Maureen. Do go back and say your goodbyes to lovely Henry and Alice. I would go myself, but there will be so much to do."

"Are you sure, Grandma?" asked Maureen, torn between the responsibility of caring for her grandmother and not wishing to disappoint Brendan.

Brendan, understanding Maureen's position, interrupted before Grandma answered. Looking at his watch, he said, "It's coming up to seven o'clock. I'm just thinking we have had no sleep: it's about fifty miles to the hotel. I'll ring them at eight and tell Ma what's happened and that we will visit them soon. I'm sure they will understand."

"Thanks, Bren," a relieved Maureen replied, giving him a hug. "Now, let's go and have some breakfast. What do you say, Grandma?" asked Maureen, trying to relieve the tension.

"Thank you, Maureen and Brendan. I'm so glad you're staying. I know Wilmslow will do all that is required. Perhaps you could have a word with him, Brendan, please."

***

"Hello, Ma."

"Hello, Brendan," replied the sleepy voice of his mother. "Why, in the name of God, are you ringing? What's happened? Where are you?"

"Sorry, Ma, but earlier this morning, we got a call from Chester that Maureen's grandfather had died."

"Yes, Pauline said he wasn't very well."

"Look, Ma, will you apologise to Pop and the others? I don't think we'll be able to get up to Liverpool before you fly back to Dublin."

"But Brendan, we've come all this way to see you and Maureen. Can the pair of you not make it? We didn't have time to have a chat."

"I know, Ma, same here. But Chester is some fifty miles from the hotel, and neither of us have had any sleep. Look, when things have settled down here, we'll both get over to you for a weekend."

"OK, Brendan, I know what you mean. What a shame. Any chance of a quick word with Maureen and maybe Pauline?"

Brendan, looking towards the two women sitting on the settee across the room, got a nod from Maureen and a negative shake of her head from Grandma.

"Here's Maureen, Ma. Grandma has gone to get her head down."

"Hello, Mrs. Alice Harris, the new Mrs. Maureen Harris here," said Mo with a bit if a laugh in her voice. "Yes, a great shock... I'll tell Grandma... We'll do our best to get over before the end of the year... Yes, lovely meeting you both and Brendan's brothers. Look, I'll give you back to Brendan and thank you so much for coming over. It is nice to be part of such a lovely family. Now, here's Bren. Goodbye...Ma."

"She is very nice, Bren. Make sure you come to see us soon. Do give us a ring during the week. Bye-bye to you both and please tell Pauline, Pop and I are so sorry to hear the sad news, goodbye again."

"Grandma, would it be all right if I go and have a word with Wilmslow that we may work together, as I believe it's going to be a busy day?"

A startled grandma, half asleep, raised her hand in acceptance and started to weep silently. Maureen comforted her and also nodded her agreement to Brendan's offer.

Brendan's eye was caught by Wilmslow, standing in the doorway, and he accompanied him into the kitchen.

"Wilmslow, you may have heard my suggestion to Mrs. Walker that we could work together to make this day as painless as possible for her. I am open to your suggestions wherever you think I am needed."

"Yes, Mr. Harris, thank you for the offer. I agree it is paramount we make today as relaxed as possible for Madam. I have called the doctor to register the major's death and expect him within the hour."

"Perhaps I may call Mr. Hardy, Mrs. Walker's brother, to inform him. Are there any other close relatives?"

And so the day progressed: the doctor called, pronounced the major dead from natural causes, and the undertaker arrived to take the body away.

The few people contacted called to offer their sympathies, led by Norman Hardy—Grandma's brother, and his wife Joyce. In conversation with Norman, Brendan discovered he owned a successful firm of investment and insurance brokers in Chester and was interested to hear about Maureen's present position with Mitchells in Southport.

Norman then said he was financial adviser for the family, and he and Pauline were executors to the will.

"Shortly after the funeral, the will will be read and we must have a family meeting to discuss the future. You and Maureen are very much part of the family, Brendan. Such a pity James was unable to appreciate he had such a lovely granddaughter." Suddenly changing his tone of voice, Norman asked, "Did you ever think of a career change?"

Taken somewhat by surprise with the question, Brendan's immediate thought was, *Is he offering me a job?* He replied, "Interesting that you ask, Norman. With Maureen's involvement with Mitchell Insurance, and her very favourable comments about financial services as a career, I am seriously considering a change."

"Glad to hear, Brendan. My company is expanding and we are looking for suitable management potential."

"Count me in, Norman, but you do know I live in Formby?"

"Taken into account, Brendan. Now, do you think Maureen would be interested in joining us?"

"Well, I'm sure she would be interested, but that, of course, will be up to her. Before we go any further, please do give me your company's name and address that I may do some research before we meet."

"My card, Mr. Harris," smiled Norman, taking out his business card from his inside pocket.

"And mine, Mr. Hardy," reciprocated Brendan, passing his business card with a smile, very conscious of the solemn atmosphere and not wishing to make it too obvious they were taking advantage of the sad moment. "Perhaps, Norman, I should call you after the funeral."

"Of course, Brendan, a sad day. Quite a man, was Major James Walker. Worked in the background in the Falklands. Became very much involved in the problems in the North of Ireland. He is a sad loss to the country, though I found him a difficult man to associate with. His standards were always related to the army standards. Whenever we met, I felt I had to stand to attention." Norman laughed behind his hand. "Look, there's Maureen beckoning to you. Now, don't forget, Brendan, do call me in a week or so."

"Shall do, Norman. Glad to meet you again. Yes, Mo, coming." Brendan acknowledged her beckoning hand.

Feeling quite elated, he was eager to discover more as he examined the business card. "Hardy Financial Services Investments and Pensions. Norman Hardy Managing Director. Company founded in 1948. *Sounds like a strong company—wonder what their expansion plans are?* "Good morning again, Grandma. Just talking to Norman, a very nice chap."

"Yes, Brendan, Norman and I are quite close. He has been a tremendous help to me over the past few difficult years. Now, I'm going to ask you a great favour, Brendan. I have spoken with Maureen and wish to put the following proposition to you both. I am getting older now, and I'm quite frightened of the future. Losing poor James has been quite a shock. Please excuse me…" Grandma took a silk handkerchief from her sleeve, dabbed her eyes and blew her nose.

"Bren, Grandma has asked me to stay over the week with her—at least until the funeral is over. What do you think?"

Taken aback by this request, Brendan's immediate reaction was to disagree. They were only just married and had a lot of planning to work on, and he didn't fancy living in the house on his own for the next week. Also, what about her job with Mitchell? He would understandably be pretty annoyed. However, the other major point was the pair of them were now getting very involved with the Walkers and could lose their independence.

"I think what is most important, Mo, is what do you think?"

"Do you mind, Grandma, if Bren and I go into another room and talk about this. We both want to help you where we can. Do you mind?" Maureen asked, taking Brendan's arm.

"Of course, Maureen. Come back to me as soon as you can." Grandma touched both of them with her hand.

"If you do what Grandma wants, Mo, I could see the end of your job with Mitchell."

"She needs me, Bren. To hell with Mitchell. It's only for a week."

"Is it, Mo?"

"What do you mean?"

"In a week's time, we're going to be in the same position. Grandma won't want to be on her own and may ask you to stay for another week. It would become hard to say no. The other very important thing is money. We've stretched ourselves to the limit over the past few weeks, and your salary with Mitchell is important."

"Oh, Bren, what do we do? I want to help Grandma all I can, and I know we're short of money. I was beginning to enjoy myself with Mitchell. I do like working in the finance business."

"I know you do, Mo, and I have a proposition to put to you."

"Go on, Bren. I'm all ears—must get my hair done."

"Another day, Mo," laughed Brendan and gave Maureen a summary of Norman's chat with him.

"That sounds exciting, Bren. Would that mean moving down to Chester?"

"I have no idea, but let's play it cautiously. I'll make some enquiries about his business. I suppose you had better stay with Grandma, at least for a few days. I'm thinking about Ma and the others—they've come all the way to see us. What's the time? Look, it's ten o'clock—we could be up to the hotel by twelve, have a quick lunch with the family and you could pick your car up from Formby and be back here by three o'clock."

"Brendan, my love. I…" She hesitated. "Yes, Bren, let's get going now. I'll tell Grandma I'll be back mid-afternoon. What time does their plane leave?"

"Three o'clock—they have to be at the airport by two."

"That doesn't give much time. It'll take at least an hour to get to the hotel. What if we meet them at the airport, say half an hour before check-in time. Give us enough time to say our goodbyes and then nip across to Formby to pick up my car."

"There's an awful lot of driving there, Mo. Go have a word with Grandma and say you've got to see off my family and you'll be back to Chester first thing on Monday morning. Don't forget, we've got a room booked for the night at the Blundellsands Hotel. I'm sure she will understand, fingers crossed."

"Leave it to me, Bren. I'll come with you to the airport, stay in the hotel for the night and tomorrow morning pick up my car and drop in to Mitchell to tell him what's happening. He'll probably dismiss me. Perhaps Great-Uncle Norman might come up with a winner."

"Great, Mo. I'll ring Ma now. Gotta keep everybody happy. Good luck with Grandma."

***

"Right, Speke Airport, here we come."

It was with some relief the newly married couple had bid their goodbyes to their new relations. Grandma took it very well and wished them all the best. Ma said they would make a point of being at the airport at one-thirty.

""I did feel a bit guilty leaving Grandma, Bren," Maureen admitted, "but I do want to make a good impression with your family, and I wanted a bit more of life together, as we are newlyweds, after all. You'll be careful with me, as I am very delicate?"

"Of course, my little piece of delicate porcelain. I shall treat you with care and feed you well, only if you produce me a pair of twins."

"Isn't a pair of two a total of four, my cut of slender sirloin steak."

"Of course, my meaty hamburger with onions. I will rephrase that. Only if you produce twins. Stop giggling, Mo, you'll have me off the road. Look, we're coming to the Runcorn Bridge again. We'll soon be there. Wish we were flying off to somewhere exotic—Naples or Venice or Hawaii, perhaps. I have a cousin there who is a hula-hula dancer."

"That would be nice. Maybe when we make our first million." After a short silence, while both considered the glory of earning a million pounds, Maureen asked, "What do you think Uncle Norman has up his sleeve, Bren?"

"He's a general insurance broker, Mo, sells cover for cars and businesses. From what we have found from Mitchell Insurance, there is a lot of money to be made in life insurance and pensions. Perhaps he's looking to expand into that side of the business."

"Before we meet Uncle Norman next, let's put together a plan based on his client base and educate ourselves on pensions and life insurance, show him we know what we're talking about. Oh!" exclaimed Maureen, rubbing her hands together. "I am looking forward to the future."

"Before we make any decisions, Mo, tell me what you think of the future with Grandma Walker?"

"That's the million-dollar question, Bren. This is what I think: I might have it all wrong, but Grandma is now on her own in a huge house, worth many thousands. She seems well off. No doubt Granddad was insured. Well, she wants my company but she knows we come as a pair. Now, listen to this, Bren. I may have it all wrong. Grandma wants us to live with her, and to encourage us, she has suggested to Norman he could have us work for him, as fortunately, we are involved in selling and insurance. Now, what do you think of that?"

"I was thinking on similar lines, Mo. Look, we're just coming to the airport. Let's talk about it when we're back at the hotel...Mrs. Harris. I'd nearly forgotten we're a married couple now, and I am sure looking forward to the years ahead."

After parking the car, they walked to the entrance lounge to find the Irish group all seated around a table groaning under plates of sandwiches, sausage rolls and mugs of tea.

"Here they are," called Jono. "Make room for the married couple." He squeezed down on the settee-style seat. "There's room for you there, Maureen, beside Ma and Pop."

"Sorry all," Brendan said as he sat down beside Jono. "As you know, Maureen's granddad died early this morning, and we felt we should go down to Chester to help her grandma. I hope you enjoyed last night, and thanks, Ma, for the entertainment. Thanks to all of you for coming over. We really appreciate it."

"I second that, everybody," agreed Maureen. "A great night."

"You've both gotta come over for Christmas. What do you say?" asked Ma. "We can have a party, or maybe the New Year. Now, help yourselves to a sandwich or two. Any tea left in the pot, Hen?"

For the next twenty minutes until their flight was called, Ma and Pop got to know a bit more about Maureen, and it was hugs and kisses all round as they left through the departure gate.

"Right, next step, Bren—out to Formby, pick up my car. It's all go, isn't it?"

"Yep, Mo. it's about twenty miles to Formby, another eight to Crosby, and then we can relax and start our honeymoon. You'd better ring, find out how she is, then tomorrow morning…"

"Don't remind me, Bren. I've got to tell Mitchell I won't be around for a couple of weeks, or maybe forever, if Norman comes up with an offer."

After another hour or so of driving, when they pulled into The Close, they were dismayed to see the front lawn was overgrown and there was a mountain of letters and advertising leaflets in the porch. The estate agent's 'Sold' notice was still standing. The whole place looked unkempt and deserted.

Fortunately, the Ford Anglia was still in the garage and started after a deal of coaxing. The boxes of Sabre razor blades were also intact. Brendan and Maureen decided to stay, have a look around and, before they left, call in to a few of the neighbours to apologise for the untidy appearance of the house.

Standing in the small porch with their arms around each other, they looked at the bald staircase in dismay. Upstairs was not much better with uncarpeted floors and empty wardrobes. The double bed looked most uninviting. Downstairs, their voices echoed in the main room with its one ancient settee in the middle of the floor facing a large gas fire in the grate. The kitchen still smelt of fried bacon, the back garden was as wild as the front, and some of the latticed fence had fallen over. Looking over the fence, all that could be seen were the backs of houses and back gardens stretching to the left and right.

Brian and Dot, a young couple with a squalling baby, from next door, were very understanding and even offered to cut the grass and take down the agent's sign. There was nobody in the house on the other side. Brendan went over the road to speak with a man, somewhat older than himself, who was cutting the grass with a motor mower—a machine almost as big as the house. He was not so friendly and complained about the dandelions carpeting their lawn and hoped Brendan was going to cut then down before they went to seed. Finishing off his tirade with a final flourish as he revved his motor mower, he muttered, "You modern-day youngsters have no idea of responsibility. Owning a house an' you're not even out of nappies."

"Careful, old man, or you might wet yourself," shouted Brendan over the roar of the mower, giving the driver a friendly wave. "Let's get going, Mo. Time is passing: must get back in time for a splash-up meal at the hotel, look through the post and…get to bed early."

"Yes, let's, Bren. Though, wait a minute—I'll give Grandma a ring first and find out how things are. Hope the phone works. You did tell them to reconnect?" she asked, looking doubtfully at Brendan.

"Go on, try it, Mo. I did tell the Post Office.

"Well done, Bren, there is a dialling tone. Now, where's her number?"

"Hello, Maureen Harris, here. Oh, hello, Norman. How are things? Is Grandma keeping well?... Could I have a word with her?... Gone to bed. Please tell her I shall be down to see her tomorrow about twelve and stay until the funeral... Next Thursday at eleven o'clock, you say... Yes, it has been lovely meeting you and Joyce... Goodbye, Norman, I'll put Brendan on—Norman would like a word with you." She handed the phone to Brendan.

"Hello, Norman, what can I do for you?... Yes, I am still very interested... Certainly... Your house for dinner... Both of us. Good... seven o'clock. That's fine, see you then, goodbye, Norman." Replacing the receiver, Brendan turned to Maureen. "It's looking good, Mo."

"Don't be building up your hopes, Bren. It might all come to nothing," a cautious Maureen warned. "The bill from the hotel will leave us with £100 in the bank. I'll put the facts to Mitchell tomorrow morning. I'll ring him at nine, make sure he's in, and you get back here and get working with Sabre."

"Let's get going, Mo. Forget about old misery across the road—he can come over and have fun chopping the dandelion heads off." Brendan caught sight of Brian, from next door, trundling his lawnmower towards their front garden.

"Brian, how very good of you," Brendan said as he and Maureen went to their cars. "I'll unlock the back gate—you could drop the clippings and dandelions in the back. And again, our many thanks to you and Dot. I'll be back tomorrow to live here. Will give you a call. Goodbye, Brian, and thanks again."

"That's OK, Brendan. What are neighbours for but to help each other?"

With a feeling that all was right in the world when somebody could be as generous as their neighbour, Brendan and Maureen drove over to the hotel in their respective cars, where Brendan spent most of the evening preparing his calls for the following week. He was not too enamoured with the prospect of endeavouring to encourage the many retailers in the North West, from chemist shops to newsagents, to display Sabre razor blade units and advertising stickers. However, come nine o'clock in the evening, after a satisfying meal, they repaired to their room, and Brendan put Sabre razor blades to bed.

28

The Funeral

"As you say, Brendan…whatever…we've got each other. I'll work out something with Mitchell now…that's what I was waiting for, a hug and a kiss," agreed Maureen as they put their arms around each other and shared a long and satisfying kiss.

That morning, Brendan called upon the four chemists in Formby, two men's hairdressers and three small self-service shops and was successful in five of the calls. He installed a display pillar with twenty-five packs of blades and a sticker in the doorway in three of the chemists and one of the hairdressers. He called in to an insurance broker and picked up a few glossy brochures on pensions and investment to be prepared in even a little way to impress Norman when they met later in the week.

The afternoon was spent at three wholesalers negotiating deals, so it was a very satisfied Brendan Harris who returned to the house in Formby that evening, delighted to find the grass cut both front and rear. He immediately went next door to thank Brian and Dot.

The news from Maureen was as expected. Mitchell, whilst he understood her problem, dismissed her but offered the opportunity to reapply for the post when her family problems had resolved themselves.

In their telephone conversation, Maureen told Brendan about the stream of visitors calling to offer their sympathies to Grandma. "Dozens of them, or well," she said, "maybe ten." She then continued with the quite surprising news that Grandma wanted them both to come and live with her in Chester. "She's offering us our own rent-free part of the house, and were Norman to agree to employ us in whatever situation determined, she would finance us with a loan on a competitive rate of interest if we wanted one."

"God, Mo! How amazing. Sounds too good to be true. There's a catch somewhere. How possessive would Grandma become? Is Wilmslow staying? It all depends on what Norman has to offer."

"There's also a change to the meal on Thursday evening at Norman's. Grandma is coming."

"They're ganging up on us, Mo. We've got to be careful. Roll on Thursday. What time shall I get to the house? Lucky my suit is dark—I'll only have to buy a black tie. What about you, Mo? Have you any suitable clothing?"

"Hold on a minute, Bren. Be here before ten and definitely get a black tie. Your business suit will be fine. Grandma and I are going out tomorrow to tog me out. The point you mentioned—ganging up on us—I'm enjoying myself, but I know what you mean. Let's be cautious and talk things over at the weekend."

"OK, Mo. Who would have thought we would be in such a position. See you Thursday. Bye, love."

Over the next two days, Brendan worked from the house in Formby and opened up a number of new accounts, but his heart and soul were not in it. He kept speculating what Norman was thinking about. Hoping to impress Norman, he spent a lot of time reading about pensions, investments and mortgages and bought the *Financial Times*—the pink newspaper devoted to financial matters.

He had rung his immediate boss in Sabre, Kenneth Shanks, to tell him he would be unable to work the Thursday due to the funeral in Chester. Shanks was somewhat annoyed and told Brendan he was to report to him at the hotel on the M62 close to Manchester the following Friday at ten-thirty to discuss his position.

Well, just keep my fingers crossed Sabre accepts my mitigating reasons and looks at my figures. Most importantly keep up a good front with Norman to show him the Brendan Harris team are what his company needs.

Thursday morning arrived. Brendan had had a poor night's sleep worrying about his position with Sabre and hoping he was ready to meet Norman. With his head full of information about pensions and life insurance, the present state of the stock market, and with knowledge about mortgages, he felt he was ready to impress. So, after a good breakfast, he set off in the sunlight to find what the future had in store for him and Maureen.

"Good morning, Brendan," Grandma welcomed. She was dressed in an expensive back dress, black shoes and a severe black hat with a white carnation. James had been proud of his flower garden. "Would both of you like to come with me in the limousine? The funeral director has arranged everything."

"Yes, we'd like that," agreed Brendan, taking Maureen's hand and leading her down to the six-seater limo. The hearse, with the coffin on display with white lilies arranged on the lid, had silently pulled up at the entrance to the house.

"Oh, there you are, Norman, Joyce. Come along, we are in the first limo," Grandma ordered, full of nervous energy. "The other two have some close friends and distant relatives."

"All right, Pauline, calm down," Norman said gently. "It's going to be a long day. Hello, Brendan, Maureen." He nodded to them. "All right for tonight?"

Both acknowledged Norman's question with a smile as they all settled down in the luxury of the limousine with the hearse ahead of them. Wilmslow was seated in the front passenger seat. The hearse pulled away from the kerb with the three limos silently following their leader alongside the River Dee, heading to Christ Church in Gloucester Street, Chester.

"What's this?" asked Brendan. "The police have closed the road?"

"Should have told you, Brendan," answered Norman. "The army has granted a twenty-one-gun salute in the major's honour. There will be top brass in the church; also, I believe, the MP will attend. Major James Walker was very well known and respected."

The three cars were allowed inside the barrier and parked a short way from the church. There was a group of soldiers all from the major's regiment, the Cheshire Fusiliers, gathered before the church entrance. A uniformed officer came down to Grandma, saluted and requested all close family to stand behind the coffin, now draped with the Union Jack. Whilst the officer was arranging the family, another was ordering the soldiers to line up facing each other to form a corridor. The coffin, carried by six soldiers, was taken down this corridor of saluting soldiers, followed by the immediate family.

Brendan and Maureen with Grandma and other close relatives followed the coffin into the church and took their seats in the reserved aisles. This was all done to the sound of the organist playing the regimental march. Then, after a short silence whilst all were seated, the vicar conducted the service.

Norman spoke the eulogy in which he emphasised the very impressive and important role Major James Walker had conducted in his life in the army and politics. The MP for Chester spoke about the work the major had done for the community after his retirement. At the end of the service, all left the church again to the sound of the organist playing the regimental march.

What a man, thought Brendan. For his life to end as it had seemed so unfair.

At the cemetery, whilst all listened to the vicar go though the service, seven soldiers lined up and fired three volleys from rifles as the coffin was lowered into the grave. Grandma had bravely held back her emotions throughout the service but broke down weeping and was consoled by Norman's wife Joyce, and Maureen.

On their return to the house, Wilmslow, who had liaised with the funeral director to provide the caterers, hurried inside to ensure light food and drinks were set out as he expected, and was there to welcome Grandma and party.

After everybody had freshened up, Grandma, holding onto Maureen's arm, welcomed and thanked everybody and introduced Maureen, her long-lost granddaughter. Brendan stayed in the background, getting the odd glance from Maureen with raised eyebrow and a trace of a smile that seemed to say, *Bear with me, I'll be with you shortly. This is Grandma's day.*

By five o'clock, everyone had conveyed their sympathies to Grandma, had their choice of drink from tea to whiskey, their cucumber sandwich and their chat with those whom they hadn't seen since the last funeral.

After the caterers had cleared away, Brendan and Maureen got together in Grandma's room to have a rest and prepare for the evening.

"I've given Wilmslow the evening off. He's been working long hours over the past weeks," said Grandma. "Norman's house is only about a mile along the Dee. Would you care to take us, Brendan?"

"I'd love to, Grandma, but I have an important appointment in Liverpool tomorrow morning and want to get back to Formby reasonably early tonight. What about using your car, Mo?"

Brendan knew he had to get back to Formby; he had the feeling that Shanks the sales manager was going to do a spot check on him.

29

Accept Offer

As with the building they had just left, Norman and Joyce lived in an impressive property on the riverbank. The short, tree-lined driveway led to the front door of an imposing double-fronted house with Virginia creeper covering the walls. Grandma, Maureen and Brendan were greeted at the doorway by Wilmslow's double—another butler with a dignified manner, formally dressed in butler uniform—who escorted them into the drawing room. "I shall tell madam and sir you have arrived, ladies and sir. Perhaps you would care for a drink?"

"Gin sling, please, Brabinger," said Grandma, looking across to Maureen.

"A glass of orange juice will be fine for me."

"And you, Brendan?" Grandma prompted.

Deciding it was best to keep a clear head for the evening, and aware of the long drive ahead afterwards, Brendan replied, "The same for me, please. An orange juice will do fine."

The butler bowed and left.

"What a lovely room," Maureen said, turning on the spot to take it in. "And look at the piano. Reminds me of your ma, Brendan. Wasn't she good, Grandma?"

"Yes, that was quite a night, Maureen. Alice could certainly make a lot of tuneful noise from the one in the hotel." Grandma walked across the carpeted floor to pat the lid of the gleaming expensive grand piano. "This is one of the latest—a Baldwin grand with a Steinway stool to complete the picture. We must get Joyce to play a piece this evening."

"That's something to look forward to," agreed Maureen. "What do you say, Bren?"

Brendan—thinking the evening looked as if it was going to be a long one, and also a bit put off by the belittling of his mother's piano-playing ability—nonetheless thought he had better play his allotted place in the performance.

"Yes, Grandma, I do look forward to hearing her play. What is her repertoire, by the way?"

Before Grandma could answer, Norman and Joyce made their entrance into the drawing room, both dressed in light evening clothes. Norman was wearing a grey smoking jacket over a pair of grey slacks whilst Joyce was dressed in an off-the-shoulder three-quarter-length cream dress.

Norman, moving smoothly and silently over the Axminster, gave Grandma the customary peck on the cheek, as did Joyce, before both turned to the slightly out of place couple. In his somewhat worn grey business suit, Brendan felt underdressed, though Maureen, in her green summer dress, looked very fetching and youthful.

"And what do we have here, Pauline? Is it the future of the old firm? I do hope so. Welcome to our humble abode, Brendan and Maureen." Norman shook Brendan's hand and kissed Maureen. Joyce, in a more subdued tone, followed with a greeting to Maureen and peck on the cheek, with a welcoming smile and gentle hug for Brendan.

Taking the initiative but feeling a mite self-conscious, Brendan took Maureen's hand and raised his free hand for silence. "Joyce, Norman, and especially you, Grandma…my wife—" he looked affectionately at Maureen "—my lovely wife and I, through great fortune, have been accepted into your family. It is very hard to believe that only a few months ago, we—that is, Maureen and I—did not even know each other.

"However, fate was so kind and introduced to us the wonderful matter of love and understanding. We were planning our future—had even thought of emigrating to Australia—I had been tentatively offered a post in Melbourne—but fate proceeded with its many tempting offers.

"So, we decided to get married and buy a small house, and strive to succeed in our chosen professions, when fate intervened again, and it was discovered that Maureen was the daughter of your son—" Brendan looked to Grandma "—Captain Rupert Walker. This gave Maureen the wonderful chance to be part of a family. I thank you, Grandma, for your welcome reception, and you, Norman and Joyce, for offering the opportunity for both of us to join your family business."

Norman glanced to Joyce, who smiled, nodding in agreement. "Thank you, Brendan, and you, Maureen," Norman said. "Joyce and I—and, of course, your grandma—are delighted that we may consider expansion of the firm and keep…it within the family." Norman stopped speaking and smiled at Grandma, who returned the smile with delight. "Now, there is a lot to be considered—let us continue over dinner…"

***

After reminiscences about the major and the striking man he had been, the conversation turned to the future and the proposed expansion of Hardy Financial Services. Firstly, Norman outlined his ambitions.

"My proposal is to open a life and pensions company to run alongside the general insurance business under the group title of Hardy Financial Services or HFS. The life company—let's call it Hardy Life for the moment—will use the client base provided by HFS. My proposal is that Maureen comes on the board of HFS to run the admin and business side of HL and Brendan runs the sales side. What are your thoughts on that, Maureen, Brendan?"

Maureen looked at Brendan to see what he thought, as it would be a lower-status role for him.

"I'll go along with that, Norman," Brendan agreed.

Everyone was watching Maureen, as it all depended on her decision.

"I agree, too," Maureen said.

The sense of relief was apparent all around the table.

To Brendan, this was the answer to his dissatisfaction with his present occupation with Sabre, although there were numerous unanswered questions.

To Maureen, it was obvious that there was a lot of Grandma's will behind the offer—could Maureen cope with such an exalted position as being on the board of a company?

To Grandma, this could be the answer to the future. She was keen to grant the couple use of the self-contained guest rooms in her large home rather than sell up and move into a smaller property.

Norman, aware of the young couple's lack of business experience but encouraged by their attitude, felt that, with support, they could succeed. "Phew!" he said. "Well, that's very satisfactory. Now, Joyce and I are directors of HFS. We have already created the subsidiary company, Hardy Life Investment and Pensions—or Hardy LIP—and the general insurance arm, Hardy's General Insurance—HGI. We can get the new company up and running within the month. One final thought, before we start on the dessert: finance. You will both be self-employed and live on your earnings in the company. As there will be some time before you earn anything, HFS will advance Hardy LIP £5,000, to be repaid over time."

To Brendan's ears, this was marvellous news. Five thousand pounds was a small fortune…but where would they live? He realised they would need to sell the house in Formby and move to Chester, and, of course, as she had planned, Grandma had the answer.

"Maureen, Brendan," she said with a great deal of satisfaction in her voice. "I am more than willing to let you have the self-contained guest section as living accommodation, rent free."

In spite of Brendan's misgivings, it would certainly suit in the short term, and both immediately jumped at the offer.

Brendan raised his glass, and all drank to the success of the venture. Norman, grinning mightily, rose from his chair with his hand outstretched. He approached the seated Brendan, who reciprocated by rising from his chair to meet Norman, and they shook hands on the deal. Everyone else followed suit, shaking hands and hugging each other.

***

Later that evening, after a relaxing coffee, Brendan explained he had to return to Formby as he was meeting the management of Sabre Sword Edge first thing in the morning.

"I shall feel quite guilty giving in my notice so soon after joining the company. You asked, Norman, how soon I could start work on Hardy LIP. Well, the agreement with Sabre is a month's notice either side, but I am aware the company generally gives a month's salary and dismisses the employee immediately. Hopefully, that's what will be offered."

"What about you, Maureen?" asked Norman.

"I can start whenever required, Norman. However, as this is a big, big career change for us both, is it all right if we have some time together to talk about yours and—" she smiled at Joyce "—Joyce's offer."

"Of course, of course, Maureen," replied Norman and Joyce in unison, laughing together. "If there are any problems, we could probably resolve them before you leave."

"Certainly, Norman, Joyce—perhaps we could have a few moments on our own?"

"Yes, of course. It's only eight o'clock. Do you want to go into the morning room—Oh! I forgot to mention, Brendan. As transport might be one of your problems, we could let you use the Morris. It's been in the garage for the past year. It's an old Morris Oxford—we've had it for a few years."

Brendan sat back in relief. "That's very good of you, Norman. I may need transport after my meeting with Sabre tomorrow."

"Why not stay with us and leave early in the morning?" Grandma suggested. "What do you say?"

"I'm all for it, Grandma. It's been an exciting day today and, I must admit, I wasn't looking forward to the drive tonight. Thank you. I'll have a glass of that wine you offered earlier, if you don't mind, Norman…"

***

"Mo, I can't really believe what is being offered," said Brendan as he and Mo settled down in the morning room with their drinks. "A car, a business, capital to start the business, free accommodation—what's the catch?"

"Apart from getting two bright ambitious youngsters?" Mo replied with a bashful smile. "If we succeed, it means the continuation of the

Hardy Company. It also seems there is one underlying condition, husband dear, and that is we are expected to live with Grandma."

"Yep, I gathered that, Mo. We would have to lay down some rules."

"We have our own rooms and our own keys," Maureen pointed out.

"And the £5,000 advance—wow! It will have to be used initially as income. What would be the conditions? Will the parent company want a cut on profits?"

"Let's make out a quick business plan for the first year, Bren. Provided its realistic, I think Norman will accept it. Fingers crossed."

The next ten minutes were spent putting together the semblance of a business plan using Maureen's knowledge of the commissions offered by insurance companies to insurance advisers.

With everything agreed in principle, the rest of the evening was spent with Grandma talking about the many adventures she and the major had had over the years. Brendan told a few of his funny stories, and Norman gave a bit of a lecture on the success of the company.

Staggering slightly, Brendan and Maureen walked back to Grandma's house, and after a very comfortable night, Brendan was awakened by Wilmslow at six the next morning.

Maybe I'll get a manservant like Wilmslow one day, he thought as he tucked into his Irish breakfast.

30

Leave Sabre Sword Edge

After a two-hour drive, Brendan arrived back at the house in Formby to find a bundle of post with one from the NHS bringing forward his consultation on his wonky eyesight to Thursday of the following week.

He wasn't sure what to do—did he have to go to Manchester just to give his notice? He decided to give Ken Shanks a call and say he was resigning from Sabre.

"Good morning, Ken. Brendan Harris."

"Yes, Brendan." Ken sounded surprised.

"I'm offering my notice to quit Sabre…"

"Not surprised, Brendan. Whilst your sales were acceptable, your commitment to the company required some correction," Ken answered with a resigned tone in his voice. "Your notice is accepted, Brendan. Can you drop the car over to my house?"

"Could do, Ken. I take it you don't want me to work my notice?"

"No, Brendan, it's company policy to pay you in lieu. Actually, can you hang on at your home? I'll arrange to have your car collected with your stock of blades and calling cards."

"Certainly, Ken. By the way, I sent my resignation letter to personnel with a copy to you."

"Thanks. I'll come back to you within the hour, Brendan, with the time."

Putting the phone down with some satisfaction, Brendan sat back on the settee to collect his thoughts. *Must call Maureen to tell her the good news and ask her to come up to bring me back to Chester. Hope Norman has insured the Morris… Now, who were the estate agents we bought the house through? Wonder how soon we can move into Grandma's? It's all go, but everything's finally falling into place. Wonder when the hitch happens?*

Within the hour, Ken called back with the arrangements. Maureen agreed to drive up from Chester to collect Brendan and take him back to the house. As there were a few hours before the car would be collected, Brendan called in to the estate agent in Southport to have them put the house up for sale.

***

"Grandma, that was a lovely meal, and thank you, Wilmslow, for preparing the guest rooms for us."

"You're welcome, sir," replied the manservant as he poured out the chosen wine. "The Morris is also ready to be used. I have had the local garage prepare it for you, sir. The car keys are in your rooms, along with the insurance—a cover note, I believe."

"Thank you, Wilmslow," Grandma said. "We are all very grateful to you, aren't we, Maureen?" She was delighted to find her plans had born fruit. Maureen was coming to live with her, with her husband—the big lad with the eye patch.

"Yes, Wilmslow, we both would like to thank you," said Maureen, giving Wilmslow a grateful smile.

Later that evening, the three of them went for a drive in the Morris Oxford: a staid, black, four-door, heavy, well-made car with a powerful engine. It had been the major's car, and it brought back memories for Grandma.

A respectable car, suitable for a gentleman to drive, thought Brendan as they drove out into the country. *Not as sleek as the Cortina...*

***

"Mo, what do you think?" asked Brendan as he relaxed in the double bed with his arm around Maureen.

"I feel like the cat that got the cream—do you hear me purring? Grandma is so generous, and Norman is putting a lot of faith in both of us to run the life and pensions business. I'm a bit scared about next week, when we go to Norman's office to meet the staff and tell Norman how we're going to run the business. Still, we've got the weekend to prepare. Now, give me a kiss and let's have a go at making those twins you married me for."

***

After breakfast with grandma, they excused themselves, telling her they had a lot of preparation to do for the meeting with Norman.

"Right, Bren, we have all these magazines and textbooks about insurance and mortgages and pensions—where do we begin?" Maureen looked at the mound of sales literature on the table.

"Well, Mo, what do we know about insurance and mortgages for a start?"

For the next half hour, they pored over the different types of mortgage-related life insurances and briefly looked at the different pension plans on the market.

"There are two sorts, Bren: company pensions and pensions for the self-employed. There's a lot of reading and study ahead of us. At this stage, we'll just read up about the insurance plans that we will be expected to advise on. Oh, God, Bren, have we taken on more than we can chew?"

Over lunch, Grandma surprised the two of them by saying, "Maureen, Brendan, I am very much aware you are quite short of money, so I make the following offer. For the next six months, I will finance your living costs. During that time, we will also see if we can live together. I do so want it to work. Do you agree?"

"Grandma," said Maureen glancing at Brendan, "that is quite wonderful, and we will, of course, pay you back when the six months end. By that time, we should be making lots of lovely money."

"Of course, my love," answered Grandma. "We'll work something out then, but the most important thing is that you make a success of Norman's offer. I know there will be a lot of hard work, successes and disappointments, but I am certain the two of you will succeed." Grandma stopped for a moment to wipe a tear from her cheek, saying, "Oh, if only my James could be here to share this adventure."

"Grandma, I have another adventure within the next week," said Brendan, commanding immediate attention from Pauline.

"And what would that be, Brendan dear?"

"As you will have no doubt noticed, I wear an eye patch."

"Yes—to correct the diplopia you suffer from? Am I right?"

"Yes, Grandma—diplopia, double vision. Well, in a few days, I am having an operation, in Liverpool, on the left eye, hopefully to correct it. I had one some time ago, in Ireland, which was unsuccessful, but the Walton Hospital is pretty confident they will get it right this time."

"That's great news, Brendan, but I'll be sorry to see your charming eye patch go," laughed Grandma in mock distress. "What do you think Maureen, dear?"

"I'll be glad to see it go, but it will be strange to see my Brendan with two eyes." She laughed. "That's Thursday next week, but before that, we're meeting Norman at his office on the Tuesday. Another busy week…"

It was then decided that the two of them would return to Formby, see the estate agent to get the house ready for sale for £3,800, and arrange to have the furniture disposed of and…to cut the grass.

***

"Good morning, Mr. and Mrs. Harris, do come in. Mr. Hardy is in the back office. I'm Miss Annabel Sweeny, Mr. Hardy's secretary." Pointing to the female with her back to the room on the telephone, she offered in a louder voice, "The young lady on the phone is Miss Agnes Winterbotham."

Agnes Winterbotham, still with her back to them, showed a small figure of a much older female with her grey hair tied in a bun on top of her head. However, when she swung around on the swivel chair, there was a transformation. Her smile lit up the room, and they discovered she was dressed in very stylish office wear: a black jacket, open to show a white blouse, with a black skirt. Covering the phone with her right palm, she mouthed a good-morning welcome. Maureen and Brendan waved their acknowledgment.

Miss Sweeny, looking very severe in similar dress with long greying hair to her shoulders, said through her thin lips, "Agnes is only new to the office. Joined five years ago."

"You've been a long time here, then, Miss Sweeny," stated Brendan, his tall body overshadowing the smaller figure of the woman.

Miss Sweeny looked up at Brendan, but before she could answer, the office door swung open and a middle-aged man in suit and tie exited. He acknowledged the presence of the visitors and Miss Sweeny with a brusque, "Good morning," and strode away to the side of the office.

"Mr. Hopkins, senior clerk and sales," said Miss Sweeny through pursed lips without any further detail.

Maureen nudged Brendan behind Miss Sweeny's back. *Bad blood there*, she mouthed.

"Come in, come in, the pair of you," was the sound of Norman's welcoming voice. "Now, both of you…still keen to start? I am looking forward to the next few months, as you no doubt are yourselves. You are, aren't you?" he questioned with a smile. "Please, abide with me for rabbiting on. It is such a pleasure to have some young blood in the office. You agree, Miss Sweeny—Anna?"

"Yes, Mr. Hardy, a breath of fresh air."

"Oh, of course, I never introduced you, Anna," exclaimed Norman, hitting his forehead with his right hand in frustration. "As you say, a breath of fresh air. This is Brendan and Maureen Harris, who are going to open a life and pensions department in the office here." Norman pointed to the couple and continued, "Maureen, Brendan, allow me to introduce you to the mainstay of Hardy General Insurance—Miss Anna Sweeny."

After handshakes all round, Norman asked Anna to arrange coffee for the visitors and to have Agnes bring it and introduce herself at the same time.

"Thank you, Agnes," acknowledged Norman as Agnes passed the steaming cups around. "As you have already heard, Agnes, Maureen is the daughter of Captain Rupert, my nephew, and she and her husband Brendan are going to open a new investments and pensions arm to Hardy General Assurance. Captain Rupert died in the last war, and we were not aware of Maureen's existence until quite recently. Oh, drat it, there's the phone. Could you answer it, please, Agnes."

For the next few hours, they were shown around the office and the room allocated to Hardy Life, Investment and Pensions. Later that evening, resting in their new accommodation, they had a drink to celebrate their good fortune. But uppermost in their minds was the expected operation on Brendan's eyes to correct the double vision.

31

The Operation

"Yes, ladies and gentlemen, Mr. Harris has kindly agreed to talk about the cause of his problem." The consultant surgeon, dressed in his white gown and with a surgical eye piece positioned on his forehead like a coal-miner's lamp, announced to the group of seated students, indicating Brendan seated beside him. "Thank you, Mr. Harris," he continued in his marked London accent, "will you kindly tell the group before you the reasons why you are wearing the eye patch?"

Brendan, ever the showman taking the stage, stood up in his rather short white hospital robe, adjusted the eye patch to a more comfortable position over his left eye and said, "Good morning, everybody. It was over three years ago when a car driven by a drunk came out of a side road and wham! I bashed into it on my brother's Vespa scooter. I was unconscious for three weeks." Some heads nodded in sympathy; Brendan continued, "Apparently, bouncing your head off the roof of a car when you're going at thirty miles an hour isn't the recommended way of stopping, as, when I regained consciousness, I could see two of everything and had also lost my memory."

There was a spontaneous muted burst of sympathetic laughter from the audience.

"Yes, yes, thank you, Mr. Harris, for that," the consultant said. "Now, everybody, what is the name given to Mr. Harris's problem? Yes, you in the glasses with your hand up."

"This would appear to be a case of diplopia, commonly known as double vision, sir."

"Yes, thank you. Now, as most of you probably know, double vision—as the name implies—is, and I quote, 'the simultaneous perception of two images of a single object that may be displaced horizontally, vertically, diagonally—that is both vertically and horizontally in relation to each other'. What is your trouble, Mr. Harris? What happens when you remove the eye patch?"

"I see two of everything. When I look to the right, I see two images of the chosen object, quite far apart, and as I gradually move my eyes to the left, the vertical gap reduces to nil."

"Thank you, Mr. Harris. Now, ladies and gentlemen, what is the answer to Mr. Harris's problem?"

The wearer of the glasses shot his hand up and replied without being asked, "Sir, a muscle in the right eye appears to have been weakened. Could not the same muscle in the left be adjusted to reduce its strength?"

"An excellent answer, young man," agreed the consultant. "Before we discuss the details of the operation, perhaps Mr. Harris might repair to the preparation room. Thank you, Mr. Harris," said the pleased consultant as Brendan was escorted from the room, pulling his short robe down to his knees.

In the preparation room, Brendan, having been transferred to a bed, was approached by another smiling, white-robed figure wielding a syringe of anaesthetic. Bidding Brendan a pleasant morning, he instructed him to count to ten, aloud, as he injected the knockout drops into the vein on the back of Brendan's hand. Before the anaesthetic had reached a count of four, Brendan was in the land of nod.

***

"...how many pencils do you see, Mr. Harris. Yes, open both eyes. Don't be worried if you still see two of them."

I've been here before. I'll humour the man, he seems confident.

"I see two pencils, one above the other," he admitted grudgingly.

"Good, as expected. Whilst you were asleep, Mr. Harris, we tied two…strings…around the muscle at the back of the left eye. Now, tell me if there is any change as I tighten them."

"Yes, there is, the pencils are closer to each other. The bottom one is moving nearer to the other. Oh, God, is this really happening?"

"Yes, it is, Mr. Harris," answered the smiling consultant. "Now, tell me when the two pencils become one."

"Yes, yes, they are close. Now, they are together."

"Are you certain, Mr. Harris?"

"Yes!" replied Brendan in excitement.

"Now, Mr. Harris, the final moment of magic."

The consultant, with deft movements resulting in some small discomfort to the eye, tightened and then removed the 'string' and said slightly triumphantly, holding the wonderful singular pencil in front of Brendan, "Hold your head steady, Mr. Harris. Look to the left. One pencil as usual? Now, follow it as I move it to the right. Yes, Mr. Harris, from the big grin on your face I can see the pencil remained single throughout. Mr. Harris," he announced, "your double vision is cured!"

"Thank you so much! I can't believe this has happened. May I have the pencil as a memento of this marvellous day?"

***

That evening, the very happy couple booked a table at a local restaurant to run over the many exciting events of the recent past.

"What a year, Mo," declared Brendan with a delighted smile. "I met you on the toy floor of Lewis's department store…"

"Yes," said Maureen. "I remember seeing this tall young man with a black eye patch and thinking, not a bad-looking guy, wonder about the patch… Now look at us, married, with a house for sale, amazing new relations, a business to start up and the operation on your eyes was a success." Maureen stopped speaking, then continued with a smile upon her lips, "And, by the way, Brendan love, the doctor has confirmed I'm pregnant. The start of a new life for us both, in more ways than one."

About the Author

David R. McCabe grew up in the countryside south of Dublin, Ireland and now lives with his partner Joan, in the north of England. Happily retired, David spends much of his time fly fishing with Joan and working on his next book.

Website: www.anirishlad.co.uk
Facebook: www.facebook.com/pg/brendanharris11

By the Author

Pinkeens to Diddies (An Irish Lad #1)
Brendan Afloat (An Irish Lad #2)
Brendan Ashore (An Irish Lad #3)

Beaten Track Publishing

For more titles from Beaten Track Publishing, please visit our website:

http://www.beatentrackpublishing.com

Thanks for reading!